GRAND OAK BOOKS

The Complete Short Stories of Émile Zola

Published by:
Grand Oak Books Publishing, Ltd

ISBN-10 0982957971
ISBN-13 978-0982957974

Library of Congress Cataloging-in-Publication Data:

Zola, Émile (1840-1902)/The Complete Short Stories of Émile Zola, Vol. 1
        p.   cm.

First Edition

The Complete Short Stories of Émile Zola

VOL 1.

Edited by Stephen R. Pastore

Introduction by Emily Pardoe

Grand Oak Books

2011

The Complete Short Stories of Émile Zola

VOL 1.

INTRODUCTION to
The Complete Short Stories
of Émile Zola in Four Volumes

by Emily Pardoe

The relative or sometimes complete unavailability of texts has been the major factor in depriving non-French admirers of Zola's novels of the rewarding and exciting literary experience of reading his tales and short stories. The present volume is unique in providing a conspectus of these works, ranging from his first collection, Contes à Ninon, published in 1864, to his last story, 'The Haunted House' (Angeline), which appeared more than thirty years later. The stories provide many pleasures of recognition: readers will find a variety of theme, a dramatic power, a minute observation of physical detail, the narrative invention, the social scope, which bring a whole epoch of French life into vigorous relief, and with which his novels have made them familiar. There are also, however, stimulating differences: they will be spared the irritation they may have felt at the novelist's occasional jejune determinism and his tendency to over-play (though not, thank God, in his best novels) the importance of so-called laws of heredity and environment. They will meet in the short stories no attempt to apply his half-baked and totally misplaced theories as to the possibility of turning the novel into a sort of experimental research laboratory to observe and deduce the laws of human behavior. They will even find the novelist's dramatic sense enhanced by the enforced concision of the short story form. And they will discover an accuracy of details that owes more to experience and intuition than to documentation, as the more anecdotal nature of the stories gives them an added liveliness.

But above all, from the very first tale (which is, significantly, in the first-person narrative), readers will become aware of a new dimension, a noticeable difference in tone, which may best be described as a sort of wry playfulness, used variously to mitigate or heighten an underlying seriousness. This different tone covers a wide range. It takes the form, for instance, of broad, even farcical humor, in 'Coqueville on the Spree' (La Fête à Coqueville)—a particularly interesting example, since Coqueville, as the epitome of the closed society, isolated in space and time, could have lent itself excellently to a painstaking study of the influence of heredity and environment, whereas Zola chooses to treat the village and its inhabitants, largely as a huge joke. Mainly, however, this playfulness finds expression in a wide range of irony: the savage irony of 'The Attack on the Mill' (L'Attaque du moulin); the cruelest irony of all, with 'Captain Burle' (Le Capitaine Burle), perhaps the only story where the tone is almost unrelievedly tragic; and, more frequently, a gentler irony, as in the story of Monsieur Chabre (Les Coquillages de Monsieur Chabre), or in 'The Girl Who Loves Me' (Celle qui m'aime). The irony is sometimes blatant: sections of 'Priests and Sinners' offer good examples of this; at other times far subtler, as in 'Absence Makes the Heart Grow Fonder' (Jacques Damour), which ends on at least two different levels. Whatever form it takes, the irony is rarely unadulterated, and here again, I think, readers of Zola's short stories will have a further advantage over someone who knows only his novels, where irony is generally in rather short supply, and often obtrusive when it does appear. The

eponymous anti-hero Burle, for example, excites compassion at the same time as he evokes an ironical smile of contempt, and the same can be said of Jacques Damour. Indeed pity, aroused, be it noted, obliquely in accordance with Zola's tenet of realistic impartiality, by ostensibly objective depiction rather than direct appeal to the reader's emotions, is a predominant element in many of these stories, and this skilful blending of contrasting suggestions arouses a similarly ambiguous reaction in the reader, a reaction more complex than that provoked by most of his novels, and which for many readers will more than adequately compensate for the lack of the epic quality of the better novels, well-nigh impossible to produce in a short story-although the spree at Coqueville is a binge of epic proportions, albeit on a mock-heroic scale.

Quite apart from the differences inherent in the genres, there is a deeper underlying distinction to be drawn between the novels and the short stories. For Zola the novelist, ambition and fame are the spur and the epic tone clearly forms part of the grand manner which will enable him to challenge a giant such as Balzac; but the charm of the short stories springs from the more urgent spur of economic necessity, the need to survive. The majority of these stories, in fact, form an important part of Zola's considerable and sometimes feverish production as a journalist, most of which falls between 1864 and 1880.

In 1865 when he left his job as head of the publicity department of the newly formed publishing firm of Hachette which he had joined two years before, Zola had to support his mother as well as himself, for his father had died when Émile was only seven years old; and incidentally, it should be mentioned that being the only son of a widow proved to have compensations: he was exempted from military service and had the additional bonus—his war stories make it plain that he must have considered this a bonus—that he escaped the servitudes and hardships and dangers of soldiering during the Franco-Prussian war. It is interesting to reflect that his numerous writings on the subject of war were based on hearsay and imagination, not on experience, which may explain why he fails to realize, in 'The Attack on the Mill", that in modern warfare, shells had replaced cannon-balls.

Zola's economic straits, already bad enough, were shortly to become even worse when, very soon, a further mouth was added to the two he had to feed: that of his mistress Gabrielle-Alexandrine Meley, whom he was to marry in 1870. Something had to be done; it had to be done quickly; but it takes a long time, weeks or months, even for someone of Zola's methodical and industrious routine, to write a novel. It can take even longer to reap any considerable benefit from royalties, even if, with luck, you have the good fortune to have your novel accepted for publication in serial form, a method which Zola was able to adopt in later life. But as an unknown writer, there was only one possibility: journalism. Articles and short stories can be dashed off in a few days or even hours and, with luck and a reliable editor, you can eat and drink.

Zola's journalistic output never consisted solely of short stories; throughout his career as a journalist, a large part of his time and energy was devoted to criticism and reviews, not only of literary and dramatic works but also of painting, as we are reminded when reading 'Fair Exchange' (Madame Sourdis); and Zola, like young Ferdinand Sourdis, was a modernist, not surprisingly since he was a schoolmate of Paul Cézanne whom he continued to frequent for many years. One of his earliest public controversies arose from his support of the unfashionable and 'iconoclastic' painter, Édouard Manet.

Zola in his day, however, was best known as a journalist for his short stories and tales, some barely a couple of pages long, others of thirty pages or more, of which he wrote more than eighty over a period of more than thirty years, although of this number only 'Angeline' was written after 1880. The reason for the cessation of his activity after this date was simple: the resounding success of his proletarian novel L'Assommoir in 1877 brought him fame overnight and proportionate wealth shortly afterwards. The spur of financial necessity had gone; the contract which he had secured in 1875 through the good offices of the friendly Turgenev to provide articles and stories to the Russian periodical Vestnik Evropy (European Messenger) was to expire in 1880. The years of grinding poverty which Zola had experienced in the mid-sixties were now but a memory; they had, however, been

11

useful in providing personal knowledge of a way of life which appeared in both his novels and his short stories. Henceforth his novels were to bring him enduring fame of a magnitude that he could never have expected as a critic or a short story writer. All the same, as a journalist, Zola obviously learned many of his skills during this period and it could be argued that he might even have done well to carry some of them over more fully into his novels. If journalism has disadvantages, it can also bring benefits.

The potential disadvantages are obvious. Paid by the word or by the page, a journalist can easily sacrifice quality to quantity. A very stern critic might, I fancy, find some wordiness in parts of Zola's short stories; but we should not forget that a more leisurely age than ours would be happy to linger over charming descriptions of Guérande and Piriac (in 'Shellfish for Monsieur Chabre') or of L'Estaque, in 'A Flash in the Pan' (Naïs Micoulin), all the more willingly if such descriptions have the charm of exoticism as well, since many of these short stories were written for Russian readers. Furthermore, as a realist, Zola is concerned to create as complete an atmospheric background as possible. And the occasional lengthy description, far from being purely decorative, serves to prolong our suspense and even, as in a good detective story (I think again of 'A Flash in the Pan'), the trivial, apparently unnecessary detail can provide a clue to the dramatic dénouement.

Another danger facing the journalist is that topicality is often expected to be one of his ingredients; especially in his earlier works, Zola takes his starting point from a contemporary event or a matter of current interest. Here again, Zola manages to survive relatively unscathed, and in any case, his output was sufficiently considerable to enable a selection to be made which avoids minutiae unlikely to interest a modern reader. In much of his later work, Zola avoids any such danger by deliberately choosing a topic of general import (as in 'Priests and Sinners') and inventing a dramatic framework to illustrate his point.

But the benefits of journalism are so considerable, at least for someone of Zola's temperament, as to outweigh the disadvantages. Writing quickly, you will find yourself writing briskly and crisply; you will seek to be lively. Writing for different editors and different reading publics gives you practice in flexibility. Parisian readers have different attitudes from those of the provincials, while Russian readers—for most of the stories were written under contract to a Russian periodical—require a good deal of background information, a requirement which admirably suits Zola's technique; and they have their special expectations and preconceptions with regard to French society. Could this perhaps explain some of the flippancy—'French sauciness' is perhaps the better word—of 'The Party at Coqueville?' But, above all, people will not, I suggest, read short stories to be preached at or indoctrinated, even if they are not averse to having their prejudices flattered. So didacticism, that scourge of Zola's criticism and his later novels, has no place in his short stories, although he has his own methods of inferring a moral. In fact, the best way of entertaining males—and more females than they may perhaps care to admit—is by the slightly scabrous or the quasi-erotically suggestive. However, from what we know of Zola, such a tone was not one which represented his own inclinations and here again this sort of constraint can only have furthered his development as an artist: he has to be careful to avoid too forthright an expression of strongly held personal views; artistry is more important than outspoken sincerity. It is, of course, an attitude which squares very well with the realist's avowed aim of depicting people and society in their everyday life, however dull and even hateful, people as they are and not as we would have them be. Such suppression of personal feelings is bound to have its limits, of course: particularly as a young man, Zola was much given to sentimentality which can sometimes sink to mawkishness and he had a strong melodramatic tendency which he never threw off. The sentimentality diminished with age and self-discipline but he never seemed able to accept Hardy's dictum that while nothing is too strange to have happened, there is a good deal that is too strange to be believed. Once again, we have been saved by the quantity of Zola's output: with over eighty stories to choose from, it is easy to weed out the mawkish or over-melodramatic, which might, indeed, have appealed to a Victorian reader but would now be found unacceptable.

Zola's short story writing falls into two easily distinguishable periods, with 1875 as the dividing line, when he was, in fact, at thirty-five, in the middle of his career, though his life was to be forcibly abridged. The first period contains largely very short pieces, some little more than a couple of pages long; the majority are mere sketches illustrating Parisian life (one of the collections of this typically journalistic production, first published in 1866, was called Esquisses Parisiennes). These sketches were a very prevalent genre at the time, a chronicle, and its author, the chronicler, writes of his personal impressions, usually basing his story on an odd event, an anecdote, real or imagined, a genuine or fictitious personal memory; he strolls through Paris noting things that strike his fancy or people who seem perhaps odd or even 'typically Parisian'; topics on which he can talk out loud, personally, inviting the reader's complicity. Occasionally, the tale will invite the expression of a hope or a non-censorious moral, although we should beware of accepting any such expression of emotion or judgment at its face value. It is pleasant chat and much of it, where Zola's contribution to the genre is concerned, is now read only by critics in search of influences or anxious to find in it the seeds of his future novels. These chronicles were largely published in the many newspapers and magazines which proliferated in Paris in the declining years of the Second Empire; and they tend to have a sameness of tone, a sort of slickness which quickly palls. All the same, some have sufficiently strong ironic edge and an observation of permanent human foibles accurate enough to amuse a modern reader. Five have been included here, out of a total of over fifty.

The second period of Zola's activity as a short story writer is very different; no longer sketches, the stories all have a plot and characters. Although still writing for a periodical, he is relieved of the need to crave the suffrage of the French reading public and can avoid any direct editorial pressure; the obligation to provide slick entertainment and instant dramatization is lifted. On his much broader canvas of more than ten thousand words, he can exercise his realistic technique of detailed observation, he is free to develop situations in accordance with views that from other evidence we know to be closer to his heart but which he has learned to express with artistic discretion. All except one of the remaining translations of the stories are taken from this collaboration: ten stories in all, exactly half of Zola's total output of short stories for the Russian periodical (he also wrote more than forty other pieces, articles on literary and other topics). One or two of the stories have retained the impressionistic stamp of his earlier journalism, not surprisingly since he occasionally borrowed from earlier sketches to put his Russian pieces together; and one or two of them are too essentially topical for inclusion here, for instance, a series of short sketches recounting some of the electioneering and voting in the important French general election of 1878, which are of greater interest for the historian than for the general reader.

We have mentioned the importance of drama in the short story to offer the reader an unexpected twist, a surprising turn of events or a sudden striking revelation of character. Zola well understood the desirability of this technique and in many of these stories he keeps the reader on tenterhooks. What exactly is going to become of the sexually obsessed Captain Burle? Who is going to be shot—or is anyone going to be shot—in 'The Attack on the Mill'? In 'Absence Makes the Heart Grow Fonder', what possible solution can be found for Jacques Damour's agonizing problem? Is that rather unpleasant young Frédéric Morand, so perfectly adapted to his rich middle-class background, none the less riding for a serious, if not fatal, fall? These are a few of the major dramas which combine with interlocking minor dramas to provide complex suspense for the reader. But it would be underestimating Zola's inventive narrative talent to assume that he places exclusive reliance on what are, after all, fairly ordinary basic skills which, if indulged in to excess, can turn into mannered devices. Zola has other strings to his bow and in all his full-length stories the questions are more subtly posed: it is not so much what is going to happen, as when and how is what we can expect to happen actually going to happen. Far less common is the question why something happens. Zola rarely probes motives nor, indeed, does he generally need to do so for the mainsprings of most characters' behavior are plain, although not necessarily simple. All the same, in one or two of these stories, there is greater ambiguity: Jacques Damour's final resolution, in "Absence Makes the Heart Grow Fonder' is not explained. When Zola does choose thus to respect the uncertainty of human motive, his realistic technique stands him in good stead, relying as it does on the external recording of behavior rather than on omniscient authorial probing: here actions or even gestures speak louder than words and the reader can ponder the motives at leisure.

But there is no doubt that the question of how something happens is most important for Zola and is worth examining in some greater detail. 'Shellfish for Monsieur Chabre' is as good an example as any. Now, it is surely not necessary to be particularly sophisticated or cynical to realize very early in the story that Monsieur Chabre's balding head is going to be adorned with horns and we know quite well who is going to put them there. The main suspense thus centers on the question of how, and this is where Zola shows his artistry. We see in great detail the physical background and contributory events which foster the growth of a relationship between a shy young man, becoming progressively and charmingly less shy, and a respectable and spirited young wife, becoming progressively less respectable; a relationship which not only unites two bodies—both equally beautiful bodies—but reveals a marriage of minds which share the same feeling for nature and a similar sense of beauty as well as the same sense of fun, the same interest in life's oddities. All these aspects of the links between the two young people are observed with careful and selective realistic detail, never over-explicit: the reader is not taken into the exact workings of the protagonists' minds or the minute development of their feelings but is left to surmise and deduce—and to be amused. Woven into the tale are Zola's own holiday impressions of a specific district of France which is realistically portrayed in considerable detail for the foreign Russian reader, no doubt fascinated—as American readers may well also be—by a glimpse into an excitingly beautiful landscape or a charmingly picturesque old town. More importantly, the impact of such joint impressions on the young couple in creating a stimulating bond between them is central to the plot; it seems clear that here is no description for the sake of description and even the long drawn out account of the shrimping expedition has an important functional role; it increases our suspense as well as suddenly revealing a breakthrough in the couple's relationship. The net result is that what could have been a banal and sordid adultery, a quick seaside 'petticoats up and trousers down' on the beach, becomes a lyrical celebration of the beauty of natural forces set in a convincing and fascinating specific French background, in a specific French milieu. Even the chief victim is not entirely a caricature black-and-white character. Paunchy and absurd though he is, Monsieur Chabre is a living person and not really a bad sort of fellow—he's mannerly and considerate towards his wife; and, in the end, Zola lets him come to no harm. He's nobly eaten his loathsome shellfish and the reader is delighted when he gets his reward in the shape of a bouncing son and heir; it's a sort of nineteenth-century form of in vitro fertilization. And quite apart from the sexual problem, we may feel that, through his truth to life, Zola has, as it were incidentally, given us an intriguing and plausible glimpse into a perennial mystery: how can rich businessmen, so shrewd and expert in their particular sphere, prove so ineffectual and stupid outside these activities?

I have spent time on 'Shellfish for Monsieur Chabre' because it is an excellent example of Zola's narrative technique, albeit one of many, whereby he succeeds in turning a relatively predictable what into a far more uncertain how. Beyond simple comedy or drama, we are taken into more enriching regions of the mind while at the same time our attention is constantly held by the convincing and accurate depiction of many different milieus. By the manner of their telling, we are persuaded to overlook the familiarity or even banality of the events being told; the realist Zola has, strangely, achieved a sort of classicism, the classicism of 'what oft was said but ne'er so well expressed'.

Zola's stories extend through a very wide range of French society, almost as wide as his novels, though the typical nouveau riche character of the period is not well represented; Durandeau in 'Rentafoil' (Les Repoussoirs) is the nearest approach to the crafty Second Empire speculator lavishly depicted in the novels. Apart from this, we see specimens from the aristocracy down to the peasantry and proletariat: indeed, in two of the stories here reproduced, 'How People Die' (Comment on meurt) and 'Priests and Sinners', there is a deliberate juxtaposition of the attitudes of different classes, although in the second of these, the emphasis is placed more on a particular type of priest rather than on the class of society to which he was ministering. If realism is deemed to depend exclusively on observation, there must be some difficulty in considering such works as realistic: Zola had no direct or personal experience of most of the milieus he was depicting, the aristocracy, the upper-and lower-middle classes, the proletariat or the peasantry. His own frequentations were largely of journalists, of literary and artistic Parisian bohemians. However, in his years of poverty in the early and mid-sixties, he would certainly have rubbed shoulders with the working and poorer artisan classes and he would have seen something of provincial life and peasantry in his boyhood in Provence. The life of the aristocracy and the upper-middle classes must have remained a closed book to him, to be learnt about from other writers' works or from other people's conversation. Critics have taken Zola to task over this. However, Zola had very sensitive antennae and a lively imagination; he was to need less than a week 'in the field' in Beauce when gathering material for his superb peasant novel La Terre and since both Balzac and Proust, in their different ways, seem to have overcome similar shortcomings in their novels, it would be prudent to let readers judge for themselves as to the authenticity of Zola's portrayal of classes of which he had limited direct knowledge.

From our knowledge of Zola's strong feelings about social injustice, we might have expected the aristocracy to have suffered harshly at his hands; in fact, they do not come off too badly. True, they appear as heartless, hypocritical and sexually promiscuous but they are shown as possessing good manners, decorum and a certain panache, a conventional picture, of course, but Zola's invention of incident, the petit fait vrai of Stendhal, and the accurate background detail make perfectly plausible and interesting stories out of this unoriginal material. The middle classes at all levels had been the butt of most of the important poets and novelists of the nineteenth century in France and Zola similarly belabors them for their materialistic greed, their snobbery and, particularly the women, for their bigotry; again, it is the manner rather than the matter that is original. Predictably, the lower-middle classes, harder pressed by economic circumstances, are treated more sympathetically, although Monsieur Rousseau, the stationer in the third section of 'How People Die', however sincerely he may mourn his wife, still has a nagging grievance against her: what a pity she had to die on a day which forced him to close the shop! It is far easier to arouse compassion for the wretched working classes and Zola does so; nonetheless, his code of impartiality leads him to show a few warts: the working-class inhabitants of the tenement block in the fourth section of 'Priests and Sinners' are notably uncharitable in their judgments as well as drunk and dis-

17

orderly in their communal lives. On the whole, the peasantry come out best; they have a simple fatalistic dignity springing from their close contact with natural forces; but this does not prevent Zola from drawing a devastating picture of their appalling superstitions in the first section of 'Priests and Sinners'.

In a word, Zola's view of mankind is unflattering but it must be said that if there are few wholly admirable characters, there are also not many really despicable ones. Indeed, it could be argued that his characterizations in his short stories, because of his frequent humorous or ironic touches, is more rounded than in his novels; and the narrower canvas still gives him room to etch in some convincing, often slyly funny vignettes of minor characters.

As we might expect, one of the major characters of his short stories is the carefully drawn environment. Zola invites the readers' close attention to the influence of social and other circumstantial conditioning on our behavior; and this conditioning not only helps to explain our complexities, it also serves as an extenuating circumstance. In 'A Flash in the Pan' (Naïs Micoulin), for instance, Naïs' father is a wife-beater, a harsh father who knocks his daughter about, and a would-be murderer; yet this sort of uncouth savagery is shown as rooted in the desperate struggle to survive in a pitiless drought-ridden region, as well as in the still living tradition of a French male-dominated society whose pride in family honor is the mainstay of his existence. Similarly, the stupid Father Pintoux in the first part of 'Priests and Sinners' is as much a victim of circumstance as his pathetically superstitious flock of Breton peasantry; his life is almost as hard as theirs and his belief in hell fire as strong; and if the Monsignor of the fifth section of the same group is ruthlessly ambitious, it is his early military training which is partly to blame for his insensitivity. Zola obviously considers professional military training as one of the most pernicious environments. It results in a besetting sin which incurs his ultimate condemnation of any human being: lack of imagination. No amount of courage or loyalty can make up for this failure: the jaunty, gallant French officer in 'The Attack on the Mill' as well as the dour, pathetic, doggedly courageous and strictly honorable Major Laguitte in 'Captain Burle' are both ultimately condemned, insofar as Zola allows anyone to be condemned, as blinkered automata.

A further reason for Zola's distaste for the military is that, through their association with war, which he vies as a deplorable but inevitable human infirmity, they are closely associated with death. Zola had a streak of morbidity which finds explicit expression in 'Dead Men Tell No Tales' (La Mort d'Olivier Bécaille), and which no doubt will find an echo with many a reader. We know from other sources not only of his fear, which proved to be prophetic, of meeting an untimely death but also of being buried alive, and the story plainly owes much of its initial impact to this autobiographical element. However, as always, Zola constructs a plot and a situation which go far beyond any personal feelings. Fear of death and of burial alive turn out to be the most superficial, if perhaps the most dramatic, of the levels at which the story works; the real subjects are the fragility of the marriage vows, the pressure of economic necessity, the portrayal of women as creatures possessing habits and customs rather than morals, and finally, a favorite theme in Zola's short stories, the justification of sexual desire, an interesting contrast to the depressing view of sexuality revealed in the novels of the Rougon Macquart cycle; it seems almost as if in this portrayal of the successful fulfillment of young love, a vein of sentimentality persists from the early Contes à Ninon which was ruthlessly excised from the later novels. Let it be noted, by the way, that if women are sternly treated at times, the men have nothing to crow about: the motives of men's actions are usually social advancement or material gain, with love as a secondary commodity.

In later life, Zola became a very active political figure in his support for Dreyfus; but politics and politicians are skeptically viewed in his stories. The political Monsignor of 'Priests and Sinners' is a rabidly reactionary self-seeker while, at the other end of the spectrum, the left-wing Berru of 'Absence Makes the Heart Grow Fonder' is a rascally rabble-rousing firebrand who takes good care of his own skin. Big Michu's father, in 'Big Michu' (Le grand Michu), is mentioned as a brave and honest 1848 Republican; but Jacques Damour, in 'Absence Makes the Heart Grow Fonder', also brave and honest, is shown as a credulous simpleton whose Communard activity is closely linked to the few francs a day which he receives as a National Guardsman. Politics are in fact largely the preserve of a corrupt aristocracy and a conservative and ambitious upper-middle class and Zola shows us no evidence to suggest that any of the lower-class aspirants to political power are likely to be very different. In a word, politicians are members of the human race, of which someone wrote:

> I wish I liked the human race,
> I wish I liked its silly face,
> And when I'm introduced to one
> I wish I thought: What jolly fun!

Such indeed, here expressed in humorous Anglo-Saxon terms, which need not exclude a hidden anguish, is a sentiment that can be seen to run through Zola's short stories. It is a cry from the heart of many French writers, from Molière and La Rochefoucauld, Chamfort and Voltaire, Flaubert and Céline. In Zola, it is no isolated disenchantment, for his picture is very complete. He takes us into aristocratic bedrooms and dining rooms, into drawing-rooms in Paris and in the provinces, into little shops and wretched garrets, into a garrison town, seaside resorts, the Faubourg Saint-Germain and Ménilmontant, a Lorraine village and an assortment of cemeteries. He peoples his accurate backgrounds with convincing characters: men-about-town, middle-class money-makers, pretty bourgeois, soldiers, fishermen, peasants, bricklayers, shopkeepers, artisans and other manual workers, not forgetting the odd kept woman; conservative reactionaries as well as un-easy liberals and opportunistic republicans; and they are all seen in action, often dramatically and frequently ironically. We see a well-composed and authoritative fresco, of a wide range in full color, of French society in the second half of the nineteenth century. But this is not just a period piece: Zola's themes—love, young and fierce or tired and disillusioned, maternal, paternal, filial, married or adulterous; death, natural or violent; money (or lack of it); religion (or lack of it); work (or lack of it)—are always with us and to many of them he gives a strikingly modern, even prophetic, slant. His general theme is, after all, various forms of recognizably modern con-flict: the dilemma of the tormented Abbé de Villeneuve is similar to that of the worker-priest; fundamentalist religious fanatics, in the line of poor Father Pintoux, are today, in many parts of the world, a commonplace; we can all think of gifted men destroying themselves through drink and dissi-pation; the lures of high pressure are familiar bogies; and many people have an uneasy suspicion that there may still exist those who hope to be able to cry, like the French captain in 'The Attack on the Mill', 'We've won! We've won!' on piles of corpses and flattened buildings. It would seem very likely therefore that, having survived for a century, these brilliant stories, so var-ied in theme and tone, will continue to engross and entertain readers for a long time to come.

The Complete Short Stories of Émile Zola

Volume I

TO NINON

Here they are then, my friend, these unfettered narratives of our young days, which I related to you out in the country in my dear Provence, and to which you listened with an attentive ear, while vaguely following with your eyes the great blue lines of the distant hills.

On May evenings, at the moment when heaven and earth glide slowly into supreme peace, I left the city and reached the fields; the barren slopes, covered with brambles and juniper bushes; or else the banks of the little river, that December torrent, so unobstrusive in fine weather; or again an out-of-the-way corner of the plain, warm with the embrace of the south, a broad stretch of red and yellow land, planted with almond trees with slender branches, old olives turning grey, and vines with their entangled offshoots trailing along the ground.

Poor parched earth, it stands out glaring, grey, and naked in the sun, between the fertile meadows of the Durance and the orange groves on the sea-shore. I love it for its harsh beauty, its doleful-looking rocks, its thyme and lavender. There is, I know not what burning air of desolation about this sterile valley; a strange whirlwind of passion seems to have passed over the country; then, great oppression followed, and the fields, which were still full of generous warmth, fell asleep, so to say, in a final desire. At present, amidst my forests of the north, when I recall to mind that stone and dust, I feel most profound love for that rugged country which is not mine. Doubtless the merry child and the sad old rocks formerly felt tender affection for each other; and now the child, who has become a man, disdains damp fields and submerged verdure; he is in love with the broad white roads and calcinated mountains, where his mind, in all the freshness of its fifteen summers, dreamed its first dreams.

I reached the fields. There, when I had half laid me down on the cultivated land, or on the slabs on the hillside, lost in that peacefulness which came from the profound depths of heaven, I found you, on turning my head, extended comfortably on my right, thoughtful, your chin resting in your hand, gazing at me with your great eyes. You were the angel of my solitude, my good guardian angel whom I perceived near me wherever I might be; you read my secret wishes in my heart, you sat down beside me everywhere, unable to be where I was not. At present, this explains to me your presence every night. In days gone by, without ever seeing you approach, I experienced no astonishment in constantly meeting your bright look; I knew you were faithful, always within me.

My dear soul, you brought sweetness to the sadness of my melancholy evenings. You possessed the forlorn beauty of those knolls, their marble pallor blushing at the last kisses of the sun. I know not what perpetual thought elevated your forehead and enlarged your eyes. Then, when a smile played upon your idle lips, one would have said in presence of the youthfulness and sudden brightness of your face, that it was that ray of May which causes all the flowers and verdure of this palpitating earth to grow, flowers and verdure of a day that are scorched by the June sun. Between you and the horizon was secret harmony that made me love the stones on the footpaths. The little river had your voice; the stars, when they rose, your look; everything around me smiled with your smile. And you, lending your gracefulness to this nature, assumed its impressive severity. I confounded you one with the other. When I saw you, I was conscious of nature's free sky, and when my eyes searched the valley, I recognized your lithe, bold lines in the undulations of the ground. It was by comparing you thus that I took to madly loving you both, not knowing which I adored the most, my dear Provence or my dear Ninon.

Each morning, my friend, I feel a new necessity to thank you for bygone days. It was charitable and tender of you to love me a little and live within me; at that age when the heart suffers at being alone, you brought me yours to spare all pain to mine. Ah! if you only knew how many poor souls at present die of solitude. Times are hard for those who are made of love. I have not known that misery. You showed me at all times the face of an adorable woman, you peopled my desert, mingling your blood with mine, living in my thought . And I, lost in this profound love, I forgot, feeling you in my being. The supreme joy of our hymen caused me to pass in peace through that rugged land of sixteen years, where so many of my companions have left shreds of their hearts.

Strange creature, now that you are far away and I can see clearly within me, I experience keen pleasure in examining our love-making piece by piece. You were a beautiful and ardent woman, and I loved you as a husband. Then, I know not how, at times you became a sister, without ceasing to be a sweetheart; then I loved you both as a brother and a sweetheart, with all the chastity of affection, all the passion of desire. At other moments I found a companion in you, the healthy intelligence of man, and always, also, an enchantress, a well-beloved, whose face I smothered with kisses, while pressing her hand like an old comrade. In the folly of my tenderness, I gave your beautiful frame, which I so much adored, to each of my affections. Divine dream, which caused me to worship in you each creature, body and soul, with all my strength, apart from sex and blood. You satisfied at the same time the warmth of my imagination and the requirements of my intellect. You thus realized the dream of ancient Greece, the mistress made man, gifted with exquisite elegance of shape coupled with a masculine mind, worthy of knowledge and wisdom. I adored you in all the different forms of love, you, who sufficed for my being, you, whose exquisite beauty filled me with my dream. When I felt your supple frame within me, your sweet childlike face, your thoughts made of my thoughts, I tasted in its entirety, that unheard-of voluptuousness, sought for in vain in antiquity, of possessing a creature with all the sinews of my flesh, all the affection of my heart, all the power of my intelligence.

I reached the fields. Lying on the ground, your head resting on my bosom, I talked to you for long hours, my gaze lost in the azure immensity of your eyes. I spoke to you, careless of my words, according to the whim of the moment. Sometimes bending forward as if to nurse you, I addressed a naive little girl, who will not close her eyes, and whom one sends to sleep with pretty stories, lessons of charity and moderation; at other moments, my lips on your lips, I related to one whom I cherished, the loves of the fairies, or the charming affection of young sweethearts; still more frequently, on days when I was the victim of the silly unkindness of my companions, and those days together, have made up years of my youth, I took your hand, with irony on my lips, doubt and negation in my heart, complaining to a brother of the miseries of this world, in some afflicting tale, a satire dipped in tears. And you, bending to my whims, while still remaining a wife and woman, were in turn a naive little girl, a well-beloved and a consoling brother. You heard each of my styles of language. Without ever answering, you listened to me, allowing me to read in your eyes the emotion, the gaiety, the sadness of my tales. I lay my conscience quite bare to you, being anxious to hide nothing. I did not treat you as those ordinary sweethearts to whom lovers measure out their thoughts. I gave myself away entirely without ever bridling my tongue. And what long gossips they were, what strange stories born of a dream! What disjointed tales, where invention was left to chance, and the only supportable episodes of which were the kisses we exchanged! If some passer-by had spied us out at night at the foot of our rocks, I know not what singular look he would have had on hearing my free language, and seeing you understand it, my naive little girl, my well-beloved, my consoling brother.

Alas! Those delightful evenings are no more. A day came when I had to leave you, you and the fields of Provence. Do you remember, my darling, we said adieu to each other, one autumn evening, beside the little river. The naked trees rendered the horizon more vast and gloomy; the country at that advanced hour, covered with dry leaves, damped with the first rains, spread out black, with great yellow spots, like a huge coarse carpet. The last rays of light were leaving the sky, and night arose in the east with threatening fogs, a dark night to be followed by an unknown dawn; with my life it was as with that autumnal sky; the planet of my youth had just disappeared, the night of age was rising, reserving I knew not what future for me. I felt the burning necessity of experiencing reality; I was weary of the dream, weary of the spring, weary of you, my dear soul, who escaped from my embrace, and in presence of my tears could only smile at me sadly. Our divine love was quite at an end; it had had its season, like all things. It was then, perceiving you were dying within me, that I went to the bank of the little river in the expiring country, to give you my kisses of departure. Oh! That evening so full of love and sadness! I kissed you, my distressed pale one; I endeavored, for the last time, to give you back the robust health of your happy days: I could not, for I was your executioner. You rose within me higher than the body, higher than the heart, and you were nothing more than a souvenir.

It is now nearly seven years since I left you. Since the day of our farewell, in enjoyment and in grief, I have often listened to your voice, the caressing voice of a souvenir asking me for the tales of our Provencal evenings.

I know not what echo of our sonorous rocks responds in my heart. You, whom I left far away, plead so touchingly from your exile, that I seem to hear you in my innermost being. That sweet throb which past delight leaves within one, urges me to give way to your desire. Poor shadow that has disappeared in the solitude where the dear phantoms of our vanished dreams reside, if I must console you with my old stories, I feel the comfort I shall experience in listening to myself talking to you, as in our young days.

I comply with your request. I am going to relate the tales of our love-making again, one by one, not all, for there are some that could not be told a second time, the sun having faded those delicate flowers, which were too divinely simple for broad daylight, at their birth, but those with a robust constitution, which that clumsy machine called human memory is able to keep in mind.

Alas! I fear I am preparing great grief for myself in acting thus. To confide our conversations to the passing wind is violating the secret of our tenderness, and indiscreet lovers are punished in this world by the cold indifference of their confidants. I have still one hope, namely, that not a single person in this country will be tempted to peruse our stories. Our century is really much too busy to be attracted by the remarks of two unknown lovers. My detached pages will pass unperceived in the crowd, and will still reach you in their virginity. Thus I can indulge in folly at my ease; I can be as adventuresome as formerly, and as careless of the paths. You alone will read me, and I know with what indulgence.

And now, Ninon, I have satisfied your wishes; here are my stories. Raise no more your voice within me, that voice of remembrance, which brings tears to my eyes. Leave my heart, which requires rest, in peace; come no more, amidst the struggle, to remind me of our idle nights. If you must have a promise, I undertake to love you again, later on, when I shall have sought in vain in this world for other darlings, and when I shall return to my first love. Then I will go back again to Provence, and meet you on the bank of the little river. Winter will have come, a winter both sad and sweet, with a clear sky and earth giving hope for a future harvest. Believe me, we shall adore each other for another whole season; we will resume our peaceful evenings out in the country we love; we will complete our dream.

Wait for me, dear soul, faithful vision, sweetheart of the child and of the old man.

SIMPLICE

Once upon a time—listen attentively, Ninon, an old shepherd told me this story—once upon a time, on an island which the sea has long since engulfed, there were a king and queen who had a son. The king was a great monarch: his glass was the deepest in his kingdom; his sword the heaviest; he slaughtered and drank royally. The queen was a lovely queen: she painted herself so much that she did not appear more than forty. The son was a simpleton.

But a simpleton of the worst kind, said the witty people of the kingdom. When he was sixteen he was taken to battle by the king: it was a matter of exterminating a neighboring nation which was guilty of the atrocious crime of possessing territory. Simplice behaved like a fool: he saved two dozen women and three-and-a-half dozen children from the slaughter; he almost wept at every sabre-cut he gave; in a word the sight of the battlefield, streaming in blood and encumbered with corpses, struck such pity into his heart that he did not eat anything for three days. He was a great fool, Ninon, as you see.

When he was seventeen, he had to be present at a banquet given by his father to all the great gluttons of the kingdom. There again he committed stupidity on stupidity. He was satisfied with a few mouthfuls, spoke little, and did not swear at all. As there was a risk that his glass would always remain full in front of him, the king, to save the family dignity, was compelled to empty it from time to time on the sly.

When he was eighteen and hair began to grow on his chin, one of the queen's maids of honor noticed him. Maids of honor are dreadful, Ninon. This one wanted the young prince to kiss her. The poor child had never dreamt of such a thing; he shook with trembling when she spoke to him, and ran away as soon as he caught sight of the hem of her skirt in the palace grounds. His father, who was a good father, saw all, and laughed in his sleeve. But as the lady continued the pursuit more ardently than ever without obtaining the kiss, he was ashamed at having such a son, and himself gave the required kiss, always for the purpose of saving the dignity of his race.

"Ah! The little jackass!" exclaimed the great monarch, who was a man of parts.

II

It was at twenty that Simplice became a perfect idiot. He came across a forest and fell in love.

In those olden times people did not beautify trees by clipping them with shears, and it was not the fashion to raise grass by sowing it, or to sprinkle gravel on paths. The branches grew as they pleased; God alone undertook to moderate the brambles and preserve the footways. The forest Simplice came across was an immense nest of verdure, multitudes of leaves and impenetrable masses of yoke-elms intersected by majestic avenues. The moss, inebriated with dew, reveled in a debauchery of growth; the sweetbriers, extending their flexible arms, sought one another in the glades to perform frantic dances round the great trees; the great trees themselves, while remaining calm and serene, distorted their roots in the shade, and rose tumultuously to kiss the rays of summer. The green grass grew anywhere, on the branches as on the ground; the leaves embraced the wood, while the Easter daisies and myosotis, in their haste to bloom, sometimes made a mistake and blossomed on the old fallen trunks. And all these branches, all these herbs, all these flowers sang; all mingled, crowded together, to babble more at ease, to relate to one another, in whispers, the mysterious love-making of the corolla. A breath of life ran to the depths of the gloomy coppices, giving voice to each bit of moss in the matchless concerts at dawn and twilight. It was an immense festival of the foliage.

The lady-birds, beetles, dragon-flies, butterflies, all the beautiful sweethearts of the flowering hedges, met at the four corners of the wood. They had established their little republic there; the paths were their paths; the brooks their brooks; the forest their forest. They stretched themselves out commodiously at the foot of the trees; on the low branches, in the dry leaves, living there as at home, quietly and by right of conquest. They had, for that matter, like civil persons, left the lofty branches to nightingales and other songsters.

The forest which already sang by its branches, its leaves, and flowers, sang also by its insects and birds.

III

In a few days Simplice became an old friend of the forest. They gossiped so madly together that he lost the little reason that still remained to him. When he left the forest to shut himself up between four walls, to seat himself at a table, to lie in a bed, he was all in a dream. At length, one fine morning, he suddenly abandoned his apartments, and took up his quarters beneath the beloved foliage.

There, he chose himself an immense palace.

His drawing-room was a vast circular glade, about a thousand hectares in extent. It was decked with long green drapery all round; five hundred flexible columns supported a veil of emerald-colored lace; the ceiling itself was a large dome of blue shot satin, studded with golden nails.

For bedroom he had a delicious boudoir, full of mystery and freshness. Its floor and walls were hidden beneath soft carpeting of inimitable workmanship. The alcove, hollowed out of the rock by some giant, was lined with pink marble, while the ground was strewn with ruby dust.

He also had his bath-room, with a spring of sparkling water and a crystal bath, buried in a cluster of flowers. I will not tell you, Ninon, of the thousand galleries that intersected the palace, nor of the ball-room, the theatre, and gardens. It was one of those royal residences such as God knows how to build.

Henceforth the prince could be a simpleton at his ease. His father thought he had been changed into a wolf, and sought an heir more worthy of the throne.

IV

Simplice was very busy on the days following his installation. He struck up an acquaintance with his neighbors, the beetle of the grass and the butterfly of the air. All were good creatures, and had almost as much wit as men.

At the commencement, he experienced some difficulty in learning their language, but he soon perceived that he had only his early education to thank for that. He soon conformed to the concise tongue of the insects. One sound ultimately sufficed for him, as for them, to designate a hundred different objects, according to the inflection of the voice and length of the note. So that he became unaccustomed to speak the language of men, so poor in spite of its wealth.

He was charmed with the manners of his new friends. He marveled above all at their way of expressing their opinion anent kings, which is not to have any. In short, he felt ignorant among them, and decided to go and study at their schools.

He showed more discretion in his intercourse with the mosses and hawthorns. As he could not yet catch the words of the flowers and blades of grass, his acquaintance with them was of a somewhat reserved character.

Altogether the forest did not look at him askance. It understood that his was a small mind and that he would live in good understanding with the creatures. They no longer hid from him. It often happened that he surprised a butterfly at the bottom of a path ruffling the frill of a daisy.

The hawthorn soon conquered its timidity so far as to give the young prince lessons. It amorously taught him the language of the perfumes and colors. Henceforth the purple corollas greeted Simplice every morning when he rose; the green leaf related to him the tittle-tattle of the night, the cricket confided to him in a whisper that he was madly in love with the violet.

Simplice had chosen a golden dragon-fly, with a slender waist and fluttering wings, for sweetheart. The pretty beauty showed herself despairingly coquettish; she gamboled, seemed to call him, then cleverly fled just as his hand was on her. The great trees, which saw the sport, smartly rebuked her, and gravely said among themselves that she would end badly.

Simplice all at once became anxious.

The lady-bird, who was the first to notice their friend's sadness, endeavored to ascertain from him what it was all about. He replied amidst tears that he was as gay as at the commencement.

He now: rose with the sun and wandered through the copses until night. He put the branches softly aside and examined each bush. He raised the leaves and gazed at its shadows.

"What can our pupil be looking for?" inquired the hawthorn of the moss.

The dragon-fly, astonished at being abandoned by her lover, fancied he had gone mad with love. She came teasing around him. But he did not look at her. The great trees had formed a correct opinion of her. She promptly consoled herself with the first butterfly she met at the cross-roads.

The leaves were sad. They watched the young prince questioning every tuft of grass, searching the long avenues with his eyes; they listened to him complaining of the thickness of the brambles, and said:

"Simplice has seen Flower-of-the-Waters, the undine of the spring."

V

Flower-of-the-Waters was the daughter of a ray of light and a drop of dew. Her beauty was so limpid that a lover's kiss would make her die; she exhaled such sweet perfume that a kiss from her lips would kill a lover.

The forest knew it, and the jealous forest hid its darling child. For sanctuary it had given her a spring shaded with its most bushy boughs. There Flower-of-the-Waters beamed, in silence and shade, amidst her sisters. Being idle she resigned herself to the stream, her little feet half veiled by the wavelets, her fair head crowned with limpid pearls. Her smile delighted the water-lilies and gladiolus. She was the soul of the forest.

She lived unattended with care, knowing nothing of the earth but her mother, the dew, and of heaven naught but the ray of light, her father. She felt herself loved by the wavelet that rocked her, by the branch that gave her shade. She had thousands of sweethearts and not one lover.

Flower-of-the-Waters was aware that she must die of love; that thought gave her pleasure, and she lived hoping for death. Smiling she awaited the well-beloved.

Simplice had seen her one night by starlight, at the bend of a path. He sought her for a long month, fancying to meet her behind the trunk of each tree. He was always thinking he saw her glide into the coppice; but on running there he only found the great shadows of the poplars waving in the breath of Heaven.

VI

The forest was now silent; it distrusted Simplice. It thickened its foliage; it cast all its gloom over the young prince's footsteps. The peril threatening Flower-of-the-Waters grieved it; there were no more caresses, no more amorous chatter.

The undine returned to the glades, and Simplice saw her again. Mad with desire, he dashed off in pursuit of her. The child, seated on a ray of the moon, did not hear the sound of his footsteps. She flew along in this way, as light as a feather borne upon the wind.

Simplice ran, ran after her without being able to catch her. Tears streamed from his eyes, he was in despair.

He ran, and the forest anxiously watched his mad flight. Shrubs barred the road. Brambles encompassed him with their thorny arms, stopping him suddenly on his way. The whole wood protected the child.

He ran, and felt the moss become slippery beneath his feet. The branches of the coppice were interlaced more closely and presented themselves to him as rigid as brass rods. Dry leaves collected in the glens; trunks of fallen trees placed themselves across the paths; rocks rolled themselves before the prince. The insect stung him in the heel; the butterfly blinded him by beating its wings against his eyelids.

Flower-of-the-Waters, without seeing or hearing him, continued to fly on the ray of the moon. Simplice with agony felt the moment approaching when she would disappear.

And, breathless, in despair, he ran, ran.

VII

He heard the old oaks shouting to him in anger:

"Why did you not say you were a man? We would have hidden from you; we would have refused you our lessons, so that your gloomy eye might not see Flower-of-the-Waters, the undine of the spring. You presented your-self to us with the innocence of animals, and now you display the mind of man. Look, you are crushing the beetles, tearing away our leaves, breaking our branches. The wind of egoism bears you along; you want to rob us of our soul."

And the hawthorn added, "Simplice, stop, for pity's sake! When a capricious child wants to breathe the perfume of my starry nosegays, why does not he leave them to bloom in freedom on the branch! He plucks them and only enjoys them for an hour."

And the moss said in its turn, "Stop, Simplice; come and dream on my cool, velvety carpet . Far away, between the trees, you will see Flower-of-the-Waters at play. You will see her bathing at the spring, casting collets of watery pearls about her neck. We will give you a half share in the joy of her look; you can live and gaze on her as we do."

And all the forest resumed, "Stop, Simplice, a kiss must kill her; give not that kiss. Are you not aware of it? Did not our messenger, the breeze of night, tell you? Flower-of-the-Waters is the celestial pearl whose perfume brings death. Alas! Pity for her, Simplice, drink not her soul on her lips."

VIII

Flower-of-the-Waters turned round and saw Simplice. She smiled; she made him a sign to approach, saying to the forest: "Here comes the well-beloved."

The prince had been pursuing the undine for three days, three hours, three minutes. The words of the oaks were thundering behind him; he was tempted to fly.

Flower-of-the-Waters was already pressing his hands. She raised herself tip-toe on her little feet, mirroring her smile in the young man's eyes.

"You have delayed coming," she said. "My heart knew you were in the forest. I mounted a ray of the moon and sought you for three days, three hours, three minutes."

Simplice was silent, he withheld his breath. She made him sit down at the edge of the spring; she fondled him with her eyes; and he contemplated her for a long time.

"Do you not know me?" she continued. "I have often seen you in my dreams. I went to you, you took my hand, then we walked, silent and trembling. Did you not see me? Do you not remember your dreams?"

And as he at length opened his mouth:

"Do not say anything," she resumed again. "I am Flower of-the-Waters, and you are the well-beloved. We are going to die."

IX

The great trees bent forward to get a better view of the young couple. They shuddered with grief, they said to one another, from coppice to coppice, that their soul was about to fly away.

All the voices were silent. The blade of grass and the oak experienced immense pity. There was no longer any cry of anger among the foliage. Simplice, Flower-of-the-Water's well-beloved, was the son of the old forest.

She had rested her head on his shoulder. Bending over the brook they smiled at one another. Sometimes, raising their foreheads, they followed with their eyes the gold dust fluttering in the last rays of the sun. They clasped each other slowly, slowly. They awaited the appearance of the first star to be blended together in one and fly off for ever.

Not a word troubled their ecstasy. Their spirits rising to their lips were exchanged in their breath.

Day was on the wane, the lips of the two lovers approached closer and closer. The silent, motionless forest experienced terrible agony. The huge rocks from which the springs burst forth, threw great shadows over the couple who shone in the coming night.

And the stars appeared, and the lips were united in the supreme kiss, and the oak trees gave a prolonged sob. The lips were united, the spirits flew away.

X

A clever man was wandering in the forest. He was in the company of a learned man.

The clever man made profound remarks on the unhealthy dampness of woods, and spoke of the beautiful fields of lucerne that might be obtained by cutting down all the great ugly trees.

The learned man dreamed of making himself a name in the world of science by discovering some new plant. He searched about everywhere and came upon nettles and couch grass.

On reaching the edge of the spring they found the corpse of Simplice. The prince was smiling in the slumber of death. His feet were in the water, his head resting on the grassy bank. He pressed to his lips, which were for ever closed, a small pink and white flower, exquisitely delicate in form, and with a strong perfume.

"The poor idiot!" said the clever man, "he must have been trying to pick a nosegay, and drowned himself."

The learned man cared little about the corpse. He had taken the flower, and under pretence of examining it, tore away the corolla. Then, when he had pulled it to pieces, he exclaimed—

"Precious find! In memory of this simpleton, I will name this flower Anthapheleia litnnaia."

Ah, Ninette, Ninette, the barbarian named my ideal Flower-of-the-Waters Anthapheleia litnnaia!

THE BALL-PROGRAM

I

Do you remember our long run in the woods, Ninon? Autumn had begun to sprinkle the trees with yellow purple leaves, which were still gilded by the rays of the setting sun. The grass beneath our feet was thinner than at the commencement of May, and the russety moss hardly afforded shelter for a few rare insects. Lost in the forest, which abounded in melancholy sounds, it seemed as though we heard the bitter lamentations of a woman who believes she has discovered the first wrinkle on her forehead. The foliage, which this pale, mild evening could not deceive, felt the winter coming in the breeze which had freshened, and submitted sadly to being rocked by the wind while weeping over its reddened verdure.

We wandered for a long time in the coppices, caring little for the direction of the paths, but choosing the most shady and secluded. Our frank peals of laughter frightened the thrushes and blackbirds that were whistling in the hedges; and sometimes we heard a green lizard, troubled in his ecstasy by the sound of our footsteps, slipping noiselessly beneath the brambles. Our ramble was without object: after a cloudy day, we had seen the sky, towards evening, wearing a brighter aspect; we had dashed out to enjoy this ray of sunshine. We advanced thus, raising a perfume of sage and thyme beneath our feet, at times running after one another, at others walking leisurely hand in hand. Then I plucked you the last flowers, or sought to reach the red berries of the hawthorns, which you coveted like a child. And you, Ninon, in the meanwhile, crowned with blossoms, you ran to the neighboring spring under pretence of drinking, but rather to admire your headdress, O coquette and idle girl!

All at once distant peals of laughter became mingled with the vague murmurs of the forest; a fife and tabor were heard, and the breeze brought us the subdued sound of dancing. We had stopped, listening attentively, quite expecting to find that this music came from the mysterious ball of the sylphs. We slipped from tree to tree, guided by the sound of the instruments; then, when we had cautiously put aside the branches of the last thicket, this is the sight we saw.

In the center of a glade, on a strip of turf surrounded by wild juniper and pistachio trees, some ten peasants of both sexes were moving backward and forward in time. The women, who were bare-headed, with throats covered up by neckerchiefs, skipped about freely, giving utterance to those peals of laughter we had heard; the men, to dance with greater ease, had thrown their jackets among their implements of labor, which glittered in the grass.

These honest folk paid little attention to the measure. A thin, raw-boned man, leaning with his back against an oak-tree, was playing the fife, while he struck a sharp-sounding tabor with his left hand, after the custom of Provence. He seemed to follow the hurried, noisy measure with delight. Sometimes his glance wandered to the dancers; then he pitifully shrugged his shoulders. Accredited musician of some large village, he had been stopped as he passed that way, and it was not without anger that he saw these inhabitants of the inner country thus breaking all the rules of fine dancing. Aggrieved during the quadrille at the leaping and stamping of the peasants, he blushed with indignation when, at the end of the air, they continued their paces for five long minutes, without appearing to have any idea even of the absence of the fife and tabor.

It would have been charming, no doubt, to have surprised the hobgoblins of the forest at their mysterious frolics. But, at the least breath, they would have vanished; and running to the ball-room, we would hardly have found a few blades of slightly bent grass, to indicate their passing presence. It would have been a mockery: make us hear their laughter, invite us to share their joy, then run away at our approach, without allowing us a single quadrille.

We could not have danced with sylphs, Ninette; with peasants, never was reality more engaging.

We suddenly left the thicket. Our noisy dancers showed no disposition to take to flight. It was only a long time after we had been there that they perceived our presence. They had begun capering again. The player on the fife, who had pretended to withdraw, having seen a few pieces of money shine, had just taken to his instruments again, beating and blowing afresh, while sighing at the thought of prostituting melody as he was doing. It seemed to me that I recognized the slow, imperceptible measure of a waltz. I was encircling your waist, watching the moment to whirl you along in my arms, when you eagerly tore yourself away to laugh and skip, just like a bold, sun-burnt peasant girl. The man with the tabor, who was becoming consoled at the sight of my preparations as a fine dancer, had only to shroud his face after that, and bewail the decline of art.

I know not how it was, Ninon, that I recalled those follies last night, our long run, our dances full of freedom and laughter. Then, this vague souvenir was followed by a hundred other vague reveries. Will you pardon me if I relate them to you? Traveling along at hazard, stopping and running without any reason, I trouble myself but little about the crowd; my tales are only very faint sketches: but you told me you were fond of them.

The dance, that chastely wanton nymph, charms rather than attracts me. I, a simple spectator, love to see her jingling her little bells throughout the world; voluptuous, twisting herself into all sorts of attitudes, blowing fiery kisses, beneath the skies of Spain and Italy; gliding along amorously in a long veil, like a dream, in blond Germany; and even when walking, reserved and skilful, in the drawing-rooms of France. I like to see her everywhere; on the moss in the woods as on costly carpets; at village weddings as at glittering parties.

Gracefully bending backward, with moist eyes and lips half parted, she has passed through ages, clasping and unclasping her arms above her fair head. All doors have opened at the measured sound of her footsteps; those of temples, those of joyous retreats; there perfumed with incense, here with her gown reddened with wine, she has harmoniously struck the ground; and after so many centuries she reaches us, smiling, without her supple limbs ever hastening or delaying the melodious cadence.

Let the goddess then appear. Groups are formed, the dancing-girls camber beneath the clasp of their partners. Here is the immortal. Her extended arms hold a tambourine; she smiles, then gives the signal; the couples move, follow her steps, imitate her attitudes. And I, 1 love to watch that nimble rotation; I endeavor to catch all the glances, all the words of love, in the corner where I am dreaming; I experience the enthusiasm of rhythm, thanking the immortal, if she has left me ignorant and clumsy, for having given me at least the sentiment of her harmonious art.

To tell the truth, Ninette, I would prefer her, the fair goddess, in her amorous nudity, unclasping and waving her white girdle without following any rule; I would prefer her far from the ball-room, fancying herself hidden from all profane eyes, tracing her most capricious steps upon the turf. There, barely veiled, softly pressing the grass with her rosy feet, she would move about in innocent liberty; she would discover the secret of the melody of movement. There, I would go, hidden in the foliage, to admire her lovely form, slim and supple, and watch the gambols of the shadow on her shoulders, according as her caprice bore it away or brought it back.

But, sometimes, I have taken to detesting her, when she appeared to me in the shape of a young coquette, well starched and foolishly decent; when I have seen her blindly obeying an orchestra, pouting, appearing weary, stifling a yawn while acquitting herself of her steps as of a task. I will say all: I have never admired the immortal in a ballroom without a feeling of sorrow. Her taper legs become entangled in those long skirts of our ladies of fashion; she finds herself too much clogged, she who only wants to be free and capricious; and, in trouble, she clumsily conforms to our silly curtsies, always losing her gracefulness and often becoming ridiculous.

I would like to close our doors to her. If I bear with her sometimes beneath the chandeliers, without feeling too sad, it is, thanks to her tablets of love, to her ball-program.

Do you see it in her hand, Ninon, that little book? Look; the clasp and pencil-holder are gold; never was paper more soft or more nicely perfumed; never was there binding more elegant. That is our offering to the goddess. Others have given her the wreath and girdle: we, out of kindness of heart, have made her a present of the ball-program.

She had so many adorers, the poor child, she was so pressed with invitations, that she hardly knew what to do. Each came to admire her, begging for a quadrille, and the coquette always consented. She danced, danced, lost her memory, was overwhelmed with reproaches, and made other mistakes; hence dreadful confusion and frightful jealousy. She withdrew with aching feet and her memory gone. One took pity on her and presented her with the little golden book. Since then no more forgetfulness, no more confusion nor injustice. When lovers besiege her she hands them her program; each writes his name there; it is for those who are the most in love to come first . Let them be a hundred, the white pages are numerous. If all have not squeezed her slender waist when the lights of the chandeliers begin to pale, they have only to complain of their own indolence, and not of the child's indifference.

No doubt the system was simple, Ninon. You must be surprised at my exclamations anent a few leaves of paper. But what charming leaves, exhaling a perfume of coquetry, full of sweet secrets! What a long list of handsome sweethearts, the name of each of whom is an homage, each page an entire evening of triumph and adoration! What a magic book, containing a life of tenderness, in which the profane can only spell out vain names, while the young girl reads off-hand an account of her beauty and the admiration she excites!

Each comes in turn to make submission, each comes and signs his love-letter. Are they not, indeed, the thousand signatures to a declaration under the rose? Ought one not, if one were of good faith, to write them on the first page, those eternal phrases that are always young? But the little book is discreet; it will not make its mistress blush. It and she alone know what to dream of.

Frankly, I suspect it of being very artful. See how it dissembles, how simple and necessary it makes itself. What is it, if not an aid for memory? Quite a primitive means of doing justice, by giving each one his turn. It speak of love, it agitate young girls! You make a great mistake. Turn over the pages; you will not find the smallest "I love you." It says truly, nothing is more innocent, more simple, more primitive than I. And, indeed, parents notice it in their daughters' hands without alarm. While the note signed with a single name is hidden in the bodice, the letter bearing a thousand signatures is boldly exhibited. One meets with it everywhere in broad daylight, in the drawing-room and in the child's bedchamber. Is it not the least dangerous little book one knows of?

It deceives even its mistress. What danger can there be in an object of such common use, approved, moreover, by one's parents? She turns the leaves over without fear. It is here that one can accuse the ball-program of absolute hypocrisy. What do you think it whispers in the child's ear when all is silent? Simple names? Oh! not at all! but real, long, amorous conversations. It has put aside its air of necessity and disinterestedness. It chats and caresses; it is burning, and stutters out tender words. The young girl feels oppressed; trembling, she continues. And all at once the party reappears, the chandeliers sparkle, the orchestra resounds amorously; suddenly each name is personified, and the ball, of which she was the queen, begins again with its ovations, its fondling and flattering words.

Ah! you rogue of a book, what a procession of young partners! That one there, while gently squeezing her waist, extolled her blue eyes; this one, here, bashful and trembling, could only smile at her; while that other talked, talked, without ceasing, paying her all those gallant compliments, which, in spite of their being devoid of sense, say more than long speeches.

And, when the virgin has once forgotten herself with him, the sly rascal knows she will do it again. As a young woman, she turns over the leaves, consults them anxiously to discover what has been the increase in the number of her admirers. She pauses with a sad smile at certain names which are not repeated on the last pages, flighty names which have no doubt gone to enrich other programs.

Most of her subjects remain faithful to her; she passes them in review with indifference. The little book laughs at all that. He knows his power; he will receive the caresses of a whole lifetime.

Old age comes, the program is not forgotten. The gilt edges are faded and the leaves hardly hold together. Its mistress, who has become aged as well, seems to like it the more. She still often turns over the pages, and becomes intoxicated with its distant perfume of youth. Off to sleep again, but so light was her slumber that the sudden cracking of a piece of furniture made her half sit up. She thrust back her hair falling in disorder on her forehead, rubbed her eyes swollen with sleep, brought ail the corners of her bedclothes over her shoulders, crossing her arms to hide herself the better.

Isn't that a charming part, Ninon, that of the ball program? Isn't it , like all poetry, incomprehensible to the crowd, and only read fluently by the initiated? Confident of woman's secrets, it accompanies her through life like an angel of love, smothering her with hopes and remembrances.

II

Georgette had only just left the convent. She was still of that happy age when dreams and reality make one; sweet and short-lived epoch, the mind sees what it dreams of and dreams of what it sees. Like all children she had allowed herself to he dazzled by the blazing chandeliers at her first balls; she honestly imagined herself in a superior sphere, among beings who were demi-gods, in whom the bad side of life had been remitted.

Her cheeks, which were slightly brown, possessed that golden reflex which is peculiar to the bosom of a Sicilian girl; her long black lashes half veiled the flash of her eyes. Forgetting she was no longer under the eye of an assistant schoolmistress, she checked the fierce fire that was burning within her. In a drawing-room she was never anything more than a little timid and almost silly girl, blushing at a word and casting down her eyes.

Come, we will hide behind the great curtains; we shall see the indolent creature stretch her arms and uncover her rosy feet as she awakes. Do not be jealous, Ninon: all my kisses are for you.

Do you remember? Eleven o'clock was striking. The room was still dark. The sun was lost in the thick hangings at the windows, while a fairy lamp that was dying out, struggled in vain against the darkness. On the bed, when the flame of the fairy lamp brightened, appeared a white form, a pure forehead, a throat lost in waves of lace; further down, the delicate extremity of a small foot; a snow-like arm with an open hand, hung outside the bed.

Twice the lazy creature turned round on the couch to go

When she was well awake, she stretched out her hand towards a bell-rope hanging beside her; but she rapidly brought it to her again, she sprang to the floor and drew aside the window hangings herself. A bright ray of sunshine filled the room. The child, surprised at the broad daylight, and catching sight of herself in a looking-glass, half nude and with her dress in disorder, felt very much alarmed. She went back and buried herself in bed, all red and trembling at her fine performance. Her chambermaid was a silly curious girl; Georgette preferred her own reverie to that person's gossip. But, goodness gracious I how light it was, and how indiscreet looking-glasses are I

Now, on the chairs scattered about the room one perceived a ball toilette that had been negligently-cast there. Here the young girl, half asleep, had left her gauze skirt, there her sash, a little further on her satin shoes. Her jewels sparkled in an agate bowl close to her; a faded bouquet was dying beside a ball-program.

With her forehead resting on one of her naked arms, she took up a necklace and began toying with the pearls. Then she set it down, opened the program, and began turning it over. The little book had a weary and indifferent air. Georgette ran her eye over it without much attention, thinking apparently of something else.

As she turned the pages, the name of Charles written at the head of each of them, ended by trying her patience.

"Always Charles," she said to herself. "My cousin has a fine handwriting; those long sloping letters have a very serious aspect. His hand rarely trembles, even when he presses mine. My cousin is a very sedate young man. One of these days he is to be my husband. At each ball he takes my program, without asking me, and writes himself down for the first dance. That is no doubt a husband's right. That right displeases me."

The program became more and more cold. Georgette gazing into space, seemed to be working out some momentous problem.

"A husband," she resumed, "that is what frightens me. Charles always treats me as a little girl; because he won eight or ten prizes at college, he considers himself compelled to be pedantic. After all I don't know exactly why he should be my husband; I never asked him to marry me; he on his side has never asked my permission. We played together formally; I remember he was very unkind. Now he is very polite; I should like him better if he were unkind. So, I am going to be his wife; I had never seriously thought of that: his wife, I really don't see the reason why. Charles, always Charles! One would think I belonged to him already. I shall ask him not to write so big on my program: his name occupies too much space."

The little book, which also seemed tired of Cousin Charles, almost closed itself with weariness. I suspect ball-programs of feeling the most candid hatred for husbands. This one turned over its pages and slyly presented other names to Georgette.

"Louis," murmured the child. "That name recalls a singular dancer. He came, almost without looking at me, and asked me to grant him a quadrille. Then, at the first sounds of the instruments, he dragged me to the other end of the ball-room; I cannot understand why, opposite a tall, fair lady, who was following him with her eyes. At times he smiled at her, and so absolutely forgot my presence, that on two occasions I was obliged to pick up my bouquet myself. When the dance brought him near her, he spoke to her in an undertone; as for me, I listened, but could understand nothing. Perhaps it was his sister. His sister, oh! no: he trembled when he took her hand; then when he held that hand in his, the orchestra summoned him in vain to my side. I stood there like a stupid, with my arm stretched out which looked very bad; the figures were all in confusion. It was perhaps his wife. How simple I am! His wife, really, yes! But Charles never speaks to me when dancing. It was perhaps"

Georgette remained with parted lips absorbed in reflection, like a child placed before an unknown toy, not daring to approach and opening her eyes to see better. She listlessly counted the tassels on the counterpane, her right hand extended and wide open on the program. The latter began to show signs of animation; it stirred about and seemed to know perfectly well who the fair lady was. I am unaware whether the libertine confided the secret to the young girl. She drew back the lace which was slipping down, over her shoulders, completed scrupulously counting the tassels on the counterpane, and at last said in an undertone:

"It's singular, that beautiful lady was neither M. Louis' wife nor his sister."

She resumed turning over the pages. A name soon stopped her."

"This Robert is a wicked man," she continued. "I should never have thought that any one with such an elegant waistcoat could be so base-minded. For a full quarter of an hour he was comparing me to a thousand beautiful things—the stars, flowers, and I know not what else. I felt flattered. I experienced so much pleasure that I did not know what to answer. He spoke well, and for a long time without stopping. Then he led me back to my seat, and there he almost wept at leaving me. Afterwards I went to a window; I was hidden by the curtains which hung down behind me. I was thinking a little, I fancy, of my chatter-box of a partner, when I overheard him laughing and talking. He was speaking to a friend of a silly little thing, who blushed at the slightest word, of a novice just fresh from a convent, who cast down her eyes and made herself ugly by her over modest demeanor. No doubt he was alluding to Therese, my dear friend. Therese has small eyes and a large mouth. She is a very good girl. Perhaps they were alluding to me. So young men tell falsehoods, then! So, I am ugly. Ugly!

Therese, however, is more so. They must certainly have been alluding to Therese."

Georgette smiled, and felt a sort of inclination to run and consult her mirror.

"Then," she added, "They made fun of the ladies at the ball. I continued listening, and at last I failed to understand. I fancied they were using ugly words. As I could not get away I courageously stopped my ears."

The ball-program was convulsed with laughter. It proceeded to quote a swarm of names to prove to Georgette that Therese was indeed the silly little thing who made herself appear ugly by a too modest demeanor.

"Paul has blue eyes," it said. "Paul assuredly does not tell falsehoods, and I have heard him say very sweet things to you."

"Yes, yes," repeated Georgette, "M. Paul has blue eyes, and M. Paul does not tell falsehoods. He has fair moustaches, which I like much better than those of Charles."

"Don't speak to me of Charles," continued the program; "his moustaches do not deserve the faintest smile. What do you think of Édouard? He is timid, and only dares speak with his eyes. I don't know if you understand that language. And Jules? He affirms that you alone know how to waltz. And Lucien, and Georges, and Albert? They all consider you charming, and for long hours beg the charity of a smile."

Georgette recommenced counting the tassels on the counterpane. The program's chattering began to alarm her. She felt the book was burning her hands; she would have liked to close it, but had not the courage.

"For you were the queen," continued the demon. "Your lace wouldn't hide your arms; your forehead of sixteen summers put your tiara in the shade. Ah! My Georgette, you could not see all, otherwise you would have shown pity. The poor fellows feel very sad at the present moment!"

And there was a silence signifying of commiseration. The child who was listening, smiling and on the alert, seeing the program remain silent, murmured:

"A bow had fallen from my gown. Surely that made me look ugly. The young men must have made fun as they passed. Those dressmakers are so careless!"

"Did not he dance with you?" interrupted the program.

"Who do you mean?" inquired Georgette, blushing so much that her shoulders became quite pink.

And pronouncing, at last, a name she had had before her eyes for a quarter of an hour, and which her heart was spelling out to her, while her lips spoke of a torn gown, she said:

"M. Edmond seemed sad last night. I saw him looking at me from a distance. As he was afraid to approach, I rose and went over to him. He could not do otherwise than ask me to dance."

"I am very fond of M. Edmond," sighed the little book. Georgette pretended not to understand. She continued: "In dancing I felt his hand trembling on my waist. He stammered out a few words, complaining of the heat. Seeing he cast a look of envy at the roses in my bouquet, I gave him one. There was no harm in that."

"Oh no! Then, in taking the flower, his lips by a peculiar chance came close to your fingers. He gave them a little kiss."

"There is no harm in that," repeated Georgette, who for a few moments had been very restless in bed.

"Oh no I But I must really scold you for having made him wait for that poor kiss so long. Edmond would make a charming little husband."

The child, more and more troubled, did not notice that her fichu had fallen off and that one of her feet had thrown back the bedclothes.

"A charming little husband," she repeated again.

"I am very fond of him," continued the tempter. "If I were in your place I would willingly return him his kiss."

Georgette was scandalized. The good apostle continued, "Only a kiss, there, softly on his name. I won't tell him about it"

The young girl vowed by all she respected that she would not do it. And I know not how it was that the page came to her lips. She knew nothing about it herself. Amidst her protests, she kissed the name twice.

Then, she perceived her foot, which was smiling in a ray of the sun. All in confusion she pulled up the bedclothes, and completely lost her head on hearing the handle of the door turn.

The ball-program slipped amidst the lace and disappeared in great haste under the pillow. It was the chambermaid.

SHE WHO LOVES ME

Is she who loves me a grand lady, smothered in silk, lace and jewels, dreaming of our love on the sofa of a boudoir? Marchioness' or duchess, graceful and light as a dream, languidly trailing a profusion of white petticoats across the carpets, and making a little pout sweeter than a smile?

Is she who loves me a smart grisette, tripping along, catching up her skirt to jump over the gutters, searching with her eyes for a compliment on her taper leg? Is she the good-natured girl who drinks out of every one's glass, clothed in satin to-day, in coarse calico to-morrow, and who finds a little love for each in her wealth of heart?

Is she who loves me the blond child kneeling down to say her prayers beside her mother? The foolish virgin calling on me at night in the darkness of the narrow streets? Is she the sunburnt country-girl who looks at me as I pass, and carries a remembrance of me away with her amongst the corn and ripe vines? Is she the poverty-stricken creature who thanks me for my charity? Is she the mate of another, lover or husband, whom I followed one day, and saw no more?

Is she who loves me a daughter of Europe, as white as dawn, a daughter of Asia yellow and gold like sunset, or a daughter of the desert as dark as a stormy night?

Is she who loves me separated from me by a thin partition? Is she beyond the seas? Is she beyond the stars?

Is she who loves me still to be born? Did she die a hundred years ago?

Yesterday I sought her at a fair. The Faubourg was holidaymaking, and the people, dressed in their Sunday clothes, were noisily ascending the streets.

The illumination lamps had just been lit. The avenue, from distance to distance, was decked with yellow and blue posts, affixed to which were small colored cups, burning smoking wicks that were blowing about in the wind. Venetian lanterns were vacillating in the trees. The footways were bordered by canvas booths with the fringe of their red curtains dragging in the gutters. The gilded crockery, the freshly painted sweets, the tinsel of the wares mirrored in the raw light of the Argon lamps.

There was a smell of dust, of gingerbread and waffles made with fat, in the air. The organs resounded; the Merry-Andrews, smothered in flour, laughed and wept beneath a shower of cuffs and kicks. A warm wave weighed upon this joy.

Above this wave and noise expanded a summer sky of pure melancholy depths. An angel had just lit up the azure blue for some divine fete, a supremely calm festival of the infinite.

Lost in the crowd, I felt how solitary was my heart. I advanced, following with my eyes the young girls who smiled at me as I passed along, saying to myself that I would never see those smiles again. That thought of so many amorous lips, perceived for a moment and lost for ever, caused me anguish.

In this manner I reached a cross way, in the middle of the avenue. On the left, against an elm was an isolated booth. In the front, a few ill-joined planks served as a platform, and a couple of lanterns lighted the door which was nothing more than a strip of canvas caught up like a curtain. As I stopped, a man wearing the costume of a magician, a long black gown and pointed hat scattered over with stars, was addressing the crowd from the height of the planks.

"Walk-up," he shouted, "walk-up, my fine gentlemen, walk-up, my beautiful young ladies! I have come in all haste from the interior of India to make young hearts rejoice. It was there that I conquered, at the peril of my life, the mirror of love, which was guarded by a horrible dragon. My fine gentlemen, my beautiful young ladies, I have brought you the realization of your dreams. Walk-up, walk-up and see 'She who loves you!' For two sous 'She who loves you!'"

An old woman, attired as a guard, raised the piece of canvas. Her eyes wandered over the crowd with an idiotic expression: then, she cried in a husky voice:

"For two sous, for two sous 'She who loves you!' Walk-up and see 'She who loves you!'"

The magician beat a captivating fanciful rumble on the big drum. The guard hung on to a bell and accompanied him.

The public hesitated. A learned ass playing at cards offers lively interest; a strong man raising 100-lb. weights is a sight one would never tire of; it is impossible to deny, moreover, that a half-naked female giant is a fit subject to give pleasant amusement to people of all ages. But to see "She who loves us," is what one cares about the least, and a thing that does not foreshadow the slightest emotion.

I had listened to the appeal of the man with the long gown with rapture. His promises responded to my heart's desire; I saw the hand of Providence in the hazard that had directed my footsteps. This worthless fellow rose singularly in my estimation, by reason of the astonishment I experienced in hearing him read my secret thoughts. It seemed to me that I saw him fixing flaming eyes on me, beating the big drum with diabolical fury, shouting out to me to walk-up in a voice louder than the sound of the bell.

I was placing my foot on the first step, when I felt myself stopped. Having turned round, I saw a man at the foot of the platform holding me by my coat. This man was tall and thin; he had large hands covered with cotton gloves that were still larger, and wore a hat that had become russety, a black coat white at the elbows, and dreadful-looking kerseymere trousers, all yellow with grease and mud. He bent himself double in a long and exquisite reverence, then, in a fluty voice, addressed me in the following language:

"I am sorry, sir, that a young man who has been well brought up should set a bad example to the crowd. It is showing great levity to encourage the impudence of this rascal, who is speculating on our bad instincts; for I consider those words shouted out in the open air, which call boys and girls to a debauchery of sight and mind, profoundly immoral. Ah! The people are weak, sir. We men, rendered strong by education, we have, bear it in mind, grave and imperious duties to perform. Let us not give way to guilty curiosity, let us be worthy in all things. The morality of society depends on us, sir."

I listened to what he said. He had not let go of my coat, and could not make up his mind to complete his reverence. He discoursed hat in hand, with such courteous calmness, that I never dreamt of getting angry. When he had concluded, I was content to look him in the face without answering. He took this silence for an inquiry.

"Sir," he said, with another bow, "sir, I am the People's Friend, and my mission is the happiness of humanity."

He pronounced these words with modest pride, suddenly drawing himself up erect. I turned my back on him and ascended to the platform. As I raised the piece of canvas before entering, I looked at him for the last time. He had delicately taken the fingers of his left hand with those of his right, and sought to efface the wrinkles of his gloves which he was threatened with losing.

Then, the People's Friend, crossing his arms, tenderly surveyed the guard.

I let the curtain fall and found myself in the temple. It was a sort of long narrow place devoid of seats, with canvas walls and lighted by a single Argon lamp. A few people, inquisitive girls and youths making a noise, were already assembled there. The arrangements had been made with every regard to decency: a cord stretched down the centre of the booth, separated men from women.

The Mirror of Love, to tell the truth, was nothing more than a couple of pieces of glass without tinfoil, one in each compartment, little round windows, in fact, looking into the inner part of the booth. The promised miracle was accomplished with admirable simplicity: it sufficed to apply the right eye to the glass, and, without its being a question of thunder or sulphur, the well-beloved appeared on the other side. How would it be possible to disbelieve so natural a vision!

I did not feel the strength to attempt the trial at the outset. The guard had cast a look on me as I passed her that froze my heart. How could I tell what awaited me beyond that piece of glass? Perhaps a horrible countenance with sparkless eyes and violet lips; a centenarian thirsting for young blood, one of those deformed creatures whom I see at night in my bad dreams. I thought no more of those blond creatures with whom I charitably people the void in my heart. I remembered all the ugly ones who showed me some affection, and I asked myself in terror if it were not one of these whom I was about to see appear.

I retired into a corner. To regain courage I watched those who, bolder than myself, consulted destiny without so much ado. It was not long before I took peculiar pleasure at the sight of these different faces, the right eye wide open, the left closed with two fingers, each having his particular smile, in conformity with the vision pleasing him more or less. The glass was rather low, and it was necessary to bend slightly forward. To my mind nothing could be more grotesque than these men following one another to see the sister soul of their own soul through a hole a few centimeters round.

First of all two soldiers advanced: a sergeant bronzed beneath Africa's sun and a young conscript, a lad still savoring of the plough, whose arms were ill at ease in a greatcoat three times too large for him. The sergeant gave a skeptic laugh. The conscript remained a long time stooping, particularly flattered at having a sweetheart.

Then came a fat man in a white jacket, with a red, puffy face, who gazed quietly without making a grimace of either joy or displeasure, as if it were quite natural that he should be loved by some one.

He was followed by three schoolboys, bold-faced youths of fifteen or sixteen summers, pushing one another to make believe that they enjoyed the honor of being tipsy. All three vowed they recognized their aunts.

Thus the inquisitive came one after the other to the piece of glass, and it would not be possible for me to remember now, the different expressions of features that struck me then. O vision of the well-beloved! What severe truths you made those expanded eyes say! They were the real Mirrors of Love, mirrors in which the gracefulness of woman was reflected in a surreptitious glimmer, where lust and stupidity were blended together.

The girls, at the other piece of glass, were amusing themselves in a much more respectable way. I read nothing but a great deal of curiosity on their faces; not the least look of naughty desire, not the smallest wicked thought. They came each in turn to cast an astonished glance through the small aperture, and withdrew, some a trifle thoughtful, others laughing like madcaps.

To tell the truth, I hardly know what they were doing there. If I were a woman and only a trifle pretty, I would never have the silly idea of troubling to go and see the man who loved me. On days when my heart would be sad at being alone —those would be bright, sunny spring days—I would go off to a flowery lane and make all who passed adore me. In the evening, I would return with a wealth of love.

Of course, these curious creatures were not all equally pretty. The handsome ones laughed at the magician's science; they had long since ceased to have need of him. The ugly ones, on the contrary, had never enjoyed such a treat. Amongst them came one with thin hair and a large mouth, who could not tear herself away from the magic mirror. She preserved on her lips the joyous and heartrending smile of an indigent person satisfying hunger after a prolonged fast.

I was wondering what were the beautiful ideas that had been awakened in those giddy heads. It was but a poor problem. All had assuredly dreamt of a prince casting himself at their feet; all wished to gain a better idea of the lover of whom they had but a confused recollection on awakening. There were, doubtless, many deceptions; princes are becoming rare, and the eyes of our souls which open at night-time on a better world, are otherwise accommodating than those which we make use of in broad daylight. There was also great joy: the vision was realized, the lover had the silky moustache and the raven hair dreamt of.

Thus each of them, in a few seconds, lived a life of love. Simple romances, as swift as hope, which could be guessed in their high-colored cheeks and the more amorous heaving of their bosoms.

After all, these girls were perhaps fools, and I am a fool myself for having seen so many things, when there was no doubt nothing to see. Anyhow, by studying them I recovered my pluck. I noticed that men and women in general appeared very satisfied with the apparition. The magician would assuredly never have had the unkindness to cause these honest folk, who gave him two sous, the least displeasure.

I approached and applied my eye to the glass without too great excitement. I perceived a woman leaning over the back of an arm-chair, between red curtains. She was brilliantly lit up by Argon lamps, which were invisible, and stood out in relief against a piece of painted canvas, stretched in the background. This canvas, which was torn in places, must formerly have represented a lover's grove of blue trees.

"She who loves me" wore, as a well-bred vision should do, a long white gown, just caught in at the waist, and falling on the boards like a cloud. From her forehead hung a long veil, also white, fastened by a wreath of May blossoms. The dear angel, thus attired, was all white and all innocence.

She leant coquettishly forward, turning her eyes towards me—great caressing blue eyes. She looked bewitching under the veil: flaxen tresses disappearing amidst the muslin, the candid forehead of a virgin, delicate lips, dimples that were nests for kisses. At the first glance I took her for a saint; at the second, I found she had the air of a good-natured girl, in no way prudish and very accommodating.

She carried her fingers to her lips and sent me a kiss, with a bow which had nothing of the abode of spirits about it. Noticing that she did not make up her mind to fly away, I fixed her features in my memory and withdrew.

As I left, I saw the People's Friend enter. This grave moralist, who seemed to avoid me, was hastening to set the bad example of guilty curiosity. His long back-bone, curved in a half-circle, was quivering with desire; then, not being able to go any lower, he kissed the magic glass.

I went down the three stairs; I found myself again among the crowd decided on seeking "She who loves me," now that I knew her by her smile.

The lamps smoked, the tumult increased, the throng of people threatened the safety of the booths. The fete had reached that ideal hour of joy, at which one runs the risk of enjoying the happiness of being stifled.

Standing on my toes, I had a horizon of cotton caps and silk hats. I advanced, jostling the men and turning with precaution round the ample petticoats of the ladies. Perhaps it was this pink hood; perhaps this tulle cap trimmed with mauve ribbons; perhaps this delicious straw toque with an ostrich feather. Alas! The hood was sixty years of age; the cap, abominably ugly, was leaning amorously on the shoulder of a sapper; the toque was shouting with laughter, enlarging the finest eyes in the world, and I did not recognize them in the least.

Hovering above crowds is a sort of anguish, a kind of immense sadness, as if a breath of pity and terror came from the multitude. I have never found myself in a great gathering of people without experiencing vague uneasiness. It seems to me that a terrible misfortune threatens these men assembled together, that a single flash will suffice in the exaltation of their movements and voices, to strike them with immobility and eternal silence.

Little by little I slackened my pace, contemplating this joy which lacerated my heart. An old beggar, with a stiffened body, horribly distorted by paralysis, was standing upright at the foot of a tree, in the yellow light of the lamps. He raised his pallid face towards the passers-by, blinking his eyes in a most lamentable way, in order to excite more pity. He gave his limbs sudden fits of shivering, which shook him like a dead branch. The fresh and blushing young girls passed before this hideous sight laughing.

Further on, two workmen were fighting at the door of a wine-shop. The glasses had been upset in the struggle, and the wine, streaming on the pavement, had the appearance of blood that had come from deep wounds.

The laughter seemed to change into sobs; the lights became an immense fire, the crowd turned about struck with horror. I moved along, feeling intensely sad, peering into the youthful faces and unable to find "She who loves me."

I saw a man standing before one of the posts to which the lamps were affixed, and contemplating it with the air of a person profoundly engrossed in thought. From his anxious look I imagined he was seeking the solution to some serious problem. That man was the People's Friend.

Turning his head, he perceived me.

"Sir," he said, "the oil used at these festivals costs twenty sous the liter. In a liter, there are twenty small glass cups like those you see there: that is to say a sou of oil for each cup. This post has sixteen rows of eight cups each: one hundred and twenty-eight cups in all. Moreover—follow my calculations carefully—I have counted sixty similar posts in the avenue, which makes seven thousand six hundred and eighty cups, consequently seven thousand six hundred and eighty sous, or rather three hundred and eighty-four francs."

While speaking thus, the People's Friend gesticulated, accentuating the figures with his voice, curving his long body, as if to put himself within reach of my weak understanding. When he was silent he threw himself triumphantly backward; then, he crossed his arms, looking me in the face with deep concern.

"Three hundred and eighty-four francs worth of oil," he exclaimed, scanning each syllable, "and the poor are in want of bread, sir! I ask you, and I ask you with tears in my eyes, would it not be more honorable for humanity, to distribute these three hundred and eighty-four francs to the three thousand indigent people in this Faubourg. Such a charitable measure would give each of them about two sous and a half of bread. This thought is worthy of being pondered over by tender-hearted people, sir."

Seeing that I contemplated him with curiosity, he continued in a low voice, assuring the safety of his gloves between his fingers:

"The poor should not make merry, sir. It is absolutely dishonest for them to forget their poverty for an hour. Who would weep over the people's misfortunes if the government were often to treat them to such saturnalias?"

He wiped away a tear and left me. I saw him enter a wine-shop where he drowned his emotion in five or six drams taken one after the other at the counter.

The last illumination lamp had just gone out. The crowd had dispersed. By the vacillating light of the gas, I saw only a few dark forms strolling beneath the trees, couples of belated lovers, drunkards, and policemen giving their melancholy thoughts an airing. The grey and silent booths stretched along on either side of the avenue, like tents in a deserted camp.

The morning wind, a wind damp with dew, made the leaves of the elms rustle. The sour emanations of the evening had given place to delicious freshness. Soft silence and the transparent shadow of the infinite fell slowly from the depths of heaven, and the festival of the stars succeeded that of the illumination lamps. Respectable folk would at last be able to amuse themselves a little.

I felt quite a man again, the hour of my delight having arrived. I was going along at a smart pace, ascending and descending the walks, when I saw a grey shadow flitting along the houses. This shadow came towards me, rapidly, without seeming to see me; by the light step, by the cadenced rhythm of the clothing, I knew it was a woman.

She was about to knock up against me, when she instinctively raised her eyes. I saw her face by the light of a neighboring lamp, and then I recognized "She who loves me:" not the immortal in the cloud of white muslin; but a poor girl of the earth, attired in washed-out calico. She still appeared charming in her misery, although pale and tired. There was no room for doubt: there were the great eyes, the fondling lips of the vision; and, moreover, gazing at her thus at close quarters, one could perceive that the gentle aspect of her features was the result of suffering.

As she stopped for a second, I grasped her hand, which I kissed. She raised her head and gave me a vague smile without seeking to withdraw her fingers. Seeing I remained silent, and that emotion was choking me, she shrugged her shoulders and resumed her rapid walk.

I ran after her, accompanied her, my arm round her waist. She laughed to herself; then shivered and said in a low voice:

"I'm cold: let us walk quickly."

Poor angel, she was cold! Her shoulders trembled beneath the thin black shawl in the fresh night wind. I kissed her on the forehead and inquired softly:

"Do you know me?"

She raised her eyes a third time and answered without hesitation:

"No."

I know not what rapid reasoning passed through my mind. In my turn I shuddered.

"Where are we going to?" I asked her.

She shrugged her shoulders with an unconcerned little pout, and answered in her childlike voice:

"Wherever you like, to my place, to yours; what does it matter?"

We were still walking, descending the avenue.

On a bench I perceived two soldiers, one of whom was gravely descanting, while the other listened respectfully. It was the sergeant and the conscript. The sergeant, who seemed very much affected, made me a mocking bow, murmuring:

"The rich sometimes lend, sir."

The conscript, who was a tender and simple soul, said to me in a doleful voice:

"I had but her, sir: you are stealing from me 'She who loves me.'"

I crossed the road and took the other path.

Three boys advanced towards us, holding one another by the arm and singing at the pitch of their voices. I recognized the schoolboys. The unfortunate little fellows no longer needed to feign intoxication. They stopped, bursting with laughter, then followed me for a few paces, each of them shouting after me in an unsteady voice:

"Hi! Sir, the lady is deceiving you; the lady is 'She who loves me !'"

I felt a cold sweat moisten my temples. I hurried along, being anxious to fly, thinking no more of this woman whom I was bearing away in my arms. At the end of the avenue, just as I was stepping from the pavement, at last about to quit this inauspicious neighborhood, I stumbled over a man lying comfortably in the gutter. With his head resting on the curb-stone and his face turned towards heaven, he was engaged in a very complicated calculation on his fingers.

He moved his eyes, and, without quitting his pillow, spluttered out:

"Ah! It is you, sir. You ought to help me count the stars. I have already found several millions, but I'm afraid of forgetting one of them. The happiness of humanity, sir, depends solely on statistics."

He was interrupted by a hiccup. Tearfully he continued:

"Do you know what a star costs? Providence must assuredly have made a great outlay up there, and the people are in want of bread, sir! What is the use of those lights? Are they eatable? To what practical purpose are they adaptable, if you please? What need had we of this eternal festival? Ah! Providence never had the least shadow of an idea of social economy."

He had succeeded in sitting up ; and cast a troubled glance around him, shaking his head indignantly. He then caught sight of my companion. He started, and with his countenance all purple, eagerly stretched out his arms towards her.

"Eh! Eh!" he continued, "it's ' She who loves me!'"

"This is how it is," she said to me. "I am poor, I do what I can for a living. Last winter, I passed fifteen hours a day bent over an embroidery frame, and I hadn't always bread. In the spring I threw my needle out of the window. I had found employment which caused me less fatigue and was more lucrative.

"I dress myself up every evening in white muslin. Alone in a sort of shed, leaning against the back of an arm-chair, all the work I have to do consists in smiling from six o'clock till midnight. From time to time I make a bow, I kiss my hand into space. For that I am paid three francs a sitting.

"Opposite me, behind a small glazed aperture in the partition, I see an eye staring at me ceaselessly. It's sometimes black, sometimes blue. Without that eye I should be perfectly happy; but that spoils the whole thing. At times, seeing it always there, alone and fixed, I am seized with such frightful terror that I am tempted to scream and fly.

"But one must work to live. I smile, bow, kiss my hand. At midnight I wipe off my paint, and put on my calico gown again. Bah! How many women do the amiable before a wall without being compelled to!"

THE LOVE-FAIRY

Do you hear the December rain beating against our windows, Ninon? The wind moans in the long corridor. It is a nasty evening, one of those on which the poor shiver at the doors of the rich, whom the ball bears away in its dances beneath the gilded chandeliers. Leave your satin shoes where they are, and come and sit on my knee, beside the warm grate. Leave your costly jewels alone; I want to tell you a tale tonight, a beautiful fairy tale.

You must know, Ninon, that, once upon a time there was a dark and dismal castle on the summit of a mountain. It was naught but towers, ramparts, and drawbridges loaded with chains. Men encased in steel mounted guard night and day on the battlements, and soldiers alone met with courteous welcome from Count Enguerrand, the lord of the manor.

If you had seen the old warrior walking down the long galleries, if you had heard his brief and threatening explosions of voice, you would have trembled with fright, just as his niece Odette, the pious and handsome young lady, trembled. Have you never, of a morning, noticed a daisy opening at the first kisses of the sun among the stinging-nettles and brambles? In a like manner this young girl was blooming among bluff knights. She was a child when, in the midst of play, she perceived her uncle; she stopped, and her eyes filled with tears. Now, she was grown up and handsome; her bosom was always heaving with gentle sighs; and each time Lord Enguerrand appeared her fright became more acute.

She resided in a distant turret, passing her time in embroidering beautiful banners, and resting from her work by praying to the Almighty, while contemplating the emerald green country and azure blue sky from her window. How often of a night, rising from her couch, had she gone to gaze at the stars, and, when there, how often had her heart of sixteen summers bounded towards celestial space, inquiring of those radiant sisters what it was that affected it so. After these sleepless nights, after these transports of love, she felt inclined to hang round the old knight's neck; but a harsh word, a cold look stopped her, and she tremblingly resumed her needle-work. You pity the poor girl, Ninon; she was like the fresh, balmy flower, whose brilliancy and perfume are disdained.

One day Odette, the disconsolate, was dreamily following with her eye the flight of two doves, when she heard a tender voice at the foot of the castle. She leant out of the window, and saw a handsome youth, who, with a song on his lips, was asking for hospitality. She listened, and could not understand the words; but the tender voice weighed upon her heart, and tears coursed down her cheeks, wetting a sprig of sweet marjoram that she held in her hand.

The castle gate remained closed, and a warrior, armed, shouted from the walls:

"Withdraw: there are none but warriors within."

Odette continued looking. She let the sprig of sweet marjoram, wet with tears, which she held in her hand, fall at the singer's feet. The latter raising his eyes, and seeing that lovely fair head, kissed the sprig and departed, turning round at each step.

When he had disappeared, Odette went to her prayer-desk and said a long prayer. She thanked Heaven without knowing why; she felt happy, without understanding the cause of her joy.

That night she had a beautiful dream. She fancied she saw the sprig of sweet marjoram that she had thrown down. Slowly, from amidst the rustling leaves, rose a fairy, but such a charming fairy, with shining wings, a wreath of myosotis and a long green gown, the color of hope.

"Odette," she said melodiously, "I am the Love-Fairy. It was I who sent you Lois this morning, the young man with the tender voice; it was I who, seeing your tears, wished to dry them. I wander about the world gleaning hearts and bringing those who sigh together. I visit both the cottage and the manor-house, I have often found pleasure in uniting the shepherd's crook to the king's scepter. I scatter flowers beneath the footsteps of my favorites, I enchain them with such brilliant and precious thread that their hearts leap with joy. I live among the plants in the lanes, among the bright embers on the hearths in winter, amidst the drapery of the nuptial bed; and wherever my foot alights, come kisses and tender words. Weep no more, Odette: I am the Loving-One, the good fairy, and I have come to dry your tears."

And she returned into her flower, which closing its leaves became a bud again.

You know very well, Ninon, that the Love-Fairy exists. Look at her dancing on our hearth, and pity the poor people who do not believe in my beautiful fairy.

When Odette awoke, the sun was shining in her room, the song of a bird ascended from the outside, and the morning breeze, perfumed with the first kiss it had just given to the flowers, fondled her flaxen locks. She arose full of happiness, and passed the day singing, having hope in what the good fairy had told her. At times she gazed at the country, smiling at each bird that flew by, and feeling an impulse within her that made her leap and clap her little hands together.

In the evening she went down into the large hall of the castle. Beside Count Enguerrand was a knight listening to the old man's stories. She took her distaff, seated herself in front of the hearth, where a cricket was singing, and the ivory spindle spun round rapidly between her fingers.

While busy at her work, she cast a glance at the knight, and perceived that he had her sprig of sweet marjoram in his hands, and then she recognized Lois of the tender voice. She almost shrieked with joy. To conceal her blushes she bent down towards the fire; stirring up the embers with a long iron rod. The burning wood crackled, burst into flames, gave out reports and threw up sheaves of sparks; and suddenly in the midst of the latter appeared the Loving-One, smiling and ardent. She shook from her green silk gown the pieces of live charcoal, which were sprinkled over it like golden spangles; and springing into the room, went, invisible to the count, and placed herself behind the young people. There, while the old knight was relating a frightful battle with the infidels, she softly said to them:

"Love one another, my children. Leave remembrances to austere old age, leave to it the long stories beside the burning embers. Let naught but the sound of your kisses be mingled with the crackling of the fire. Later on it will be time enough to soothe your sorrow by recalling these happy moments. When one is in love at sixteen, there is no need for the voice; a single look says more than a long speech. Love one another, my children; let old age talk."

Then she enveloped them so thoroughly with her wings, that the count, who was explaining how the giant Buch-Iron-Head was slain by a terrific blow from Giralda-the-Heavy-Sword, did not notice Lois imprinting his first kiss on Odette's quivering forehead.

I must tell you, Ninon, about those beautiful wings of my Love-Fairy. They were as transparent as glass, and as thin as the wings of gnats. But, when the sweethearts were in danger of being seen, they enlarged, enlarged and became so obscure, so thick that they stopped the look and smothered the sound of kisses. And so the old man went on with the prodigious story for a long time, and for a long time did Lois fondle Odette the fair, under the wicked suzerain's nose.

Good heavens! Good heavens! What lovely wings they were! Young girls, they tell me, sometimes find them again; and it is thus that more than one of them is able to hide herself from the eyes of her parents. Is it true, Ninon?

When the count had got to the end of his protracted story, the Love-

Fairy disappeared in the flame, and Lois went off, thanking his host, and sending Odette a final kiss. The young girl slept so happy that night that she dreamt of mountains of flowers lighted by thousands of stars, each of which was a thousand times more brilliant than the sun.

The next day she went down to the garden, searching in the most obscure arbors. She met a warrior, bowed to him, and was about to withdraw when she noticed in his hands the sprig of sweet marjoram bathed in tears. And so she again recognized Lois of the tender voice, who had just succeeded in re-entering the castle under a new form of disguise. He made her sit down on a turfy seat beside a spring. They gazed at one another, delighted at seeing each other in broad daylight. The fauvettes were singing, and there was something in the air which indicated that the good fairy must be wandering in the neighborhood. I will not repeat to you all the things that the discreet old oak-trees heard; it was a pleasure to listen to the lovers chattering together so long, so long that a fauvette which happened to be in a neighboring bush had time to build a nest. BLOOD

All at once the heavy tread of Count Enguerrand resounded along the walk. The two poor lovers trembled. But the water at the spring sang more softly, and the Loving-One emerged, laughing and ardent, from the clear stream of the source. She surrounded the lovers with her wings, then lightly tripped along with them, passing beside the count, who was astonished at having heard voices and finding no one.

She soothes her cherished ones, she walks on, saying to them in a very low voice:

"I am she who protects love-making, she who closes the eyes and ears of those who love no more. Fear nothing, handsome lovers; love one another in broad daylight, in the lanes, beside the springs, wherever you may be. I am there, and I watch over you. Providence has placed me here below so that men, those mockers of all righteousness, may never come and trouble your feelings. It gave me my beautiful wings and said to me, 'Go, and may young hearts rejoice.' Love one another; I am there, and I watch over you."

And she walked on, imbibing the dew which was her only food, leading along Odette and Lois, whose hands were interlaced, in a joyful roundabout dance.

You want me to tell you what she did with the two lovers. Really, my pet, I dare not do so. I am afraid you will not believe me, or else that, jealous of their good fortune, you will cease returning me my kisses. But now you are very curious to know, naughty girl, and I can see that I shall have to satisfy you.

So, know that the fairy wandered about thus until night. When she wished to separate the lovers, she saw them so pained, but so pained at having to leave one another, that she began to speak to them in a whisper. It seems that she told them something very beautiful, for their faces were beaming, and their eyes expanded with delight. And, when she had spoken and they had consented, she touched their foreheads with her wand.

Suddenly—oh! Ninon, what great wondering eyes! How you would tap your foot, were I not to tell you the end!

Lois and Odette were suddenly transformed into sprigs of sweet marjoram, but such lovely marjoram that only a fairy could make any like it. They found themselves placed side by side, so close to one another that their leaves entwined together. Marvelous flowers grew there, which were always to remain in bloom, exchanging their perfume and dew everlastingly.

As to Count Enguerrand, they say that he consoled himself by relating every night how the giant Buch-Iron-Head was slaughtered by a terrific blow from Giralda-Heavy-Sword.

And now, Ninon, when we go into the country, we will seek for the enchanted sweet marjorams, to ask them in which flower the Love-Fairy is. Perhaps, my pet, a moral is concealed in this tale. But I have only told it you, with our feet before the grate, to make you forget the December rain which is beating against our windows, and to instill a little more love in you, tonight, for the young story-teller.

Here already are many sunbeams, many flowers, many perfumes. Are you not tired, Ninon, of this everlasting spring? Always loving, always chanting that dream of sixteen summers. You fall asleep at night, naughty girl, when I talk to you at great length of the coquetry of the rose, and the infidelity of the dragon-fly. You close your great eyes wearily, and I, who no longer find inspiration there, stammer on, without coming to a conclusion.

I'll vanquish your idle eyelids, Ninon. To-day I am going to relate such a terrible tale to you, that you'll not close them for a week. Listen. Terror is delicious after a deal of laughter.

Four soldiers, on the night of a victory, had encamped in a deserted corner of the battle-field. Night had come, and they were supping joyously among the dead.

Seated on the grass round a camp fire, they were grilling slices of lamb on the burning embers, and eating them when only half done. The red glare of the fire threw a faint light over the companions, casting their gigantic shadows to a distance. Every now and then, the arms lying around them, slightly flashed, and then amidst the night, one perceived men sleeping with their eyes open.

The soldiers laughed with long peals of merriment, without perceiving the staring gaze that was fixed upon them. The day had been a hard one. Not knowing what the morrow reserved for them, they were enjoying the rations and repose of the moment.

Night and Death flew across the battle-field, their great wings agitating its silence and horror.

When the meal was over, Gneuss sang. His sonorous voice uttered false notes in the sad, mournful air; the song, which burst joyfully from his lips, echoed in sobs. Astounded at these accents issuing from his mouth, and which he failed to recognize, the soldier sang in a higher key, when a terrible cry, proceeding from the darkness, sped through space.

Gneuss was silent, as if seized with uneasiness, and said to Elberg:

"Go and see what corpse is awakening."

Elberg took a flaming brand and disappeared. His companions were able to follow him for a few instants by the light of the torch. They saw him stoop down, examining the dead, piercing the bushes with his sword. Then he disappeared.

"Clerian," said Gneuss after a silence, "the wolves are wandering about to-night: go and look for our friend."

And Clerian in his turn was lost in the darkness.

Gneuss and Flem, tired of waiting, wrapped themselves up in their cloaks and both lay down beside the smoldering fire. Their eyes were just closing, when the same terrible cry passed over their heads. Flem arose in silence, and walked towards the darkness where his two companions had disappeared.

Then Gneuss found himself alone. He was afraid, afraid of the darkness through which ran the death-rattle. He threw some dry roots on to the fire, hoping that the bright light would dispel his fright. A red flame burst out, and the ground was lit up in a wide luminous circle; in this circle, the bushes were dancing fantastically, and the dead, sleeping in the shadow of them, seemed shaken by invisible hands.

Gneuss was afraid of the light. He spread out the flaming stalks, and extinguished them beneath his heels. As the darkness returned, more dense and weighty, he shuddered, dreading to hear the cry of death pass by. He sat down, then rose up to call his companions.

The high notes of his voice frightened him; and he feared he had attracted the attention of the corpses.

The moon appeared, and Gneuss, terrified, noticed a pale beam of light gliding across the battle-field. Night no longer hid its abominations. The devastated plain, strewn with fragments and corpses, extended before his eyes, wrapped in a winding-sheet of light; and this light, which was not the light of day, lit up the darkness without dispelling its silent horror.

Gneuss, erect, his forehead bathed in perspiration, thought of ascending the hillock to extinguish the pale torch of night. He wondered what the dead were waiting for, to arise and surround him, now that they saw him. Their immobility caused him anguish; and expecting some terrible event to happen, he closed his eyes.

And, as he stood there, he felt a tepid warmth at his left heel. He bent down towards the ground, and saw a narrow streak of blood escaping from beneath his feet. This streak bounding from stone to stone, ran along with a merry murmur; it came out of the darkness, twirled about in the light of the moon, to fly away and return into the night; one would have taken it for a serpent with black scales, the rings gliding along and following one another without end. Gneuss started back without being able to close his eyes again; they kept wide open, fixed on the sanguinary brook.

He saw it slowly swell, increase the breadth of its bed. The brook became a stream, a slow and peaceful stream that a child could have cleared at a bound. The stream became a torrent, and passed rumbling over the ground, casting a reddish spray on either side. The torrent became a river, an immense river.

This river bore away the corpses, and this blood which had poured from the wounds in such abundance that it carried away the dead, was a horrible prodigy.

Gneuss continued to retreat before the rising flood. He could no longer see its opposite bank; it seemed to him that the valley had changed into a lake.

All at once he found himself with his back against a rocky slope; he had to pause in his flight. Then he felt the waves beating against his knees. The dead, who were borne along by the current, insulted him as they passed by; each of their wounds became a mouth that jeered at his fright. The thick ocean rose, continued rising; now it moaned around his hips. He made a supreme effort, and stretching up, clutched the crevices in the rocks; the rocks gave way, he fell, and the flood covered his shoulders.

The pale, sad moon looked down upon this sea, and fell on it without reflex. Light floated in the sky. The immense expanse of firmament, full of shadows and riotous sounds, seemed like the gaping opening to an abyss.

The wave rose, rose and reddened Gneuss' lips with its foam.

Elberg's arrival at daybreak awakened Gneuss, who was sleeping with his head on a stone.

"Friend," he said, "I lost myself in the bush. As I was sitting at the foot of a tree, sleep overcame me, and my soul's eyes saw strange scenes unrolled before them, which remained impressed on my memory when I awoke.

"The world was in its infancy. The sky resembled an immense smile. The earth, which was still virgin, expanded its chaste nudity, in the rays of the May sun. The blade of grass grew green and larger than the largest of our oaks; the trees spread leaves out into the air that are unknown to us. The sap coursed copiously in the veins of the world, and its flood was so abundant, that being unable to limit itself to the plants, it streamed into the entrails of the rocks and gave them life.

"The horizons extended calm and radiant. Holy nature was awakening. Like the child who kneels down in the morning, and thanks the God of light, it poured out all its perfumes, all its songs to heaven, penetrating perfumes, unutterable songs, which my senses could hardly bear, so divine was the impression they produced on me.

"Sweet and fruitful earth, engendered without pain. Fruit trees multiplied at will. Fields of corn bordered the highways, as fields of nettles do now. One felt in the air that human toil was not mingled with the breath of heaven. The Almighty alone worked for his children.

"Man, like the bird, lived on the food Providence gave him. He went about blessing God, picking fruit from the trees, drinking water at the spring, sheltered at night beneath the foliage. His lips had a horror of flesh; he knew not what the taste of blood was like, he found savor only in such viands as dew and sun prepared for his meals.

"It was thus that man remained innocent, and that his innocence crowned him king of the other animals of creation. Concord reigned everywhere. The world was of inconceivable whiteness, and was rocked in infinity by inconceivable supreme peace. The birds' wings did not beat to fly away; the thickets in the forests were not places of refuge. All God's creatures lived in the sun, and formed but one people, having but one law—goodness.

"I walked among these people, amidst this nature, and felt myself becoming stronger and better. My chest inhaled a full provision of the air of heaven. Suddenly leaving our impure winds for these breezes of a less infected world, I experienced the delicious sensation of a miner ascending to the open air.

"As the angel of dreams continued rocking me in my sleep, this is what my mind saw in a forest where it seemed lost.

"Two men followed a narrow path lost in the foliage. The younger walked in front; happiness beaming upon his lips, and his eyes having a caress for each blade of grass. Sometimes he turned round and smiled at his companion. I know not by what sweet expression it was that I recognized the smile was that of a brother.

"The lips and eyes of the other man continued mute and gloomy. He cast a look of hatred upon the youth, hastening on, stumbling behind him. He seemed to be pursuing a victim who did not fly. I saw him cut a tree which he roughly fashioned into a club. Then fearing to lose his companion, he ran, hiding his weapon behind him. The young man who had sat down to wait for him, arose at his approach, and kissed him on the forehead, as if after a long absence. They set out walking again. Daylight was drawing in. The child perceiving in the distance, between the large trunks of the forest, the soft lines of a hill that looked yellow in the sun's farewell, hastened on. The gloomy man thought he was flying, and raised the club.

"His young brother turned round with a happy word of encouragement on his lips. The club smashed his face and blood spurted from it. The blade of grass which received the first drop, shook it with horror on the earth. Earth, shuddering and terrified, swallowed this drop; a long cry of repugnance escaped from its bosom, and the sand on the path turned the hideous beverage into blood-stained moss.

"At the victim's cry, I noticed the creatures disperse in terror. They fled all over the world, avoiding the roads; they gathered together in the glades, and the strongest attacked the weakest. I saw them when alone, polishing their fangs and sharpening their claws. The great brigandage of creation was commencing.

"Then passed before me an everlasting flight. The hawk pounced on the swallow, the swallow seized the fly on the wing, the fly settled on the corpse. From worm to lion, all creatures found themselves threatened. The world bit its tail, and went on devouring itself for evermore.

"Nature itself, struck with horror, had a prolonged convulsion. The pure lines of the horizon were broken. Sunrises and sunsets were attended by blood-like clouds; the waters heaved with eternal sobs, and the trees, twisting their branches, cast dead leaves every year upon the earth."

As Elberg ceased speaking, Clerian appeared; he seated himself between his two companions and said to them:

"I know not whether I saw or dreamed what I am about to relate to you, the dream was so like reality, and reality so like a dream.

"I found myself on a road crossing the world. It was bordered by cities, and the multitudes followed it in their journeys.

"I saw the paving stones were black. My feet slid, and I perceived they were black with blood. The road sloped down on either side; a brook of thick, red water ran in the centre of it.

"I followed this road on which a crowd was stirring. I went from group to group, watching life pass before me.

"Here fathers sacrificed their daughters whose blood they had promised to some monstrous divinity. The fair heads bowed beneath the knife, and turned pale at the embrace of death.

"There proud, trembling virgins killed themselves, to escape the kiss of shame, and the tomb was the white raiment of their virginity.

"Further on, lovers died amid kisses. This one, weeping at being abandoned, expired at the waterside, her eyes fixed on the flood which had borne away her heart; that one, murdered in the arms of her lover, met her end clinging to his neck, and both expired in a supreme strain.

"Further on, men tired of darkness and misery, sent their souls to seek, in a better world, the liberty they had searched for, in vain, on this earth.

"Everywhere, the feet of kings left sanguinary imprints on the stones. This one walked in the blood of his brothers; that one, in the blood of his people; this other, in the blood of his God. Their crimson footprints in the dust made the people exclaim: 'A king had been this way.'

"The priests slaughtered victims then stupidly bending over their palpitating entrails, pretended they read the secrets of heaven there. They wore swords beneath their robes, and preached warfare in the name of their god. Nations at their bidding set upon one another, devouring each other for the glorification of the common Father.

"All humanity was intoxicated; it battered down walls, wallowed on the flagstones soiled with hideous mire. With closed eyes and grasping a double-edged blade in both hands, it struck into the night and massacred.

"A damp breath of carnage passed over the crowd which was hidden in the distance in a reddish mist. It ran, borne along in an outburst of panic, it plunged into orgies with shouts that continued increasing in fury. It trampled on those who fell, and made their wounds yield the last drops of blood. It panted with rage, cursing the corpse, when it could no longer tear a groan from it.

"The earth drank, drank eagerly; its bowels ceased to feel repugnance for the bitter liquor. Like a being degraded by intoxication, it gorged itself with lees.

"I hastened on, anxious not to see my brethren any more. The dark road continued stretching ahead as broad as ever at each new horizon; the stream I was following seemed to be bearing the sanguinary flood to some unknown sea.

"And as I advanced, I saw nature becoming somber and harsh. The bosom of the plains was profoundly lacerated. Masses of rock divided the ground into sterile hills and dismal dells. The hills rose higher and higher, the dells sank deeper and deeper; stone became mountains, the fields a chasm.

"There was not a leaf, not a piece of moss; naught but barren rocks with the summits bleached by the sun and the base gloomy and overshadowed. The road passed through these rocks and was enshrouded in death-like silence.

"At last it made a sudden bend, and I found myself on a dismal site.

"Four mountains, resting heavily against one another, formed an immense basin. Their sides, which were steep and smooth, towered up like the walls of a cyclopean city and formed a gigantic well, the breadth of which extended to the horizon.

"And this well, into which the stream discharged itself, was full of blood. The thick, smooth ocean rose slowly from the chasm. It seemed sleeping in its rocky bed. The sky reflected it in purple clouds.

"I then understood that all the blood spilt by violence was running there. From the first murder, each wound had shed its tears into this pit, and tears had poured in there in such abundance, that the pit was full."

"Last night," said Gneuss, "I saw a torrent that was running into this accursed lake."

"Struck with horror," resumed Clerian, "I approached the brink, judging the depth of the flood with the eye. I could tell by the dull sound that it penetrated to the centre of the earth. Then, glancing at the rocks forming the enclosure, I saw that the flood was approaching the top of them. The voice of the abyss cried out to me: the flood, which is rising, will continue to do so and will attain the summit of the rocks. It will rise higher, and then a river, escaping from the terrible basin, will pour down on to the plains. The mountains, weary of struggling with the flood, will sink down. The entire lake will then fall upon the world and inundate it. It is thus that men who are to come, will die drowned in the blood shed by their fathers.'"

"That day is near at hand," said Gneuss: "the flood was high last night."

The sun was rising, when Clerian had completed the account of his dream. The sound of a bugle wafted by the morning breeze, was heard towards the north. It was the signal for the soldiers dispersed over the plain to assemble round the flag.

The three companions rose and took their arms. As they were setting out, casting a last glance at the extinguished fire, they saw Flem advancing towards them, running in the tall grass. His feet were white with dust.

"Friends," he said, "I have ran so fast that I know not whence I come. I have seen the trees flying behind me in a disorderly dance for hours. The sound of my footsteps lulling me made me close my eyelids, and, while still running, without slackening my speed, I slept a strange sleep.

"I found myself on a desolated hill. The scorching sun fell upon the great rocks. I could not set my feet down without the flesh being burnt. I hastened to reach the summit.

"And, as I bounded onward, I perceived a man walking slowly. He was crowned with thorns; a heavy burden weighed upon his shoulders and his face was bathed in blood-like sweat . He advanced slowly, stumbling at each step.

"The ground was burning hot, I could not bear his torment; I went up and waited for him beneath a tree at the top of the hill. Then I saw he was carrying a cross. By his crown, his purple robe stained with mud, it seemed to me that he was a king, and I felt great joy at his suffering.

"Soldiers were following him, hurrying him on with their iron-tipped lances. On reaching the highest rock they stripped him of his garments, and made him lie down on the forbidding timber.

"The man smiled sadly. He held his hands out wide open to the executioners, and the nails made two ghastly holes in them. Then, bringing his feet together, he crossed them, and one nail sufficed.

"He lay silent on his back gazing at the sky. Two tears coursed slowly down his cheeks, tears which he did not feel and which were lost in the submissive smile upon his lips.

"The cross was erected, the weight of the body increased the size of the wounds horribly. The crucified man gave a prolonged shudder. Then, he cast his eyes up to heaven again.

"I gazed at him. Observing his courage in the face of death, I said, 'This man is not a king.' Then I felt pity, and cried out to the soldiers to pierce his heart.

"A feathered songster was singing on the cross. Its song was sad, and sounded in my ears like the voice of a virgin in tears.

"' Blood colors the flame,' it sang, 'blood gives purple to the flower, blood reddens the naked. I stood upon the sand and my claws were covered with blood; I grazed the branches of the oak and my wings were red.

"' I met a just man and followed him. I had been bathing at the spring, and my coat was pure. My song said: Be joyful, my feathers; on this man's shoulder you will not be soiled with the rain of murder.

"' My song says now : Weep, warbler of Golgotha, weep for your coat stained by the blood of him who kept a shelter for thee in his bosom. He came to give the warblers back their purity, Alas! And men made him wet me with the dew of his wounds.

"' I doubt, and I weep over my soiled coat. Where shall I find thy brother, O Jesus! So that he may open his linen garment to me? Ah! Poor master, what son born of thee will wash my feathers reddened with your blood?'

"The crucified man listened to the warbler. The breath of death made his eyelids quiver; agony distorted his lips. He cast his eyes up towards the bird, and they bore an expression of sweet reproach; his smile was bright and as serene as hope.

"Then, he uttered a loud cry. His head fell upon his breast, and the warbler flew off, borne away in a sob. The sky turned black, earth shuddered in the darkness.

"I continued running, and I still slept. Dawn had come, the valleys were awakening, smiling in the morning mist. The storm of the night had cleared the sky, and had given greater strength to the green leaves. But the path was bordered by the same thorns as tore me on the previous evening. The same hard, sharp flints rolled beneath my feet; the same serpents stole along in the thickets, and threatened me on the way. The blood of the Just One had ran into the veins of the old world, without giving it back the innocence of its youth. "The warbler passed overhead, and cried to me: "' Ah! Ah! I am very sad. I cannot find a spring pure enough to bathe in. Look, the earth is as wicked as formerly. Jesus is dead, and the grass has not flowered. Ah! Ah! It is but one more murder.'"

The bugle continued sounding the departure.

"Boys," said Gneuss, "our calling is an unpleasant one. Our slumber is troubled by the phantoms of those whom we strike. I, like you, have felt the demon of nightmare weighing on my chest for long hours. For thirty years I have been killing, and I need sleep. Let us leave our brethren there. I know of a glen where ploughs require hands. Shall we taste the bread of toil?"

"We will," answered his companions.

Thereupon the soldiers dug a great hole at the foot of a rock, and buried their arms. They went down and bathed in the river; then, all four arm in arm disappeared at the turn of the pathway.

THE THIEVES AND THE ASS

I know a young man, Ninon, to whom you would give a good scolding. Leon is passionately fond of Balzac and cannot bear George Sand; Michelet's book almost made him sick. He naively says that woman is born a slave, and never utters the words love and modesty without laughing. Ah! How ill he speaks of you! No doubt, he communes with himself at night the better to tear you to pieces during the daytime. He is twenty.

Ugliness seems to him a crime. Small eyes, a mouth too large, set him beside himself. He pretends that as there are no ugly flowers in the fields, all girls should be born equally beautiful. When by chance he meets an ugly one in the street, he fumes for three whole days about her scanty stock of hair, large feet and thick hands. When on the contrary the woman is pretty, he smiles wickedly, and his silence then is so full of naughty thoughts that it seems quite dreadful.

I know not which of you would find favor in his eyes. Blondes and brunettes, young and old, graceful and deformed, he envelops you all in the same malediction. The naughty boy I and how laughingly tender are his eyes! How soft and fondling his speech!

Leon lives in the midst of the Latin Quarter.

And now, Ninon, I feel very much embarrassed. At the least thing, I would hold my tongue, regretting I ever had the singular idea to commence this story. Your inquisitive mind is eager for the scandal, and I hardly know how to introduce you to a world where you have never placed the tips of your little toes.

This world, ray well-beloved, would be Paradise, if it were not Hell.

Let us open the poet's volume and read the song of twenty summers. Look, the window faces the south; the garret, full of flowers and light, is so high, so high in the sky, that sometimes one hears the angels chatting on the roof. Like the birds that select the loftiest branch to hide their nests from man, so have the lovers built theirs on the last storey. There the sun gives them his first kiss in the morning and his last farewell at night.

What do they live on? Who knows? Perhaps on smiles and kisses. They love each other so much, that they have no leisure to think about the missing meal. They have no bread, and yet they throw crumbs to sparrows. When they open the empty cupboard, they satisfy their hunger by laughing at their poverty.

Their love dates from the blooming of the first blue corn flower. They met in a wheat field. Having long known one another, without ever having seen each other, they took the same path to return to the city. She wore a large nosegay at her bosom, like one betrothed. She ascended the seven floors, and, feeling too tired, was unable to go down again.

Will she have strength to do so to-morrow? She does not know. In the meantime she is resting, while tripping about the garret, watering the flowers, looking after a home which does not exist. Then she sews, while the youth works. Their chairs touch; little by little, for greater comfort, they end by taking only one for both of them. Night comes. They scold each other for their idleness.

Ah! What fibs that poet tells, Ninon, and how delightful his falsehoods are! May that unalterable child never become a man! May he continue to deceive us when he can no longer deceive himself! He comes from Paradise to tell us of its love-making. He met two saints there, Musette and Mimi, whom it pleased him to bring among us. They only just grazed the earth with their wings, and went off again in the ray that brought them. Hearts twenty summers old are seeking for those saints, and weeping at not finding them.

Must I, in my turn, tell you fibs, my well-beloved, by bringing them from Paradise, or must I confess that I met them in Gehenna? If there, near the fire, in that arm-chair where you are rocking yourself, a friend were listening to me, I would boldly raise the golden veil with which the poet has decked such unworthy shoulders! But you—you would close my lips with your little hands, you would get angry, you would vow it was false, because it was so true. How could you believe in lovers of our age drinking in the gutter when they feel thirsty in the street? How angry you would be if I dared tell you that your sisters, the loving ones, have unfastened their fichus and unbound their hair! You live laughing and serene in the nest I built for you; you are ignorant of the ways of the world. I shall not have the courage to confess to you that flowers are very sick of those ways, and that to-morrow, perhaps, the hearts that are there will be dead.

Close not your ears, darling: you will not have to blush.

Leon, then, lives in the midst of the Latin Quarter. His hand is more grasped than any other in that land where all hands know one another. His frank look makes each passerby his friend.

The women dare not forgive him the hatred he bears them, and are furious they cannot confess they love him. They detest him while doting on him.

Previous to the facts I am about to relate to you, I never knew him to have a sweetheart. He says he is blasé, and speaks of the pleasures of this world as would a Trappist, were he to break his long silence. He has a weakness for good living, and cannot bear bad wine. His linen is very fine, and his garments are always exquisitely elegant.

I see him sometimes stop before pictures representing virgins of the Italian school with moist eyes. A fine marble procures him an hour's ecstasy.

Leon, moreover, leads a student's life, working as little as possible, strolling in the sun, lounging obliviously on all the divans he meets with. It is particularly during these hours of semi-slumber that he gives utterance to his worst abuse of women. With closed eyes, he seems to be fondling a vision while cursing reality.

One May morning I met him looking quite cheerless. He did not know what to do, and was rambling through the streets on the look-out for something to interest him. The pavement was muddy; and although the unforeseen was encountered from place to place by the pedestrian's feet, it was only in the form of a puddle. I took pity on him, and suggested going into the fields to see if the hawthorn were in flower.

For an hour I had to listen to a lot of long philosophical orations, all of which pointed to the nihility of our pleasures. Houses gradually became scarcer. Already on the thresholds of the doors, we perceived dirty brats rolling over fraternally with great dogs. As we reached the real country, Leon suddenly stopped before a group of children playing in the sun. He fondled one of them, and then owned to me that he adored fair heads.

For my part I have always liked those narrow lanes, confined between a couple of hedges, which are free from the ruts of great wagon-wheels. The ground is covered with fine moss, as soft to the feet as a velvety carpet. One treads amid mystery and silence; and when an amorous couple lose themselves there, the thorns in the verdant wall compel the fond girl to press against her lover's heart . Leon and I found ourselves in one of these out-of-the-way walks, where kisses are only overheard by feathered songsters. The first smile of spring had vanquished my philosopher's misanthropy. He experienced prolonged tenderness for each drop of dew, and sang like a schoolboy who had broken out of bounds.

The lane continued to stretch ahead. The high thick hedges were all our horizon. This sort of confinement, and our ignorance as to where we were, made us doubly merry.

The pathway gradually became narrower; we had to walk in single file. The hedges began to take sudden turns, and the lane was transformed into a labyrinth.

Then, at the narrowest part, we heard a sound of voices; next, three persons appeared at one of the leafy corners. Two young men marched in front, putting aside the branches that were too long. A young woman followed them.

I stopped and bowed. The young fellow facing me did the same. After that we looked at each other. The position was delicate; the hedges shutting us in on either side were thicker than ever, and neither of us seemed inclined to turn round. It was then that Leon, who was behind me, standing up on tip-toe, perceived the young woman. Without uttering a word, he dashed bravely in among the hawthorns; his clothes were torn by the brambles, and a few drops of blood appeared upon his hands. I had to do as he had done.

The young men passed by, thanking us. The young woman, as if to reward Leon for his self-sacrifice, stopped before him, wavering, gazing at him with her great black eyes. He immediately sought to frown, and could not.

When she had disappeared I came out of the bush, sending gallantry to the deuce. A thorn had torn my neck, and my hat was so beautifully suspended between two branches that I had the greatest difficulty imaginable in getting it down. Leon shook himself. As I had given the pretty passer-by a friendly nod, he inquired if I knew her.

"Certainly," I answered. "Her name's Antoinette. She was three months my neighbor."

We had begun walking on again. He held his tongue. Then I talked to him of Mademoiselle Antoinette.

She was a fresh and delicate little party, with a half mocking, half-tender look, a determined air, and a smart, nimble gait; in a word, she was a nice girl. She could be distinguished among her fellows by her open-heartedness and probity, qualities peculiarly rare in the society in which she lived. She expressed an opinion about her own self without vanity, as also without modesty, and announced openly that she was born to love and take her pleasure where fancy led her.

For three long winter months I had seen her living, poor and] alone, on the produce of her labor. She acted thus without display, without uttering that big word virtue, because that was her idea at the time. So long as her needle sped on, I never knew her to have a lover. She was a good comrade to the men who came to see her; she pressed their hands, laughed with them, but bolted her door at the first pretence of a kiss. I confess I had tried to court her a bit. One day when I offered her a ring and pendants, she said:

"My friend, take back your jeweler. When I give myself away it is only for a flower."

When in love she was idle and indolent. Lace and silk then took the place of calico. She carefully got rid of all traces of the needle, and the work-girl became a grand lady.

Besides, when in love, she maintained her liberty. The man she was enamored of soon knew it; he knew quite as quickly when she loved him no more. She was not, however, one of those pretty, capricious creatures who change their sweetheart each time they wear out a pair of shoes. She had a broad intelligence and a great heart. But the poor girl often made mistakes; she placed her own hands in others that were unworthy, and rapidly withdrew them in disgust. And so she was tired of this Latin Quarter, where the young men appeared to her very old.

At each new wreck her face became a little more sad. She told men disagreeable truths, and scolded herself for being unable to live without loving. Then she shut herself up, until her heart broke the bars.

I had met her the previous evening. She was in great grief: a sweetheart had just thrown her over, while she still cared for him a little.

"Of course I know," she had said to me, "that in a week's time I should have left him myself: he was an unkind fellow. But I still kissed him tenderly on both cheeks. It's a loss of at least thirty kisses."

She had added, that since then she had had two suitors at her heels who overwhelmed her with bouquets. She let them do so, and sometimes held this language to them: "My friends, I love neither of you; you would be great fools to quarrel for my smiles. Be amicable, instead. I can see you are good chaps; we will amuse ourselves like old chums. But, at the first quarrel, I leave you."

The poor fellows, therefore, warmly shook hands, while wishing each other at the deuce. It was probably them whom we had just met.

Such was Mademoiselle Antoinette: a poor loving heart gone astray in the land of debauchery; a gentle, charming girl who sprinkled her crumbs of tenderness to all the thieving sparrows on the road.

I gave Leon these details. He listened to me without showing much interest, without encroaching on my confidence by the least question. When I was silent he said:

"That girl is too frank; I don't like her way of understanding love."

He had tried so hard to frown that he had at length succeeded in doing so.

We had at last got away from the hedges. The Seine was running at our feet; on the opposite bank a village was reflected in the river. We were in a familiar neighborhood; we had often wandered in the islands down stream.

After a long rest beneath a neighboring oak, Leon announced that he was dying of hunger and thirst, just as I was about to tell him I was dying of thirst and hunger. Then we held council. The result was touching in its unanimity. We would go to the village; there, we would procure a large basket; this basket would be nicely filled with viands and bottles; finally all three, the basket and ourselves, would make for the most verdant isle.

Twenty minutes later, it only remained for us to find a boat. I had obligingly taken charge of the basket. I say basket, and the term is modest enough. Leon walked on ahead, inquiring of each angler along the river bank for a boat. They were all engaged. I was on the point of suggesting to my companion that we should spread our table on the continent, when some one directed us to a place where he said we might perhaps find what we required.

The man lived in a cottage standing at the corner of two streets, at the end of the village. And it happened that, on turning this corner, we again found ourselves face to face with Mademoiselle Antoinette, followed by her two lovers. One of them, like myself, was bending beneath the weight of an enormous basket; the other, like Leon, had the busy appearance of a man in search of something he could not find. I cast a look of pity on the poor fellow who was bathed in perspiration, while Leon seemed to be thanking me for having accepted a burden that made the young woman laugh rather wickedly.

The man who let out the boats was smoking on the • threshold of his door. For fifty years he had seen thousands of couples come and borrow his oars to reach the desert. He loved those amorous blondes who set out with starched fichus and came back with them a trifle crumpled, and with their ribbons in great disorder. He smiled at them on their return, when they thanked him for his boats, which were so familiar with the isles where the grass grew highest, that they went there almost of their own accord. As soon as the worthy man caught sight of our baskets he advanced to meet us.

"Young people," he said, "I have only one boat left. Those who are too hungry had better sit down to table over there under the trees."

That remark was certainly a very clumsy one : you never own before a woman that you are too hungry. We held our tongues, hesitating, not daring after that to refuse the boat. Antoinette, who still had a mocking air about her, nevertheless took pity on us.

"You gentlemen," she said, addressing Leon, "made a sacrifice for us this morning; we will do the same now."

I looked at my philosopher. He hesitated; he stuttered like a person who is afraid to say what he thinks. When he saw me fix my eyes on him, he exclaimed:

"But there is no question of self-sacrifice now: one boat will suffice. These gentlemen will put us ashore at the first island we come to, and will pick us up on their return. Do you agree to that arrangement, gentlemen?"

Antoinette answered that she accepted. The baskets were carefully placed at the bottom of the boat. I took a seat close to mine, and as far away from the oars as possible. Antoinette and Leon, not being able to do otherwise no doubt, sat down side by side on the seat remaining vacant. As to the two sweethearts, they continued to vie with each other in showing good humor and gallantry, and seized the oars in brotherly harmony.

They reached the current. There, as they balanced the boat, allowing it to descend the stream, Mademoiselle Antoinette pretended that the islands up the river were more deserted and shady. The oarsmen looked at one another disappointed. They turned the boat round and pulled laboriously up stream, struggling against the current, which was very strong at that spot. There is a kind of tyranny that is very oppressive and very sweet: it is the desire of a tyrant with rosy lips, who, in one of her moments of caprice, can ask for the world and pay for it with a kiss.

The young woman had leant over the side of the boat and dipped her hand in the water. She withdrew it full; then, dreamily, seemed to be counting the pearly drops escaping between her fingers. Leon watched her and held his tongue, apparently uncomfortable at finding himself so close to an enemy. Twice he opened his lips, no doubt to utter some stupidity; but he closed them quickly on noticing me smile. Yet neither of them seemed very pleased at being such close neighbors. They even slightly turned their backs to one another.

Antoinette, weary of wetting her lace, talked to me about her recent bereavement. She told me she had got over it. But she was still sad; she could not live without love in summer time. She did not know what to do until autumn came round again.

"I am looking out for a nest," she added. "It must be all in blue silk. One ought to love longer when furniture, carpets, and curtains are the color of the sky. The sun would make a mistake, would forget itself there of an evening thinking it was slumbering in a cloud. But I seek in vain; men are so unkind."

We were opposite an island. I tell the oarsmen to put us ashore. I had already one foot on the bank, when Antoinette protested, finding the island ugly and devoid of foliage, and declaring she would never consent to abandon us on such a rock. Leon had not moved from his seat. I returned to my place, and we continued to ascend the river.

The young woman, with childlike delight, began to describe the nest she had set her mind on. The room must be square; the ceiling high and arched. The hangings on the walls would be white, strewn with blue cornflowers bound together in bunches with ribbon. At the four corners would be pier tables loaded with flowers; another table in the centre also covered with flowers. Then a sofa, but a small one, so that two persons could hardly sit there together while pressing very close to one another; no glass to attract the eyes and make one egotistically coquettish; very thick carpets and curtains to drown the sound of kisses. Flowers, sofa, carpet, curtains would be blue. She would put on a blue gown, and would not open the window on days when the sky was cloudy.

I wanted, in my turn, to ornament the room a bit, and spoke of the fireplace, a clock, a wardrobe.

"But," she exclaimed in astonishment, "we shall not warm ourselves and we shall not want to know the time. I consider your wardrobe ridiculous. Do you think me so stupid as to drag our miseries into my nest? I wish to live there free, without care, not always, but for a few happy hours each summer evening. If men became angels they would get tired of Paradise itself. I know all about it . I should have the key of Paradise in my pocket."

We were opposite a second green isle. Antoinette clapped her hands. It was the most charming little deserted nook that any Robinson Crusoe of twenty summers could have dreamt of. The bank, which was rather high, was bordered by great trees, between which sweet-briars and grass struggled for supremacy in growth. An impenetrable wall built itself up there each spring, a wall of leaves, branches, moss, which continued to rise and reflected itself in the water. Outside, a rampart of interlaced boughs; within, one knew not what. This ignorance as to what the glades were like, this broad curtain of verdure quivering in the breeze, without ever opening, made the island a mysterious place of seclusion, which the passer-by on the neighboring banks might easily have taken to be peopled by the pale nymphs of the river.

We rowed a long way round this enormous mass of foliage, before we found a landing-place. It seemed as if it had determined that it would only have the free birds for inhabitants. At last we were able to step on shore under a great bush spreading over the water. Antoinette watched us land, and straining her neck endeavored to see beyond the trees.

One of the oarsmen who was keeping the boat in position while holding on to a branch, let the craft go. Then the young woman, feeling herself drifting away, extended her arm and seized a root. She clung to it, called for help, and cried out that she did not want to go any further. Then, when the oarsmen had secured the boat, she sprang on to the grass and came to us, all rosy from the effects of her achievement.

"Don't be afraid, gentlemen," she said to us, "I do not wish to be in your way; if it pleases you to go to the north, we will go to the south."

I had taken up my basket again, and gravely set out to look for the plot of turf that was the least damp. Leon followed me, and was followed himself by Antoinette and her sweethearts. In this order we walked round the island. On returning to our point of departure, I sat down, decided not to make any further search. Antoinette took a few steps, appeared to hesitate, then returned and placed herself opposite me. We were at the north, she did not think of going to the south. Leon then found the site charming, and vowed I could not have made a better selection.

I do not know how it occurred, the baskets happened to be side by side, the provisions went together so perfectly, when they were spread out on the grass, that neither party was able to distinguish which was which. We had to have but one cloth, and in a spirit of justice, we shared the viands.

The two lovers had hastened to seat themselves on either side of the young woman. They anticipated all her wishes. For one piece of anything she asked for, she regularly received two. Her appetite, however, was good.

Leon, on the contrary, ate little, but watched us devouring. Being obliged to sit next to me, he held his tongue, giving me a mocking look each time Antoinette smiled at his neighbors. As she was receiving food on both sides, she held her hands out right and left with equal complacency, tendering thanks each time with her soft voice. Leon, on seeing this, made energetic signs to me which I did not understand.

The young woman was desperately coquettish that day. With her feet drawn under her petticoats, she almost disappeared in the grass; a poet would have made no difficulty about comparing her to a large flower gifted with looks and smiles. She, who was generally so natural, gave herself roguish airs, and there was a simpering tone in her voice which I had never noticed before. The lovers, confused at her kind remarks, looked at each other triumphantly. For my part, astonished at this sudden coquetry; seeing the wicked creature laughing every now and then in her sleeve, I wondered which of us was transforming this simple girl into a shrewd woman.

The repast was almost over. We laughed more than we talked. Leon changed his seat continually, unable to make himself comfortable anywhere. As he had resumed his disagreeable manner, I was afraid a speech was coming, and with a look I begged our lady-friend to pardon me for having such a sulky companion. But she was a plucky girl: a philosopher of twenty, however serious he might be, could not put her out of countenance.

"Sir," she said to Leon, "you are sad; our merriment seems to annoy you. I am afraid to laugh any more."

"Laugh, laugh, madam," he answered. "If I hold my tongue, it is because I am unable to find fine phrases to delight you, like these gentlemen."

"Does that mean that you do not flatter? In that case speak out at once. I am all attention, I want brutal truths."

"Women do not like them, madam. Besides, when they are young and pretty, what fib can one tell them that is not true?"

"Come, you see, you are a courtier like the rest. Now you are making me blush. When we are absent, you men tear us to pieces; but let the most insignificant of us appear, and you cannot bow low enough or find language sufficiently tender. That's hypocrisy! As for myself I am frank, I say: Men are cruel, they do not know how to love. Look here, sir, be straightforward too. What do you say of women?"

"Have I full liberty?"

"Certainly."

"You will not get angry?"

"Eh! No, I will laugh rather than do so." Leon struck the attitude of an orator. As I knew the speech by heart, having heard it more than a hundred times over, I began to throw pebbles into the Seine to divert myself and bear with it."

"When our Maker," he said, "perceived a being was wanting in His creation, and had used up all the mud, He did not know where to find the necessary material wherewith to repair His forgetfulness. He had to turn to the dumb animals; He took a little flesh from each of them, and with these contributions from the serpent, she-wolf, vulture and so on, He created woman. And so the wise who are familiar with this circumstance, omitted from the Bible, are not surprised to see woman whimsical and everlastingly a prey to contrary Humours, as she is a faithful image of the different elements of which she is composed. Each creature has given her a vice; all the evil dispersed throughout creation has been assembled in her; hence her hypocritical caresses, her treachery, her debauchery"

Any one would have said that Leon was repeating a lesson. He held his tongue, searching for the continuation. Antoinette applauded.

"Women," resumed the orator, "are born coquettish and giddy, just as they are born dark or fair. They give themselves away by egotism, and take little care to choose according to merit. Let a man be foppish with the regular beauty of a fool, and they will fight over him. Let him be simple and affectionate, satisfied with being a man of intelligence, without proclaiming it from the housetops, and they will not even know of his existence. In all matters they must have playthings that sparkle: silk petticoats, golden necklaces, precious stones, lovers combed and pomaded. As to the springs of the amusing machine, it matters little whether they work well or badly. They have nothing to do with minds. They know all about black hair and amorous lips, but they are ignorant of things connected with the heart. It is thus that they throw themselves into the arms of the first simpleton they meet, having full confidence in his grand appearance. They love him because he pleases them; and he pleases them, because he pleases them. One day the simpleton thrashes them. They then talk about being martyrs ; they are plunged in grief, and say a man cannot touch a heart without breaking it. What foolish creatures. Why do they not seek for the flower of love where it blooms?"

Antoinette applauded again. The speech, as I knew it, stopped there^ Leon had delivered it straight off, as if in a hurry to reach the end. When he had uttered the last sentence, he gazed at the young woman and seemed dreaming. Then, declaiming no longer, he added:

"I never had but one sweetheart. She was ten and I twelve. One day she threw me over, for a big dog who let himself be teased without ever showing his teeth. I wept bitterly and vowed I would never love again. I have kept that vow. I know nothing about women. If I were in love I should be jealous and disagreeable; I should love too fondly; I should make myself hated; they would deceive me, and that would be my death."

He said no more, and, with moist eyes, sought in vain to laugh. Antoinette was no longer joking. She had listened to him very seriously; then, leaving her neighbors, looking Leon in the face, she went and placed her hand on his shoulder.

"You are a child," she simply said to him.

A last beam of the sun gliding over the surface of the river, transformed it into a ribbon of creamy gold. We waited for the first star, so as to descend the current in the cool of the evening. The baskets had been carried back to the boat, and we had laid down, here and there, each according to fancy.

Antoinette and Leon had seated themselves beneath a large sweet-briar, which extended its limbs above their heads. They were half hidden by the green branches. As their backs were turned to me, I could not see whether they were laughing or crying. They spoke in an undertone, and appeared to be quarrelling. As for myself, I had selected a little mound covered with fine grass; and stretching out lazily, I saw at the same time the heavens and the turf on which my feet were resting. The two lovers, appreciating, no doubt, the charm of my attitude, had come and laid down, one on my right and the other on my left.

They profited by their position to talk to me both at the same time.

The one on my left nudged me slightly with his arm when he found I was no longer listening to him.

"Sir," he said to me, "I have rarely met a more capricious woman than Mademoiselle Antoinette. You cannot imagine how her head turns at the least thing. For example, when we met you this morning we were on our way to dine two leagues away from here. You had hardly disappeared, when she made us retrace our steps; the country didn't please her, she said. It's enough to drive one crazy. For my part, I like doing things one can understand."

The man who was on my right said at the same time, obliging me to listen to him:

"Sir, I have been seeking an opportunity to speak to you in private since this morning. My companion and I think we owe you an explanation. We have noticed your great friendship for Mademoiselle Antoinette, and we very much regret to interfere with your plans. If we had known of your love a week earlier, we would have withdrawn, so as not to cause a gentleman the least pain; but now it is rather late: we no longer feel strong enough to make the sacrifice. Besides, I will be straightforward: Antoinette loves me. I pity you, and am ready to give you satisfaction."

I hastened to allay his fears. But although I vowed to him that I never had been, and never would be Antoinette's sweetheart, he nevertheless continued to lavish the most tender consolation upon me. He found it so delicious to think that he had robbed me of my love.

The other, annoyed at the attention I was paying to his companion, bent over towards me. To compel me to lend him an ear, he confided to me a great secret.

"I want to be straightforward with you," he said; "Antoinette loves me. I sincerely pity her other admirers."

At that moment I heard a peculiar sound; it came from the bush beneath which Leon and Antoinette were sheltering themselves. I couldn't tell whether it was a kiss or the note of a frightened animal.

In the meanwhile, my right-hand neighbor had surprised my left-hand neighbor, telling me Antoinette loved him. He raised himself and looked at him defiantly. I slipped away from them, and slyly gained a hedge, behind which I ensconced myself. Then they found themselves face to face. My cluster of brambles was admirably situated. I could see Antoinette and Leon, but without, however, hearing what they said. They were still quarrelling; only they seemed closer to one another. As to the men in love, they were above me, and I could follow their dispute. The young woman was turning her back to them, so they were able to give vent to their fury at ease.

"You have behaved very badly," said one; "you should have withdrawn two days ago. Haven't you sufficient intelligence to see? Antoinette prefers me."

"No indeed," answered the other, "I have not that intelligence. But you have the stupidity, you, to take for yourself the smiles and glances intended for me."

"Rest assured, my poor gentleman, that Antoinette loves me."

"Rest assured, my happy sir, that Antoinette adores me."

I looked at Antoinette. There was certainly no animal in the bush.

"I am tired of all this," resumed one of the suitors. "Are not you of my opinion, that it is time for one of us to make himself scarce?"

"I was about to suggest to you that we should cut one another's throats," answered the other.

They had raised their voices; were gesticulating, getting up and sitting down again in their anger. The young woman, attracted by the increasing noise of the quarrel, turned her head. I saw her look astonished, then smile. She called Leon's attention to the two young men, and said a few words to him which made him quite merry.

He rose and went towards the river, leading his companion along with him. They stifled their bursts of laughter, and avoided kicking the stones as they walked along. I thought they were going to hide themselves, so as to cause a search to be made for them afterwards.

The two wooers were shouting still louder; having no swords, they were making ready to use their fists. In the meantime Leon had reached the boat; he helped Antoinette into it, and quietly began to undo the cord; then he jumped in himself.

Just as one of the suitors was about to strike the other, he caught sight of the boat in mid-stream. Thunderstruck, forgetting to hit, he pointed it out to his companion.

"Heh! heh!" he shouted, running to the bank, "what's the meaning of this joke?"

I had been entirely forgotten behind my bush. Happiness and misfortune, alike, make persons egotists. I rose.

"Gentlemen," I said to the poor fellows who stood gaping and bewildered, "don't you remember the fable? The joke means this: Antoinette, whom you thought you had stolen from me, is being stolen from you."

"The comparison is gallant!" Leon shouted out to me. "Those gentlemen are thieves, and madam is an"

Madam kissed him, and the kiss smothered the ugly word.

"Brothers," I added, turning towards my stranded companions, "here we are without food and without a roof above our heads. Let us build a hut, and live on wild berries until a vessel comes to take us off our desert island."

And then?

And then, what do I know! You are asking me too much, Ninette. Antoinette and Leon have been living for two months, now, in the sky-blue nest. Antoinette continues a frank and good girl. Leon speaks ill of women more impetuously than ever. They dote on each other.

A SISTER OF THE POOR

At the age of ten, the poor child seemed so delicate, that it was pitiful to see her working as hard as a farm-servant. She had great, wondering eyes, and the sad smile of those who suffer without complaining. The rich farmers who met her of an evening coming out of the wood, ill-clad and loaded with a heavy burden, sometimes offered, when the corn had sold well, to buy her a good petticoat in thick fustian, and she would then answer: "I know of a poor old man, who stands under the church porch, exposed to this December cold, and who has only one blouse; buy him a cloth jacket, and to-morrow, when I see him so well clad, I shall feel warm." It was for that reason they had nicknamed her Sister-of-the-Poor; and some called her so in derision, on account of her old clothes, while others did so as a reward for her kind heart.

Sister-of-the-Poor, in her early days, had had a fine lace cradle and enough playthings to fill a room. Then, one morning, her mother did not come to kiss her when it was time to get up. As she cried at not seeing her, they told her that one of God's angels had borne her away to Paradise, and that dried her tears. A month previous, her father had gone in the same way. The dear little thing thought he had just called her mother from the sky, and that the two being united, unable to live without their daughter, would soon send an angel to carry her away in her turn.

She had forgotten how she had lost her playthings and cradle. From a rich young lady, she became a poor girl, without any one seeming astonished: no doubt wicked people had come, who had stripped her of everything, while presenting the appearance of honest folk. All she remembered was having one morning seen her uncle Guillaume and her aunt Guillaumette beside her bed. She felt very much afraid, because they did not kiss her. Guillaumette hurriedly dressed her in a frock of coarse material; Guillaume, holding her by the hand, led her away to the wretched hut where she was now living. Then, that was all she felt very weary every night.

Guillaume and Guillaumette had also been very wealthy. But Guillaume was partial to the society of boon companions, and to nights passed in drinking, without giving a thought to the barrels that were being emptied; Guillaumette was fond of ribbons, silk gowns, and of wasting long hours in vain endeavors to make herself look young and beautiful; and so they continued, until at last there was no more wine in the cellar, and the mirror was sold to purchase bread. Up till then they had shown that good nature of certain wealthy people, which is often only an effect of their own well-being and satisfaction; they enjoyed happiness more thoroughly by sharing it with others, and thus mingled much egotism with their charity. And so they were incapable of suffering and remaining kind. Regretting the wealth they had lost, having tears only for their own misery, they became hard for the poor world.

They forgot that their poverty had been brought about by their own selves, they accused each other of their ruin, and felt at heart immense necessity for vengeance; they were exasperated at having to eat black bread, and sought to console themselves by the sight of greater suffering than their own.

And so the rags of Sister-of-the-Poor, and her thin little cheeks all pale with tears, pleased them. They would not own, even to themselves, the wicked delight they took in the child's weakness, when she tottered back from the spring, clutching the heavy pitcher in both hands. They beat her for a drop of spilt water, saying that bad temper must be punished; and they struck her so readily and spitefully, that it was easy to perceive the chastisement was undeserved.

Sister-of-the-Poor bore all their misery. They gave her the most tiring work to do, sent her to glean in the mid-day sun, and to pick up dead wood in snowy weather. Then as soon as she returned, she had to sweep, wash, and put everything in order in the hut. The dear little creature had ceased complaining. Happy days were such a long way off, that she did not know one could live without weeping. She never dreamt of there being young ladies who were petted and gay; in the absence of playthings, and kisses of an evening, she accepted strokes and dry bread, as forming also part of her existence. And men of wisdom were surprised to see a child of ten display so much pity for all who suffered, without giving a thought to her own misfortune. But, one night, I know not what anniversary Guillaume and Guillaumette were feasting, they gave her a beautiful new sou piece, and allowed her to go out and play for the remainder of the day. Sister-of-the-Poor went slowly down to the town, very much troubled with her sou and not knowing what to do to play. In that frame of mind she reached the principal street . There was there, on the left, near the church, a shop full of sweets and dolls, which were so beautifully lit up, that the children of the neighborhood dreamed of them, as of a paradise. On that particular evening a lot of little creatures stood on the pavement with gaping mouths and dumb with admiration, while their hands were pressed against the window panes, as near as possible to the marvels displayed there. Sister-of-the-Poor envied their audacity. She stopped in the middle of the street, allowing her little arms to fall beside her, and bringing together her rags which were blown apart by the wind. Feeling somewhat proud at being rich, she clutched her new sou very tight and selected with her eyes the plaything she meant to buy. At last she decided on a doll which had hair like a grown-up person; this doll, which was as tall as she was, wore a white silk gown similar to that of the Holy Virgin.

The little girl made a few steps forward. She was ashamed, and as she gazed around her before entering the shop, she perceived an ill-clad woman sitting on a stone bench, and nursing a child who was crying in her arms. She stopped again, turning her back to the doll. Her hands, at the child's cries, became locked together in pity; and, this time without shame, she hurried toward the poor woman and gave her beautiful new sou.

The latter had been observing Sister-of-the-Poor for some time. She had seen her stop, then approach the playthings, so that when the child came to her, she understood her good heart. She took the sou with tearful eyes; then she retained the little hand that gave it her in her own.

"My child," she said, "I accept your charity, because I see a refusal would grieve you. But are you beyond necessity yourself? Ill-clad though I be, I can satisfy one of your wishes."

As the poor woman spoke, her eyes shone like stars, while around her head ran a halo, as if formed by a ray of the sun. The child, who was now asleep on her knees, smiled divinely in its slumber.

Sister-of-the-Poor shook her fair head.

"No, madam," she answered, "I have no wish. I wanted to buy that doll you see opposite, but my aunt Guillaumette would have broken it for me. As you will not take my sou for nothing, I would like you to give me a nice kiss in exchange for it."

The beggar bent forward and kissed her on the forehead. Sister-of-the-Poor, at this kiss, felt herself raised from the earth; it seemed to her that her interminable fatigue had quitted her; at the same time her heart became better.

"My child," added the unknown, "I will not let your charity go unrewarded. I have a sou which I, like you, did not know what to do with until I met you. Princes, highborn dames, have thrown me purses filled with gold, and I have not thought them worthy of it. Take it. Whatever happens, act according to your heart."

And she gave it to her. It was an old brass sou, jagged at the edges, and with a hole in the centre of it as big as a great lentil. It was so worn that it was impossible to discover from what country it came, but one could still see a half-obliterated hallowed crown on one of its faces. Perhaps it was a piece of heavenly money.

Sister-of-the-Poor, noticing it so thin, extended her hand, understanding that such a present could not deprive the beggar of anything, and looking upon it as a token of her friendship.

"Alas!" she thought, "the poor woman does not know what she says. Princes and fine ladies could do nothing with her sou. It is so ugly that it would not pay for an ounce of bread. I shall not even be able to give it to the poor."

The woman, .whose eyes shone brighter and brighter, smiled, as if the child had spoken aloud. Softly she said to her:

"Take it all the same, and you will see."

Then Sister-of-the-Poor accepted it, so as not to disoblige her. She bent down in order to place it in the pocket of her skirt; when she raised her head again, the bench was vacant . She felt very much astonished, and returned home pondering over her recent meeting.

Sister-of-the-Poor slept in the garret, a sort of loft strewn with pieces of old furniture. On moonlight nights, thanks to a narrow dormer-window, she had light to go to bed by. On others she was obliged to grope her way to reach her couch, a poor one, made of four badly joined planks, and a straw bed, which was so lumpy that in places the two sides of the tick touched each other.

On that particular night the moon was at its full. A luminous stream ran along the beams, filling the garret with light.

When Guillaume and Guillaumette were in bed, Sister-of-the-Poor went upstairs. On dark nights she sometimes felt very much afraid at sudden moans, at the sound of footsteps she fancied she heard, and which were nothing more than the cracking of woodwork and the scampering of mice. And so she was very fond of the beautiful satellite whose friendly rays dispersed her fears. On nights when it shone, she opened the dormer-window, and thanked it in her prayers for having returned to see her.

She was very much pleased to find light in her room. She was tired, and would sleep very tranquilly, feeling herself watched over by her good friend the moon. She had often felt it in her sleep wandering thus about the room, silent and gentle, driving away the bad dreams of winter nights.

She ran and knelt down on an old chest, in the midst of the white light . There she prayed to God. Then, going towards the bed, she unhooked her skirt.

The skirt slid to the ground, and in doing so a quantity of big sous fell out of the distended pocket. Sister-of-the-Poor, motionless and in terror, watched them rolling about.

She stooped down and picked them up one by one, taking hold of them with the tips of her fingers. She piled them up on the old chest, without seeking to ascertain how many there were, for she could only count up to fifty, and she could see very well that there were several hundred of them. When she could find no more on the ground, she picked up her skirt, and understood by the weight that the pocket was again full. Then, for a good quarter of an hour, she pulled handfuls of sous out of it, thinking she would never reach the bottom. At last she could only feel one more. When she looked at it, she recognized it was the sou the beggar-woman had given her that same evening.

She then said to herself that the Almighty had just performed a miracle, and that this ugly-looking sou which she had disdained, was a sou such as the wealthy never had. She felt it vibrate between her fingers, ready to multiply again. And she was all of a tremble lest it should take the fancy to fill the whole garret with wealth. Even now she knew not what to do with those piles of new money that were shining in the moonlight, and she gazed around her quite troubled

Like a good work-girl she had always a needle and cotton in her apron pocket, and she looked about her for a piece of old sacking to make a bag. She made it so narrow that she could hardly get her little hand into it; material was wanting, and besides, Sister-of-the-Poor was pressed for time. Then, having placed the poor woman's sou right at the bottom, she began to slip the pieces covering the chest into the bag, pile by pile. As each lot fell, the bag became full, and was immediately empty again. The hundreds of big sous had plenty of room there, and it was easy to see that it could have held four times as many.

After that, Sister-of-the-Poor, who was tired, hid the bag under the paillasse, and went to sleep. She laughed in her dreams, thinking of all the alms she would be able to distribute the next day.

When Sister-of-the-Poor awoke the following morning, she fancied she had been dreaming. It was necessary to touch her treasure to believe in its existence. It was a little heavier than on the previous evening, and this made the child understand that the wonderful sou had been at work again during the night.

She dressed herself hurriedly, and went downstairs with her wooden shoes in her hand so as not to make a noise. She had hidden the bag under her fichu and pressed it to her bosom. Guillaume and Guillaumette, who were fast asleep, did not hear her. She had to pass in front of their bed, and she almost fell down with fright at the thought that they were so close to her; then she began to run, threw the door wide open, and rushed off forgetting to close it again.

It was in winter, and one of the coldest mornings in December. Day was just breaking. The sky with its pale glimmers of dawn seemed the same color as the earth which was covered with snow. This general whiteness, which extended to the horizon, made all the surroundings look very calm. Sister-of-the-Poor walked quickly along, following the path leading to the town. All she heard was the cracking of the snow under her wooden shoes. Although very much absorbed in thought, she chose the deepest ruts by way of amusement.

As she approached the town, she remembered she had forgotten in her hurry to pray to God She knelt down at the roadside. There, alone, lost in the immense and sad serenity of slumbering nature, she pronounced her orison in that childish voice which is so sweet, that God cannot distinguish it from that of angels. She soon arose again, and feeling a chill, hurried on her way.

There was great poverty in the surrounding country, especially that year, the winter being a hard one, and bread so dear, that only well-to-do folk could purchase it. Poor people, those who lived on sunshine and pity, went abroad in the early morning to see if spring were not coming, bringing more bountiful charity along with it. They walked along the roads, or seated themselves on the boundary stones at the gates of the towns, beseeching the passers-by to assist them; for it was so cold in their lofts, that they might just as well take up their lodging on the highway. And there were such numbers of them there, that one might have peopled a large village with them.

Sister-of-the-Poor had opened the little bag. On entering the town, she saw a blind man coming towards her, led by a little girl who gazed sadly in her face, taking her for a sister in misfortune she was so ill-clad.

"My father," she said to the poor old man, "Hold out your hands. Jesus has sent me to you."

She spoke to the old man because the little girl's fingers were too small, and could not have held more than a dozen big sous. And so, to fill the hands the blind man extended to her, she had to plunge into the sack seven times, they were so long and broad. Then, before passing on, she told the little one to help herself to a final handful of money.

She was in a hurry to get before the church, near the stone benches where the poor assembled in the morning; God's house sheltered them from the north winds; the sun, when it rose, cast its rays right on the porch. She had to stop again. At the corner of an alley, she found a young woman who had no doubt passed the night there, she was so chilled and shivering with cold; with closed eyes, her arms pressed against her breast, she seemed asleep, hoping for nothing but death. Sister-of-the-Poor stood before her with her hand full of sous, not knowing how to bestow her charity upon her. She wept, thinking she had come too late.

"Good woman," she said, and she touched her softly on the shoulder, "Look, take this money. You must go and breakfast at the inn and have a sleep before a big fire."

At that sweet voice, the good woman opened her eyes and held out her hands. She, perhaps, thought she was still sleeping, and dreaming that an angel had descended beside her.

Sister-of-the-Poor hurried to the great square. There was a crowd there under the porch awaiting the first ray of sunshine. The beggars, seated at the feet of the saints, were shivering with cold and huddled against one another without speaking. They were slowly rolling their heads as the dying do. They crowded in the corners, so as not to lose any of the sun, when it made its appearance.

Sister-of-the-Poor began on the right, throwing handfuls of sous into the felt hats and the aprons, and with such good heart that many of the pieces rolled on the pavement. The dear child did not count. The little sack performed wonders; it would not become empty, it swelled out so at each fresh handful the young girl took from it, that it overflowed like a vase which is too full. The poor people stood dumbfounded at this delightful windfall: they picked up the sous that fell, forgetting the sun that was rising, and repeating hurriedly: "God will give it you back." The charity was so bountiful that some good old fellows fancied the stone saints were throwing them this fortune; and they even still believe so.

The child laughed at their delight. She went three times round, so as to give the same sum to each; then she stopped; not because the little bag was empty, but because she had much to do before evening. As she was about to go away, she perceived a crippled old man in a corner, who, being unable to advance, extended his hands towards her. Feeling sorry at not having seen him, she advanced and tilted up the bag so as to give him more. The sous began to run from this miserable-looking purse like water from a spring without stopping, and so abundantly that Sister-of-the-Poor soon closed the opening with her fist, for the heap would have risen in a few minutes as high as the church. The poor old man would not have known what to do with so much wealth, and perhaps the rich would have come and robbed him.

Then, when those on the grand square had their pockets full, she set out towards the country. The beggars, forgetting to comfort themselves, began to follow her; they gazed at her in astonishment and respect, borne along by an outburst of brotherly feeling. She, standing alone, looking round about her, advanced the first. The crowd came afterwards.

The child, dressed in a ragged printed calico gown, was indeed a sister to the poor people who formed her suite, sister by her rags and sister by tender pity. She found her

self there in a family gathering, giving to her brothers, forgetting herself; she walked along gravely with all the strength of her little feet, happy to act the big girl; and this little fair thing of ten, followed by her escort of old men, was beaming with naive majesty.

With her narrow purse in her hand, she went from village to village distributing charity throughout the country. She advanced without picking her way, taking the roads of the plains and the paths of the hills. Sometimes she turned aside, crossing the fields to see if some vagabond were not sheltered beneath the hedges or in the hollow of the ditches. She stood on tiptoe, gazing at the horizon, regretful that she was unable to call all the poverty of the neighborhood around her. She sighed when she reflected that she was perhaps leaving some one in suffering behind her; it was that thought that made her sometimes retrace her footsteps to examine a bush. And, whether she slackened her speed at bends in the roads, or ran forward to meet some person in want, her retinue followed her wherever she went.

And so it happened that as she was crossing a meadow, a flight of sparrows swooped down before her. The poor little creatures, lost in the snow, chirped in a lamentable way, asking for the food they had sought for in vain. Sister-of-the-Poor stopped, taken aback at meeting unfortunates to whom her big sous could be of no assistance; she gazed at her bag in anger, execrating the money which could not be employed in charity of this kind. In the meanwhile the sparrows surrounded her; they said they belonged to the family, and asked for their share of her favors. Ready to burst out sobbing, not knowing what to do, she drew a handful of sous from the bag, for she could not make up her mind to dismiss them with nothing. The dear child had assuredly lost her head, imagining big sous were sparrows' money, and that these children of God have millers to grind and bakers to knead their daily bread. I know not what she thought of doing, but the fact is that the charity which was given out in handfuls of sous fell in handfuls of corn on the ground.

Sister-of-the-Poor did not seem surprised. She gave the sparrows a regular feast, offering them all sorts of grain, and in such quantity that when spring came, the meadow was covered with grass as thick and high as a forest. Since then, that corner of the earth has belonged to the birds of the air; they find abundance of food there in all seasons, notwithstanding that they come by thousands, from more than twenty leagues around.

Sister-of-the-Poor resumed her walk, delighted at her new power. She no longer limited herself to distributing big sous. According to the people she met, she gave good smocks, which were very warm, thick woolen petticoats, or boots that were so light and tough that they barely weighed an ounce and yet wore down the stones. All this came from an unknown factory. The materials were wonderfully strong and flexible; the seams were so finely sewn, that in the hole which one of our own needles would have made, magic needles had easily found room for three of their stitches; and the most extraordinary thing was that each article of clothing fitted the poor person who put it on. No doubt a workshop of good fairies had been established at the bottom of the bag, and they had brought a pair of fine gold scissors, which cut ten cherubs' gowns out of a roseleaf. It was, certainly, heavenly labor, for the work was so perfect and so quickly sewn.

The little bag showed no pride on that account. The opening was slightly worn, and the hand of Sister-of-the-Poor had perhaps enlarged it a little; it might now have the dimensions of a couple of linnets' nests. In order that you may not charge me with telling fibs, I must explain to you how the large articles of clothing came out of it, such as petticoats and cloaks five or six yards wide. The truth is, they were folded up like the flower of the poppy before it has burst from the calyx; and they were folded so cleverly that they were no bigger than the bud of that flower. Then Sister-of-the-Poor took the packet between two fingers and slightly shook it. The material was unfolded, extended in length, and became a garment, no longer any good for angels, but suitable for broad shoulders. As to the shoes, I have never been able to ascertain up to this day in what form they left the sack. I have, however, heard say, although I affirm nothing, that each pair was enclosed in a bean, which burst open on touching the ground. And all that, of course, did not interfere with the handfuls of big sous which fell as thick as hail in March.

Sister-of-the-Poor continued walking. She did not feel fatigued, although she had done more than twenty leagues since the morning, without eating or drinking. To observe her passing along the roads, leaving hardly a trace of her footsteps, one would have said she was borne along by invisible wings. She had been seen that day at the four corners of the neighborhood. You would not have found an angle of land, plain or mountain, where the slight imprint of her little feet was not marked in the snow. In truth, if Guillaume and Guillaumette were pursuing her, they risked running a whole week before catching her. Not that there was any reason to hesitate about the road she took, for she left a crowd behind her, as kings do on their way; but because she walked so pluckily that she herself, in other times, would have been unable to make such a journey in less than six full weeks.

And her retinue continued increasing at each village. All those whom she assisted walked in her train, so that, towards evening, the crowd extended behind her for several hundred yards. It was her good actions that were thus following her. Never had a saint gone before God with such a royal escort.

However, night set in. Sister-of-the-Poor was still walking, and the little bag was still at work. At length the child was seen to stop on the summit of a hill; she remained motionless, gazing at the plains she had just been enriching, and her rags stood out black against the whiteness of the twilight. The beggars formed a circle round her; they swayed about in great dark masses with the hollow murmuring of crowds. Then there was silence. Sister-of-the-Poor, high up in the air, with a people at her feet, smiled. Then, having grown a great deal taller since the morning, and standing upright on the hill, she pointed with her hand to heaven, saying to her people, "Thank Jesus; thank Mary."

And all her people heard her sweet voice.

It was very late when Sister-of-the-Poor returned home. Guillaume and Guillaumette had fallen asleep, worn out by their anger and threats. She went in by the stable door, which was only closed by a latch, and quickly reached her loft, where she found her good friend the moon, looking so clear and joyful, that it seemed to know how she had been passing her day. Heaven often thanks us thus, by brighter beams of light.

The child felt in great need of rest; but before going to bed she wanted to see the miraculous sou again—the one that was at the bottom of her bag. It had worked so hard and well that really it deserved a kiss. She seated herself on the chest and began to empty the purse, placing the handfuls of money at her feet. For a quarter of an hour she tried to get to the bottom; the pile reached up to her knees, and then she was in despair. She could see very well that she would fill the loft without getting on any further with her work.

In her perplexity she could think of nothing better than to turn the little bag inside out. The result was a prodigious rush of big sous; the garret for the nonce was three-parts full of them. The bag was empty.

The noise, however, awoke Guillaume. Although the floor coming in would not have disturbed the poor fellow's sleep, not the smallest piece of money could have fallen on the flags without him opening his eyes.

"Heh! Wife," he exclaimed; "do you hear?"

And as the old woman grumbled in a bad humor, he resumed:

"The child has returned home. I think she must have robbed some one, for I can hear the jingle of a full purse up there."

Guillaumette sat up in bed wide awake, thinking no more of grumbling. She promptly lit the lamp, saying, "I knew very well that child was full of vice."

Then she added, "I will buy a cap with ribbons and a pair of cloth shoes. I shall be proud of myself on Sunday."

Then both of them, half-dressed, ascended to the garret, Guillaume leading the way and Guillaumette following, holding up the lamp. Their thin, strange-looking shadows extended along the walls.

They stopped in amazement at the top of the ladder. On the floor was a mass of coins three feet deep, filling every corner, so that it was impossible to perceive a piece of board as large as the hand. In some places the money lay in heaps, which one might have taken for the waves of this sea of big sous. In the centre of it, between two of the heaps, Sister-of-the-Poor was sleeping in a ray of the moon. The child, overcome by slumber, had been unable to reach her bed; she had let herself slip softly down, and was dreaming of heaven on this couch of doles. With her arms crossed over her breast she grasped the beggar's magic present in her right hand. Her light, regular respiration could be heard amidst the silence, while the beloved planet reflecting around her on the new money enveloped her, as it were, in a circle of gold.

Guillaume and Guillaumette were not people to be long astonished. The miracle being to their advantage, they did not trouble much about seeking to fathom it, caring very Rule whether it was the work of the Almighty or Satan. When they had counted the treasure for an instant with their eyes, they wanted to make quite sure that it was not merely an effect of shadow and reflection of the moon. They eagerly stooped down with their hands wide open.

But what occurred then, is so little worthy of belief that I hesitate to relate it. Guillaume had hardly taken up a handful of the pieces, when they were transformed into enormous bats. He parted his fingers in terror and the nasty creatures escaped, giving utterance to shrill cries and striking him in the face with their long, black wings. Guillaumette, on her side, caught hold of a litter of young rats, with sharp white teeth, which bit her dreadfully as they escaped down her legs. The old woman, who fainted at the sight of a mouse, was half dead when she felt these creatures running about her petticoats.

They had stood up, no longer daring to play with this money which looked so new in appearance but was so unpleasant to the touch. They gazed at each other ill at ease, encouraging one another with those half laughing, half angry looks of a child that has just burnt itself with a piece of hot pudding. Guillaumette was the first to give way to the temptation the second time; she stretched out her skinny arms, and took two fresh handfuls of sous. As she closed her fists so that nothing could escape, she shrieked with pain, for in truth she had clutched hold of two handfuls of needles, which were so long and pointed that her fingers seemed as if sewn to the palms of her hands. Guillaume, seeing her stoop down, wanted his share of the treasure. He lost no time, but his booty consisted only of two shovelfuls of red-hot cinders, which burnt his skin like gunpowder.

Then, mad with pain, they fell upon the big sous, plunging right into them, endeavoring to get the best of the miracle by the rapidity of their movements. But the big sous were not to be taken by surprise. Hardly were they touched than they flew away in the form of locusts, wriggled as serpents, ran along as boiling water, were dispersed in smoke; any form seemed suitable to them, and they did not leave without having slightly burnt or bitten the thieves.

The fecundity was frightful, so rapid, giving birth to so many different kinds of creatures that unutterable terror reigned there. Flying-toads, owls, vampires, night-moths, rushed to the dormer-window, flapping their wings, and escaping in great flights. Scorpions, spiders, all the hideous denizens of damp places reached the corners in long affrighted columns. Although the loft was full of chinks and crevices, there were not sufficient holes for them, and they were there, hustling one another, and crushing themselves in the cracks.

Guillaume and Guillaumette, mad with fright, began to run, borne along in the giddy movement of this strange creation. To the right and left, everywhere, they hastened the bursting into existence of new creatures. Life streamed from their fingers. The living flood rose. This treasure, on which the moon a moment before had been casting its rays, was nothing more than a blackish mass which swayed heavily to and fro, rising, sinking upon itself, as wine in the vat.

There was soon not a big sou left. The entire heap had become alive. Then Guillaume and Guillaumette, unable to take anything but reptiles fled, casting two handfuls of snakes in their own faces.

And, as they had removed all the monsters in these two last handfuls, the loft was empty. Sister-of-the-Poor had heard nothing and was slumbering, calm and smiling.

When Sister-of-the-Poor awoke, she was troubled with a feeling of remorse. She said to herself that she had been searching out the poverty of the neighborhood far and wide, without thinking of relieving that of her uncle and aunt.

The dear child had compassion for all suffering. With her, the fact that the poor were poor, came before the question as to whether they were good or bad. She made no distinction among those who wept. She did not consider she had the task of meting out punishments and rewards, but the mission to dry tears. No grand idea of justice found a place in her small mind of ten summers; she was all charity, all alms. When she thought of the damned in hell, a feeling of pity gained her heart, which she never experienced in so great a measure for souls in purgatory.

When somebody, one day, told her that a certain poor person did not deserve the bread she gave him, she failed to understand. She refused to believe that it was not sufficient to be hungry, to eat.

So, Sister-of-the-Poor, to make amends for her forgetfulness, took her little bag again, and ran and bought, in beautiful new money, a piece of land adjoining her relatives' hut. She also purchased a pair of white and brown oxen, with coats as glossy as silk. She took care not to forget the plough. Then she hired a farm-laborer, who drove the yoke of cattle to the edge of the field, at the door of the cottage. While this was being done, she purchased in the town a quantity of stores of all sorts; old vine roots, which make a bright fire, the best flour, salt provisions, dry vegetables. She made three large carts follow her, and went from shop to shop, loading them with what she thought necessary for a home. And it was marvelous to see how she spent God's money like a grown-up girl, not purchasing any useless things, as might have been expected of a child so young, but strong furniture, pieces of linen, copper cooking pots, all that a housewife of thirty could dream of.

When the three carts were full, she came and stood them beside the bullocks and plough. Then it struck her that the cottage was very wretched, very small, to hold all this wealth, and she was grieved that she could not buy a farm, not because she had not the money, but because there was no farm in that part of the country. She resolved to send for the masons and make them build a large house on the same site as the humble dwelling. But, in the meanwhile, as she was in a great hurry, she merely poured a few heaps of big sous on the ground, in front of the carts, to meet the expense of building.

She set about her work so briskly that it took her less than an hour to arrange everything. Guillaume and Guillaumette were still asleep, having heard neither the sound of the wheels nor the laborer's whip.

Then Sister-of-the-Poor went to the door, with an artful smile on her lips, for she sometimes had a roguish way of doing good. She had hurried a little, out of obsession, and was pleased that she had everything ready before her relatives awoke.

She cast a last look at her purchases, and then began to cry out, as she clapped her hands with all her might, "Uncle Guillaume! Aunt Guillaumette!"

And as the two old people did not move, she struck the badly-adjusted planks of the shutters with her fist, repeating several times in a louder tone, "Uncle Guillaume, Aunt Guillaumette, open quickly, fortune wants to come in!"

Now, Guillaume and Guillaumette heard this as they slept, and they jumped out of bed, without troubling to wake up. Sister-of-the-Poor was still shouting, when they appeared on the threshold, pushing against each other, rubbing their eyes, to see better; and they had been in such a hurry, that Guillaume had on the petticoats and Guillaumette the breeches. They had no idea of this, having so many other subjects for amazement. The heaps of big sous rose as high as hay-ricks in front of the three carts which had a magnificent aspect, the caldron and oak furniture standing out against the snow. The bullocks were breathing loudly in the morning breeze. The ploughshare looked so white, in the rays of the early sun, that it seemed as if made of silver.

The laborer advanced and said to Guillaume, "Master, where shall I take the yoke of oxen? This is not the time of year for ploughing. Have no anxiety: your fields are sown and you will have an ample harvest."

And, during this time, the carters had gone up to Guillaumette.

"Good lady," they said to her, "here is your furniture and winter stores. Be quick and tell us where we are to unload our carts. One day is hardly enough to get all these things into the house."

The two old people, with gaping mouths, knew not what to answer. They looked timidly at these goods which they had never seen before, and thought of those horrid sous that had made such dreadful fun of them on the previous night. Sister-of-the-Poor, hidden in a corner, was laughing at their bewildered looks; she did not want to take any other revenge for the slight friendship they had shown her in days of misfortune. The poor little girl had never laughed so much in her life. I assure you, you would have been as merry as she was, to have seen Guillaume in petticoats and Guillaumette in breeches, undecided as to whether they ought to laugh or cry, and pulling the most amusing faces in the world.

At last, as she saw they were on the point of going in and closing the door and window, she showed herself.

"My friends," she said to the laborer and carters, "put all this into the cottage; don't be afraid of cramming the rooms up to the ceilings. I never thought of the smallness of the place, I have purchased so much that we shall now require a country-house. But there lies the money for the masons."

She spoke thus so as to be heard by her relatives, for she thought with reason, to set their minds at ease, by making them understand that she was the good fairy who brought them these presents. Now Guillaume and Guillaumette had resolved, since the previous night, to flog her, as a punishment for having left them a whole day; but, when they heard her speaking thus, when they saw the men putting down their furniture and stores at their door, they looked at her and burst out sobbing, without knowing why. It seemed to them that a hand was clutching them at their throats. They remained there, standing, ready to choke, not knowing what to do amidst this feeling of emotion which was so strange to them. And, all of a sudden, they discovered that they loved Sister-of-the-Poor. Then, laughing amidst their tears, they ran and kissed her, and that relieved their feelings.

A year afterwards, Guillaume and Guillaumette were the richest farmers in the district. They owned a large new farmhouse; their fields stretched so many leagues around, that they went beyond the horizon.

For a poor person to become rich, is not a rare occurrence; no one nowadays thinks of being surprised at it. But, when Guillaume and Guillaumette from unkind became good, there were people who refused to believe it. It was the truth notwithstanding. Sister-of-the-Poor's relations, having ceased to suffer from cold and hunger, recovered their former good nature. As they had shed many tears, they felt themselves akin to the unfortunate, and relieved them without egoism.

Tears, I know, are good advisers. However, if Guillaumette was not over fond of lace, if Guillaume gave up drinking and preferred work, it is my opinion that the big sous possessed some secret virtue which assisted the miracle; for they were not like ordinary sous which consent to be spent improperly; they would not allow evildoers to make use of them, but when in the possession of worthy souls, they caused them to be charitable by guiding their hands. Ah! The honest big sous, they had none of the gloomy stupidity of our ugly gold and silver coins!

Guillaume and Guillaumette kissed Sister-of-the-Poor from morning till night. At first they spared her all fatigue, and got angry when she spoke of working. It was easy to see they hoped to make a fine young lady of her, with delicate white hands, suitable for tying ribbons. "Carry your head high," they said to her every morning; "don't bother yourself about the rest." But the young girl was not of that mind; she would have died of sadness if she had remained all day long without any other occupation than that of watching the clouds sail by; her wealth gave her less distraction than polishing her oak furniture and carefully folding up her fine linen sheets. She therefore amused herself in her own way, saying to her relations: "Let me be, I am warmly clothed and have no use for lace; I prefer household cares to those of dress."

And she spoke so seriously, that Guillaume and Guillaumette understood that she possessed great intelligence, and ceased interfering with her inclinations. That gave her great pleasure. She rose, as formerly, at five o'clock, and went about her household duties; not that she swept or washed as in the days of misfortune, for she was not strong enough to keep such a large house clean; but she looked after the servants, and was not prevented by any feeling of false pride from assisting them in the dairy and poultry yard. She was assuredly the wealthiest and most active young girl in the neighborhood. Every one marveled that she did not alter on becoming the owner of a large farm, apart from having more rosy cheeks, and working more merrily. "Dear poverty," she often said, "you taught me how to behave when rich."

She was very thoughtful for her age, and that sometimes made her sad. I do not know how it was she perceived her big sous had become of little use to her. The fields gave her bread, wine, oil, vegetables, fruit; the flocks supplied her with wool for clothing and meat for meals; she had everything within arms' reach, and the produce of the farm was ample for her requirements, as well as for those of her people. The share of the poor was also large, for she no longer distributed alms in money, but in meat, flour, wood for firing, lengths of linen and cloth, and she showed her wisdom in doing so, giving away what she knew the indigent stood in need of, and thus sparing them the temptation of turning the sous of charity to bad account.

And so, amidst this abundance of riches, several large heaps of big sous remained in the loft, where Sister-of-the-Poor was grieved to see them occupying the place of twenty or thirty trusses of straw. She would have much preferred the straw, the reward of labor, to this money which she amassed without much merit. And so, little by little, she began to feel great disdain for this sort of wealth, which was good to remain idle in the chests of misers, or to be worn smooth in the hands of dealers in the towns.

She was so weary of this inconvenient fortune that one morning she determined to make it disappear. She had kept the little bag that devoured the big sous so easily; it did its duty in a conscientious way, and soon cleaned out the loft. Sister-of-the-Poor had had recourse to a cunning artifice, for she took care not to place the beggar-woman's sou at the bottom of the bag and the money went away for good, without having the temptation to return.

Thus, she was careful not to become too rich, feeling there would be danger for her heart if she were so. Little by little she gave away a part of her property, which was too extensive for the support of only one family. She arranged her revenue according to her requirements. Then, as there was no need of more hands on the farm, when, in spite of all she did, the sous accumulated in the loft, she went up there, on the sly, and took pleasure in diminishing her wealth. To assure contentment she all her life retained possession of the enchanted purse, which gave so generously in times of distress, and in the hour of fortune knew only how to receive.

Sister-of-the-Poor had another care. The poor woman's present embarrassed her. She was alarmed at the power it gave her; for, even when one has no mistrust of oneself, there is more pleasure in feeling one is humble than powerful. She would willingly have cast it in the river; but then some wicked person might find it in the sand and make use of it to the disadvantage of all; and, in truth, if that party expended half the money in doing harm that she had laid out in doing good, there could be no doubt that he would be the ruin of the neighborhood. And she then understood that the beggar-woman must have sought for a long time, before giving away her alms. It was a present that would cause people joy or despair, according to the hand that received it.

She kept the sou. As it had' a hole in it, she hung it on a ribbon round her neck, so she could not lose it. But it grieved her to feel it on her bosom. She would have done anything in the world to have found the poor woman again. She would have begged her to take back the deposit, which was too heavy to be retained for long, and to let her live the life of a good girl, performing no miracles but those of work and merry humor.

But having sought for her in vain, she despaired of ever meeting her.

One evening as she passed by the church, she entered to say a short prayer. She went right to the end of it, into a little chapel that she loved on account of its obscurity and silence. The colored-glass windows of a dull blue, lit up the flagstones on the ground like a reflection of the moon; the rather low vaulted roof was echoless. But, on that particular night, the little chapel was quite gay. A stray ray of light, after crossing the nave, fell in full on the humble altar, showing up the gilded frame of an old picture in the darkness.

Sister-of-the-Poor, who had knelt down on the bare stones, had a short fit of abstraction at the sight of this lovely farewell of the sun as it sank below the horizon on that frame which she was not aware was there. Then, bowing her head, she began her prayer. She beseeched the Almighty to send her an angel to take charge of the big sou.

In the middle of her supplication she raised her forehead. The sun's kiss was slowly ascending; it had left the frame for the painted canvas. One might have thought that a pale light was issuing from the sacred subject. It reflected on the black wall; and it was as if some cherub had put aside a corner of the veil of heaven, for one saw the Virgin Mary hushing Jesus to sleep on her knees.

Sister-of-the-Poor stared, searching in her mind. She had, perhaps, seen this beautiful saint and divine child in a dream. They also recognized her no doubt, for she saw them smile at her, and she even saw them leave the canvas, and descend towards her.

She heard a sweet voice that said:

"I am the saintly beggar of Heaven. The poor of the earth offer up to me their tears, and I extend my hand to all who are wretched in order to relieve them. I take these alms of suffering to heaven, and it is they that, collected one by one through centuries, form on the last day treasures of bliss for the elect.

"It is for that reason I wander through the world in poor attire, as becomes a daughter of the people. I console the indigent, my brethren; I save the wealthy by charity.

"I saw you one evening, and recognized in you the person I was in search of. My work is very hard. When I meet an angel upon earth, I entrust her with part of my mission. For that purpose I have heavenly sous which have power to do good and which render pure hands fairy-like.

"Look, my Jesus is smiling at you; He is satisfied with you. You have been the beggar of Heaven, for they have all given you their souls in alms, and you will lead your retinue of poor to paradise. Now, give me that sou which is a burden to you; cherubs only, have the strength to carry good eternally on their wings. Be humble, be happy."

Sister-of-the-Poor listened to the divine word. There she was, bending forward, mute, in ecstasy; and the blaze of the vision was reflected in her astonished eyes. She remained motionless for a long time. Then, as the ray of light continued to rise, it seemed to her that the gates of heaven were closed; the Virgin, having placed the ribbon round her neck, slowly disappeared. The child still looked, but she only saw the top of the gilded frame shining feebly in the last rays of light.

Then, no longer feeling the weight of her sou on her breast, she believed in what she had just seen and went away, thanking the Almighty.

It was thus that she had no more care, until the day when the angel she had been awaiting from infancy, bore her away to her mother and father, who, grieved at the separation, had been calling her to paradise for so long. She found, beside them, Guillaume and Guillaumette, who had also left her one day when they felt too weary.

And more than a century after her death, it was impossible to discover a single beggar in the district; not that our ugly gold and silver pieces were stored away in the family cupboards, but because there were always to be found, no one knew how, some of the produce of the Virgin's sou, of those big sous in yellow copper, which are the money of those who labor and of the simple-minded.

THE ADVENTURES OF BIG SIDOINE AND LITTLE MEDERIC

I. THE HEROES

At a distance of a hundred feet, Big Sidoine had somewhat the appearance of a poplar, except that he was perhaps taller in stature and of a thicker build. At fifty feet one could clearly distinguish his satisfied smile, his large blue eyes starting out of his head, and his enormous fists, which he swung about in a timid and embarrassed manner. At twenty-five feet one summed him up without hesitation to be a goodhearted fellow, as strong as an army, but a perfect simpleton. Little Mederic, on his side, bore, as regards stature, a strong resemblance to a lettuce, I mean a young lettuce; but on noticing his fine, restless lips, his clear, broad forehead, on seeing his graceful bow, the ease of his gait, one easily attributed to him more intellect than to the learned brains of forty tall men. His round eyes, similar to those of a tit-mouse, darted looks as penetrating as steel gimlets, which certainly would have caused him to be considered ill-natured, if long fair lashes had not veiled the malice and boldness of those orbs, with a soft shadow. He wore his hair in curly locks; he laughed so engagingly that one could not help loving him.

Although it was difficult for Big Sidoine and Little Mederic to converse freely, they were nevertheless the best friends in the world. Both were sixteen, were born the same day, at the same hour, and had known each other from that time; for their mothers, who happened to be neighbors, used to place them together in a wicker cradle at the time when Big

Sidoine was still satisfied with a bedstead three feet long, No doubt it is a strange thing that two children fed on the same pap should grow up so utterly unlike. This circumstance puzzled the learned folk of the neighborhood all the more, as Mederic, contrary to accepted custom, had certainly dwindled down some inches in height. The five or six learned pamphlets written on this phenomenon by specialists, y(proved that Providence alone could account for the secret of this strange growth, as it also knows that of the Seven League Boots, of the Sleeping Beauty, and a thousand other truths so beautiful and simple that one requires the innocence of childhood to understand them.

The same learned people, whose business it was to account for what cannot be, had set themselves another difficult problem. "How is it," they inquired of one another, without ever giving an answer, "that this great simpleton Sidoine loves that little scamp Mederic so tenderly? And how can this little scamp bestow so many caresses on that great simpleton?" It is a deep question, calculated to disturb inquiring minds, that of the brotherhood between the blade of grass and the oak.

I should not pay so much heed to these men of learning, if one of them, the one least considered in the parish, had not said one day, shaking his head, "Well, well! Good people, don't you see the meaning of it all? Nothing is simpler. The little fellows are changelings. When they were in the cradle, when their skin was tender and their skulls thin, Sidoine assumed Mederic's body, and Mederic Sidoine's mind; so that one grew in body and legs while the other grew in intelligence, hence their affection. They are one person in two beings; which is, unless I am mistaken, S, the definition of perfect friendship."

When the good man had thus spoken, his colleagues roared with laughter and treated him as a madman. A philosopher condescended to point out to him that souls do not transmigrate in this manner; a naturalist exclaimed simultaneously in his other ear, that there was no precedent in zoology, of a brother yielding his shoulders to his brother, as he would a piece of cake; the good man continued, tossing his head: "I have given my explanation, give yours; we shall then see which of the two is the most reasonable."

I have pondered for a long time on these words and found them full of wisdom. While awaiting a better explanation, if, indeed, I require one to continue this story, I will keep to that given by the old scholar. I know it will interfere with the clear and geometrical views of many; but, as I am determined to welcome with gratitude the fresh solutions of the mystery which my readers will no doubt find, I believe I am acting fairly, in so delicate a matter.

What, thank goodness, was not a subject for controversy— for all right-thinking minds agree often enough on some point—is that Sidoine and Mederic were all the better for their friendship. Each day they discovered such advantages in being what they were, that they would not have changed body or mind for anything in the world.

When Mederic attracted Sidoine's attention to a magpie's nest at the top of an oak tree, the latter declared himself to be the sharpest child in the neighborhood; and when Sidoine stooped to take possession of the nest,

Mederic honestly believed that he himself had a giant's stature. It would have been bad for you, if you had treated Sidoine as a simpleton believing he could not answer you back; Mederic would have convinced you in three sentences that you were on the verge of idiocy. And Mederic, too, if you had chaffed him on his tiny fists; only just equal to crushing a fly, it would have been quite another tune: I cannot tell how you would have escaped Sidoine's long arms. Mederic' and Sidoine were both strong and intelligent, as they were never apart, and it had never suggested itself to them that they lacked anything, except on those days when chance separated them.

To be frank, I must admit that they led somewhat the life y of vagrants, having lost their parents when they were quite young; moreover, they felt themselves capable of eating at all times and in all places. Apart from this, they were not boys to settle down quietly in a hut. I leave you to imagine what kind of a shed would have been required for Sidoine; while as for Mederic, he would have been content with a cupboard. So that, in order to suit the convenience of both, they lived in the fields, sleeping on the grass in summer, setting the cold at naught in winter beneath a blanket of leaves and dry moss.

They thus constituted a singular household. It was Mederic's part to think; he did that wonderfully, saw at the first glance the fields where the best and most savory potatoes were to be found, and knew, to within a minute, the time they must be in the cinders to be done to a turn. Sidoine worked; he dug up the potatoes, which was no small task I can tell you, for, though his companion only ate two or three, he required two or three cart-loads for his share; then he lit the fire, covered the potatoes with embers, and burnt his fingers in withdrawing them.

These petty domestic cares required neither great cunning nor strength of wrist. But it was good to see the two companions in the more serious circumstances of life, such as when they had to protect themselves from wolves during winter nights, or to clothe themselves decently without loosening their purse-strings, which offered considerable difficulty.

Sidoine was very busy keeping the wolves at a distance; right and left he distributed kicks which would have over thrown a mountain. On most of these occasions he overthrew nothing at all, for he was very clumsy. He generally emerged from the struggle with his garments in tatters. Then Mederic's part began. It was out of the question to repair the clothes. The sharp boy preferred providing new ones, as either way he had to draw on his imagination. Having a mind fertile in expedients, he provided a fresh texture for each torn smock. It was not so much quality as quantity that troubled him; imagine a tailor who would have to clothe the towers of

Notre Dame.

On one occasion, in pressing need, he petitioned the millers, asking for the old sails of all the windmills in the neighborhood. As he uttered his request with a charm without its equal, he soon obtained sufficient linen to make a magnificent bag, which did the greatest honor to Sidoine.

Another time, he had a still more ingenious idea. As a revolution had just broken out in the country, and the people, to convince themselves of their power, destroyed the armorial bearings and tore to shreds the standards used in the last reign, he obtained without difficulty all the old banners which had done duty at public festivals. You can imagine whether the smock made of these silken shreds was splendid to behold.

But these were court clothes, and Mederic sought for a material which would show greater resistance to the claws and fangs of wild animals. On the night of one of the battles, when the wolves had finally eaten up the standards, he was seized with a sudden idea while contemplating the dead left on the field. He told Sidoine to skin them nicely, and dried the skins in the sun. A week later his big brother walked about carrying his head high, gloriously clad in the spoils of their enemies. Sidoine, who like all big men was a little bit vain, was much impressed by these fine new clothes; so each week he made a frightful carnage among the wolves, clubbing them more cautiously, for fear of spoiling the fur.

From that moment Mederic had no further anxiety as regards the wardrobe. I have not told you how he clothed himself, but you have, no doubt, understood that he succeeded in doing so without so many contrivances. The tiniest scrap of ribbon was sufficient for him. He was very graceful, well proportioned, though small; the ladies quarreled over him in order to bedeck him with velvet and lace; and so, one always met him attired in the latest fashion.

I cannot say that the farmers were over delighted at having the two friends as neighbors; but they held Sidoine's fists in such regard, and had so much affection for Mederic's sweet smiles, that they allowed them to live in their fields as though they belonged to them. The lads, besides, did not encroach on the hospitality; they only appropriated a few vegetables when they were tired of game and fish. Had they been of a more desperate character, they would have ruined the country in three days; a walk through the cornfields would have sufficed. Therefore, the harm they did not do was borne in mind. Gratitude, even, was felt for the wolves they destroyed by hundreds, and for the number of inquisitive strangers they attracted from the neighboring towns.

I hesitate entering on the subject of my story without having given you full details concerning the affairs of my heroes. Can you picture them to yourself? Sidoine, as tall as a tower, clad in grey fur; Mederic, adorned with ribbons and spangles, sparkling in the grass at his feet like a golden bottle. Can you see them taking their walks abroad by the river-side, supping and sleeping in the glades, living in freedom beneath God's sky? Do you realize how simple Sidoine was, with his huge fists, and what ingenious expedients, what sharp repartee found their abode in Mederic's little head? Do you grasp the idea that their union was their strength, that, born far from one another, they would have been poor and very incomplete creatures, compelled to live in accordance with the habits and customs of all the world? Have you thoroughly understood that if I had bad intentions, I might hide some philosophical problem beneath all this? Are you, finally, prepared to thank me for my giant and dwarf whom I have brought up with special care, in order that they may constitute the most marvelous couple in the world? Yes? Well, without further delay I will commence the astounding account of their adventures?

II. THEY START ON THEIR TRAVELS

An April morning—the air was still keen, and slight mists were rising from the damp earth—Sidoine and Mederic were warming themselves at a large brushwood fire. They had just breakfasted, and were waiting till the embers had died out to take a short walk. Sidoine, seated on a large stone, watched the fire thoughtfully; but it was well to mistrust that look, for it was a recognized fact that the good fellow never thought of anything. He was smiling blissfully, his fists resting on his knees. Mederic, who was lying down opposite, affectionately contemplated his companion's fists; for although he had seen them grow, he experienced boundless joy and astonishment in gazing at them.

"Oh the fine pair of fists!" thought he; "what powerful fists they are! How massive and well set are the fingers! I should not care to receive the slightest fillip from them for all the wealth in the world: it would suffice to fell an ox. This dear Sidoine does not seem to have the least idea that he balances our fortune at his finger tips."

Sidoine, who enjoyed the fire, was stretching out his hands in an indolent manner. He wagged his head, and was absorbed in utter forgetfulness of the things of this earth. Mederic drew nearer to the fire, which was dying out.

"Is it not a pity," he resumed in an undertone, "to use such fine weapons against a few mangy wolves. They deserve to be turned to better account, such as crushing whole battalions and overthrowing the walls of citadels. We, who were surely intended for a high destiny, are now in our sixteenth year, and have achieved nothing. I am tired of the life we lead in the depths of this lonely valley. I think it high time we conquered the kingdom that God has in store for us somewhere; for the more I gaze on Sidoine's fists the more I am convinced they are the fists of a king."

Sidoine was far from suspecting the great destiny dreamed of by Mederic. He had just dozed off, having slept but little the previous night. One felt, on hearing his regular breathing, that he did not even trouble himself to dream.

"Hallo I my beauty," shouted Mederic to him.

He raised his head, cast an anxious look on his companion, opened his eyes wide, and pricked up his ears.

"Listen," resumed Mederic, "and try to understand, if possible. I am thinking of our future, I consider that we neglect it greatly. Life, my beauty, does not consist in eating fine golden potatoes and in clothing one's self in magnificent furs. It is necessary, also, to make a name in the world, to make a position for one's self. We do not belong to the common run of people, who can rest satisfied with the condition and name of vagrants. Certainly I don't despise the calling, which is that of lizards, animals that are certainly happier than many men; but we can resume it at any time. It is therefore a question of leaving this country, which is too small for us, at the earliest opportunity and of seeking a wider sphere where we can show ourselves off to advantage. Surely, we shall soon make our fortunes, if you render me the assistance in your power. I mean by distributing blows as I advise and counsel. Do you understand me?"

"I think so," answered Sidoine modestly. "We are going to travel and to fight throughout the journey. It will be delightful."

"Only," resumed Mederic "we shall require an object in view to prevent our indulging dilly-dallying on the way. You see, my beauty, we are too fond of sunshine. We should be capable of spending our youth in warming ourselves beneath the hedgerows, if we did not know, from hearsay at all events, of the country we wish to reach. I have therefore sought for a country worthy of possessing us. I admit, that, at first, I found none. Fortunately, I recalled a conversation I had, some days ago, with a bullfinch of my acquaintance. He told me he had come in- a direct line from an extensive kingdom, called the Kingdom of the Happy, celebrated by the fertility of its soil and the good character of its inhabitants; it is governed at present by a young queen, the charming Primrose, who, in her kindness of heart, is not satisfied with allowing her subjects to live in peace but is also anxious that the animals of her realm should share the blessedness of her reign. One of these nights, I will tell you the strange stories that my friend the bullfinch has related to me on this subject. Perhaps—for you seem to be uncommonly inquisitive today—you wish to know how I propose behaving in the Kingdom of the Happy. To begin with, judging things from a distance, it seems to me advisable to cause the charming Primrose to fall in love with me, and to marry her, in order that we may live in clover ever after, regardless of the other kingdoms of the world. We will create a position for you in accordance with your tastes, allowing you to keep in training. My beauty, I vow that sooner or later I will plan out such a noble task for you, that in a thousand years, he would talk of your fists."

Sidoine, who had understood, would have hugged his brother had it been possible. He whose imagination was usually very dilatory, saw in his mind's eye, battle-fields as extensive as oceans, a charming outlook which caused his arms to quiver with joy. He rose, buckled the belt of his smock frock, and struck an attitude before Mederic.

The latter was lost in thought, casting sad looks around.

"The inhabitants of this country have always been good to us," he said at last. "They have tolerated us in their fields. But for them we should not make such a good appearance. We are bound to give a proof of our gratitude, before leaving. What can we do to afford them pleasure?"

Sidoine ingenuously thought this question was addressed to him. He had an idea.

"Brother," answered he, "what do you think of a huge bonfire? We might burn the next town to the great delight of the inhabitants; for, if their tastes are a bit like mine, nothing would entertain them so much as beautiful crimson flames on a very dark night." Mederic shrugged his shoulders.

"My beauty," said he, "I advise you never to meddle in what concerns me. Let me think for a moment. If I stand in need of your arms then you shall work in your turn."

"I have it," he resumed, after a pause. "There is a mountain in the south which, I am told, inconveniences our benefactors. The valley lacks water, their land is so dry that it produces the worst grapes in the world, which is a constant source of grief to the tipplers of the district. Tired of sour wine, they recently assembled all their learned societies. Such an erudite gathering would certainly invent rain without more trouble than if God had interfered. The scientists therefore set to work; they made remarkable studies on the nature and incline of the lands, deciding that nothing would be easier than to turn the course of the neighboring stream and bring it into the plain, if that nuisance of a mountain were not exactly in the way. What short-sighted creatures men, our brethren, are. A hundred were there measuring, leveling, making magnificent plans. They stated, without being in error, what the mountain consisted of, marble, chalk, or limestone; if they had wished, they could have weighed it to within a few kilograms, yet not one, not even the biggest, thought of removing it somewhere else, where it would no longer be in the way. Take that mountain, Sidoine, my beauty. I am going to see where we can place it without doing damage."

Sidoine opened his arms and delicately encircled the rocks with them. Then, he made a slight effort, throwing himself back, and rose up again, pressing the burden to his chest. He supported it on his knee, waiting until Mederic had made up his mind. The latter hesitated.

"I would have it cast into the sea," he muttered, "but such a stone would surely cause a fresh flood. Neither can I have it put down brutally on the earth at the risk of damaging a town or two. The farmers would make a fine ado if I were to thus encumber a field of turnips or carrots. Sidoine, my beauty, observe the dilemma I am in. Mankind has portioned out the earth in an absurd manner. One cannot shift a miserable mountain without crushing a neighbor's cabbage patch."

"You speak truly, brother," answered Sidoine; "only please come to a decision as rapidly as possible. It is not that this stone is heavy, but it is so large that it slightly inconveniences me."

"Come along, then," resumed Mederic. "We will place it between those two hillsides you see on the north of the plain; there is a gorge there through which a bitter wind blows over the country. Our stone will completely block it, and shelter the valley from the March and September gales."

When they had reached the spot, Sidoine was preparing to cast the mountain down from his arms, like the woodcutter throws his faggot from him on returning from the forest .

"Good heavens! My beauty," exclaimed Mederic, "let it slide softly if you don't wish to shake the earth for fifty leagues round. Good: do not be in a hurry, and never mind about the scratches. I think it wobbles about; it would be advisable to steady it with some rock, so that it may not take into its head to slip when we are no longer here. That is done. Now the worthy people will drink good wine. They will have water for their vines, and sun to ripen the grapes. Listen, Sidoine, I am glad to call your attention & the fact that we are cleverer than a dozen learned societies. In our travels we can alter at our pleasure the temperature and fertility of the countries we traverse. It is only a question of re-arranging the land a little, of establishing a screen of mountains in the North, after having seen that there is a slope for the waters. I have often noticed that the earth is badly disposed; and am doubtful whether mankind will ever have sufficient brains to make it an abode worthy of civilized nations. We will work a bit in that direction in our spare time. To-day, we have paid our debt of gratitude. Shake your smock, my beauty! Which is white with dust, and let us start."

It must be admitted that Sidoine only heard the last word of this speech. He was not a philanthropist; his mind was too simple for that. He troubled little about a wine he was never to drink. The idea of traveling delighted him. Scarcely had his brother mentioned starting, when joy made him take two or three strides, which outdistanced Mgdenc by several dozen kilometers. Fortunately, Mederic had seized hold of the tail of his smock.

"Hallo! My beauty," he shouted, "could not you make your movements less rough? Stop for goodness' sake. Do you think that my small legs are equal to such jumps? If you contemplate making strides like that I shall let you go ahead and may perhaps overtake you in a few centuries. Stop, sit down."

Sidoine sat down; Mederic caught hold of the edge of his fur trousers with both hands. As he was marvelously active, he climbed lightly on to his companion's knee with the assistance of the tufts of fur and rents he met with. Then he advanced along the thigh which seemed to him a fine spacious highway, straight, broad, and without a rise. Arrived at the end, he placed his foot in the lowest buttonhole of the smock, caught higher up into the second, and thus climbed on to the shoulder. There, he went through his preparations for the journey, and settling in Sidoine's left ear, made himself comfortable. He had selected this lodging for two reasons: first of all he found himself sheltered from rain and wind, the ear in question being an exceptionally large ear; besides, he could communicate numberless interesting remarks to his companion, and be sure of being heard.

He bent over the side of a black hole he discovered in the depths of his new abode, and, in a piercing voice, shouted into that abyss:

"Now, my beauty, you can run if you think fit . Don't loiter in the lanes, and see that we travel quickly. Do you hear me?"

"Yes, brother," replied Sidoine. "I would even ask you not to talk so loud, for your breath tickles me unpleasantly." And they started off.

III. A SHORT DISCOURSE ON MUMMIES

Sidoine would never have petitioned the Board of Works for the erection of bridges and roads. He usually walked across country, paying little heed to ditches and still less to hillocks; he expressed disdain for the angles of trodden paths. The good fellow practiced geometry unawares, as he had found out, without assistance, that the straight line is the shortest road from one point to another.

He thus went through a dozen kingdoms, taking heed not to place his foot in the center of a town, for he felt this would have displeased the inhabitants. He strode over two or three seas without wetting himself overmuch. He did not deign to bother about the streams, taking them for those narrow streaks of water with which the earth is furrowed after heavy rain. The travelers he met amused him greatly; he saw them perspire as they went up the inclines, go to the north in order to reach the south, read the fingerposts by the roadside, anxious about wind, rain, ruts, floods and the pace of their horses. He was indirectly aware of the absurdity of these poor people, who light-heartedly risk being thrown over a precipice when they might remain so comfortably by their fireside.

"Devil take it I" Mederic would have said, "When you are so constituted you should stay at home." But for the time being Mederic was not watching the earth. At the end of a quarter of an hour's walk, however, he wanted to take his bearings. He thrust out his nose, bent over the plain, turned to the four points of the compass, and saw nothing but sand, nothing but an extensive desert filling up the horizon. The site displeased him.

"Good heavens!" thought he, "how thirsty the people here must be. I notice the ruins of many towns, and I could swear the inhabitants have died for want of a glass of wine. Surely this is not the Kingdom of the Happy. My friend the bullfinch described it as prolific in vineyards and fruits of all kinds; 'you even find there,' he added, 'springs of clear water,' which is excellent for rinsing bottles. That madcap of a Sidoine has certainly lost his way." And turning towards the depths of the ear he exclaimed: "Hallo! My beauty! Where are you going to?" "Straight ahead of course," replied Sidoine without stopping "You are a fool, my beauty," resumed Mederic. "You do not seem to understand that the earth is round, and that by always going straight ahead you will get nowhere. We have clearly lost our way."

"Well!" said Sidoine, running all the faster, "it does not matter to me; I am at home everywhere."

"Pray stop, simpleton!" again exclaimed Mederic. "It makes me perspire to see you walk thus. I ought to have kept a look-out on the road. No doubt you stepped across the residence of the charming Primrose, without paying any more attention to it than to the hut of a charcoal-burner; palace and cottage are the same to your long legs. Now, we must scurry through the world haphazard. I will watch empires pass, from the height of your shoulder, until the day when we shall discover the Kingdom of the Happy. Meanwhile there is no hurry; we are not expected. I think it advisable to sit down a moment, in order to consider the peculiar country we are crossing at present, in greater comfort. Sit down, my beauty, on that mountain at your feet."

"That's a mountain!" answered Sidoine, sitting down; "It is a paving-stone, or may the devil take me!"

To tell the truth this paving-stone was one of the great pyramids. Our comrades, who had just crossed the African desert, found themselves at that time in Egypt. Sidoine, possessing no exact historical knowledge, looked upon the Nile as a muddy brook; as for the Sphinx and obelisks, they seemed to him heaps of gravel of a peculiar and extremely ugly shape. Mederic, who knew everything, without having learnt anything, was vexed at the little attention his brother gave to this mud and stones, which had been visited and admired for over five hundred leagues around.

"Hallo! Sidoine," he said, "Endeavour to assume, if possible, a look of respectful astonishment and admiration. It is the worst possible taste to keep calm in view of such a scene. I dread lest any one should notice you wagging your head thus, before the ruins of ancient Egypt. We should sink in the estimation of cultured people. Bear in mind it is not a question of understanding, no one cares to do that, but to appear deeply impressed at the great interest felt in these stones. You have just sufficient sense to extricate yourself with honor. There, you see the Nile, that yellowish water which stagnates in the mud. I am told it is a very ancient stream; however, I presume it is no older than the Seine or the Loire. The people of antiquity were satisfied in knowing its mouths: we inquisitive persons, taking pleasure in interfering with what does not concern us, have sought to find its sources for some centuries, without succeeding in discovering the smallest reservoir. Men of learning are divided; according to some, a spring exists somewhere, which it is only a question of thoroughly searching for; others, who seem to be in the right, maintain that they have explored everywhere, and that the stream has certainly no source. I have no decided opinion on the subject, as I seldom think of it; besides which, no solution would benefit me in any way. Now look at those hideous animals which surround us, scorched by millions of suns; it is affirmed that it is out of sheer spite that they do not speak; they know the secret of creation, and the everlasting smile they assume, is simply to scoff at our ignorance. For my part I do not consider them so vindictive; they are good blocks of stone, very simple-minded, and know less than people believe. Continue listening, my beauty; never fear learning too much. I will tell you nothing about Memphis, the ruins of which we can see on the horizon, I will tell you nothing about it for the best of reasons, that I did not live in the time of its greatness. I mistrust the historians who have mentioned it. Like others, I might read the hieroglyphics on the obelisks and ruined walls; but as I am scrupulous on all historical points, apart from the fact that it would not entertain me, I should be in constant dread of mistaking an A for a B, and of inculcating errors into you which would have disastrous consequences for you. I prefer adding to these general remarks a slight disquisition on mummies. There is nothing pleasanter to see than a well-preserved mummy. The Egyptians, no doubt, buried each other with all this coquetry, in view of the great y pleasure we should experience, some day, in digging them up again. As to the pyramids, according to general opinion, they served as tombs, unless they were intended for another use which has escaped us. For example, judging from that on which we are sitting—for I wish you to notice that our seat is one of the finest pyramids—I should think, but for the slight comfort they afford when put to such use, that they had been erected by a hospitable people to serve as resting-places for weary travelers. I will conclude with a moral. Know, my beauty, that thirty dynasties sleep at our feet; kings repose in thousands in the sand, swathed in bandages, their cheeks are fresh, and they have still their teeth and hair. One could, by careful search, make a charming collection of them, which would be of great interest to courtiers. The misfortune is that their names are forgotten, and they could not be properly labeled. They are more dead than their corpses. If ever you become a king, remember these poor royal mummies sleeping in the desert; they have conquered the worms for five thousand years, and could not live ten centuries in the memory of mankind. I have finished. Nothing develops the mind like travel. I intend perfecting your education, in this manner, by giving you a practical course of lectures on the various objects we shall meet with on the road."

During this long discourse, Sidoine, in order to gratify his companion, had assumed the silliest expression imaginable. Bear in mind that this was precisely the expression required. But, in truth, he was gaping with weariness, gazing in despair on the Nile, the Sphinx, Memphis, the pyramids, and even doing his utmost to think of the mummies, although without any satisfactory result . He sought surreptitiously to see if he could not discover some object on the horizon which would allow him to interrupt the lecturer politely. As the latter ceased speaking, he perceived somewhat tardily, two bands of men appear on the two opposite sides of the plain.

"Brother," he said, "I am weary of the dead. Tell me who are these people advancing towards us."

IV. SIDOINE'S FISTS

I omitted to tell you that it was about noon when our travelers, seated on one of the great pyramids, discoursed in this manner. In the plain the waters of the Nile rolled heavily on their way, like the flow of molten metal. The sky was as white as the roof of some enormous oven heated for a gigantic baking; there was not a shadow on the land, which slumbered breathless, overcome by a leaden sleep. In the intense immobility of the desert, the two armies formed in columns, advanced like serpents gliding slowly over the sand.

They grew longer and longer. Soon they ceased to be mere caravans and became two large armies, two nations in countless file spreading from one horizon to the other, casting dark shadows upon the dazzling whiteness of the earth. Those coming from the north wore blue coats, the others approaching from the south were clad in green smocks. All carried long spears with steel points on their shoulders, so that, at each step, a flash of lightning silently enveloped them. They were marching against one another.

"My beauty," exclaimed Mederic, "let us take up a good position, for, unless I am mistaken, we shall witness a fine sight. These good people are not deficient in intellect . The spot is well chosen to afford an opportunity of effectually cutting the throats of a few hundreds of thousands of men. They will massacre each other at ease, and the vanquished will have a fine race-course when it is a question of decamping with the utmost speed. Tell me of such another plain for fighting to the great enjoyment of onlookers."

However, the two armies had halted facing one another, and divided by a broad strip of land. They uttered terrible yells, brandished their weapons, shook their fists at each other, but did not advance a step. Each appeared to hold the enemy's lances in great respect.

"Oh, the cowardly rascals!" repeated Mederic, who grew impatient; "do they intend sleeping here? I could vow they have come over a hundred leagues for the mere pleasure of cuffing each other. And, now, they hesitate to exchange a single blow. I ask you, my beauty, is it right for two or three million men to assign a meeting in Egypt, on the stroke of noon, merely to stand face to face and vilify one another. Will you fight, knaves? But just look at them; they are yawning in the sunshine like lizards; they don't appear to consider that we are waiting. Hallo, arch cowards! Will you fight or not?"

The Blues took two steps forward as if they had heard Mederic's exhortations. The Greens, perceiving this maneuver, prudently took two steps back. Sidoine felt scandalized.

"Brother," said he, "I feel a strong inclination to take part in the fray. The dance will never begin unless I set it going. Don't you think this a good opportunity to try my fists?"

"Of course," answered Mederic; "you have had a brilliant idea for once in your life. Turn up your sleeves and do some good work."

Sidoine turned up his sleeves and rose.

"Which shall I begin with?" asked he, "the Blues or the Greens?"

Mederic considered a moment.

"My beauty," he answered, "the Greens are certainly the most cowardly. Cuff them well, so as to teach them that fear is no protection against blows. Wait a minute. I do not wish to miss any part of the show; first of all I will settle myself comfortably."

Saying this, he climbed on to his brother's ear, lay there flat on his face, careful to show only his head; then he seized a lock of hair which he found at hand, so as not to be thrown during the medley. Having thus made his arrangements he announced himself ready for the fight.

Sidoine without a word of warning, immediately fell on the Greens. He beat time with his fists, using them as flails, and administering blows to the army in rapid succession, just as if it were corn on the threshing-floor. At the same time, when some closer ranks stopped his way, he sent his feet right and left into the very midst of the battalions. It was a fine fight I assure you, and deserved to be celebrated in an epic poem of twenty-four cantos. Our hero trod on the spears without paying any more heed to them than if they had been blades of grass. He went hither and thither making large gaps on every side, crushing some against the earth, throwing others twenty or thirty yards high. The poor creatures died without even having the consolation of knowing what rough hand had fallen upon them. For at first, when Sidoine was quietly resting on the pyramid, he could not be clearly distinguished from the blocks of granite. Then, when he rose, he had not given the enemy time to look at him. Observe that it required two full minutes to follow the outline of that huge body before reaching the face.

The Greens had therefore no definite idea as to the cause of the vigorous cuffs which overthrew them by hundreds. The greater number no doubt thought when dying, that the pyramid was falling down upon them, for they could not conceive that a man's fists could bear such a striking resemblance to hewn stones.

Mederic, amazed at this exploit, quivered with delight; he clapped his hands, bent over at the risk of falling, lost his balance, and quickly clung again to the lock of hair. At last, unable to remain silent under such circumstances, he leapt on to the hero's shoulder, where he kept his footing by holding to the lobe of the ear. From there he at times gazed across the plain, and at others turned to shout out a few words of encouragement.

"Oh! Dear, dear I" he cried; "what blows, by Jove I What a -fine sound of hammers on the anvil. Hey, my beauty, strike to your left; polish off that cavalry man who is preparing to escape, for me. Now hurry up; strike to your right, yonder, on that knot of warriors bedecked with gold and embroidery; strike with feet and fists together, for I think we have to do with princes, dukes, and other swaggerers. Well I those are good thumps. The ground is as clear as if the scythe had been over it. Evenly, my beauty, evenly! Work methodically and the task will be more rapidly accomplished. That's good! They fall by hundreds in perfect order. I like regularity in everything. What a marvelous sight; one might compare it to a cornfield on harvest-day when the sheaves are stacked in long symmetrical rows alongside the furrows. Strike, strike, my beauty! Don't trouble to crush the fugitives one by one; bring them back speedily by the seats of their trousers, and catch at least two or three dozen at a time. Oh, dear me, what clouts, what shoves, what triumphant kicks!"

Mederic burst into raptures, turning on all sides, unable to find sufficiently choice expressions to express his delight. Of a truth Sidoine did not strike any harder or quicker. At the beginning he had assumed an easy gait, continuing his task phlegmatically without increasing his pace. He was only surveying the edge of the army. When he noticed a fugitive, he was satisfied with bringing him back to his post with a fillip, in order that he might take part in the feast when his turn should come. After a quarter of an hour of these tactics, all the Greens found themselves lying nicely on the plain without a survivor to carry the news of the defeat to the remainder of the nation—a rare and distressing incident which has not since been repeated in the annals of the world.

Mederic rose to see the blood flow. When all was over he said to Sidoine, "As you have annihilated this army, my beauty, it seems to me fair that you should bury it."

Sidoine having looked around, noticed five or six sand heaps at hand; he sent them on to the battle-field with vigorous kicks, and smoothed them out with his hand so as to make a single hillock of them, which served as a grave for about eleven hundred thousand men. In similar cases a conqueror rarely bestows such care on the vanquished. This showed how good-natured my hero could be, hero though he was, when occasion offered.

During the affray, the Blues, amazed at this reinforcement which came to them from the top of one of the great pyramids, had had time to realize that this was not an avalanche of paving-stones, but a man in flesh and bone. First of all they thought of rendering him some assistance; then, seeing the easy way in which he worked, realizing that they would rather be in the way, they discreetly retired to a distance in fear of the splinters. They stood on tip-toe, hustled one another to see better, and welcomed each blow with a round of applause. When the Greens were annihilated and buried, they uttered loud shrieks, congratulated themselves on the victory, moving about in tumultuous confusion, and all speaking at once.

Sidoine, however, being thirsty, went down to the edge of the Nile to drink a draught of fresh water; he dried it up at a mouthful. Fortunately for Egypt he found the beverage so hot and tasteless that he hastened to eject the stream back to its bed without swallowing a drop. See on what a country's fertility rests.

In a very bad temper he returned to the plain, and, rubbing his hands, looked at the Blues.

"Brother," he said, in an insinuating tone, "what if I were now to knock these about a little. They make a great noise. What do you think of a few fisticuffs to reduce them to respectful silence?"

"Mind you don't," replied Mederic. "I have been watching them for a moment, and I believe they have the best intentions in the world. They are certainly talking of you. Endeavour, my beauty, to assume a majestic attitude; for, unless I am mistaken, your great destiny is about to be accomplished. See, here comes a deputation."

A solemn silence had succeeded the tumult of a million of men, each giving vent to his individual opinion without hearkening to his neighbor's. The Blues had no doubt come to an understanding; which is surprising, for in the assemblies of our country, where the members do not exceed a few hundred, they have hitherto been unable to agree over the slightest trifle.

The army filed off in two columns. Soon it formed an immense circle. In the midst of this circle was Sidoine, embarrassed to know what to do with himself; he cast down his eyes, ashamed to see so many people looking at him. As for Mederic, he realized that at this decisive moment, his presence would give rise to needless and even dangerous surprise. He prudently retired into the ear that had served as his abode since morning.

The deputation stopped within twenty steps of Sidoine. It did not consist of warriors, but of old men, bald-headed, with magisterial beards flowing in silvery waves on their blue coats. The hands of these old men had assumed the dry wrinkles of the parchments they constantly fingered; their eyes, accustomed solely to the light of smoky lamps, only bore the splendor of the sun's rays by blinking the lids, as would an owl astray in broad daylight; their spines were curved, as though they were constantly at a desk; while spots of oil and streaks of ink—mysterious signs which were of no small account in their high renown for science and wisdom—formed the strangest patterns on their gowns.

The oldest, driest, blindest, most age-spotted of the learned company advanced three steps, bowing low; after which, having drawn himself up, he spread out his arms, in order to accompany his words with suitable gestures.

"My lord giant," said he in a solemn tone, "I, prince of orators, senior member and dean of all academies, grand officer of all the orders, address you in the name of the nation. Our king, a wretched creature, died a couple of hours ago from a stomach complaint, with which he was seized at the sight of the Greens on the opposite side of the plain. We are therefore without a master to load us with H?" taxes, and to have us slaughtered for the public weal. This is, as you know, a state of freedom which is generally displeasing to a people. We need a king immediately; and, in our haste to prostrate ourselves at royal feet, we have thought of you, who fight so bravely. We hope, in offering you the crown, to express our gratitude for your devotedness to our cause. I feel that such a circumstance requires a speech in a learned language—Sanskrit, Hebrew, Greek, or, at all events, Latin—but may the necessity I am under to improvise, the certainty that later on I can make amends for this lack of propriety, be my excuse." The old man paused.

"I was sure," thought Mederic, "that my beauty's fists were those of a king."

V. MEDERIC'S SPEECH

"My lord giant," continued the prince of orators, "it remains for me to tell you what the nation has resolved, and what proof of your fitness for regal power it requires at your hands before placing you on the throne. It is weary of having as masters, men who resemble their subjects in all points, who are unable to strike the slightest blow without injuring themselves, and who cannot make a long-winded speech every third day without dying of consumption at the end of four or five years. In a word, it requires a king who will entertain it, and it is persuaded that, amongst pleasures in good taste, there are two, especially, of which it could never tire—thrashings sharply administered, and the empty and resonant phrases of a royal proclamation. I admit I am proud to belong to a nation that appreciates the transitory pleasures of this life so thoroughly. Its desire to have an entertaining king on the throne appears to me even more praiseworthy. What we require amounts to this. Princes are gilt toys which nations bestow on themselves, in order to procure entertainment and diversion by watching them glitter in the sun; but these playthings almost always cut and bite, just like steel knives— bright blades with which mothers frighten their children to no purpose. Now we wish our plaything to be harmless, to entertain, to divert us in accordance with our tastes, without our running the risk of wounding ourselves in turning it over and over between our fingers. We require heavy blows, for that game makes our warriors laugh and amuses them thoroughly, while giving them courage; we need long-winded speeches to provide occupation for the good folk of the kingdom in applauding and criticizing them, smartly rounded sentences which will keep the orators of the day in good temper. You have already, my lord giant, supplied part of the programme to the perfect satisfaction of the most unaccommodating. I speak truthfully; never have fists made us laugh more heartily. Now, to crown our desires, you must go through the second ordeal. Choose your own subject, tell us of the love you bear us, of your duty towards us, of the great events which will mark your reign. Instruct us, entertain us; we will listen to you."

The prince of orators, having thus spoken, bowed again. Sidoine, who had listened with uneasiness to the exordium, and had followed the various issues with anxiety, was very much alarmed at the peroration. To make a long speech in public seemed to him an absurd idea, out of keeping with his usual habits. He looked cunningly at the learned grey beard, fearing some cutting jest; wondering to himself if a good blow well aimed at that yellow brow would not solve the difficulty. But the worthy fellow was not spiteful. This old man had spoken to him with so much courtesy, that it seemed hard to answer him so roughly. Having sworn not to open his lips, appreciating, besides, the awkwardness of his position, he shifted from one foot to the other, twirled his thumbs, and laughed his simplest laugh. As he became more and more idiotic, he thought he had come across an ingenious idea. He bowed lowly to the old gentleman.

But at the end of five minutes the army became impatient. I think I told you these incidents were taking place in Egypt on the stroke of noon. As you know, nothing tries one's temper so much as waiting in the midday sun. Increasing murmurs from the Blues bore witness to the fact that the lord giant must be quick, or they would throw him over and seek a more talkative king elsewhere.

Sidoine, surprised that these good people were not satisfied with a bow, immediately made three or four more, one upon the other, turning from side to side, so that each might have his share.

Then arose a storm of oaths and laughter, one of those popular tempests in which every one makes fun of some sort —some whistling like blackbirds, others clapping their hands in mockery. It became a surging tumult decreasing to swell again, resembling the noise of the ocean's waves. It was a capital apprenticeship for royalty as regards a nation's spirit.

Suddenly, during a few moments' silence, a sweet, melodious voice was heard issuing from the heights of Sidoine—a sweet soft child's voice like a silver bell, with delightful modulations.

"My well-beloved subjects," it said. Deafening cheers interrupted it at these first words. What a delightful sovereign! With fists that could crush mountains, and a voice which would make the May breeze envious!

The prince of orators, amazed at this phenomenon, turned to his learned colleagues.

"Gentlemen," he said to them, "here is a giant who possesses a peculiar voice for his species. I would not have credited it had I not heard it, that a throat capable of swallowing an ox and its horns, could utter such marvelously delicate sounds. There is some anatomical curiosity here which we must study and explain at all costs. We will discuss this important subject at our next meeting; we will make a fine scientific fact of it, which shall be expounded at our universities."

"Come, my beauty," Mederic whispered softly in Sidoine's ear, "open your jaws wide; keep them going in time, as though you were cracking nuts. It is well that you should move them vigorously, as those who do not hear you will at least see you are speaking. Do not omit the gestures either: curve your arms gracefully during well-toned periods; wrinkle your brows and throw out your hands when there are bursts of eloquence, endeavor even to cry at pathetic parts. Above all, no blunders. Follow the lead. Do not stop suddenly in the midst of a sentence, nor continue when I am silent. Insert full stops and commas, my beauty. It is not difficult; the greater number of our statesmen do nothing more. Attention I am about to begin."

Sidoine opened his mouth frightfully wide and began to gesticulate, with the look of one of the damned. Mederic expressed himself in these terms, "My beloved subjects, allow me, in accordance with custom, to express my surprise and declare myself unworthy of the honor you are bestowing upon me. I do not believe a single word I have just uttered; I believe I deserve, as every one does, to be a bit of a king in turn; and I do not know why I was not born a prince's son, which would have saved me the trouble of founding a dynasty.

"In the first instance, in order to secure my future freedom, I must call your attention to present circumstances. You look on me as a good engine of war; it is indeed on that account alone that you offer me the crown. I comply. Unless I am mistaken, this is what is called Universal Suffrage. The invention seems excellent; nations will be all the better for it when it is perfected. Therefore be so good as to blame yourselves when occasion offers, if I fail to keep all the fine promises I am making, for I might unintentionally forget some of them, and it would not be fair to punish me for a slip of memory, when you, yourselves, may have been lacking in judgment.

"I am anxious to deal with the programme I long since sketched out in view of the day when I should have leisure to be king. It is charming in simplicity, and I commend it to my brethren—those sovereigns who may find themselves encumbered with their people. This is it in its innocence and simplicity; as is abroad, peace at home.

"War abroad is like an enema: It rids the nation of quarrelsome people, allowing them to go and be maimed out of the country. I allude to those who are born with clenched fists, who, owing to their temperament, would from time to time feel the need of a slight revolution, if they had not to thrash some neighboring state. In each nation a certain number of blows have to be distributed; prudence demands that these blows should be given some five or six hundred leagues from the capital. Let me express myself clearly. The organization of an army is simply a prudent measure, taken to separate riotous from reasonable men; the aim in making war is to cause as many of these rioters as possible to disappear, and so allow the sovereign to live in peace, having only reasonable men as subjects. I know one hears of glory, conquest and other stuff and nonsense. Those are idle words which gratify fools. If kings launch their armies against each other at the least provocation, it is because they understand one another, and enjoy bloodshed. I intend following their example with a view to impoverish the blood of my subjects. Otherwise they might develop high fever. But one thing perplexes me. The further one goes the more difficult it is to find cause for war; we shall soon be compelled to live at peace for want of a pretext to fight one another. I have had to draw on my imagination. Fighting to avenge an injury is not to be thought of: we have nothing to avenge, for no one provokes us, our neighbors are courteous and have good manners.

"The seizure of border lands, under the pretence of enlarging our dominions, is an old idea which has never succeeded when put into practice, and which conquerors have always regretted. To fall out over a few bales of cotton, or some hundredweight of sugar, would cause us to be looked upon as vulgar merchants, as thieves who object to be robbed; while our great aim is to be a charming people, dreading the cares of business, and devoted to the ideal and witty sayings. No acknowledged system in the matter of warfare would satisfy us. But, after deep thought, a brilliant idea has occurred to me. .We will always fight for others and never for ourselves, which will always be aware that we must account for the blows we strike. Just imagine how convenient this method will be, and the honor we shall derive from such enterprises. We will assume the title of benefactors of nations, we will publish abroad our disinterestedness, we will assume the part of upholders of good causes, of faithful followers of great ideas. This is not all. As those we do not assist might express their surprise at this strange policy, we will answer boldly that our passion for lending our armies to those who ask for the loan of them, is due to a generous wish to pacify the world, to pacify it thoroughly by means of pike-thrusts. We will say that our soldiers go forth as civilizers, cutting the throats of those who do not promptly become civilized, sowing the most fruitful ideas in pits dug on battle-fields. They will baptize the earth with a baptism of blood, to hasten the birth of liberty. But we will not add that they will have an endless task, waiting in vain for a harvest which cannot rise on graves.

"That, my dear subjects, is what I have planned. The idea has all the magnitude and absurdity requisite for success. Therefore, those among you who feel a desire to proclaim one or two republics are requested not to do so in my dominions. I charitably grant them access to the kingdoms of other monarchs. Let them liberally distribute provinces, change the order of governments, consult the will of the peoples; let them go and get killed in neighboring countries, in the name of freedom, and leave me to govern my own dominions as arbitrarily as I please.

"My reign will be a martial reign."

"To ensure peace at home is a harder problem to solve. In spite of ridding one's self of evildoers a spirit of rebellion always exists in the multitude against their chosen master. I have often thought of that latent hatred that nations have for all time experienced towards their sovereigns; but I admit that I could never find a sensible or logical reason for it. We will give this subject for competition at our universities, so that our men of learning may hasten to tell us whence the evil comes and what the remedy is. But, while awaiting the aid of science, we will employ the simple means bequeathed to us by our predecessors to allay the unhealthy anxiety of our subjects. They are certainly not infallible. If we employ them, it is because no ropes have yet been invented, which are sufficiently long and strong to bind down a nation. Progress advances so slowly. We will therefore select our ministers with care. We do not require excessive intellectual and moral qualities; it will suffice if they are second-rate in everything. But what we shall exact is that they have powerful lungs, and have been well exercised in shouting 'Long live the King!' in the loudest and most exalted manner possible. To utter a fine - Long live the King' according to rule, raising it artistically, making it die away in a whisper of love and admiration, is a rare merit which cannot be too handsomely rewarded. However, to be candid, we depend but little on our ministers; they hinder rather than assist. If our opinion had sway, we would dispense with these gentlemen and combine the duties of king and ministers in our own person. We set great hopes on certain laws we propose enforcing. They will permit of a man being seized by the collar and cast into the river without further explanation, after the excellent method of the mutes of the seraglio. You can easily foresee how convenient such an expeditious law will be; it is so troublesome to have to abide by form, to have to believe candidly that a crime has been committed, to find a person guilty. We shall, moreover, enlist the services of well subsidized newspapers which will sound our praises, conceal our faults, conferring more virtues upon us than on all the saints in Paradise. We shall have others paid more handsomely, which will attack our policy, discuss our politics, but in such a dull, clumsy manner, that they will bring all sensible and intelligent people over to our side. As to the newspapers we shall not subsidize, they will not be allowed either to blame or praise us; in any case we shall suppress them at the earliest opportunity.

"We must also protect art, for there is no great reign without great artists. In order to create as many as possible, we shall abolish liberty of thought. It would perhaps be as well to bestow a small pension on retired writers, I mean on all those who have succeeded in making their fortunes, and who hold patents for turning out prose or verse. As to the young men, those who merely possess talent, they will have beds reserved to them in our hospitals. If they are not quite dead by the time they are fifty or sixty, they will share the benefits we shall shower upon the world of letters. But the real pillars of our throne, the glories of our reign, will be the stonecutters and masons. We will depopulate the rural districts, summon to our side all men of good will, and make them take the trowel in hand. That will be a touching and sublime sight. Broad streets, straight streets passing through a town from one end to the other! Fine white walls, fine yellow walls, rising as by magic! Magnificent buildings adorning immense squares, ornamented with shrubs and street lamps. To build is nothing, but what a charm there is in pulling down! We shall demolish more than we shall build. The city will be razed to the ground, leveled, cleansed. We will convert a town of old plaster into one of new plaster. Such miracles will, I know, cost a great deal of money; but as it is not I who will pay, the expense troubles me but little. Anxious, above all, to leave glorious traces of my reign, I consider that nothing is more fit to astonish coming generations than a frightful consumption of bricks and mortar. Besides, I have noticed that the more a king builds, the more satisfied are his people. They do not seem to know what fools defray the cost of these buildings; they innocently believe that their good-natured sovereign is ruining himself in order to give them the pleasure of beholding a forest of scaffoldings. All will be for the best . We will make the taxpayers pay dearly for the improvements and distribute the pence to the workmen, so that they may rest quietly on their ladders. We shall thus provide bread for the people, and ensure the admiration of posterity. Is it not very ingenious? If any dissatisfied person complained, it would certainly be from sheer jealousy.

"My reign shall be a reign of masons. You see, my beloved subjects, that I am disposed to be a very diverting king. I will burden you with fine wars in the four quarters of the globe, which will bring you blows and glory: at home, I will cheer you with great heaps of ruins and interminable clouds of plaster dust. I shall not spare you speeches; I will make them as empty as possible, thus sharpening the wits of the inquisitive who will have the courage to search for what is not in them. This is enough for to-day; I am dying of thirst. But, in conclusion, I promise you to deal shortly with the serious difficulty of the budget; it is a subject which requires to be prepared a long while in advance, in order to be suitably intricate and obscure. Perhaps you would also wish to hear me deal with religion. In order not to disappoint you in your expectations, I must inform you, at once, that I never intend to express my views on this subject. Therefore spare me indiscreet questions; never urge me to hold opinions in regard to that matter which is particularly disagreeable to me. Now, my beloved subjects, may God bless you."

Such was Mederic 's speech. Of course you understand that I am giving you, here, a brief abstract of it, for it lasted six hours, and the limits of this story do not allow of my transcribing it in full. Had not the orator to lengthen his phrases, turn his periods, and so thoroughly drown his thoughts in a deluge of words, that the people listening to him might not grasp their meaning? In any case my abstract is conformable to the spirit of the speech. If the army heard what it chose to hear, it was thanks to the speaker's oratorical precautions and to the length of his sentences. Is it not always so under such circumstances?

Sidoine vigorously worked his arms and jaws during his brother's speech. Some of his gestures were much applauded; sometimes they were familiar without being trivial, then again they were noble and poetically attractive. To speak the truth he at times gave himself strange contortions, and made bounds which were not precisely in good taste; but this risky mimicry was attributed to inspiration. What gained the day, was the surprising manner in which he opened his mouth. He lowered his chin, then raised it again by even jerks; he caused his lips to assume all the figures of geometry from the straight line to the circle, not omitting the triangle and square; while at the last ring of each sentence he even put out his tongue, a poetical boldness which proved a prodigious success.

When Mederic ceased speaking, Sidoine understood that he must conclude by a master stroke. He took advantage of the favorable moment, then hiding his face with his hand, and without moving, he shouted in a powerful voice:

"Long live Sidoine I., king of the Blues I"

The lord giant knew when to put in a word if required. At the piercing sound of his voice, each battalion believed it had heard the battalion next to it utter the enthusiastic shout. As nothing is more contagious than a stupid blunder, the whole army sang in chorus:

"Long live Sidoine I., king of the Blues."

There was a startling noise for the space of ten minutes. Meanwhile Sidoine, becoming more and more civilized, was prodigal in bows.

The soldiers spoke of carrying him in triumph; but the prince of orators, having quickly summed up his weight, pointed out to them the difficulty of such a proceeding. He undertook to settle the matter with Sidoine. He rendered him homage as his king, in the name of the people, while bestowing on him the titles and privileges of his new position. He afterwards invited him to march at the head of the army and make his entry into his kingdom, which was about ten miles away.

Mederic, meanwhile, was holding his sides, and thinking he would die of laughter. His own speech had greatly amused him. It was quite another matter when Sidoine acclaimed himself

"Bravo, pretty majesty!" he said in a whisper. "I am pleased with you; I no longer despair as regards your education. Allow these good people to do as they like. Let us try the calling of kings; we can give it up in a week if it bores us. For my part, I shall not be sorry to sample it before marrying the charming Primrose. Apart from this, continue to avoid blunders, walk regally, rest satisfied with gestures, and leave speech to me. It is needless to inform this good people that we are two, for that might authorize them to consider themselves under a republic. Now, my beauty, let us quickly enter our capital."

The annals of the Blues thus relate the accession of the great king Sidoine I. to the throne. The incidents recorded here, can be perused in full detail therein, and it may also be remarked that the official historian draws attention in various passages to the fact that these events took place in Egypt, on the stroke of noon, in a temperature of a hundred and nine degrees.

VI. MEDERIC EATS BLACKBERRIES

I will spare you the description of the triumphal entry of our heroes, and of the public rejoicings which took place on that occasion.

Sidoine played the part of a ruler nobly. He graciously received some fifty deputations which came to swear allegiance to him; he even listened without yawning overmuch to the speeches of the heads of the different state bodies. In truth he was in great need of sleep; he would willingly have sent these worthy people off to bed, in order to seek repose himself, if Mederic had not whispered to him that a king, belonging to his people, only slept when the rascals of his kingdom consented to his doing so.

At length the grand functionaries conducted him to his palace, a kind of huge barn, before which the schoolboys raised their hats. Ants greet thus the stones by the wayside. Sidoine, who had made use of a pyramid for a stool, showed by an expressive gesture how restricted he considered this dwelling. Mederic, in his sweetest tones, said that he had noticed an extensive cornfield at the gates of the town, and suggested that this was a more worthy abode for a great prince. The ears of corn would make him a lovely golden couch, which would be marvelously soft, and he would have as canopy the great celestial curtains which God's golden nails secure to the walls of Paradise.

As the people were very fond of shows and masquerades, he announced his intention, with a view to attaining popularity, of giving up the former palace to bear-keepers, rope-dancers, and fortune-tellers. Furthermore, a show of puppets, so perfectly constructed as to be mistaken for live actors, would be established there. The multitude received this proposal with gratitude.

When the question of an abode was settled, Sidoine retired, being anxious to get to bed. He soon perceived a detachment of armed men following him respectfully. Like a good king, he took them for enthusiastic soldiers, and did not trouble himself any more about them. However, when he had stretched himself out voluptuously on his pallet of fresh straw, he saw the soldiers post themselves at the four corners of the field, marching backward and forward with drawn swords. This maneuver excited his curiosity. He partly raised himself, while Mederic, anticipating his wish, called to one of the men who had drawn quite close to the royal couch.

"Hallo! My friend," he shouted, "can you tell me what makes you and your companions leave your beds at this hour to roam around mine? If you have evil designs on wayfarers, it is unseemly to expose your king to the necessity of bearing witness against you in order that you may be hanged. If you are waiting for your sweethearts, though naturally interested in the increase of my subjects, I do not care to assist at these family details. Now, candidly, what are you doing here?"

"Sire, we are keeping guard over you," answered the soldier.

"You are keeping guard over me? And against whom, may I ask? The enemy is not at the frontier that I am aware of, and it is not with your swords that you will protect me from gnats. Come, speak up. Against whom are you protecting me?"

"I do not know, Sire. I will summon my captain." When the captain came up and heard the king's question, he exclaimed, "Good heavens! Sire, how can your majesty ask such a simple question? Is your majesty unacquainted with these minor details? All kings are protected from their subjects. There are here a Hundred good fellows whose sole duty consists in spearing the curious. We are your bodyguard, Sire. But for us, your subjects, a people who absorb monarchs, would already have destroyed a fearful number."

Sidoine laughed till tears filled his eyes. The thought of those poor fellows keeping guard over him had at first seemed a rare joke; but when he learnt that they were protecting him from his subjects, he gave a fresh roar of laughter, which almost choked him. As for Mederic, his cheeks were bursting, letting loose a perfect storm in his beauty's ear.

"Come, clowns," he shouted, "take up your baggage and clear off as quick as possible. Do you think I am such a simpleton as to follow the example of your timorous kings who close ten or twelve doors upon themselves, and station a sentinel in front of each? I look after myself, my worthy friends, and I do not like to be gazed at when asleep; for my foster-mother always told me I was not beautiful when snoring. If you must absolutely watch over some one, I beg you to protect the people against the king, instead of protecting the king against the people; you will be making better use of your night watches, aria" be earning your money more honestly. On summer evenings, if you wish to give me pleasure, send your wives with fans, or, if it rains, vote me an army of umbrellas. But as to your swords, what in the name of patience do you think is their use to me? Now, good night, gentlemen of the bodyguard."

Captain and soldiers withdrew without further ado, delighted with a prince who was so easy to serve. Then our friends, glad that they were alone, were able to talk freely about the astonishing adventures that had befallen them since morning. I mean to say, you understand, that Mederic chattered away for half an hour, moralizing on everything, begging his beauty to carefully follow the thread of his reasoning. At the first words the beauty snored like a top. Our chatterbox no longer understanding what he meant himself, postponed the remainder of his observations to the following day. It was thus that King Sidoine I. spent his first night in the open air, in a deserted field, at the gates of his capital.

The events which took place on the following days are not worthy of being recorded in detail, though they were as strange and marvelous as all those I have selected in which the heroes took part. Our king in two persons—see on what a mystery rests !—having accepted the crown out of sheer good nature, avoided attempting the slightest reform. He allowed the people to act according to their own will, which is recognized to be the best way of reigning; the easiest for the sovereign, the most profitable for the subjects.

At the end of a week Sidoine had already won five pitched battles. He felt called upon to lead his army to the two first. But he soon perceived that instead of rendering him assistance, it impeded him by getting between his legs, and running the risk of receiving kicks. He therefore determined to disband the troops, declaring that in future he, alone, would take the field. This was the subject of a fine proclamation, which began in this remarkable manner: "There is nothing so satisfactory in fighting as to know why one does so. Therefore, as the king, when he declares war, alone knows the cause of his good pleasure, logic demands that the king, alone, should fight." The soldiers greatly appreciated these ideas; in truth, for want of a good reason for going on fighting, they had turned tail in many battles. They had also often expressed astonishment, when talking at evening in the ambulances with wounded foes', of the peculiar custom of princes, who had fists like all the world, and yet who caused thousands of men to be killed to satisfy their private quarrels but if you recollect the charter, you will remember that the Blues had chosen a master with the sole object of being diverted by seeing and hearing him act with his fists and tongue. The army therefore obtained leave to follow its chief at a distance of two kilometers. In this manner it had the pleasure of witnessing battles, without running any of the attendant risks.

Mederic spoke even more than Sidoine fought. By the end of a week he had already enriched the literature of the country with thirteen bulky volumes. When he awoke on the third day he discovered that he knew Greek and Latin without having learnt these languages at any college; he was thus able to quote ten pages of Demosthenes in answer to the prince of orators, who had thought to puzzle him by reciting five pages of Cicero. From that moment, which was that when the nation ceased to understand him, the orator-king acquired even more popularity than the warrior-king.

In point of fact the Blue nation was in rapturous transports. It at length possessed the long-dreamt-of prince, an ideal prince, devoting his energies to its pleasures, never interfering in serious matters. Still as a people, even a satisfied people, always grumbles a little, the worthy man was credited with peculiar tastes; as, for example, his obstinacy in insisting on sleeping in the open air. Besides, I believe I told you that Sidoine was a great fop; so soon as he had a budget within reach, he quickly discarded his wolves' skins for magnificent garments of silk and velvet, finding some compensation in gazing at himself, for the cares of his new profession. He was blamed for this innocent pleasure though he entailed no other expense; he was accused of requiring too much satin, of tearing too much lace. Dew, it is true, spots fine materials, and there is nothing that cuts them like straw. Now, Sidoine slept without undressing himself.

In conclusion, there were scarcely more than five or six thousand discontented persons in this kingdom of thirty million men ; loafers without occupation who had put their backs up, people with deep anger whom the long speeches made feverish, and more especially perverse creatures who were angry at public peace. After reigning a week, Sidoine could have appealed to universal suffrage without fear.

When Mederic awoke on the ninth day, he was seized with a longing to run about the fields. He was tired of living confined to the house, I mean in Sidoine's ear; he was bored at playing the part of a mere mind. He descended slowly. His beauty was still sleeping, and as he only intended to be away a quarter of an hour, he did not inform him of his proposed walk.

A fresh April morning is a delightful thing. The sky was vaulted pale and high. A clear sun, with a white glow and without heat, was rising above the mountains. The leaves which had expanded on the previous day shone in green tufts in the country; the rocks and land stood out in large yellow and red patches. One might have said, on seeing how clean everything appeared, that all nature was new.

Mederic, before proceeding further, paused on a hillock. Then, having sufficiently admired the great place as a whole, he thought of taking advantage of the pleasures of the lanes without troubling about the horizon. He went along the firs' path he came to; then, when he reached the end, took another. He lost his way amidst the sweet-briers, ran in the grass, stretched himself on the moss, tired out the echo with his voice, endeavoring to make a great noise because he found himself surrounded by absolute silence. He admired the fields in detail and in his own way, which is the correct one, catching glimpses of the sky through the trees, creating a universe for himself from a hollow bush, discovering fresh worlds at each turn of the hedges. He became tipsy by inhaling too much of the pure and rather chilly air he found]n the avenues, and ended by stopping, out of breath, delighted with the white rays of the sun and the charming tones of the landscape.

Now, he paused at the foot of a high bramble hedge, those brambles with coarse leaves and long thorny branches, which certainly produce the best fruit a man of refined taste can eat. I am speaking of those luscious clusters of wild blackberries, pervaded with the perfume of the neighboring lavender and rosemary. Do you remember how appetizing they are, black beneath green leaves, and the fresh flavor, partly sweet and partly sour, which they have for palates worthy of appreciating them?

Mederic, like all who love freedom and a vagabond life, was a large consumer of blackberries. He was rather proud of it, having only met, during his meals along the hedges, simple-minded creatures, dreamers and lovers; which led him to conclude that fools could not appreciate this savory fruit, and that they were a feast bestowed by angels in paradise on the good souls in this world. Simpletons are far too stupid to appreciate such a treat; they are only comfortable when seated at a table cutting huge pears which melt into pure water. A fine task, indeed, requiring only a knife; whereas in order to eat blackberries a dozen rare qualities are necessary: the correct eye which discovers the most exquisite hedges, those where the sun's rays and the dew have ripened the fruit to a turn; the knowledge of thorns, that marvelous power of searching in a thicket without scratching one's-self; the wit to know how to waste one's time, to spend an entire morning over one's breakfast, while walking two or three leagues along a path fifty strides long. I am passing over other qualities that are equally deserving of mention. Some people will never attempt to lead this life of poets, feed on pure air, moralize or sleep between two morsels. Idlers, chosen children of heaven, alone know the refinements of this pleasant occupation.

That is why Mederic prided himself on his love for blackberries.

The brambles in front of which he had just stopped were laden with an abundance of rich bunches. He was in raptures.

"Good gracious," he exclaimed, "what fine fruit, what a marvel. Blackberries in April, and blackberries of such a size; this seems to me as surprising as a pail of water turned into wine. It has been well said that nothing strengthens faith like the sight of the supernatural; for the future I will believe all the old women's tales told me in childhood. Personally I appreciate miracles when they fill my glass or my plate. Now to breakfast, as it has pleased Providence to alter the course of the seasons in order to provide me with what I like."

Saying this, Mederic gracefully stretched out his fingers and seized a large berry which would have provided a meal for two sparrows. He enjoyed it leisurely, then smacked his lips, nodding his head in a satisfied manner, like a connoisseur tasting old wine. Then the brand being sampled, the breakfast began. The glutton went from bush to bush, inhaling the sunshine in the intervals, discovering differences in taste, unable to make up his mind. While walking, he discoursed aloud, having acquired the habit of soliloquy when in company with the silent Sidoine; when alone, he nevertheless addressed his friend, concluding that his presence was of little importance to the conversation.

"My beauty," he said, "I do not know of any more philosophical task than that of eating blackberries along the lanes. It is quite a lifelong apprenticeship. See what skill one must display to reach the high branches, which, bear in mind, always present the choicest fruit. I make them bend by drawing the lowest boughs down by degrees; a fool would break them, but I let them spring back to provide for next season. There are also the thorns, which scratch clumsy people. I utilize them; they serve me as hooks in performing this delicate operation. If you wish to judge a man and know him as thoroughly as God who created him, place him with an empty stomach in front of a bramble bush laden with berries on a bright morning. Ah! Poor fellow! A blackberry at the end of a high branch suffices to awaken the seven deadly sins."

And Mederic, quite pleased to exist, ate, made speeches, and blinked his eyes so as to take in his little scene of action more satisfactorily. Apart from this he had utterly forgotten his majesty Sidoine I., the Blue nation, and all the regal comedy. The king in two persons had left his body amongst his subjects; his mind was roaming in the fields, lost among the hedges, thoroughly enjoying itself. It is thus, at night, that the soul takes its flight on the wings of a dream to sport in some unknown corner, oblivious of the prison from which it has escaped. Is not this comparison very ingenious? And though I denied concealing a philosophical truth beneath this slight veil of fiction, does it not tell you the opinion you should form of my giant and dwarf?

However, as Mederic was making sweet eyes at a blackberry, he was recalled to the sad realities of life in the most unforeseen manner. A bulldog, and not one of the smallest, suddenly came dashing along the pathway, barking loudly, and showing his white teeth and bloodshot eyes. Have you noticed, Ninette, the nice hospitable character of dogs in the country? When these faithful animals have received the benefits of education from man, they possess the sense of ownership in the highest degree. They consider it a crime to tread on another's ground. This one, who would have devoured Mederic for merely removing the quantity of earth that clings to the boots of a passer-by, became furious on seeing him eat the blackberries that grew freely at the will of sun and rain. He rushed at him with open jaw.

Mederic certainly did not expect him. He had a confirmed hatred for those great beasts of brutal appearance that are considered amongst animals what gendarmes are amongst men. He scampered off, full speed, frightened and alarmed as to the consequences of this ill-fated meeting. He did not reason on this occasion; but as from habit he had become very logical, though he had lost his head, he set himself the following proposition: This dog has four legs; I have two, which are weaker and less fit. He deduced from it: He is able to run farther and quicker than I. He was naturally led to think: I shall be devoured; and ended in victoriously concluding: It is merely a question of time. The conclusion gave him cold shivers. He turned and saw the dog ten paces off; he ran faster, the dog ran faster still; he jumped a ditch, the dog followed him. Breathless, with outstretched arms, he continued without a will; he felt sharp fangs entering his flesh, and with closed lids saw two bloodshot eyes shining in the dark. The dog's bark encompassed him, made him choke, as waves do a drowning man.

Two jumps more and all would have been over with Mederic. And here, Ninon, allow me to complain of the lack of assistance rendered by our mind to our body when the latter finds itself in a fix. What, I ask, had Mederic's intellect dwindled to while his body had but two wretched legs to depend on? A fine idea fleeing to save one's-self! Every one does the same thing. If his mind had not been wool-gathering, the ingenious child would, at the outset, have quietly climbed up a tree, as he did at the end of a quarter of an hour's mad race, instead of growing breathless and running the risk of pleurisy. That is what I consider a stroke of genius; he was inspired from above. When he was astride a strong branch he was astonished at having thought of such a simple thing.

The bull-dog, in a furious spring, struck violently against the tree, then set about walking round and round its trunk, barking ferociously. Mederic took it easy, and recovered speech.

"Alas! Alas I" he exclaimed, "my poor beauty, I am severely punished for wishing to go out unaccompanied by your fists. This is another proof of how indispensable we are to one another; our affection is the work of Providence. What are you doing without me, having only your arms to help you out of a dilemma? What am I doing here myself up a tree, unable to strike the slightest blow on this dog's muzzle? Alas! Alas! It is all over with us."

The dog, tired of barking, had gravely settled himself on his hind-legs, his neck outstretched, his snout drawn up. He gazed at Mederic without moving a muscle. The latter, seeing the brute paying him unremitting attention, appeared to think it invited him to speak He determined upon utilizing such an auditor, anxious to be listened to for once in his life. Besides, words were his only resource to help him out of his difficulty.

"My friend," he said, in a honeyed voice, "I do not wish to detain you any longer. Go about your business. I shall easily find my way again. I will even admit to you, that at a few leagues from here are a good people who must be greatly concerned at my absence. I am a king, if you must know everything. You are aware that kings are precious jewels, whom nations do not like to lose. Withdraw, therefore. It would be most improper to have to set down in history, one of these days, how the stupid obstinacy of a dog sufficed to overthrow a great empire. Would you like a post at my court? To be keeper of the food at the palace? Tell me what position can I offer you that your Excellency may deign to withdraw?"

The dog did not move. Mederic thought to have got over him by the bait of an official post; he prepared to come down. The dog was undoubtedly not ambitious, for he growled afresh, standing up against the tree.

"The devil take you !" muttered Mederic.

Having exhausted his eloquence, he felt in his pockets. This is a means which usually proves successful, in so far as mankind is concerned. But what is the use of throwing a purse to a dog, unless to raise a bump on his head? Besides, Mederic was not a fellow to carry a purse about him; he looked on money as being absolutely useless, having always lived on principles of free trade. He found something better than a handful of coppers;

I mean to say that he found a lump of sugar. As my hero was very greedy by nature, this find must in no way surprise you. I am anxious to point out to you how naturally all the details connected with this story occur, and how truthful they are.

Mederic, holding the sugar between his finger and thumb, showed it to the dog, who opened his mouth without more ado. Then the besieged came slowly down. When he was near the ground he let the prize drop; the dog snapped it up, swallowed it, and did not even lick his snout before setting upon Metric.

"You villain," shouted the latter, briskly ascending to his branch again, "you eat my sugar and want to bite me! Well, I can see you have been carefully brought up; you are an apt pupil of the egotism of your masters, cringing before them, and always eager for the flesh of passers-by."

VII. WHEREIN SIDOINE BECOMES TALKATIVE

Mederic was about to continue in this strain, when he heard a rumbling noise behind him like the sound of a distant cataract. Not a breath of wind disturbed the leaves; the neighboring stream flowed with too discreet a murmur to utter such complaints. Mederic, surprised, set aside the branches questioning the horizon. At the first glance he could see nothing; the landscape on this side spread out grey and barren, like a plain stretching from hillock to hillock, till it reached the mountains which formed its boundaries. But as the noise increased he looked more attentively, and then perceived a rock of peculiar construction rising from a dip in the earth. This rock—for it was difficult to take it for anything but a rock—was of the shape and color of a nose, but of a gigantic nose, out of which several hundred ordinary noses might easily have been made. This nasal organ, turned in a despairing manner towards the sky, had the appearance of a nose which had had its placidity disturbed by some great sorrow. Without doubt it was this nose that was making the noise.

When Mederic had carefully examined the rock, he hesitated a moment, not daring to believe his eyes. Then finding himself on familiar ground, he could doubt no longer.

"Hallo, my beauty!" he exclaimed in astonishment, "Why does your nose parade the fields all alone? May I die, if that is not it there, ready to faint away like a calf which is being slaughtered."

At those words the nose—the rock, incredible though it seems, was nothing but a nose after all—the nose became pitifully excited. Something like a landslip occurred. A long grayish block, resembling a large obelisk lying on the ground, moved, bent itself double, rising from one end and stretching itself out from the other. A head appeared, a chest was defined, the whole joined to two legs, which, though out of proportion, would nevertheless have been called legs in all languages, both ancient and modern.

When Sidoine had assembled his limbs he assumed a sitting posture, his fists in his eyes, his knees high and wide apart He was sobbing in a heart-rending manner.

"Oh! Oh!" said Mederic, "I was sure of it; in all the world there is but my beauty who has a nose of that size. I know that nose as well as I know my village steeple. Hallo I my poor brother, so you also have serious trouble. I assure you I only intended absenting myself for ten minutes at the most; if you find me again at the end of ten hours, it is assuredly the fault of the sun and of bushes laden with blackberries. We will forgive them. By the way, just fling that dog aside; we shall then be able to speak more comfortably."

Sidoine, still sobbing, stretched out his arm and seized the dog by the nape of the neck. He swung him for a moment, and sent him howling and writhing straight into the sky, with a speed of several thousand miles to a second. Mederic thoroughly enjoyed the ascent. He followed the animal with his eyes. When he saw it enter the magnetic sphere of the moon, he clapped his hands and congratulated his comrade on having at last peopled that satellite for the gratification of future astronomers.

"Now, my beauty," he said, jumping to the ground, "what about our people?"

Sidoine, on hearing this question, began moaning afresh; rolling his head, and smearing his face with his tears.

"Pooh!" continued Mederic, "are our subjects dead? Did you annihilate them in a fit of spleen, considering the kingly people liable to abdication like all other monarchs?"

"Brother, brother," sobbed Sidoine, "our subjects have behaved badly."

"Really?"

"They lost their temper over a trifle— "The villains turned me adrift."

"The unmannerly creatures!"

"Like no nobleman ever dismissed a footman."

"Just look at the aristocrat!"

At each pause Sidoine uttered a deep sigh. When he came to a full stop in his speech, his emotion having reached its height, he again burst into tears.

"My beauty," resumed Mederic, "it is no doubt disheartening for a master to be dismissed by his footmen; but I do not see in this a cause for such distress. If your grief did not once more bear witness to your kind heart and ignorance of social intercourse, I would reprove you for lamenting what is after all but a very frequent occurrence. One of these days we will take up the study of history; you will see it is an old habit of nations to ill-treat princes when people get tired of them. In spite of what some people say, God never had the strange fancy of creating a peculiar race with the object of imposing on His children, masters elected by Him from father to son. Do not therefore be surprised if those who are governed wish in their turn to govern, for every man has a right to that ambition. It is a relief to be able to reason out one's misfortunes. Come, dry your tears. They would do credit to an effeminate creature, a braggart fed on praise who had forgotten his status as a man through practicing that of a king too long. But we, mon-archs of a day, know how to walk without other escort than our shadow, and bask in the sunshine, having for sole kingdom the dust on which we set our feet."

"You take it easy," answered Sidoine dolefully. "The profession pleased me. I fought to my heart's content; I wore Sunday clothes every day of the week; I slept on fresh straw. Reason away and explain to your heart's con-tent; as for me, I wish to cry."

And he wept; then, suddenly pausing in the midst of a sob, he said:

"This is how things came about"

"My beauty," interrupted Mederic, "you are becoming talkative. De-spair is not good for you."

"This morning at about six o'clock, as I was dreaming peacefully, I was awakened by a great noise. I opened an eye. The people surrounded my couch, and appeared very excited, awaiting my awakening with a view to some judgment. All right! Said I to myself, this concerns Mederic; let us sleep again. And I did so. At the end of I don't know how many minutes, I felt my subjects tugging respectfully at me by the corner of my royal smock. I was compelled to open both eyes. The people were growing im-patient. What is amiss with my brother Mederic? thought I, in a bad humor. Thereupon I sat up. On perceiving this the good people surrounding me ut-tered a murmur of satisfaction. Do you understand me, brother; and can-not I relate when occasion offers?"

"Decidedly; but if you relate in that style you will be relating till to-mor-row. What did our subjects want?"

"Ah! there you are. I do not think I quite understood them. An old man approached me leading a cow by a halter. He placed it at my feet, with its head turned towards me. Two groups formed on the right and left of the beast, facing each flank, and shaking their fists in each other's faces. The one on the right shouted, 'It is white!' that on the left, 'It is black!' Then the old man, bowing repeatedly, said to me in a humble tone, 'Sire, is it black, or is it white?'"

"But," interrupted Mederic, "that was deep philosophy. Was the cow black, my beauty?"

"Not exactly."

"Then it was white?"

"Oh! Certainly not. Besides, I did not at first trouble much about the beast's color. It was you who had to reply. I had merely to look on. Still you did not speak. I thought you were preparing your speech, and was about to settle down to sleep comfortably. The old fellow, who had bent himself in two to hear my answer, feeling his back ache, repeated, 'Sire, is it white, or is it black ?'"

"My beauty, you dramatize your story in accordance with all the rules of the art. If I only had time, I would make a tragic author of you. But go on."

"'Ah! The sluggard!' I said to myself at last, 'he sleeps like a king.' However, the people again became impatient. It was a question of awakening you as quietly as possible without attracting their attention. I slipped a finger into my left ear; it was empty. I slipped it into my right ear; that was also empty. It was from the moment I made those movements that the people lost their temper."

"No wonder! My beauty. Are you so ignorant of the art of pantomime? To scratch one's ear signifies that one is puzzled, and when you have a judgment to deliver you go and scratch both!"

"Brother, I was greatly concerned. I rose without paying further attention to the people. I actively searched all my pockets, those of my smock, of my breeches; every one of them, in fact. Nothing in the left-hand, nothing in the right-hand pockets. My brother Mederic was no longer about me. For a moment I hoped I might find him in some out-of-the-way gusset. I examined the seams, looked over each fold. No one. There was no more a Mederic in my clothes than in my ears. The people, astounded at this strange performance, no doubt suspected me of seeking for an answer in my pockets; they waited a few moments, then began to hoot me with no more respect than if I had been the least deserving of consideration among the peasantry. Admit, brother, it required a strong head to escape safe and sound from such a situation."

"I admit it willingly, my beauty. And what about the cow?"

"The cow! It was the cow that puzzled me. When I had ascertained that

I must speak in public, I summoned all the common-sense I could master to my aid, to enable me to survey the cow without prejudice. The old man had just risen, calling out to me in an angry tone that everlasting sentence which was taken up in chorus by the people, 'Is it white? Is it black?' On my word of honor, brother Mederic, it was both black and white. I perceived that while some would have it black, the others would have it white, and that is exactly what worried me."

"You are very simple-minded, my beauty; the color of objects depends on the position of the people. Those on the left and those on the right, only seeing one side of the cow at a time, were equally right and equally in error. You, looking straight at it, formed another opinion about it. Was this the correct one? I dare not say; for bear in mind that some one standing at the tail might have given utterance to a fourth opinion quite as logical as the three first."

"Well, brother Mederic, why moralize so much? I don't pretend I was the only one in the right. But I say the cow was both white and black; and I can certainly say this, as it is what I saw. My first idea was to impart to the crowd the truth revealed to me by my eyes, and I did so good-naturedly, being simple enough to think this conclusion the best possible one, as it ought to have satisfied every one, while giving offence to none."

"What! My poor beauty, you spoke?"

"Could I remain silent? The people were there, their ears wide open, thirsting for verbosity as the earth hankers for rain after two months of drought. The jocular ones, seeing my confused and stupid look, exclaimed that my warbler's voice had disappeared just at the mating season. I turned my sentence over seven times in my mouth, then partly closing my eyelids, and rounding my arms, I uttered the following words in the most fluted voice possible: 'My well-beloved subjects, the cow is both black and white !'"

"Oh dear me! My poor beauty, in what school did you learn to utter speeches consisting of one sentence? Have I ever set you such a bad example? You had there a subject to fill a couple of volumes, and you cast all the fruit of your observations into a dozen words! Of course you were understood: your speech was pitiable!"

"I believe you, brother. I had spoken very softly. One and all, men, women, children, old men, stopped up their ears, looking at each other affrighted, as though they had heard thunder rumbling overhead. Then they made a great outcry: 'And who is the uncouth person who is bellowing like that?' they inquired. Our king has been changed. This man is not our gentle lord, whose sweet voice charmed our ears. Be off with you quickly, wretched giant, whose only use is to frighten our daughters when they cry. Did you hear the simpleton affirm that this cow is white and black? It is white. It is black. Is he mocking us in stating that it is black and white?

"Come, be off with you. What a silly pair of fists! What ugly appendages, when he swings them stupidly about, as if he did not know what to do with them. Throw them aside, that you may run faster. You would cure us of having kings, if we could be cured of that ill. Come, be off quickly. Clear out of the kingdom. What possessed us to take a fancy to men several yards high? Nothing is more artistically constructed than gnats. We want a gnat."

Sidoine on recalling this tumultuous scene could no longer control his feelings; his tears started afresh. Mederic did not utter a word, for his beauty was assuredly awaiting his sympathy to yield still more to his grief.

"The people," he resumed, after a pause, "pushed me slowly out of their territory. I walked backwards, step by step, not thinking of defending myself, without daring to open my lips, trying to hide my fists which had excited such an uproar. You know I am very shy by nature, and nothing vexes me so much as to see a crowd busying itself about me. Therefore, when I found myself in the open fields, I soon made up my mind: I turned my back on my revolutionary subjects, and ran with all the speed I could command. I heard them grumble at my flight louder than they had done two minutes previously at my slowness in withdrawing. They called me coward; shook their fists at me, forgetting they ran the risk of putting me in mind of my own ; and ended by throwing s ones after me when I had outdistanced them. Alas! Brother Mederic, these are sad adventures."

"Come, cheer up," sensibly answered Mederic; "let us hold council. What do you think of a slight reproof being administered to our subjects, not with a view to subjugating them—for, after all, they were not bound to retain us once they were no longer satisfied with us—but to show them that they cannot turn out people such as are with impunity? I vote for a brief shower of clouts."

"Oh!" said Sidoine, "can one read in history of such punishments being inflicted?"

"Yes, certainly. Kings sometimes destroy a town; at others times behead kings. It is sweet reciprocation. If it will amuse you, we will belabor those on whose behalf we fought yesterday."

"No, brother; it would be a sad task. I belong to the class of people who do not care to eat chickens bred in their own poultry yards."

"Well said, my beauty. Let us then bequeath the task of making us regretted to the king who succeeds us. Besides, that kingdom was too small;

you could not move without passing the frontiers. We have tarried long enough by the wayside. We must, without further delay, seek the Kingdom of the Happy, which is an extensive kingdom, where we shall reign in comfort. Above all let us keep together. We will spend some morning in completing our education, in acquiring perfect knowledge of this world in a corner of which we shall rule. Is the matter settled, my beauty?"

Sidoine ceased weeping, he no longer thought, no longer spoke. Tears, for a brief space of time, had placed thoughts in his brain and words on his lips. All disappeared simultaneously.

"Listen and do not reply," added Mederic. "We will step across our former kingdom, and set out towards the East in quest of a new realm."

VIII. THE CHARMING PRIMROSE QUEEN OF THE KINGDOM OF THE HAPPY

It is high time, Ninon, to tell you of the marvels of the Kingdom of the Happy. Here are the particulars that Mederic had from his friend the bullfinch.

The Kingdom of the Happy is situated in a world that geographers have as yet been unable to discover, but which kindhearted beings of all ages have well known, having visited it in dreams. I cannot tell you anything concerning its extent, 'the height of its mountains, the length of its rivers; its boundaries are not clearly defined, and, up to the present, the science of geometry in this fortunate country has consisted in dividing the land into allotments, according to the requirements of each family. Spring does not reign there eternally, as you might fancy; flowers have their thorns, the plain is strewn with rocks; twilight is succeeded by dark night, which is followed in turn by dawn. The fertility, the salubrious climate, and supreme beauty of this kingdom, find their origin in the delightful harmony and wise equilibrium of the elements. The sun ripens the fruits which rain has produced; night rests the fields from the fertilizing labor of the day. The sun never scorches the crops, cold never arrests the flow of the streams. There is nothing that is supreme, everything is counterbalanced, has its part in the universal order of things; so the world, where all opposite influences are in equal quantity, is a world of peace, justice, and duty.

The Kingdom of the Happy is well peopled; from what date has this been so? No one knows; but it is certain that no one would take the nation to be ten years old. It does not appear to suspect to what height of perfection human beings can attain; it lives peacefully without having to vote daily, to maintain one law, twenty laws which will require in their turn twenty other laws, to insure them also being maintained. The edifice of iniquity and oppression has not got beyond its foundation-stone. Some great sentiments, as simple as home truths, take the place of rules: brotherhood in the sight of God, need of rest, knowledge of the insignificance of human nature, the undefined hope of eternal peace. There is a tacit understanding amongst these passers-by of an hour, who question the use of elbowing one another when the road is wide, and leads small and great to the same goal. Harmonious nature, which is ever placid, has influenced the character of the inhabitants; they have, like it, a soul rich in feeling, accessible to all sentiments. This soul, wherein the slightest increase of passion would raise a storm, enjoys a calm that nothing will destroy, owing to the just equalization of good and bad faculties.

You see, Ninon, that these people are not angels, and that their world is no paradise. A dreamer of our impulsive countries could ill adapt himself to this temperate clime, where the heart must beat regularly; or to the caresses of a pure and tepid atmosphere. He would despise those peaceful landscapes enveloped in white light, stormless, and with no dazzling middays. But what a peaceful home for those who, recently awakened from death, recall amid sighs, the delightful slumber they enjoyed in the eternity of the past, and who from hour to hour await the rest of future everlastingness. Those beings refuse to suffer, they aspire to that equality, that holy calm which recalls their true nature, that of non-existence. Feeling both good and wicked, they have made it a rule to annihilate mankind as far as possible, to cause him to resume his place in creation, by regulating the harmony of their soul by that of the universe.

Among such a people there cannot be much hierarchy. It is satisfied with existing, and does not divide itself into hostile castes, which dispenses with the necessity of having a history. It declines to submit to that selection of fate which appoints certain men as rulers over their fellows, by giving them a larger part of intellect than the usual share heaven is able to assign to each of its children. Brave men and poltroons, simpletons and men of genius, good and wicked resign themselves, in this land, to being nothing, individually and the only merit they recognize is that of forming part of the human family. From this idea of justice a small society has sprung, which at first sight appears to be somewhat monotonous, possessing but slight individuality, yet forming a charming whole, which harbors no malice, and is a true people in the correct sense of the word.

And so there are neither small nor great, rich nor poor, no titles, no social scale, none above, none below, none who elbow others; the nation is without care, it lives calmly, is loving and philosophical, and consists of men who have ceased to be such. However, in the early days of the kingdom, in order not to be pointed at by their neighbors, they had fallen in with accepted notions by proclaiming a king. They did not feel the need of him, they considered the step a mere formality, and perhaps a shrewd way to shelter their liberty beneath the wing of monarchy. They selected the humblest citizen, who possessed sufficient intelligence to feel he was the brother of his subjects, and was not so foolish as to become malicious with time. This selection was one of the causes of the peaceful prosperity of the kingdom. The step once taken, the king gradually forgot that he had a people, the people that they had a king. Ruler and ruled thus went side by side, unconsciously protecting one another for centuries; laws were observed in that they did not make themselves felt; the country enjoyed perfect order, which was the result of its unique position in history; a free monarchy contained in a free people.

The annals relating to the history of the sovereigns of the Kingdom of the Happy would be curious reading. Certainly great deeds and humanitarian reforms would hold but a small place therein, and would yield but slight interest; worthy folk would, however, find pleasure in noting with what innocent simplicity that race of excellent men, who were born kings quite naturally, succeeded one another on the throne, and how they wore the crown as easily as one wears fair or dark hair in one's cradle. The nation having given itself the trouble to select a master at the commencement, did not intend to bother itself further in the matter, and understood that it had given its vote once for all. Respect for hereditary transmission did not account for its acting thus, for it ignored the meaning of the term; but this course of action seemed to it by far the simplest.

Therefore, at the time of the reign of the charming Primrose, no genealogist, in tracing back the family tree, could have followed, in its various branches, that long line of kings, descendants of a common ancestor. They succeeded to the royal inheritance throughout ages, without having to trouble themselves lest some beggar should rob them of it in transit. Many of them even appeared unaware of the high sinecure which they had inherited from their ancestors. Fathers, mothers, sons, daughters, brothers, sisters, uncles, aunts, nephews, nieces, had handed down the royal scepter from hand to hand like an heirloom.

Had it not been for the good nature of the kings themselves in coming forward, the people would in the end have failed to recognize its king for the time being, owing to the family connection which had at length become numerous and involved. Sometimes a circumstance occurred when a king became an absolute necessity. As everything considered, it is wise to follow the ordinary course of events, the nation thereupon called on their legitimate ruler to declare himself. Then the one who had the gilt stick in a corner of his house took it modestly, acted his part, and retired when the farce was over. These short appearances set the memory of the nation in order.

It must be pointed out, to the honor of the reigning dynasty, that two kings had never presented themselves in answer to the people's summons; amongst heirs, the fact is worthy of being noted : there was never any great nephew covetous of the prize which had fallen to the share of the eldest branch. However, I cannot affirm that the charming Primrose was directly descended from the king who founded the dynasty. You know that one is not always the daughter of one's father. But it is certain that the title of queen was transmitted to her according to the civil laws of consanguinity. There coursed through her veins a pink blood which perhaps did not contain a drop of the regal article, but which certainly preserved a tinge of the blood of the first man. That dynasty developing without shock, traversing ages at the will of births and deaths, is a splendid example for the peoples and princes of our shores.

The father of the charming Primrose, forgetting as he grew old the great art of his ancestors, conceived the peculiar idea of wishing to introduce some reforms in the government. A republic was on the verge of being proclaimed. Thereupon the old man died, and so spared his subjects the trouble of getting angry. They avoided changing a political system which had suited them so well for centuries, and quietly allowed the only daughter of the late king, the charming Primrose, who was twelve years old, to ascend the throne.

The child, who possessed great common sense for her age, was careful to avoid following her father's example. Having learnt the cost of insisting on making a nation happy which declared it enjoyed perfect felicity, she sought elsewhere for beings to console and for existences to soften. According to the story, heaven had endowed her with one of those women's souls embodying pity and love, puffs of breath from a better God, and of such pure essence that men have been obliged to invent quite a multitude of angels and cherubims to account for this penetrating kindness. Ah! Yes, Ninon; we people heaven with our sweethearts, with our soft-voiced sisters, with our mothers—those holy souls, the guardian angels of our prayers. God loses nothing by this belief, which is mine. If He needs a celestial army, He possesses up there, around His throne, the compassionate thoughts of all true-hearted women who love in this world.

Primrose, from her birth, evinced several proofs of her mission; she was born to protect the weak, and to perform acts of peace and justice. I will not say that the sun shone more brightly on the day she came into the world, or that there was greater happiness in human hearts. Yet, on that occasion the swallows talked over the event later than usual. If the wolves were not affected, it was because tears of joy do not belong to them by nature; the lambs on passing the door bleated more softly, glancing at one another with moist eyes. Among the beasts of the country—I mean the good beasts— there was an emotion which softened their sad state of brutes for an hour. A Messiah was born who had been expected by these poor creatures; I ask you the question, and without sacrilegious mockery, whether in their sufferings and darkness they do not hope for a Savior as we do?

Primrose, on opening her eyes in her cradle, bestowed her first smile on the family dog and cat, who were seated on their haunches, one on either side of the cot, as becomes high functionaries. She shed her first tear, stretching forth her hands towards a cage wherein a nightingale was sadly singing; when, to pacify her, the frail prison was handed her, she opened it, and smiled again on seeing the bird spread out its wings.

I cannot relate to you her youth from day to day, spent in placing handfuls of corn near ant-hills, not quite at the edge, in order not to deprive the laborers of the pleasure of work, but at a short distance, so as to spare the limbs of the tiny creatures; her happy youth, of which she made one long holiday, relieving herself of the necessity she felt of being kind, giving her heart the constant joy of doing good, of helping the unfortunate: sparrows and cockroaches saved from the hands of mischievous boys, goats consoled with a caress for the loss of their kids, domestic animals plentifully fed on bones and soups, bread-crumbs placed on the roof, bits of straw held out towards drowning insects, kind actions and gentle words of all kinds.

As I have told you, she attained the age of discretion early in life. What with her had at first been the instinct of the heart, soon became judgment and line of conduct. It was no longer her innate kindness only that prompted her to love the brute creation; that common sense which we display to hold dominion, had in her case the rare result of increasing her affection by helping her to realize how dumb creatures need to be loved. When she walked through the lanes with girls of her own age, she sometimes preached her mission, and it was a charming sight to see this rosy-lipped doctor, explaining with earnest simplicity to her disciples, the new religion which teaches us to extend a helping hand to the most unfortunate of the earth. She often said that she had formerly felt great pity, when thinking of creatures deprived of speech, and thus unable to make their wants known to us; she dreaded in her early years to pass by them when they were hungry or athirst, and to go on her way without having relieved them, giving them a hateful impression of the wicked heart of a little girl ignoring charity. It was from this, she said, that all the misunderstanding between God's children from man to worm came; they do not understand their different languages, and despise one another, because they cannot comprehend each other sufficiently, to give mutual assistance in a brotherly way.

Many a time when facing a huge ox, who fixed his mournful eyes on her for hours together, she had anxiously sought to ascertain what the poor creature that was looking at her so sadly, wanted. But now, as far as she was concerned, she no longer dreaded being thought unkind. She knew the language of each beast; she owed this language to the affection of dear unfortunate ones, who had taught it her during a long association. And when one asked her how to acquire those thousand languages to put an end to the misunderstandings which render creation wicked, she replied with a sweet smile: "Love animals and you will understand them."

Her logic, moreover, was not very profound; she judged by her own heart, without troubling herself about philosophical ideas she was unacquainted with. Her view of things possessed this peculiarity, in our era of pride: she did not consider man alone in God's work. She loved life in all its forms; she beheld creatures, from the humblest to the highest, crushed beneath the same law of suffering. In this brotherhood of tears she could make no distinction between those who possess a soul and those to whom we do not allow one. Stones alone left her unmoved, and yet during the hard frosts of January she would think of those poor stones which must have felt so cold on the highways. She had become attached to animals as we become attached to the blind and dumb, because they can neither see nor hear. She sought out the most miserable creatures to satisfy her great craving to love.

She certainly was not so foolish as to believe that a man was concealed under the skin of a donkey or a wolf; those are ridiculous inventions which might occur to a philosopher, but are not intended for the fair head of a little girl. The wise man who has declared that he loves beasts because they are men in disguise, is a perfect egotist. As for her, thank God, she looked on animals as mere animals. She loved them simply, believing they live, and experience joys and sorrows just as we do. She treated them as sisters, while realizing the difference existing between their being and ours, but at the same time telling herself that God, having given them life, has created them to be comforted.

When the charming Primrose ascended the throne, seeing that she could not perform a deed of charity in working for the welfare of her people, she determined to labor for the happiness of the animals in her kingdom. As the men declared themselves to be perfectly satisfied, she devoted herself to the well-being of insects and lions. She thus appeased her craving to love.

It must be admitted that if peace reigned in the cities it was not the same in the forests. Primrose had at all times experienced sad surprise at seeing the perpetual warfare which raged amongst the brute creation. She could not understand the spider sucking the fly's blood, the bird feeding on the spider. One of her most oppressive nightmares consisted in seeing, on rough winter nights, a kind of terrible round dance, an immense circle filling the heavens; it was formed of all creatures in single file devouring one another; it revolved unceasingly, borne along in the fury of the horrible feast. Fear brought a cold sweat to the child's brow, when she realized that this feast could have no end, that the creatures would eternally whirl round thus amidst agonizing yells.

But this to her mind was a dream; the dear child was ignorant of the fatal law of life which cannot be without death. She believed in the sovereign power of her tears.

This is the fine plan which she had formed, in her simplicity and kindness of heart, for the greater happiness of the animals of her kingdom.

She had scarcely attained power, before she had it proclaimed with sound of trumpet at the cross-roads of every forest, in the poultry-yards, and on the squares of large cities, that every animal tired of a vagrant life, would find sure shelter at the court of the charming Primrose. The proclamation stated, besides, that the pensioners, once instructed in the difficult science of happiness, according to the laws of heart and reason, would enjoy abundant board and be exempt from tears. As winter was drawing near and food becoming scarce, hungry wolves, chilly insects, all the domestic animals in the country, stray cats and dogs, and some five or six dozen curious wild animals answered the young queen's summons.

She lodged them commodiously in a spacious shed, giving them a thousand comforts which were new to them. Her system of education was as simple as her mind; it consisted in loving her pupils greatly; preaching mutual affection by example. She had a similar cell built for each, without troubling about their different natures, provided them with comfortable beds of straw and heather, clean troughs at a proper height, coverings in winter time, and leafy branches in summer. She sought as far as possible to lead them to forget their vagrant life with its pungent joys; she had therefore regretfully had the barn surrounded with strong iron railings to assist in the conversion, thus placing a barrier between the revolutionary spirit of the beasts outside and the good disposition of her disciples. Morning and night she visited them, assembled them in a common room, where she petted them according to individual deserts. She did not make them long speeches, but incited them to friendly discussions on delicate points of fraternity and abnegation, encouraging well-thinking orators and kindly rebuking those who raised their voices rather too high. Her aim was to blend them little by little into a same people; she hoped to make each species lose its individual language and customs and to lead them all unconsciously to universal unity, confusing for them, by means of continual contact, their various ways of seeing and hearing. Thus she set the weak under the paws of the strong, she brought the grasshopper with its sharp cry and the bull snorting with all the might of its nostrils, to hold converse together, she placed greyhounds beside hares, and foxes in the very midst of hens. But the step she thought the cleverest was to serve the same food in all the porringers. As this food could not be flesh or fish, the ordinary, for one and all, consisted in a basin of milk a day, which was smaller or larger according to the boarder's appetite.

Everything being planned in this manner, the charming Primrose awaited results. They could not fail to be good, she thought, as the means employed were excellent . The men of her kingdom proclaimed themselves happier and happier, losing their temper if ever a philanthropist sought to point out their misery to them. The animals, on the contrary, admitted their misfortunes and endeavored to attain perfect happiness. At this period, the charming Primrose found herself to be without doubt the best and most satisfied of queens.

Metric knew no more concerning the Kingdom of the Happy. His friend the bullfinch had given him to understand that one fine morning he had flown away from the hospitable barn, without explaining the reason for that unaccountable flight.

Candidly, that bullfinch must have been a good-for-nothing scapegrace, who did not like milk, but preferred the sun and briars.

IX. WHEREIN MEDERIC POPULARIZES ASTRONOMY, HISTORY, THEOLOGY, PHILOSOPHY, EXACT AND NATURAL SCIENCES, AS WELL AS VARIOUS OTHERS.

The giant and the dwarf traveled across country trifling away their time in the sunshine, anxious to reach their destination, but forgetting themselves at each bend of the path. Mederic had once more taken up his quarters in Sidoine's ear; he was satisfied with the lodging in every way, and continually discovered fresh comforts in it.

The two brothers walked along at random. Mederic allowed himself to be led according to the fancy of Sidoine's legs, without troubling as to the way; and as these legs easily covered twenty degrees of longitude at a step, it follows that at the end of the first morning, the travelers had already gone an incalculable number of times round the world. Towards noon, Mederic, tired of being silent, was unable to let seas and continents pass by again, without giving his companion a lesson in geography.

"See, my beauty," he said, "at this present moment there are millions of poor children, shut up in cold rooms, ruining their eyesight and puzzling their brains in studying the world on dirty scraps of paper, colored blue, green, and red, and covered with lines and strange names like a cabalistic conjuring book. Man is to be pitied for only seeing grand sights when brought down to his own level. Formerly I chanced to glance at one of those books, in which the countries that are known were comprised in some twenty or thirty leaves; it is not an entertaining collection, and is good at the best to stock a child's memory. Why cannot the sublime work spread out before us, be displayed to them so that they may behold its greatness at a glance? But the children, sons of our mothers, are not of a build to take in the whole page. Angels alone would be capable of true science, should there be some sour tempered clever old saint up above to give lessons in geography. So as it pleases God to set out this beautiful natural map before us, I wish to take advantage of this rare opportunity to draw your attention to the various manner and customs of

"Brother Mederic," interrupted Sidoine, "I am an ignoramus, and greatly fear I shall not understand you. Though talking does not tire you much, it is better for us both that you should keep silent."

"As usual, my beauty, you speak foolishly. It is just now to my interest to converse with you concerning human knowledge; for, understand, I intend nothing less than to popularize this knowledge. To begin with, do you know the meaning of popularize?"

"No; and even at the risk of again speaking foolishly, I must say that the expression seems to me a barbarous one."

"To popularize a science, my beauty, means to dilute it, to render it as insipid as possible, that it may be easily understood by the brains of children and persons of small intellect. This is what happens: learned men despise truths hidden beneath thick draperies and prefer them in their nakedness; children, concluding rightly that the time for serious study always comes soon enough, continue to play till they reach the age when they can climb the rough road to knowledge without being blindfolded; persons of weak intellect—I allude to those who are not wise enough to stop their ears—hearken as well as they can to the finest diffusion of knowledge, overcame their brains with it, and thus become utter simpletons. So that no one profits by this eminently philanthropic idea which consists in placing science within reach of all, no one, unless it be he who popularizes it. He has performed a great feat. You cannot, my beauty, in all conscience, prevent me doing the same if I feel in the least inclined."

"Talk away, brother Mederic, your speeches do not prevent my walking."

"Those are wise words. My beauty, pray look attentively at the four points of the horizon. From this height we cannot distinguish our brother men, we can easily mistake their towns for heaps of gray paving-stones, cast into the hollows of the plains or on the slopes of the hills. The world seen thus, presents a spectacle of peculiar grandeur; here long ridges of rocks; there, in the sunken parts, pools of water; then, at distant intervals, some forests forming dark patches on the light-colored earth. This view possesses the beauty of an immense extent of horizon; but man will always feel more delight in contemplating a hillside cottage with a couple of sweet-briars and a stream of water at its door."

Sidoine made a wry face on hearing this poetical detail. Mederic resumed, "It is affirmed that, at distant intervals, frightful earthquakes wreck continents, upheave the seas, and transform the horizon. A new act begins in the great tragedy of Eternity. At the present moment I can imagine I am looking at one of those anterior worlds, when geographers did not exist. Happy mountains, fortunate streams, calm oceans, you live in peace for thousands of centuries, without names in the sight of God, transitory shapes of a world that may perhaps change tomorrow. My beauty and I, look down on you from above as your Creator must see you, and we do not trouble ourselves concerning the depths of the waters, the heights of the mountains, nor the various temperatures of the countries. Listen, Sidoine, I am popularizing more than ever; I am in the midst of the physical geography of the globe. For the Eternal there must exist as many different worlds as there have been subversions. You can understand that. But man, creature of a moment, can only look on the earth from one point of view. Since the birth of Adam the landscapes have not altered; they are such as the waters of the last flood left them to our forefathers. My task is, therefore, singularly simplified. We have only to study stationary lines, a certain clearly defined configuration. The recollection of what we see will suffice.

Look and you will be learned. The map is a fine one, I fancy, and you possess sufficient intelligence to open your eyes."

"I open them, brother; I see oceans, mountains, rivers, islands, and a thousand other things. Even when I close my eyelids I see these things again in darkness; that is no doubt what you termed the recollection of what we see. But I think it would be well to give me the names of these marvels, and to tell me something of the inhabitants after describing the house."

"Well, my beauty, I have been able, in a few words, to give you a course of geography similar to that of the angels. I should not complete your education in ten years were I to teach you the frivolous things retailed to the students I mentioned previously. Man has delighted in confusing everything on earth; he has given twenty different names to the same peak; he has invented continents and disowned even more; he has founded so many kingdoms, and annihilated so many, that each stone in the fields has assuredly served as boundary to some vanished nation. Those well-defined lines that eternity of selfsame boundaries exist for God alone. When human nature is introduced upon this vast scene terrible confusion ensues. It is so easy every hundred years to take a sheet of paper and sketch a new world, the one existing for the time being. If the Creator's world had undergone all the changes of the world of man, we should have the strangest medley of colors and lines spread out before us, instead of this natural map, which is so clear. I cannot appreciate the whims our brethren have indulged in. I again tell you to look attentively. In a glance you will learn more than all the geographers in the world know; for with your own eyes you will have seen the great boundaries of the terrestrial crust, which these gentlemen are still seeking with their levels and compasses. Unless I am mistaken, this is rather a very popularized lesson in physical and political geography."

As the teacher ceased speaking, the pupil, who for the time being was traveling over fields of ice, stepped across the pole, without more ado, and placed his foot on the other hemisphere. It was noon on one side and midnight on the other. The comrades, leaving a bright April sun behind them, continued their journey in the clearest moonlight that could ever be seen. Sidoine, simple-minded by nature, almost fell backward in astonishment at the want of logic the sun and moon appeared to him to display at that moment. He looked up and studied the stars.

"My beauty," Mederic shouted in his ear, "now or never is the time to popularize astronomy for your benefit. Astronomy is the geography of the planets. It teaches that the earth is a speck of dust cast into space. It is amongst all a whole some science when taken in reasonable doses. But I will not dwell on that branch of human knowledge; I know you are modest and not inquisitive as regards mathematical formulas. But if you possessed the least pride I should have, in order to cure you of the bad habit, to bring to your notice, proof in hand, the appalling truths of space. No man, however insane he may be, could be so stupid as to believe for a moment, when contemplating the stars on a clear night, that God created the universe for the greater enjoyment of humanity.

"There is in the vault of heaven an everlasting denial of those false theories which, taking man only into account in the midst of creation, dispose of God's will towards him, as though God had solely the earth to consider. What is done with other worlds? If the work has an aim, will not the entire work be devoted to attaining that aim? We, the infinitely small, study astronomy in order to learn what place we hold in creation. Look at the sky, my beauty, observe it well. Giant though you be, you have infinity overhead, with all its mysteries. If ever you should have the unfortunate idea to philosophies on your origin and end, this infinity would prevent you drawing any conclusions."

"Brother Mederic, popularizing is an amusing game. I should like to know the cause of night and day. These are strange phenomena which I have never before thought about."

"My beauty, it is thus with all things. We see them constantly without understanding them in the least. You ask me what day is. I dare not popularize this serious physical question for you. Know simply that, like you, scientists are unable to account for light. Each one has formed his own pet theory in support of his argument; yet the world is none the less lit up. But, to my great honor be it said, I can attempt to popularize the phenomenon of night. First of all understand that night does not exist."

"Night does not exist, brother Mederic? Yet I see it."

"Well, my beauty, close your eyes and listen to me. Do you not know that man's intelligence alone sees clearly. The eyes are a gift than can easily mislead. It is certain that night does not exist, if day does. You will soon understand me. In summer, at harvest time, when the sun scorches and travelers cannot bear the glare of the white roads, they seek a wall, in the shadow of which they walk in comparative darkness. We are at the present moment walking in the shade of the earth, in what is popularly called complete darkness! Though travelers walk in the shade, do not the neighboring fields still enjoy the sun's rays? And though we cannot see and do not know where to place our feet, has the infinite lost a single ray of light? Therefore night does not exist if day does."

"Why this last restriction, brother? Can it be possible day does not exist?"

"Certainly, my beauty, day does not exist if night does. Oh! The fine diffusion of knowledge and how I wish I had a few dozen children here that I might make them forget their toys! Listen : light is not one of the essential conditions of space; it is undoubtedly an entirely artificial phenomenon. Our sun is waning, they say; the stars will forcibly be extinguished. Then total darkness will again hold sway in its kingdom, that kingdom of space from which we sprang. Everything considered, night exists, if day does not."

"As for me, brother, I am inclined to think that neither exists."

"It may be so, my beauty. If we could command the necessary time to acquire an abstract of all knowledge, I mean the length of several men's lives, I would prove to you by means of a third argument, that both night and day exist . But we have devoted sufficient time to physical science; let us turn to the natural ones."

Mederic and Sidoine did not stop to speak. As, after all, the only aim of their journey was to discover the Kingdom of the Happy, they descended the globe from north to south, from east to west without pausing. This way of seeking an empire certainly possessed great advantages, but it could not be said to be free of annoyance. Since the previous evening, Sidoine had risked getting colds and chilblains, by going without transition from oppressive tropical heat to the icy winds of the poles. What annoyed him most was the sudden disappearance of the sun, when he passed from one hemisphere to the other. All the lectures in the world could not have made him understand this phenomenon, which produced in his mind the same effect as the irritating alternation of light and darkness which occurs in a room when a shutter is opened and closed rapidly. You can judge from this how quickly the comrades walked. As for Mederic, more comfortably settled in his beauty's ear than on the cushions of the best hung carriage, he did not trouble much about the incidents of the journey, but sheltered himself from the cold and heat. Besides, he cared little about the flashes of day and night. The travelers had now re-entered the hemisphere where daylight reigned. Mederic popped out his head.

"My beauty," he said, "the most interesting study in natural science is that of the various races of the same animal species. On the other hand, the study of the human species offers peculiar attraction to scientists, as it claims having cost the Creator an entire day's labor, and that it does not belong to the same order of creation as other creatures. We will therefore examine the various races of mankind. Keep in the sunlight so as to see our brethren, and to be able to read the truth of my statements on their faces. You can convince yourself, at the first glance, that to a disinterested observer the countenances are equally ugly in all countries. I know that in every land they discern features of rare beauty in some; but this is mere imagination, as the different races do not agree on the subject of absolute beauty, each worshipping what his neighbor despises; a truth is true, if it be always true and true for all. I will not lay greater stress on universal ugliness. There are four human races——you see them at your feet——the black, red, yellow, and white. There are certainly intermediate shades; by seeking, one could manage to establish the entire scale, from black to white, passing through all colors. One question, the only one I intend to go deeply into to-day, presents itself at the outset to the man who wishes to popularize successfully. Here it is. Was Adam white, L yellow, red, or black? If I affirm he was white, being white' myself, I do not know how to explain the peculiar changes of color which have arisen amongst my brethren. As they, no doubt, all picture the first man as like themselves, they are as perplexed as I am when they look on me. We will admit that the question is a knotty one. Learned scientists would perhaps explain the fact by the various influences of climate and food, by a hundred fine reasons difficult to foresee and comprehend. As for me, I popularize, and you will have no trouble in understanding me. My beauty, if to-day one sees men of four colors, black, red, yellow, and white, it is because God in the beginning created four Adams, one white, one yellow, one red, and one black."

"Brother Mederic, your explanation fully satisfies me. But tell me, isn't it somewhat impious? Where would be the universal brotherhood of men? Besides, is there not a holy book in existence, dictated by God Himself, which speaks of only one Adam? I am simple-minded, and it would be wrong of you to tempt me to think evil."

"My beauty, you are too exacting. I cannot be right without proving others to be wrong. No doubt my view of the matter, which is, moreover, a personal one, attacks an old belief worthy of respect on account of its great age. But how can it harm God if we study His work freely as He has allowed us this freedom? Discussing His work is not denying Him. Even were I to deny the Creator under one form, it would be to present Him to you in another. Ah, my beauty, I am popularizing theology now! Theology is the science of God."

"Good," interrupted Sidoine, "I am acquainted with that . To master it one only needs an upright mind. Here, at last, is a simple science which does not require reasoning out."

"What are you saying, my beauty? Theology a simple science! Requiring no reasoning out I It is easy, certainly, for simple minds, to acknowledge a God, and to limit science to that, for it allows of their being wise at small cost . But anxious minds, once having found God, make Him their God. Each one has his own, whom he has brought down to his own level, so that he may understand Him; each defends his idol, and attacks his neighbor's. This has given rise to a countless mass of books, to an endless subject for heated discussions; the manner of being of Him who is, the best method for worshipping Him, His manifestation on earth, the final end He has in view. Heaven preserve me from popularizing such a science as that. I care too much for my sanity."

Mederic ceased speaking; he was saddened by those thousand truths he had been heaving up. Sidoine, no longer hearing him, took a stride and landed in China. The inhabitants, their towns, and civilization, greatly astonished him. He determined to ask a-question.

"Brother Mederic," he said, "here is a nation which makes me wish to hear you popularize history. Surely this empire holds an important place in the annals of mankind?"

"My beauty," answered Mederic, "since you do not appear to tire of being taught, I will give you a course of universal history in a few words. My method is only simple; one of these days I mean to adapt it throughout. It rests on the insubstantiality of man. When the historian questions the centuries of the past, he beholds communities sprung from primeval simplicity, rise to the highest state of civilization, and then relapse into ancient barbarism. Thus empires rise and fall by turn. Whenever a nation fancies it has reached the height of science, that very science causes its downfall, and the world is brought back to its first state of ignorance. At the beginning of time Egypt erected her pyramids, and built her cities along the banks of the Nile. Within the shadow of her temples she solved the deep problems which humanity is still seeking to understand now. She was the first to have the idea of the unity of God and the immortality of the soul; then she expired at the close of Cleopatra's revels, carrying with her the secrets of eighteen centuries.

"Greece was then smiling, perfumed and harmonious; her name comes down to us amid shouts of liberty and sublime melodies; she peopled the heavens with her dreams, she deified marble with her chisel; soon weary of glory, weary of love, she became effaced, leaving naught but ruins to bear witness to her past glories.

"Then Rome arises, grown great on the spoils of the world. The warrior subjugates other nations, rules by written law, and loses liberty on acquiring power; she inherited the wealth of Egypt, the courage and poetry of Greece; she was all voluptuousness and splendor; but when the warrior became a courtesan, a hurricane from the north burst over the eternal city, and scattered art and civilization to the four winds."

If ever a speech made Sidoine yawn it was the one Mederic thus delivered.

"And China?" he modestly inquired.

"China!" exclaimed Mederic, "devil take you! Here my treatise on Universal History is incomplete. I have lost the spirit required for such a task. Does China exist? You think you see it, and I admit that appearances are in your favor; but open the first book on history you may come across; you will not find ten pages dealing with that empire, which those roguish geographers assert to be so extensive. Half the world has always absolutely ignored the history of the other half."

"Yet the world is not so large," remarked Sidoine.

"Moreover, my beauty, without popularizing further, I hold China in great esteem, I even fear it a little, like all that is unknown. I think I see in her the great nation of the future. In a little time when our civilization collapses, as all previous civilizations have done, the extreme East will no doubt inherit the science of the West, and will in its turn become the courteous and learned country above all others. This is a mathematical deduction of my historical method."

"Mathematical!" said Sidoine, who had just regretfully left China. "That is it, I wish to study mathematics."

"Mathematics, my beauty, have made many ungrateful persons. I consent, however, to let you taste of this' source of all truths. It is bitter; it requires time for man to become accustomed to the divine voluptuousness of eternal certitude. For, you must know, exact sciences alone give that certainty sought for in vain by philosophy."

"Philosophy! You could not speak better, brother Mederic. It appears to me that philosophy must be a very agreeable study."

"Assuredly it possesses certain attractions, my beauty. The poorer classes enjoy visiting madhouses, attracted by their taste for the extraordinary and the enjoyment they derive from the sight of human suffering. I am surprised they do not read the history of philosophy with avidity; for madmen, though philosophers, are nevertheless very entertaining fools. Medicine"

"Medicine! Why did you not mention it sooner? I wish to be a doctor, to cure myself when I get a fever."

"So be it . Medicine is a fine science; when it cures it will become a useful one. Up to then, one can study it as an artist, without practicing it, which is more humane. It has some connection with Law, which one merely studies as an amateur, out of curiosity, and never troubles about afterwards."

"Then, brother Mederic, I see no drawback to commencing with the study of law."

"A few words about rhetoric to begin with, my beauty."

"Yes, rhetoric suits me fairly well"

"In Greek"

"Greek, I ask nothing better."

"In Latin"

"Latin first of all, then Greek, just as you please, brother Mederic; but would it not be as well to make a start with English, German, Italian, Spanish, and other modern languages ?"

"Oh, dear me, my beauty!" cried Mederic, out of breath, "let us popularize in measure, I beg of you. My mouth is parched. I humbly admit I can only utter a certain number of words a minute. Each science, if it please God, shall have its turn. Pray let us have some method. My first lesson is not precisely remarkable for the clearness with which it was expounded, nor for the logical connection of the subjects. Let us continue talking, if it pleases you; but in future let us talk in the orderly and calm manner which signalizes the conversation of respectable people."

"Brother Mederic, your wise words give me food for thought. I care little to speak, and even less to listen, as in the second instance I have to think in order to understand, a task which is unnecessary in the first. I should certainly like to sound the depths of all human knowledge; but really I would prefer to remain ignorant of it all my life, if you cannot convey it to me in a few words."

"Well, my pet, why did you not tell me of your horror of detail? From the beginning, without speaking, I would by means of a gesture have given you the gist of a thousand and one truths. Listen no longer, look. This is supreme science."

Saying this Mederic climbed on to Sidoine's nose, the nose he had compared to the steeple of his village church. He sat astride on the tip, his legs dangling in space. Then he leant slightly back, looking at his comrade in a sly and bantering manner. He next raised his right hand wide open, placed his thumb at the tip of his own nose, and, turning to the four points of the horizon, saluted the earth by playing with his fingers in the air in the most gallant manner conceivable

"Well, then," said Sidoine, "The dunces are not those one thinks. Many thanks for your popularizing."

X. VARIOUS STRANGE AND UNFORESEEN MEETINGS WHICH HAPPENED TO SIDOINE AND MEDERIC

When night came Sidoine stopped short. I say night, and express myself badly. The periods we term night and day did not exist for people following the course of the sun, making day and night according to their fancy. In truth, our travelers had been scouring the world for about twelve hours.

"My fists itch," said Sidoine.

"Scratch them, my beauty," answered Mederic. "I can suggest no other means of relief. But, tell me, has not education softened your bellicose temperament a bit?"

"No, brother. To tell the truth, my profession of king sickened me of blows. Men are really too easy to kill."

"That, my beauty, is humanity well understood. Come! Continue walking. You and I know we are in search of the Kingdom of the Happy."

"Do I know it! Are we really seeking the Kingdom of the Happy?"

"Why, we are doing nothing else. Man never went so directly to his goal. That kingdom must be strangely situated, I admit, to escape us so completely. Perhaps it would be as well to ask our way."

"Yes, brother, let us pay attention to the roads if we wish them to lead us anywhere."

At that moment Sidoine and Mederic found themselves on a highway not far from a town. On both sides stretched extensive parks enclosed by low walls, over which hung branches of fruit-trees laden with apples, pears, and peaches, appetizing to the eye, and which would have sufficed for the dessert of an army.

As they advanced, they perceived a miserable-looking man seated against one of these walls. On their approaching him, the poor creature rose, dragging his feet and shaking with hunger.

"Charity, my kind gentlemen!" he asked.

"Charity!" exclaimed Mederic to him. "I don't know where it is to be found, my friend. Have you lost your way the same as we? You would do us a favor if you could tell us where to find the Kingdom of the Happy."

"Charity, my kind gentlemen," repeated the beggar. "I have not eaten for three days."

"Not eaten for three days!" said Sidoine, astonished. "I could not do as much."

"Not eaten for three days" resumed Mederic. "Why attempt such a thing, my good fellow? It is universally acknowledged that one must eat to live."

The man had seated himself once more at the foot of the wall. He rubbed his hands one against the other, closing his eyes from exhaustion.

"I am very hungry," he said in a low voice.

"Do you not like peaches, pears, or apples?" asked Mederic.

"I like everything, but I have nothing."

"Well, my friend, are you blind? Stretch out your hand. There, over your nose, is a magnificent peach which will give you food and drink combined."

"That peach does not belong to me," answered the beggar.

The two comrades looked at each other amazed at this answer, and not knowing whether to laugh or lose their temper.

"Listen, old chap," continued Mederic, "we do not care to be trifled with. If you have made a bet that you will die of hunger, win your wager in your own way. If, on the contrary, you wish to live as long as possible, eat and digest in the sunshine."

"Sir," answered the beggar, "I see you are a stranger in this country. You would otherwise know that one can easily die of hunger here without having made a bet to do so. Here, some eat and some do not. Each belongs to one or the other class, according to the accident of one's birth. Moreover, this is an accepted state of things; you must have come from a distance to be surprised at it."

"What strange stories. And how many are there of you who do not eat?"

"Why, several hundred thousand."

"Well, brother Mederic interrupted Sidoine, "this meeting seems to me one of the strangest and most unforeseen. I could not have believed that there existed on the earth people who possessed the peculiar gift of living without eating. You evidently did not popularize everything for me."

"My beauty, I was unaware of this peculiarity. I should advise naturalists to study it as a fresh and well-defined trait dividing the human from other animal species. I understand now that, in this country, peaches do not belong to everybody. The meanness of man has its grandeur. When all do not share a common wealth, there arises from this injustice a beautiful and supreme justice, which protects the goods of each individual."

The beggar had resumed his sweet and heartrending smile. He was bowed down as though forgetful of all, yielding himself to the will of heaven. He muttered again, in his drawling voice:

"Charity, my kind gentlemen!"

"Charity, my man," said Mederic, "I know not where it is. This peach is not yours and you do not dare take it, thus obeying the laws of your country, and conforming to those ideas of respect for the property of others, that you imbibed with your mother's milk. Those are good beliefs which must be well instilled into men if they do not wish the frail scaffolding of their society to fall beneath the attack of the first inquiring mind. I who do not belong to that society, who refuse to fraternize with my brethren, can set their laws at defiance without in the least injuring their legislation or their moral creeds. So take this fruit, poor wretch, and eat it. If I damn myself, I do it with a light heart."

While speaking thus, Mederic gathered the peach and offered it to the beggar. The latter seized the fruit which he looked at longingly. Then, instead of biting into it, he threw it back over the wall into the park. Mederic watched him without expressing surprise.

"My beauty," said he to Sidoine, "pray look at that man. He is the truest type of humanity. He suffers, he obeys; he 'is proud of suffering and of obeying. I consider him a very wise man."

Sidoine took several strides, sad at heart at thus forsaking a poor fellow dying of hunger. Yet he did not Endeavour to account to himself for the poor wretch's conduct; he would have had to have been more man than he was to solve such a problem. Before starting he had picked up the peach; and he was now looking about him for a less scrupulous beggar to whom he could give it.

As he drew near the town, he saw a party of rich lords come out from one of the gates, accompanying a litter on which an old man was reclining. When ten paces off, he perceived that the old man was barely over forty; age could not have withered his features or whitened his hair. Surely the poor wretch was dying of hunger, to judge by the pallor of his face, and the weakness that rendered his limbs so languid.

"Brother Mederic," said Sidoine, "offer my peach to this poor person. I cannot understand how he lacks everything while reclining in velvet and silk. But he looks so ill that he can only be a pauper."

Mederic thought like his beauty.

"Sir," said he politely to the man in the litter, "no, doubt you have not eaten this morning. Life has its accidents."

The man half opened his eyes.

"I have not eaten for ten years past," he answered.

"What did I say!" exclaimed Sidoine. "The poor fellow."

"Alas!" resumed Mederic, "it must be double suffering to lack bread amidst the luxury surrounding you. Here, my friend, take this peach, satisfy your hunger."

The man did not even open his eyes. He shrugged his shoulders.

"A peach," said he; "inquire if my bearers are thirsty. This morning, my maids, lovely girls with bare arms, knelt before me offering me their baskets full of the fruits they had just gathered in my orchards. The smell of all that food sickened me."

"Then you are not a beggar?" interrupted Sidoine, disappointed.

"Beggars eat sometimes. I have told you I never do so."

"And this horrible malady is called?"

Mederic understanding the complaint of this poor fellow bedecked with jewels and lace, undertook to answer Sidoine.

"This ailment is that of poor millionaires," he said. "It has no scientific name, as drugs have no effect upon it; it is cured by a strong dose of poverty. My beauty, if this nobleman no longer eats, it is because he has too much to devour."

"Well," exclaimed Sidoine, "this is a very strange world! That one does not eat, when one has no peaches, I can understand, up to a certain point; but I decline to accept as logic, the fact that one also does not eat, when one owns forests of fruit-trees. In what absurd country are we, pray?"

The man in the litter slightly raised himself, roused from his lethargy by Sidoine's simplicity.

"Sir," he replied, "you are in the heart of the country of advanced civilization. Pheasants are very expensive; silly dogs will ho longer have them. Heaven preserve you from the feasts of this world. I am going to a worthy woman of my acquaintance, to try and eat a slice of good black bread. Your healthy appearance has given me an appetite."

The man lay down again, and the procession slowly resumed its way. Sidoine, following it with his eyes, shrugged his shoulders, shook his head and snapped his fingers, thus giving very evident signs of disdain and surprise. Then he stepped over the town, his hands still holding the peach he found such difficulty in giving away. Mederic was wrapt in thought .

At the end of a dozen strides Sidoine experienced a slight resistance at his left leg. He thought his trousers had come in contact with some brambles; but, having stooped down, he was very much astonished; it was a man of covetous and cruel appearance who thus impeded his advance. This man was simply demanding the traveler's purse.

Sidoine imagined he saw naught but hungry beggars on the road, and was anxious to display his newly acquired charity. He did not clearly hear the man's request, so he seized him by the nape of the neck, and raised him to the level of his face, in order to talk more freely.

"Hallo! Poor devil," he said to him, "are you not hungry? I willingly give you this peach, if it can allay your sufferings."

"I am not hungry," answered the brigand uneasily, "I have just left an

excellent tavern, where I have been eating and drinking enough to last me
for three days."

"Then what do you require of me?"

"Mine would be a fine trade if I waylaid travelers merely to take peaches
from them. I want your purse?"

"My purse! And what for, since you will not feel hungry for three days?"

"To become rich."

Sidoine, amazed, placed Mederic in his other hand. He looked at him
seriously.

"Brother," said he, "the people of this country have agreed to make
game of us. God cannot have created beings so devoid of common sense.
Now, here is an idiot who is not hungry, and yet waylays travelers to demand
their purses, a madman who has a good appetite, and who seeks to lose it
in becoming rich."

"You are right," answered Mederic, "all this is perfectly ridiculous. Only
you seem to me not to quite understand the class of beggar you are holding in your hand. Thieves make it their business to accept only the gifts
they take."

"Listen," then said Sidoine to the brigand. "First of all you shall not
have my purse, and for a very good reason. Besides, I think it right to in-
flict a slight chastisement on you. Everything considered, that which is
should be; I cannot let you eat in peace, when I have just left a poor fellow
dying of hunger. Brother Mederic will one day read me the statutes, so that
I may return and hang you in due form. To-day I will content myself with
washing your ugly face in the pond at my feet. Drink sufficient for three
days, my friend."

Sidoine loosened his hold, and the thief fell into the pond. An honest
man would have been drowned; the rogue saved himself by swimming.

The travelers continued on their way without looking back, Sidoine still
holding his peach, and Mederic pondering over the three last meetings.

"My beauty," suddenly said the latter, "you string your sentences together in fine style now. You never spoke so well before."

"Oh !" answered Sidoine, "it is a habit easy to acquire. I no longer fight,
I talk."

"Be quiet, please, I wish to acquaint you with some serious reflections.
I am reconstructing in my mind the sad state of society, which has been able
to place before us in less than an hour, an honest man dying of hunger, a
rogue who has had enough to eat for three days, and a powerful man rendered impotent. There is much to be learned from this."

"No more teaching, for pity's sake, brother. I simply wish to believe that to-day we have met men of peculiar races which have not yet been de-scribed by any traveler."

"I understand you, my beauty. I have read many curious details in old books. There are countries where the inhabitants have but one eye in the center of the forehead, others where their bodies are half man and half horse, others still where their heads and chests are all one. Without doubt we are now crossing a country where people carry their minds in their heels, which prevents them judging things clearly, and makes them act and speak in a remarkably absurd manner. They are monsters. Man created after the image of his Maker, is a far superior being."

"That is it, brother Mederic, we are in a land of monsters. Now look! Do you see this fourth beggar whom I was expecting, coming towards us? Is he not sufficiently ragged, thin, famished, and scared? For certain he is walking on his mind, as you were saying just now."

The man who was approaching kept to the edge of the ditch, delight-ing in performing feats of equilibrium. He advanced, his hands behind his back, carrying his head high; his thin clothes hung on his poor body, his face expressed I know not what strange medley of happiness and suffering. He appeared to be dreaming, on an empty stomach, of a rich and plentiful feast.

"I shall be unable to understand the world at all," resumed Sidoine, "if this vagrant refuses my peach. He is dying of hunger, and seems to be nei-ther a rogue nor an honest man. The thing is to offer it him politely. Brother Mederic, undertake this delicate task."

Mederic stepped down to the ground. As he stood on the tip of Sidoine's shoe the man noticed him.

"Oh!" said he, "what a pretty little insect! My charming fellow, do you drink dew and feed on flowers?"

"Sir," answered Mederic, "pure water disagrees with me, and I cannot endure perfumes, for they give me the headache."

"Hallo I the insect speaks! What a fortunate meeting I You relieve me of great embarrassment, my charming beetle."

"So, you admit you are hungry."

"Hungry! Did I say that? Certainly I am ever hungry."

"And you would willingly eat a peach?'

"The peach is a fruit I appreciate, on account of the velvety down of its skin. But thank you; I cannot eat. I have at last found what I have been seeking for the past hour."

"Well," said Sidoine, out of patience, "what were you seeking, my fam-ished one, if it was not a morsel of bread?"

"Good !" exclaimed the poor fellow, "a second find! A giant in flesh and blood. Sir giant, I was seeking an ideal.

At this answer Sidoine sat down by the roadside, anticipating long explanations.

"An idea," resumed he, "what sort of dish is that?"

"Sir Giant," continued the man, without answering, "I am a born poet. You are aware that poverty is the mother of genius. I have therefore cast my purse into the stream. Since that happy day I leave to fools the sad task of seeking their food. I, who no longer need to trouble myself with this detail, seek for ideas along the roadside. I eat as little as possible, in order to acquire as much genius as I can. Do not waste your pity on me; I am really only hungry when I do not meet with my precious ideas. What fine feasts I have occasionally. Just now, on seeing your graceful little friend, two or three exquisite stanzas came to my mind; a harmonious meter, rich rhymes, and a most brilliant conclusion. Imagine if I did not have my fill. Then, when I beheld you, I honestly feared the after effects of such a treat. I had an antithesis, a very good antithesis; the most dainty morsel that can be served to a poet . You see for yourself that I cannot accept your peach."

"Good heavens!" exclaimed Sidoine after a moment's silence, "this country is even more absurd than I thought. Here is a strange madman."

"My beauty," answered Mederic, "this is a madman, but a harmless one, a generous beggar, giving men more than he receives at their hands. I feel that I love the highways and the pleasant chase after ideas as he does. Let us weep or laugh, if you will, at seeing him great and ridiculous; but pray let us not place him in the same category as the three monsters we met a while ago."

"Rank him as you please, brother," resumed Sidoine in a bad temper. "The peach is still on my hands, and these four fools have so disturbed my thoughts concerning the fruits of the earth, that I dare not bite it."

The poet, meanwhile, had seated himself by the roadside and was writing with his finger in the dust. A pleasant smile brightened his haggard face, giving a childlike expression to his worn features. In his dream, he heard Sidoine's last words, and as though waking up he said:

"Sir, is that peach really in your way? Give it me. I know of a bush near here which is idolized by the sparrows of the neighborhood. I will place your offering upon it, and I can promise you that it will not be refused. Tomorrow I will come for the stone and will plant it in some corner for the sparrows of future springs.

He took the peach and resumed writing.

"My beauty," said Mederic, "our offering is now bestowed. To ease your mind I would point out to you that we are returning to the sparrows what belonged to them. In regard to ourselves, as men do not enjoy, providential food, we will Endeavour not to eat what Heaven sends us any more. Our passage through this country has given rise in our minds to new and sad problems. We will study them shortly. At present let us be satisfied with seeking the Kingdom of the Happy."

The poet was still writing lying down in the dust, his bare head exposed to the sun's rays.

"Hallo! Sir," Mederic called out, "can you direct us to the Kingdom of the Happy?"

"The Kingdom of the Happy?" answered the madman, raising his head; "you could not have applied to any one better informed. I often visit that country."

"What! Is it near here? We have traversed the world • without finding it."

"The Kingdom of the Happy, sir, is everywhere and nowhere. Those who follow the beaten tracks with eyes wide open, those who seek it like a kingdom of the earth displaying its towns and fields to the light of day, will pass it by, their whole life long, without ever discovering it . Extensive though it be, it occupies but little space in this world."

" And the road to it, I pray you?"

"Ohl the road is plain and direct. In whatever country you may find yourself, whether at the north or south, the distance is the same, and with a stride you can cross the frontier."

"Good!" interrupted Sidoine; "this concerns me. In which direction must I take that stride?"

"It does not signify in which direction, I tell you. Come, let me introduce you. First of all close your eyes. Good. Now, raise your leg."

Sidoine, with closed eyes, and his leg in the air, waited a moment.

"Set down your foot," ordered the poet; "now you are there, gentlemen."

He had not moved from his dusty bed, and was quietly finishing a stanza.

Sidoine and Mederic were already right in the center of the Kingdom of the Happy.

XI. A MODEL SCHOOL

"Have we reached our destination, brother?" asked Sidoine. "I am tired and in great need of a throne to rest on."

"Let us walk on, my beauty," answered Mederic. "We must become acquainted with our kingdom. The country seems to me peaceful. We shall be able to lie late a-bed in the morning, I think. To-night we will rest."

The two travelers crossed towns and fields, gazing around. Earth having saddened them, they found relaxation in the clear horizons and silent crowds of this isolated corner of the universe. I have said that the Kingdom of the Happy was not a paradise of streams flowing with milk and honey, but a country of subdued light and saintly quietude.

Mederic understood the admirable equilibrium of this kingdom. A ray the less and it would have been night; one ray more and the light would have been overpowering. He said to himself that here must be the abode of wisdom, where man consented to mete out to himself both good and evil, to accept his condition under heaven without rebelling either by his affections or his crimes.

As he and his companion advanced, they came upon a barn, surrounded by iron railings, and standing in the center of a field. Mederic recognized the model school founded by the charming Primrose for her dear animals. He had long wished to know the results of this attempt at perfection.

He made Sidoine lie down at the foot of the wall; then both, resting their foreheads against the railings, were able to contemplate and follow in all its details, a strange scene which completed their education.

At first sight they did not know what curious creatures were before them. Three months' pampering, of mutual instruction and frugal diet, had quite tired out the poor animals. The lions, bald and mangy, looked like enormous gutter cats; the wolves carried their heads low, and were more crestfallen than homeless dogs; as to the other beasts of a delicate kind, they lay pell-mell on the ground, displaying naught but fleshless ribs and elongated muzzles. The birds and insects were even less recognizable, having lost their beautiful colorings and gloss. All these miserable creatures were trembling with hunger and cold, no longer being what the Almighty had created them, but finding themselves on the other hand perfectly civilized.

Mederic and Sidoine succeeded, by degrees, in recognizing the various animals. In spite of their respect for progress and the benefits of instruction, they could not help pitying these victims of good. It is sad to see creation decay.

The animals of the model school dragged themselves moaning to the center of the barn; there they ranged themselves in a circle. They were about to hold a council.

A lion, having preserved most breath, spoke first.

"My friends," said he, "the dearest wish of us all who have the happiness to be shut up here, is to persevere in the excellent spirit of brotherhood and perfection which we are following with such astonishing results."

A grunt of approval interrupted him.

"There is no need for me," he resumed, "to go through the delightful list of the rewards which await our efforts. We shall constitute a single people in the future, we shall have but one language; while it will be a great joy for each of us to be no longer himself and to ignore who he is. Have you pictured the delight of that hour when distinction of races will cease to exist, when all animals will have only one thought, one taste, one interest? What a glorious day, my friends, and how merry it will be!"

Another grunt testified to the unanimous satisfaction 0f the assembly.

As our prayers are hastening the advent of that day," continued the lion, "it would be advisable to take measures to ensure our witnessing its arrival. The regimen pursued here, up till now, is certainly excellent, but I think it is not very substantial. First of all we must live, and we are growing thinner and thinner; death cannot be far off if, in the praiseworthy desire to feed our souls, we continue to neglect feeding our bodies. It would really be too absurd .to attempt to reach a paradise which we could not enjoy, on account of the means employed to attain it. A radical reform is necessary. Milk is a very moralizing food, of easy digestion, which singularly softens customs; but I think I sum up all opinions in saying that we can no longer stand milk, that nothing is more tasteless, and finally, that we require a more varied and less sickening ordinary."

A perfect ovation of howls and a noise of opening and closing of jaws greeted the orator's concluding words. The hatred of milk was popular amongst these worthy animals, who had lived on this luscious beverage for three months. The daily bowl made them feel ill. Ah, how sweet a little gall would have seemed to them!

When silence reigned once more the lion resumed: "My friends, the subject of our discussion is therefore decided on. We are holding a council to proscribe milk, and to replace it by a food which would, while fattening us, at the same time assist us towards good thoughts. Thus we are each going to propose our dish; then we will decide in favor of that which receives the greatest number of votes. That dish will henceforth constitute the ordinary for all of us. I think it useless to impress upon you the frame of mind that should guide you in your choice. It is the utter abnegation of your personal tastes, the search for a food that would suit each one equally well, and above all afford guarantees of morality and health."

At this point of the address enthusiasm was at its height. Nothing is pleasanter than to lay stress upon morality when the stomach has been previously lined. One sole thought, a touching unanimity of feeling ruled the assembly.

The lion, on his side, discoursed in a humble and affable manner. His eyes cast down, he would have converted his brethren of the desert, he presented such an edifying spectacle. By a sign he again secured attention, and wound up with these words:

"I consider myself authorized, by reason of my long experience, to be the first to give you my advice on this delicate subject. I will do so with all the modesty which beseems a simple member of this assembly; but also with all the authority of a beast who is convinced. That is to say, I despair of our future unity if my dish is not unanimously accepted. On my soul and conscience, having long meditated on the food which would suit us best, taking into consideration our common interests, I declare, I affirm resolutely, that nothing will satisfy the stomach and the heart of each of us, so well as a large slice of raw meat eaten in the morning, a second slice at noon, and a third at night."

The lion paused to receive the just applause that his proposal seemed to him to deserve. He was of good faith, and was astonished at the paucity of grunts. Farewell unanimity. The assembly no longer approved with unreservedly. The wolves and remaining wild beasts, the birds and insects of sanguinary appetites, applauded the excellence of the choice. But animals of other species, those which live in the meadows or at the edges of pools, bore witness, by their silence and sad expressions, to the slight civilizing virtue they granted flesh.

Some minutes elapsed full of enmity and uneasiness. One risks much in disputing the advice of the powerful, especially when they talk in the name of fraternity. At length a sheep more venturesome than her sisters, decided on speaking.

"As we are here," she said, "to express our opinions frankly, let me give you mine with the simplicity which suits my nature. I admit that I have no experience of the dish proposed by my brother the lion; it may be excellent for the stomach, and of exquisite taste; I must ask to be excused in regard to that point of the discussion. But I think this food would have a bad influence on morality. One of the firmest foundations of our progress should be respect for life; it is not respecting it to feed ourselves on dead bodies. Does not my brother the lion fear being led astray by his zeal, of starting an endless war, in selecting such an ordinary, instead of arriving at that beautiful unity he spoke of so eloquently? I know we are honest beasts; it is not a question of devouring one another. Far from me so evil a thought. Since men declare they can eat us without ceasing to be good souls, creatures according to the spirit of God, we can surely eat men and remain good, brotherly animals aiming at absolute perfection. Yet I fear evil temptations, force of habit, if some day men become scarce. Therefore I cannot vote for such an imprudent diet. Believe me, one dish alone agrees with us, a food which the earth produces in abundance, healthy, refreshing, easy and amusing to collect, and extremely varied. O the luxuriant feasts, my good brothers! Lucerne, vegetables, all the grasses of the plain, all the herbs of the hillside I speak advisedly without afterthought; moved only by the innocent desire to live without killing. I tell you truly, apart from vegetarianism, there will be no unanimity."

The sheep ceased speaking and stealthily endeavored to judge the effect produced by her speech. Some faintly expressed assent rose from the quarter of the assembly occupied by horses, oxen, and other consumers of corn and herbage. As to the beasts which had approved the lion's choice, they appeared to welcome this new proposal with strange disdain, and a grimace boding ill for the orator.

A silkworm, near-sighted and devoid of tact, then began to speak. He was an austere philosopher, troubling little about the judgment of others, preaching good for good's sake.

"To live without killing," said he, "Is a fine maxim. I can only applaud the conclusion arrived at by my sister the sheep. But my sister seems to me very gluttonous. We seek for one dish and she offers us fifty; she even seems to enjoy the thought of a princely menu with numerous dishes of varied flavor. Does she forget that sobriety and a disdain for tasty morsels are virtues necessary to beasts that pride themselves on their progress? The future of a society depends on its food: to eat little and of one dish only, is the sole means of hastening the advent of high, strong, and durable civilization. I therefore propose, for my part, that we keep our appetites in check, and especially that we content ourselves with one kind of leaf. The choice being merely a matter of taste, I hope to satisfy every one's by selecting the mulberry leaf."

"Come, you old dotard," exclaimed a pelican, "are we not thin enough without running the risk of getting a stomach-ache through feeding on damp vegetation? Fraternize with the sheep. I would agree with my brother the lion, but that I think he has made a mistake in proposing red flesh. Flesh alone gives the body the strength to do good, but I mean fish's flesh, white and delicate; that is a savory food which every one likes. In conclusion, and this last argument must convince you, as the seas occupy twice the space of the continents on the globe, we could not have a more extensive larder. My brothers will appreciate these reasons."

The brothers abstained from understanding. In order to end the debate they thought it well to shout all at once. There were as many opinions as animals; no two poor minds agreeing together, no two natures alike. Each creature started gesticulating, speechifying, suggesting his food, defending it on the score of morality and gluttony. To believe them, if all the proposed dishes had been accepted, the entire world would have been made into a stew; there was nothing which was not declared to be excellent food, from leaf to wood, flesh to stone. Deep knowledge, as Mederic said, showing what the earth is, namely, a fetus but half alive, wherein life and death hold in our day contests of equal strength.

In the midst of this tumult, a young cat exerted himself to make the assembly understand that he wished to impart a decisive truth to it. He made such good use of his claws and throat that he succeeded in obtaining some quiet.

"Well," said he, "my good brethren, for pity's sake cease this discussion which grieves all tender hearts here present. My own bleeds at the sight of this painful scene. Alas! We are far from the gentle customs and wise sayings which for my part I have sought from my youth up. This is a fine subject for a quarrel, a wretched question of food, the sustenance of a perishable body. I collect your minds, and you will laugh at your anger and abandon this miserable dispute. The more or less felicitous choice of a paltry article of diet, is not worth occupying our thoughts for a moment. Let us live as we have done, merely troubling about moral reforms. Brethren, let us philosophies and drink our bowl of milk! After all, milk has a pleasant taste; I think it preferable to the dishes by which you seek to replace it."

Frightful yells greeted these last words. The young cat's unfortunate suggestion ended by making the animals furious, recalling to their minds the tasteless beverage, with which they had washed their insides for three long months. They were seized with terrible hunger, sharpened by great anger. Nature gained the upper hand. In a moment they forgot the good manners due between "civilized animals and simply flew at one another's throats. Those who had chosen flesh, having come to the end of their arguments, found it easier to preach by example. The others, having no corn, or herbage, or fish, or other dish to avenge themselves on, were content to facilitate the vengeance of their brethren.

For some minutes there was a horrible commotion. The number of famished was rapidly diminishing, without a single wounded animal remaining on the ground. It was a strange struggle in which the dead fell no one knew where. The devourer had barely time to satisfy himself, when he, in his turn, was devoured. They fattened one another; the feast began with the weakest to end with the strongest . After a quarter of an hour the ground was clear. Ten or twelve wild beasts in all, seated on their haunches, with half closed eyes, and languid limbs, satiated with food, were complacently licking their jaws.

The model school had therefore had for result the greatest possible unity, that which consists in assimilating another's soul and body to one's self. Perhaps this is the unity that man has a vague idea of, the final goal, the mysterious work of those worlds tending to confound all creatures in one being. But what bitter raillery of the thoughts of our age that promise perfection and fraternity to creatures possessing different instincts and habits, particles of dust wherein the same breath of life produces contrary effects! Without philosophizing further, lions are lions.

"Brother Mederic," said Sidoine, "there are in front of us ten or twelve scoundrels who have a heavy weight of sins on their consciences. They have spoken as well as possible, but have acted like bullies. Let me see if my fists have grown cramped."

Saying this, he struck a blow on the shed which pulverized the beams and shattered the hewn stone to pieces. The remaining animals, the sole hope of brute regeneration, did not utter a cry. Mederic seemed to regret this execution.

"Come! My beauty," he exclaimed. "Why did you not consult me? That blow will bring you sadness and remorse. Listen to me."

"What! Brother, have I not struck justly?" "Yes, according to the idea we have of right. But, between ourselves, and I say it softly so as not to disturb a necessary belief, are not good and evil part of human creation? Does a wolf really commit crime when he eats a lamb? Man, the friend of the lamb, who would take him a dish of vegetables, is he not more ridiculous than the wolf is guilty?"

"Brother, do you mean to draw from this a logical conclusion, that good and evil do not exist?"

"Perhaps so, my beauty. You see we too often seek to hasten the time appointed by God. There are certain laws, no doubt, of divine origin, which we cannot account for, and to which we have given the ugly name of fatalities. We admit, by a rare blasphemy, that evil may have been created, and we set ourselves up as judges, rewarding and punishing because our intellect is too feeble to grasp everything; and to show us justice of your blow. You have punished these beasts for acting according to the laws by which they must live. You judged them egotistically, from the purely human stand-point, influenced especially by that fear of death which has given man re-spect for life. In short, you were scandalized at seeing one race devour another, when you yourself do not scruple to feed on the flesh of both."

"Brother Mederic, speak more clearly, or I shall not feel the least re-morse for my blow."

"I understand you, my beauty. After all I am willing: evil exists, and this dispenses me with proving that absolute good is impossible. Besides, the ruins on which we are seated are a proof of it. But, tell me, did you wish to eat these wild animals?"

"Certainly not. I am not partial to big game."

"Then, my dear fellow, why kill them?"

Sidoine looked very foolish when this question was put to him. He sought for an answer which he did not find. The greatest surprise was de-picted in his large blue eyes. Then, as a man who has at last discovered a truth, he exclaimed:

"Why, my blow was absurd, as you said. One should only kill to eat. That is a very practical precept which

Perceive the absurd embodies, in the highest degree, the relative and human justice of which you have told me. Men should write it in letters of gold on the walls of their tribunals and on the standards of their armies. Alas! My poor fists! One should only kill to eat."

XII. MORAL

The sun had just disappeared behind the western hills. The earth, veiled in a soft shadow, was already half slumbering, pensive and melancholy. A white opaque sky overhung the horizon. There comes each evening a time of great sadness; it is not yet night, light is fading slowly away as though re-gretfully; and man in this farewell, feels strange anxiety, a great need of hope and faith in his heart . The first rays of morning bring songs to one's lips; the last rays of evening bring tears to one's eyes. Is it the dispiriting thought of labor constantly resumed, unceasingly abandoned; the eager wish, mingled with dread, for eternal rest? Is it the resemblance of every-thing human to that slow agony of light and sound?

Sidoine and Mederic had seated themselves on the ruins of the shed. A star shone above the dark branches of an oak tree, amid the evanescence of earth and sky. And they both looked at this consoling light, piercing with a ray of hope the mournful veil of twilight.

The sound of a sobbing voice brought their eyes back to the path. They beheld Primrose, all white in the darkness, advancing towards them between the hedges. She came along slowly with hair unbound.

She seated herself by Mederic's side. Then, resting her head on his shoulder, said:

"O friend, how wicked animals are!"

And clasping her hands together she wept freely, letting the tears run down her cheeks without seeking to wipe them away.

"Poor despised creatures," she continued, "I loved them like sisters. I thought that by petting them, I had made them forget their fangs and claws. Is it then so difficult to keep from being cruel?"

Mederic was careful not to answer. The science of good and evil was not intended for this child.

"Tell me," said he, "are you not the charming Primrose, queen of the Kingdom of the Happy?"

"Yes," she replied, "I am Primrose."

"Then, my darling, dry your tears. I am come to marry you."

Primrose wiped her eyes; and placing her hands in Mederic's, she gazed into his face.

"I am only an ignorant creature," she said softly. "Here are wicked eyes, which however do not frighten me. There is kindness, beneath I know not what sad raillery, in those orbs. Do you need my caresses to become better?"

"I need them," answered Mederic; "I have traveled the world and am weary."

"Heaven is kind," resumed the child. "It does not allow my love rest . I will marry you, dear lord."

Having said this she again sat down. She was thinking of that feeling of unknown pity which was rising within her; she had never before experienced such a desire to console. She inquired of herself, in her simplicity, whether she had not at last discovered the mission entrusted by God to the tenderhearted and charitable young queens of this world. Men enjoy such perfect happiness that they get vexed at the slightest favor; animals have a bad character difficult to understand. Surely, since Heaven had given her tears and the inclination to caress, she could not in her turn bestow them upon any other creature save her dear lord, who had told her he stood in great need of them. To conceal nothing, she felt herself quite another being; she no longer thought of her people, she completely forgot her poor pupils on whose tomb she was sitting. Her love, offered to all creation, and which creation refused, had just become greater in being fixed on a single being. She was lost in this infinity, heedless of the world, ignorant of evil, realizing that she was obeying God, and that one hour of such ecstasy is preferable to a thousand years of progress and civilization.

All three, Primrose, Sidoine and Mederic, were silent. Around them reigned immense stillness, large indistinct shadows transformed the country into a lake of gloom, with heavy and motionless waves: above their heads was a moonless sky studded with stars, a black vault riddled with golden holes. There, on the ruins of the model school, each following his own train of thought, and with the world at their feet, they sat musing in the darkness. Primrose, slight and supple, had passed her arms around Mederic's neck, and was leaning upon his breast, her eyes wide open, gazing into the night. Sidoine, half reclining, ashamed and despairing, was hiding his fists and thinking in spite of himself.

Suddenly he spoke, and his rough voice wore an accent of indescribable sadness.

"Alas! brother Mederic," he said, "how empty my poor head is since the day when you stored it with thoughts I Where are my mangy wolves which I destroyed with such glee, my fine potato-fields that the neighbors planted, my fearless Stupidity which protected me from bad dreams?"

"My beauty," asked Mederic softly, "do you regret our wanderings and the science we have acquired?"

"Yes, brother, I have seen the world and have not understood it. You endeavored to make me spell it out, but your lessons had a certain bitterness which has disturbed my peaceful tranquility. At the start I had instinctive beliefs, an implicit faith in my natural whims: at the journey's end I can no longer see my life clearly. I do not know where to go nor what to do."

"I admit, my beauty, that I have taught you in a haphazard way. But tell me, in this mass of sciences, imprudently disturbed, do you not recall some real and practical truths?"

"Well, brother Mederic, it is exactly those beautiful truths which sadden me. I know now that the earth, with its fruits and harvests, does not belong to me; I even doubt my right to amuse myself by killing flies on the walls. Could you not have spared me the terrible agony of thought? Ah, I absolve you now from your promise."

"What had I promised you, my beauty?"

"To give me a throne to fill and men to slay. My poor fists, what can I do with them now? Are they not useless enough and in the way! I shall not have courage to raise them against a gnat. We find ourselves in a kingdom which is wisely indifferent to human grandeur and misery; no war, no court, hardly a king. Alas! And it is we who are this shadow of a monarch. This is no doubt the punishment of our ridiculous ambition. Brother Mederic, I beg you, calm my troubled mind."

"Do not be anxious, do not upset yourself, my beauty, we have reached our destination. It was written-that we should be kings, but that is a fatality for which we shall be able to console ourselves. Our travels have had the excellent result of changing our former thoughts of power and conquests. In this sense, our reign over the Blues was a training as salutary as it was rough. Destiny has its logic. We must thank fate that, unable to dispense with royalty, it has given us a fine kingdom, as extensive and fertile as we could wish, wherein we will live as honest men. In following the calling of honorary king, we shall at least gain liberty, not having to bear the burden of the duty ; we will grow old in our dignity: enjoying our crown as misers, I mean by showing it to no one; thus, our existence will have a noble aim, that of leaving our subjects undisturbed, and our reward will be the peace they will give us. My beauty, do not despair. We are about to resume our careless life, forgetful of all painful sights, all the evil thoughts of the world we have just traveled over; we are going to be perfectly ignorant and have no other care than that of loving one another. In our royal domains, in the sunshine in winter, beneath the oak trees in summer, my mission will be to fondle Primrose, while hers will consist in returning me two caresses for one; you, as you could not keep your fists at rest without being bored to death, shall during this time dig our fields, sow them with corn, reap the harvests, gather the vintage, so that we shall eat bread and drink wine belonging to us. We will never kill again, not even to eat. On these points alone do I consent to remain wise. As I told you at starting, 'I will set you such a fine task that in a thousand years the world will still talk of your fists.' For laborers of the future will marvel when passing through these fields. On seeing their eternal fertility, they will say among themselves, 'King Sidoine formerly worked here.' I foretold it, my dear fellow; your fists were destined to be the fists of a king; only they will be the fists of a working king, the finest, the rarest in existence."

On hearing these words, Sidoine could not contain himself for joy. His duty in the household seemed to him by far the most agreeable, as it was that which required the greatest strength.

"Egad! brother," he exclaimed, "Reasoning is a fine thing when one reasons wisely. I am quite consoled. I am king and reign over my field. Nothing could be better. You will see my fine vegetables, my corn as tall as reeds, my vintages fit to intoxicate a province. Ah! I was born to wrestle with the earth. From to-morrow, I will work and sleep in the sun. I will think no more."

As Sidoine finished speaking he crossed his arms and went off into a half doze. Primrose was still gazing into the darkness, smiling, her arms round Mederic's neck and hearing only the beating of her friend's heart.

After a pause the latter resumed, "My beauty, I have to finish with a speech. It will be the last, I vow. All history, it is said, requires a moral. If ever some poor creature, weary of silence, takes it into his head to relate the astounding story of our adventures, he will certainly cut the silliest figure imaginable in the eyes of his readers, in that he will appear to them perfectly absurd if he sticks to the truth. I even fear he may be stoned, on account of the sound of speech and bearing of his heroes. As this poor creature will no doubt be born in later times, in the midst of a society perfect in every sense, his indifference and denials will justly offend the legitimate pride of his contemporaries. It would, therefore, be charitable before leaving the scene, to seek the morality of our adventures, so as to spare our historian the sorrow of passing for a mendacious man. However, if he has some feeling of honesty, this is what he will pen on the last page: 'Good people who have perused my work, we are, you and me, utter dunces. To our minds, nothing is so near to reason as folly. It is true I have made game of you; but before that I made game of myself. I believe man is nothing. I doubt everything else. The joke of our apotheosis has lasted too long. We lie impudently in declaring ourselves God's master-piece, the creature superior to all, for whom He created heaven and earth. No doubt, one could not imagine a more consoling fable; for if my brethren were to admit, to-morrow, what they are, they would probably go and commit suicide, each in his own corner. I do not fear to lead their reason to this extreme point of logic; they have inexhaustible charity, a copious provision of respect and admiration for their own being. Therefore, I have not even the hope of making them agree as to their nothingness, which would have been as good a morality as any other. Besides, for a belief that I should deprive them of, I could not give them a better one; perhaps I will try later on. Today, I am full of sadness; I have related my bad dreams of the past night. I dedicate the story to humanity. My gift is worthy of it; and after all, what matters one freak more amid the freaks of the world? I shall be accused of being behind my time, of denying progress in the days most rich in conquests. Well, good people, your new lights are as yet but darkness. The great mystery escapes us now as it escaped us in the past. I am saddened as each so-called truth is discovered, for it is not the one I seek, the single and entire Truth which alone would heal my diseased mind. In six thousand years we have not been able to advance a step. If, at this hour, to spare you the trouble of considering me stark mad, you must absolutely have a moral to the adventures of my giant and dwarf, perhaps I shall satisfy you in giving you this one: 'Six thousand years and yet again six thousand years will lapse without our ever completing our first stride.' That, my beauty, is what a conscientious historian would deduce from our history. But you can imagine what fine yells would greet such an inference! I positively decline to be a cause of scandal for our brethren. From this moment, anxious to see our legend, duly authorized and approved, diffused over the world, I draw the moral as follows: 'Good people who have read me,' the poor creature will write, 'I cannot give you the fifteen or twenty morals of this story in detail. There are some for all ages, and for all conditions. It suffices that you collect your wits and interpret my words correctly. But the true moral, the most moralizing one, that which I intend turning to account in my next story, is this: When you set out for the Kingdom of the Happy, you must know the way. Are you edified? I am very glad of it.' What? Sidoine, my beauty, you do not applaud?"

Sidoine was asleep. The moon had just risen in the heavens; a soft light filled the horizon, giving a bluish tinge to space, and falling in sheets of silver from the heights, down upon the plain. The gloom had disappeared; a deeper silence reigned around. Serene sadness had succeeded the dread of the previous hour. At the first ray, Mederic and Primrose, entwined and motionless, appeared at the summit of the ruins; while at their feet lay Sidoine, radiant in the broad beams of light.

He opened one eye, and still half asleep, said, "I hear. Brother Mederic, where is wisdom?"

"My beauty," Mederic replied, "take a spade."

"I hear," said Sidoine. "Where is happiness?"

Then Primrose, unclasping her arms, slowly raised herself. She stretched out her lips and kissed Mederic on the mouth.

Sidoine, satisfied, relapsed into sleep, nodding his head twirling his thumbs, more stupid than ever!

STORIES FOR NINON II

TO NINON

It is just ten years, my dear soul, since I told you my first tales. What delightful lovers we were then! I had recently come from that land of Provence, where I had grown up so free, so confiding, so full of all the hopes of life. I belonged to you, to you alone, to your tenderness, to your dream.

Do you remember, Ninon? That remembrance is now the only joy on which my heart reposes. Until twenty we ran along the same paths together. I can hear your little feet on the hard ground, I perceive the hem of your white skirt grazing the wild plants; I feel your breath among the distant wafts of sage, which reach me like puffs of youth. Those charming hours are fresh in my memory: it was a morning, on the bank, beside the barely awakened water, all pure, all rosy with the first red rays of heaven; it was an afternoon, among the trees, in a leafy recess, with the country overcome, slumbering around us, without a rustle; it was an evening, in the middle of a field, slowly becoming enveloped in the bluish flood of twilight that stole down the hills; it was a night, walking along an endless road, both advancing towards the unknown, indifferent even to the stars, finding our pleasure in leaving the city, in Vosing ourselves far, very far away, in the depths of the discreet darkness. Do you remember, Ninon?

What a happy life! We had launched into love, art, dreamland. There is not a bush that has not hidden our kisses, smothered our chat. I led you along; I walked you about like the living poetry of my childhood. We two had heaven, earth, trees and waters, even the naked rocks that bounded the horizon, to ourselves. It seemed to me, at that age, that on opening my arms, I could take all the country on my breast, to give it a kiss of peace. I felt the strength, the desires, the kind-heartedness of a giant. Our excursions, like those of schoolboys out of bounds, our love-making, like that of the free birds, had inspired me with great contempt for the world, and a quiet belief in one's own energy. Yes, it was in your constant tenderness, my friend, that formerly I laid up that fund of courage, at which my companions, later on, were so frequently surprised. The illusions of our hearts were plates of finely tempered steel, and they still protect me.

I left you, I left that Provence of which you were the soul, and it was

177

you whom I invoked, as a good angel, from the eve of the struggle. You had my first book. It was teeming with your being, all scented with the perfume of your hair. You had dispatched me to the battle, with a kiss on the forehead, like a fond sweetheart who desires to see the soldier whom she loves conquer. And as for me, that kiss was the only thing I always remembered; I only thought of you, I could only speak of you.

Ten years have passed. Ah! My dear soul, how many tempests have roared, what a quantity of dark water, what ruins have passed since then, beneath the crumbling bridges of my dreams! Ten years of hard labor, ten years of bitterness, of blows given and received, of everlasting battle! My heart and brain are all gashed with wounds. If you were to see your sweetheart of former times, that tall, supple youth who dreamed of moving mountains in a trice, if you saw him passing along in the dim daylight of Paris, with his cadaverous countenance, heavy with weariness, you would shudder, my poor Ninon, regretting the bright sun, the fiery middays extinguished for ever. Some nights I am so broken down that I feel a cowardly desire to seat myself by the roadside, at the risk of sleeping for ever in the ditch. And do you know, Ninon, what it is that unceasingly urges me on, what gives me courage, each time I waver? It is your voice, my well-beloved, your distant voice, your pure, slender voice recalling to me my vows.

I know, indeed, that you are a courageous girl. I can unbare my wounds to you, and you will only love me the more. It will ease me to complain to you, who will console me. I have not put down the pen for a single day, my friend; I have fought as a soldier who has to earn his bread: if glory comes, it will spare me eating my bread dry. What bad work and how disgusted I still feel at it! For ten years I have fed the furnace of journalism, like so many others, with the best that was in me. Of this colossal labor there remains nothing but a few cinders. Sheets of paper cast before the wind, flowers fallen in the mire, a blend of what was excellent and the worst, all spoilt in the common trough. I have touched everything; I have dirtied my hands in this torrent of turbid mediocrity running to the overflow. My love of the absolute was bleeding, in the midst of these stupidities, so full of importance in the morning, so utterly forgotten at night. When I dreamt of some stroke given in a block of granite that would be eternal, some living labor placed erect for ever, I blew bubbles that were burst by the wings of insects buzzing in the sun. I would have glided into the habit of the calling if, in my love of power, I had not had a consolation, that of this ceaseless production, which broke me to every description of fatigue.

Then, my friend, I was armed for war. You would never believe into what fits of rage nonsense threw me. I had the passion of my opinions; I would have liked to have thrust what I believed down the throats of others. A book made me ill, a picture put me in despair, as if it were a public catastrophe; I lived in a constant battle of admiration and contempt. Beyond letters and art, the world ceased to exist. And what strokes of the pen, what furious shocks to clear the platform I Now I shrug my shoulders. I am an old, hardened offender; I have preserved my faith; I think I am even still more intractable; but I am satisfied to shut myself up and work. That is the only way to discuss things in a healthy manner; for works are only arguments, in the everlasting discussion of the beautiful.

I have not come out of the battle intact, as you very well imagine. I have scars almost everywhere, as I have told you, on the brain and heart. I no longer reply; I wait for them to become accustomed to my manner. Perhaps I shall thus return to you whole. You see, my friend, I have quitted our gallant pathways of lovers, where flowers grow, where one only gathers smiles. I have taken the high-road, grey with dust, with sorry trees; I have even, I own it, stopped curiously before dead dogs lying beside the landmarks; I have spoken of truth; I have pretended that one could write everything; I have wished to prove that art is in life and not elsewhere. Naturally they pushed me into the gutter. I, Ninon, I who passed my youth in gathering daisies and blue corn-flowers for your bosom!

You will forgive me my infidelity as a lover. Men cannot always be tied to girls' petticoats. A time comes when your flowers are too sweet. Do you remember the pale autumn evening, the evening of our farewell? It was on leaving your frail arms that Truth bore me away in her hard hands. I had a mania for correct analysis. After the ordinary daily labor, I encroached upon my nights; I wrote the books that haunted me, page by page. If I am proud of anything, it is of that will which has slowly made me independent of the calling. I have lived, without departing from my opinions. I owed you this explanation, you who have a right to know what sort of man, the child, whose beginning you encouraged, has become.

At present, my only grief is in being alone. The world ends at my garden railing. I have shut myself up at home so that my life may be entirely devoted to work, and I have so thoroughly encompassed myself that people have ceased to come. That is what has made me think of you, my dear soul, amidst the struggle. I was too lonely, after ten years' separation; I wanted to see you again, to kiss your hair, to tell you I love you always. That relieves me. Come, and be not afraid, I am not so black as I am painted. I assure you I love you still. I dream of having roses again, to place a nosegay of them in your bosom. I feel an inclination to drink new milk. If I did not fear to raise a laugh, I would take you under some hedge, with a white lamb, so that we might all three tell one another tender things.

And do you know what I have done, Ninon, to keep you beside me all this night? I will give you a thousand guesses. I have rummaged in the past, I have searched among the hundreds of pages written here and there, whether I could not find some that would be sufficiently delicate for your ears. It has given me pleasure to place this plum right in the midst of thorns. Yes, I wanted this feast for us two. We will become children again and pic-nic on the grass. They are tales; nothing but tales, jam in the toy tea-service of children. Is it not charming? Three gooseberries and two raisins will be enough to satisfy our hunger, and we will get tipsy on five drops of wine in limpid water. Listen, you inquisitive creature. I have first of all some tales that are good enough; some even that have a commencement and an end; others, it is true, go bare-footed, after having cast off all sense of propri-ety. But, I must warn you that, further on, we shall meet with fanciful things that are absolutely all at sea. To be sure! I have gleaned all I had, to keep you the whole night. There, I sing the song of "Dost thou remember?" They are our remembrances, one after the other, my girl; sweetness itself to us, the best part of our love. If they seem dry to others, so much the worse! They have no need to meddle in our affairs. Then, to retain you after that, I shall commence a long story, the last, which will take us, I hope, till morn-ing. It is right at the end of the others, placed there on purpose to send you to sleep in my arms. We will let the volume fall from our hands, and will kiss each other.

Ah! Ninon, what a wealth of pink and white! However, I cannot prom-ise that, in spite of all my care to remove the thorns, there is not a drop of blood or two in my bunch of flowers. My hands are no longer pure enough to tie up nosegays without danger. But do not be alarmed: if you prick your-self, I will kiss your fingers, I will drink your blood. The nosegay will be more fragrant.

To-morrow, I shall have grown ten years younger. It seems to me that it was but yester eve, I came from the further end of our youth, with the honey of your kiss upon my lips. It will be the beginning of my task over again. Ah! Ninon, I have done nothing yet. I weep over this mountain of paper blackened with ink; I am grieved to think that I have been unable to satisfy my thirst for reality, that vast nature escapes from my arms which are too short. I feel the fierce desire to grasp the earth, strain it to me, see all, know all, say all. I should like to lay humanity on a white page, every being, every thing; and produce a work that would be an immense ark.

And do not expect me for a long time at the trysting-place, where I promised to meet you, in Provence, when the task is completed. There is so much to be accomplished. I want truth in the novel, the drama, every-where. Remind me of you in future, only at night; come on the moonbeam that glides between my curtains, at a time when I shall be able to weep with you unseen. I require all my manhood. Later on, oh! Later on, it will be I who will go and meet you out in the country still warm with our tenderness. We shall be very old; but we shall always love one another. You shall take me on a pilgrimage to the river bank, to the edge of the barely awakened water; into the leafy recesses, with the burning country slumbering around us; .amidst the meadows, becoming gently enveloped in the bluish veil of twilight; along the endless highway, indifferent to the stars, having but one desire to lose ourselves in the obscurity. And the trees, the blades of grass, even the stones, will recognize us from a distance, by our kisses, and will bid us welcome.

Listen: so that we may not be seeking each other I want to tell you be-hind which hedge I will go and find you. You know the spot where the river makes a bend, beyond the bridge, lower down than the wash-house, just opposite the great curtain of poplars? Do you remember, we kissed hands there one fine May morning? Well! On the left, there is a hawthorn hedge, that wall of verdure at the foot of which we lay down to see only the blue of heaven. It is behind the hawthorn hedge, my dear soul, that I give you the appointment, years hence, one day when the sun is pale, when your heart will know I am in the neighborhood.

A BATH

I'll give you a thousand chances, Ninon. Seek, invent, imagine: it is a real fairy-tale, something terrifying and improbable. You know the little baroness, that delightful

Adeline de C, who had vowed No, you'll never guess: I prefer relating it all to you.

Well! Adeline is positively going to be married a second time. You doubt it, don't you? You say it is necessary to be at Mesnil-Rouge, sixty-seven leagues from Paris, to put faith in such a tale. You may laugh; the wedding will none the less take place. Fancy, that poor Adeline, who was a widow at twenty-two, and whose hatred and contempt for men made so pretty! The deceased, who was certainly a worthy man, fairly well preserved, and who would have been perfect but for the infirmities that killed him, thoroughly schooled her in matrimony in a couple of months. She had declared that her experience was sufficient. And she is marrying again! See how we are!

It is true Adeline had bad luck. An adventure such as happened to her could not have been foreseen. And supposing I were to tell you who she is about to marry! You know Count Octave de R, that tall young man whom she so cordially detested. They could not meet without exchanging ill-natured smiles, without metaphorically cutting each other's throats with pleasant phrases. Ah, the poor creatures! If you only knew where they finally met I can see very well that I shall have to tell you all about it. It is quite a novel. It rains this morning. I'll put it into chapters.

I

The chateau is six miles from Tours. From Mesnil-Rouge I can see the slate roofs buried in the verdure of the park. They call it the Chateau-of-the-Sleeping-Beauty, because it was formerly inhabited by a lord who nearly married one of his milkmaids there. The dear child lived shut up in it, and I think her ghost returned to the place. Never did stones possess such a perfume of love.

The Beauty who sleeps there now is the old Countess de M, one of Adeline's aunts. For the last thirty years she has been coming to pass a winter at Paris. Each of her nieces and nephews gives her a fortnight during the fine weather. Adeline is very punctual. Besides, she likes the chateau, a legendary ruin, which is crumbling to pieces under the influence *of rain and wind, in the centre of a virgin forest.

The elderly countess has given formal orders that neither the ceilings, which are a network of cracks, nor the stray branches that bar the walks, are to be touched. She enjoys the sight of the wall of foliage that thickens there each spring, and she frequently remarks that the building is more solid than herself. The truth of the matter is that an entire wing is on the ground. Those pleasant retreats, built under Louis XV., were as transient as the love-making of the period. The plaster-work is full of fissures, the floors have given way, and moss has penetrated even to the alcoves. The damp atmosphere of the park has given to the place a freshness, through which, however, the musky perfume of the tenderness of other times still passes.

The park threatens to invade the mansion. Trees have grown up at the foot of the hills and in the clefts of the steps. Only the broad avenue can be used for driving; and even then the coachman has to lead his horses by the bridles. To right and left the undergrowth is virgin, crossed by a few rare paths, which are dark with shade, and along which you advance with your hands stretched out in front of you, putting aside the grass. And the great trees that have fallen down make blind alleys of these bits of roads, while the contracted glades resemble wells opening on the blue of heaven. Moss hangs from the branches, and the woody nightshade forms a curtain beneath the brushwood; the swarming of insects, the murmur of birds that you do not see, give strange life to this enormous mass of foliage. I have often experienced little shudders of fright, on my way to pay the countess a visit; the woods wafted a disquieting breath to the back of my neck.

But there is a particularly delicious and disturbing corner in the park: it is to the left of the chateau, at the extremity of a flower-garden, where the only things that grow now are poppies as tall as myself. There is a grotto beneath a cluster of trees, buried in a drapery of ivy, the ends of which trail on the grass. The grotto which has been overrun, concealed, is nothing more than a dark recess, in the depths of which one perceives the whiteness of a smiling plaster Cupid with a finger on his mouth. The poor boy-god has but one arm, and on his right eye is a patch of moss which makes him half blind. He seems to be watching, with his sickly smile of an invalid, over some amorous lady who has been dead for a century.

Sparkling water, issuing from the grotto, expands in a broad sheet in the centre of the glade, and then escapes by a brook which is lost beneath the leaves. It is a natural pond, with a sandy bottom, on which the great trees cast their shadows; an aperture showing blue sky forms an azure spot in the centre of the pond. Rushes have grown, and water-lilies have unfurled their round leaves there. One hears naught in the emerald daylight of this globe of verdure, which seems to have issues above and below on the lake of open air, but the melody of the water, ever falling, with an appearance of sweet lassitude. Long water-flies are skating in a coiner. A chaffinch comes to drink with dainty manners, fearing to wet its claws. A sudden rustling of the leaves produces an effect on the pond, comparable to a virgin beating her eyelids in a swoon. And, from the darkness of the grotto, the plaster Cupid ordains silence, repose, and absolute discretion on the part of woods and water, as regards this voluptuous corner of nature.

II

When Adeline grants her aunt a fortnight, this wild spot becomes civilized. The walks must be widened, so that Adeline's skirts may be able to pass along them. She arrived, this season, with thirty-two trunks, which had to be carried on men's shoulders, because the railway-van has never dared venture among the trees. It would have stayed there, I vow, if it had.

Besides, Adeline is a savage, as you know. Between you and me she is cracked—there. At the convent she was troubled with imaginations that were really very funny. I suspect her of coming to the Chateau-of-the-Sleeping-Beauty to satisfy her appetite for extravagance, far away from the inquisitive. The aunt remains seated in her arm-chair; the chateau belongs to the dear child, who must have the most extraordinary fantastical dreams there. They relieve her. When she quits this hole, she behaves herself for a year.

During a fortnight, she is the fairy, the soul of the verdure. She may be perceived in gala toilette, airing her white lace and silken bows amidst the bushes. I have even been assured that she has been seen attired as a Pompadour marchioness with powder and patches, seated on the grass in the most deserted corner of the park. At other times a little fair young man has been caught sight of walking along the alleys. I'm horribly afraid that that young man was naught else than this darling madcap.

I know she rummages about in the chateau from cellar to garret. She ferrets in all the most obscure corners, sounds the walls with her little fists, sniffs at all the dust of past ages with her pink nose. You may find her standing on steps, lost in the depths of huge cupboards, with her ear listening attentively at the windows, gazing dreamily in front of the chimneys, evidently actuated by the desire to climb up inside and have a look. Then, as she probably fails to find what she is in search of, she runs about the flower-garden where the tall poppies are, the paths dark with shade and the glades bright with sun. She is always seeking, carrying her head very high, catching the distant and vague perfume of a flower of tenderness which she cannot pluck.

Positively, I told you so, Ninon, the old chateau has an odor of love, amidst its wild-looking trees. A girl was shut up there, and the walls have preserved the perfume of that tenderness, like those old trunks in which bouquets of violets have been put away. I'd vow it is that scent that gets into Adeline's head and acts upon her senses. Then, when she has inhaled this perfume of old love, when she is overcome by it, she would set out on a ray of the moon to visit the land of fairy-tales, and would let herself be kissed on the forehead by all the cavaliers who happened to pass that way and were good enough to awaken her from her dream of a hundred years.

She has fits of languidness, and carries little stools into the wood to sit down. But, on very hot days, she finds relief in bathing, at night, in the pond beneath the lofty foliage. That is her retreat. She is the maid of the spring. The rushes show her tenderness. When she lets her skirts fall to the ground and enters the water, with all the tranquility of a Diana feeling confidence amidst the solitude, the plaster Cupid smiles at her. She has only water-lilies for a sash, but you must know that even the fish are discreetly slumbering. She swims softly, with her white shoulders protruding from the water, and any one might think it was a swan spreading out its wings and darting noiselessly along. The coolness calms her restlessness. She would be absolutely tranquil were it not for the one-armed Cupid smiling at her.

One night, she penetrated to the bottom of the grotto, in spite of the horrible fright the damp darkness gave her; and, standing on tip-toe, placed her ear to the Cupid's lips to see if he wouldn't tell her something.

III

The frightful part of the business, this season, is that when poor Adeline reached the chateau, she found Count Octave de R, that tall young man, her mortal enemy, in possession of the best bed-room. It seems he is in some degree a cousin of old Madame de M. Adeline has vowed she will dislodge him. She bravely undid her boxes, and recommenced her excursions and the endless quest. Octave quietly watched her from his window, for a week, smoking cigarettes. In the evening bitter words and sullen warfare had ceased. He was so polite, that she ended by thinking him a bore and troubled no more about him. He continued to smoke; she knocked about the park and took her baths.

She usually went to the sheet of water about midnight, when every one was asleep, and was particularly careful to find out whether Count Octave had blown out his candle. Then she crept downstairs as if she were going to meet her sweetheart, with desires that were quite sensual for the cold water. She had had exquisite little shudders of fright since she knew there was a man at the chateau. Supposing he opened a window, supposing he were to catch sight of a corner of her shoulder through the leaves! The thought of it alone made her shiver when she emerged, sparkling all over, from the water, and a ray of the moon whitened her statue-like nudity.

One night she went downstairs at about eleven o'clock. The chateau had been buried in slumber for two long hours. That night she felt particularly bold. She had listened at the count's door, and had fancied she heard him snoring. Fie! a man who snores! That had made her feel great contempt for men, and caused her to long for the honest caresses of the water, which sleeps so sweetly. She lingered beneath the trees, taking pleasure in unfastening her garments one by one. It was very dark, the moon was only just rising, and the dear child's white form merely cast a vague whiteness on the bank like that of a young birch-tree. Puffs of hot wind came from the heavens, and passed across her shoulders in warm kisses. She was quite at ease, rather languid, somewhat stifled by the heat, but full of a feeling of careless happiness, which made her try the spring with her foot as she stood on the bank.

The moon, however, was turning, and already lighting up a corner of the sheet of water. Then Adeline, in terror, perceived a head upon the surface which was gazing at her from this illuminated corner. She slid down, and when the water reached her chin, crossed her arms as if to bring all the trembling veil of the pond across her breast; then in an unsteady voice she inquired:

"Who is there?—What are you doing here?"

"It is I, madame," quietly answered Count Octave. "Don't be alarmed, I'm taking a bath."

IV

A formidable silence ensued. On the sheet of water there was naught but ripples, which spread out slowly around Adeline's shoulders, and came to an end against the count's chest with a slight flopping sound. The latter quietly raised his arms, as if about to seize hold of a branch of willow to enable him to get out of the water.

"Remain where you are; I command you to do so," shouted Adeline in a terrified voice. "Get into the water again; get into the water at once!"

"But, madame," he answered, advancing until the water was up to his neck, "I've been here over an hour."

"That doesn't matter, sir, I will not have you get out, you understand. We'll wait."

The poor baroness was going crazy. She spoke of waiting, but hardly knowing why, her mind being quite upset by the perspective of the terrible events threatening her. Octave smiled.

"But," he ventured to remark, "it seems to me that by turning one's back'

"No, no, sir! Don't you see the moon?"

As a matter of fact the moon had advanced, and was falling in full upon the pond. It was a superb moon. The pond was shining amidst the dark leaves like a silver mirror; the rushes and water-lilies at the edges formed cleverly designed shadows, as if washed-in with a brush and Indian ink. A warm shower of stars fell upon the basin through the small opening in the leaves. The stream of water ran behind Adeline with a low, mocking sound. She ventured to glance into the grotto, and saw the plaster Cupid smiling at her with a knowing look.

"The moon, certainly," murmured the count; "however, by turning one's back"

"No, no, a thousand times no. We'll wait until the moon's no longer there. You see, it is advancing. When it reaches that tree we shall be in the shade."

"But, you see, it'll take a good hour before it gets behind that tree"

"Kill three-quarters of an hour at the most. That doesn't matter. We'll wait. When the moon is behind the tree you can retire."

The count wanted to protest; but, as he moved about as he spoke, and uncovered himself to the waist, she uttered such sharp little cries of distress that, out of politeness, he had to advance into the pond until the water reached his chin. He had the delicacy not to move. Then they both remained there, tête-à-tête with a vengeance, one may say. The two heads, the baroness' adorable fair head with those great eyes that you remember, and the count's handsome head, set off with slightly ironical moustaches, stayed quietly, motionless on the smooth water, a yard or two from one another. The plaster Cupid grinned more broadly than ever from beneath his ivory drapery.

V

Adeline had thrown herself among the water-lilies. When the coolness of the bath had restored her, and she had made her preparations to pass an hour there, she perceived that the water was really shockingly limpid. She could see her naked feet on the sand at the bottom. It must be mentioned that the wicked moon was also bathing, rolling in the water, and filling it with its wriggling, eel-like rays. It was a bath of liquid, transparent gold. Perhaps the count was able to see the naked feet on the sand, and if he saw feet and head.

Adeline covered herself under the water with a sash of water lilies. Then she quietly drew the large round leaves that were floating on the surface around her, and made a broad collar of them. When dressed in that style she felt more at ease.

The count, however, had ended by taking the thing stoically. Not having come across a root whereon to sit, he had resigned himself to kneeling. And so as not to appear absolutely ridiculous, with water up to his chin like a man lost in a huge barber's dish, he had got into conversation with the countess, avoiding all that might remind her of the unpleasantness of their respective positions.

"It has been very warm to-day, madam."

"Yes, sir, oppressively hot. Fortunately, it is cooler in these shady places."

"Oh! Certainly. This good aunt is a worthy person, is she not?"

"A worthy person, indeed."

Then they spoke about the last races and the balls already announced for the forthcoming winter. Adeline, who was beginning to feel cold, reflected that the count must have seen her while she loitered on the bank. That was simply horrible. Only she had doubts as to the importance of the mishap. It was dark under the trees, and the moon had not yet risen. Then, she remembered now, that she had stood behind the trunk of a great oak tree; that trunk must have covered her. But, in truth, this count was an abominable man. She hated him; she would have liked to have seen him slip down and drown himself. It was not she, indeed, who would have extended her hand to help him. Why, when he saw her advancing, did he not shout out that he was there, that he was taking a bath? The question came so clearly to her mind that she could not withhold it from her lips. She interrupted the count, who was talking about the latest shape of bonnets.

"But I was not aware," he answered. "I assure you I was very much afraid—you were all white. I thought it was the Sleeping-Beauty who was showing herself, you know, the girl who was shut up here. I was so frightened that I couldn't call out."

VI

Within half-an-hour they were good friends. Adeline said to herself that she made no difficulty about wearing low-neck dresses at evening parties, and that she could therefore certainly show her shoulders. She had come out of the water a little, and had torn open her high gown, which inconvenienced her at the throat. Then she had risked her arms. She resembled a nymph of the spring, with her bare throat, her naked arms, and clothed in all that mass of verdure, which expanded and extended behind her like a long train of satin.

The count grew tender. He had obtained permission to make a few steps in order to get near a root. His teeth were beginning to chatter, and he gazed at the moon with great interest.

"Hey! It advances slowly," remarked Adeline.

"Eh! No, it has wings," he responded with a sigh. She laughed, adding, "We shall have to wait at least a quarter of an hour." Then he took a cowardly advantage of the situation. He made her a declaration. He explained how he had been in love with her for two years, and that if he had teased her, it was because he had found that more amusing than paying her insipid compliments. Adeline, who was beginning to feel very anxious, pulled her green gown up to her throat, and thrust her arms into the sleeves. Only the tip of her rosy nose could be seen outside the water-lilies; and as the light of the moon fell full in her eyes, she felt quite giddy and dazzled. She had lost sight of the count, when all at once she heard a loud dabbling sound, and felt the agitated element rise to her lips.

"Will you have the kindness not to move?" she exclaimed. "Will you be good enough not to walk about like that in the water?"

"But I was not walking," said the Count. "I slipped— I love you!"

"Hold your tongue, don't move; we'll talk of all that when it's dark. Wait till the moon is behind the tree."

VII

The moon hid behind the tree. The plaster Cupid burst out laughing.

THE STRAWBERRIES

One morning in June, on opening the window, I received a puff of fresh air in the face. There had been a violent storm during the night. The sky looked like new, as if the shower had scoured it in its remotest corners. The roofs and trees, the top branches of which I could perceive between the chimneys, were still dripping with rain, and this bit of horizon was smiling beneath the golden sun, while an odor of wet earth rose from the neighboring gardens.

"Come, Ninette," I cried gaily, "put on your hat, my girl—we'll go out into the country."

She clapped her hands. She was ready in ten minutes, which was very good for a coquette of twenty summers.

At nine o'clock we were in the Verrieres woods.

How discreet those woods are, and what a number of sweethearts have aired their love in them! The copses are deserted during the week and you can stroll there side by side, with arms entwining each other's waists and lips seeking lips, without fear of being seen by any save the songsters in the thickets. The broad, open walks stretch through the masses of lofty trees; the soil is carpeted with fine grass on which the sun, penetrating the foliage, casts circles of gold. And there are hollow footways, very shady, narrow paths, where you are compelled to keep close to one another. And there are also impenetrable thickets, where you may be lost, if the kisses are too sweet

Ninon left my arm and ran like a puppy, delighted at the sensation of the plants grazing her ankles. Then she returned and hung on my shoulder weary and caressing. The wood still spread out before us like a boundless sea with leafy waves. The rustling silence, the life-like shadows that fell from the tall trees troubled, intoxicated us with all the glowing sap of spring. You become a child again amidst the mystery of the copses.

"Oh! Strawberries, strawberries!" exclaimed Ninon, leaping across a ditch like a goat at liberty, and searching among the bushes.

Strawberries, alas! No, but strawberry plants, a whole bed of them spread out beneath the brambles.

Ninon did not give a thought to the insects of which she is so horribly afraid. She boldly moved her hands amongst the plants, raising each leaf, and was in despair at not meeting with the smallest bit of fruit.

"They have been before us," she said, pouting with vexation. "Oh! come, let us make a good search; there are, no doubt, some left."

And we set ourselves to search most conscientiously. We advanced prudently, step by step, with bent backs, strained necks, our eyes fixed on the ground, without risking a word, for fear we might make the strawberries fly away. We had forgotten the forest, the silence and the shadows, the broad walks and narrow paths. It was a question of strawberries, nothing but strawberries. At each clump we came to, we stooped, and our quivering hands met beneath the leaves.

We went along in this way for more than a league, bending down, straying to right and left. There was not the tiniest strawberry. There were superb strawberry plants, with fine dark-green leaves. I noticed Ninon pinch her lips and tears glisten in her eyes.

We had come to a broad slope, on which the sun fell perpendicularly, with oppressive heat. Ninon advanced towards the incline determined not to search any further afterwards. All at once she uttered a shriek. I hastened forward, afraid, thinking she had hurt herself. I found her on the ground; the emotion had brought her to a sitting posture, and with her finger she pointed out a small strawberry to me, hardly as large as a pea, and ripe on one side only.

"You pick it," she said to me, in a low, fondling tone.

I had seated myself beside her, at the bottom of the slope.

"No," I answered. "You found it, and you must gather it."

"No; do me the pleasure, pick it."

I pleaded my own cause so long and so well that Ninon at last made up her mind to break the stalk with her finger. But it was quite another matter, when the question arose as to which of us two was to eat this poor little strawberry which it had taken us a good hour to find. Ninon wanted to force it into my mouth. I firmly resisted; then, I ended by making concessions, and it was decided that the strawberry should be divided into two parts.

She placed it between her teeth, saying to me with a smile:

"Come, take your share."

I took it. I know not if the strawberry was divided in a brotherly and sisterly way. I do not know even if I tasted it, so sweet seemed the honey of Ninon's kiss to me.

The slope was overspread with strawberry plants, and they were genuine ones. The harvest was plentiful and joyously gathered. We had spread a white handkerchief on the ground, both of us solemnly vowing we would place our booty there, without pocketing any part of it. It seemed to me, however, that I several times saw Ninon put her hand to her mouth.

When harvesting was over, we decided it was time to look for a shady nook where we could lunch at ease. I discovered a charming spot, a nest of leaves, a few steps away. The handkerchief was scrupulously placed beside us.

Ye gods! How delightful it was there, on the moss, in the voluptuous enjoyment of verdure and fresh air. Ninon gazed at me with moist eyes. The sun had brought a soft pinkness to her neck. Perceiving all the tenderness of my feeling in my look, she bent towards me, holding out her two hands, with a gesture of adorable confidence.

The sun which was blazing on the lofty foliage, cast golden circles, at our feet, on the fine grass. The feathered songsters became silent and refrained from looking. When we sought for the strawberries to eat them, we perceived with amazement that we were lying right on the handkerchief.

BIG MICHU

One afternoon, at the four o'clock recreation, Big Michu took me aside in a corner of the playground He had a serious look, which somewhat alarmed me; for Big Michu was a lusty fellow, with great fists, whom I would not have liked to have had for an enemy for anything in the world.

"Listen," he said to me with his coarse peasant's voice, which had hardly any polish to it, "listen, will you be one?"

I answered frankly, "Yes!" flattered at being something with Big Michu. Then he explained to me that it was a question of a conspiracy. The thing he confided to me gave me a delicious sensation that I have perhaps never experienced since. At last I was to take part in the mad adventures of life, I was to have a secret to keep, a battle to fight. And, truly, the unspeakable terror I felt at the idea of compromising myself in this manner, counted for a good half in the intense delight that my new character of an accomplice gave me.

And so, while Big Michu spoke, I stood in admiration before him. He initiated me in rather a rough tone, such as one would employ towards a recruit in whose energy one has but scanty confidence. Nevertheless, the tremor of joy, the air of enthusiastic ecstasy that I must have shown in listening to him, ended in giving him a better opinion of me.

As the bell rang a second time, and as we both went to take our places in the ranks, to return to the school-room, he said to me in an undertone:

"That's understood, is it not? You'll be one of us. Anyhow, you won't be afraid: you won't peach?"

"Oh no, you'll see—honor bright."

He looked at me with his grey eyes straight in the face, with the true dignity of ripe manhood, and added:

"Otherwise, you know, I'll riot lick you; but I'll tell every one you're a sneak, and you'll be put in Coventry."

I still remember the singular effect that threat produced on ma "Pooh I" I said to myself, "they may give me two thousand lines if they like; I'll be Wowed if I peach on Michu I" I awaited the dinner hour with febrile, impatience. The revolt was to break out in the dining-hall

Big Michu came from the Var. His father, who was a peasant, with a few bits of land, had taken up arms in '51, at the time of the insurrection brought about by the coup d'État. Left for dead on the plain of Uchine, he had succeeded in hiding himself. When he reappeared he was left alone. Only the authorities in the neighborhood, the notabilities, persons of independent means, both great and small, alluded to him as "that brigand of a Michu."

This brigand, this worthy, illiterate man, sent his son to the college of A. No doubt he desired him to be learned for the triumph of the cause which he had only been able to support by arms. We had some vague idea of this story at the college, and this made us regard our schoolfellow in the light of a very redoubtable personage.

Besides, Big Michu was much older than we were. He was over eighteen, although he was still only in the fourth form. But no one dared make fun of him. His was one of those straightforward minds that learn with difficulty and are incapable of conjecture; only, when he did know a thing he knew it thoroughly and for ever. Being as strong as a bull, he was the master during play-hours. For all that, he was extremely gentle. I never but once saw him angry; he wanted to strangle an usher who was teaching us that all republicans were thieves and murderers. Big Michu was very nearly expelled.

. It was only later on, when I recalled my former schoolfellow to mind, that I was able to understand his gentle, and, at the same time, vigorous attitude. His father must have made a man of him in tender years.

Big Michu liked the college, and that was one of the many things that astonished us. He experienced but one torment, of which he did not dare to speak——hunger. Big Michu was always hungry.

I do not remember ever having witnessed such an appetite. He, who was very proud, sometimes went so far as to play the most humiliating comedies to cheat us out of a piece of bread, a lunch, or our morsel in the afternoon. Brought up in the open air, at the foot of the Maures chain of mountains, he suffered more than we from the paucity of the college table.

That was one of our great subjects of conversation in the playground, standing up against the wall which sheltered us with its streak of shade. We others were dainty. I particularly remember a certain dish of codfish with a brown sauce, and another of haricot beans with a white sauce, which had become the subject of general malediction. On days when these dishes appeared, we did not finish them. Big Michu, out of human respect, protested with us, although he would willingly have swallowed all the six allowances at his table.

Big Michu only complained of the quantity of provisions. Chance, as if to exasperate him, had placed him at the end of the table, beside the .usher, a puny young man who allowed us to smoke when out walking. According to the regulations, the ushers had a right to double allowances. So, when sausages were served, you should have seen Big Michu eyeing the ends of the two bags of mystery which lay side by side on the little usher's plate.

"I'm twice as big as he is," he said to me one day, "and he has twice as much to eat as I have. No fear of him leaving anything; he doesn't get too much himself!"

Now, the leaders had decided that we were at length to rebel against the codfish with brown sauce, and the haricot beans with white sauce.

The conspirators naturally proposed to Big Michu to be their chief. The plan these gentlemen had formed was of heroic simplicity. They thought it would suffice to put their appetites on strike, to refuse all food until the headmaster formally announced that the daily fare would be improved. Big Michu's approval of this idea is one of the finest specimens of courage and self-sacrifice I know of. He accepted the post of leader of the movement with the quiet heroism of those ancient Romans who sacrificed themselves for the public weal.

Just reflect a bit! He did not care a fig about seeing the codfish and the haricot beans disappear; he only wanted one thing, to have more, as much as he liked! and to crown all, they asked him to fast! He has owned to me since, that never had that republican virtue which his father had instilled into him, solidarity, the self-sacrifice of the individual in the interest of the community, been put to so severe a test, in so far as he was concerned.

The strike commenced that evening in the dining-hall——it was the day for codfish with brown sauce—with a spirit of unanimity that was really grand. Bread only was allowed The dishes came, but we did not touch them; we ate our dry bread. And we did so solemnly, without talking in an undertone as was our custom. It was only the youngsters who laughed.

Big Michu was superb. He went so far this first night as not touch his bread He had placed his two elbows on the table, and gazed disdainfully at the little usher who was devouring his own allowance.

The usher in charge, however, had been to fetch the headmaster, who entered the dining-hall like a tempest. He rebuked us roughly, asked us what we could complain about in the dinner, which he tasted and pronounced exquisite.

Then Big Michu stood up.

"Sir," he said, "it is the codfish which is rotten, and we are unable to digest it."

"Ah! well," exclaimed that puny creature of an usher, without giving the headmaster time to answer, "on other evenings you have nevertheless eaten almost the whole dish yourself."

Big Michu crimsoned to the roots of his hair. That evening they simply sent us off to bed, with the remark that we would perhaps think better of it on the morrow.

The next day and the day following, Big Michu was terrible. The usher's observation had wounded him to the heart. He encouraged us. He told us we should be cowards if we gave in. He now put all his pride in showing that when he chose not to eat, he did not do so.

He was a real martyr. We others, we hid chocolate, pots of jam, even pork butcher's dainties, in our desks, and so avoided eating the bread, with which we filled our pockets, dry. He who had no relative in the town, and who, for that matter, abstained from such delicacies, limited himself to the few crusts he was able to find.

On the second day the headmaster having stated that, as the pupils obstinately refused to touch the dishes, no more bread would be supplied, the revolt burst out at noon. It was the day for haricot beans with white sauce.

Big Michu, whose head must have been affected by his frightful hunger, suddenly rose. He took the plate of the usher, who was eating with a famous appetite, to set us at defiance and excite our envy, threw it into the middle of the room, and then burst out singing the "Marseillaise" in a powerful voice. It was like the blast of a trumpet setting us all in action. Plates, glasses, bottles, had a bad time of it. And the masters, striding over the breakage, hastened to leave us in possession of the dining-hall. The puny creature of an usher, in his flight, received a dish of haricot beans on his shoulders, and the sauce made him a broad white collar.

It was a question, however, of fortifying the position. Big Michu was appointed general. He ordered the tables to be piled up against the doors. I remember we had all taken our knives in our hands. And they were still thundering out the "Marseillaise." The revolt was becoming a revolution. Fortunately we were left to ourselves for three long hours. Apparently the military had been sent for. Those three hours of riot sufficed to calm us.

At the end of the dining-hall were two large windows looking on to the playground. The most timid, horrified at the long impunity granted us, softly opened one of the windows and disappeared. They were followed by degrees by the other pupils. Soon after Big Michu had only about a dozen rebels around him. Then he said to them roughly:

"Follow the others, a single culprit will suffice."

Then speaking to me, who was hesitating, he added, "I give you back your word, do you hear?"

When the military had burst open one of the doors, they found Big

Michu all alone, seated quietly at the end of a table, in the midst of the broken crockery. He was sent home to his father the same evening. For our part, we gained very little by this revolt. They certainly avoided for some time giving us haricot beans and codfish. Then the dishes reappeared; only the codfish was done with white sauce, and the haricot beans with brown.

It was a long time after that, when I saw Big Michu again. He had not been able to continue his studies. He, in his turn, was cultivating the few bits of land which his father had left him when he died.

"I would have made a bad lawyer or a bad doctor," he said to me, "for I had a very thick head. It's much better that I should be a peasant. It's my trade. All the same you others let me in beautifully. And I, as it so happened, was particularly fond of codfish and haricot beans."

THE FAST

When the vicar ascended the pulpit, in his ample surplice of angelic whiteness, the little baroness was sanctimoniously seated in her customary place, near a hot-air grating, opposite the chapel of the Holy Angels.

After the usual meditation, the vicar delicately passed a fine cambric handkerchief over his lips; then, he opened his arms, like a seraph about to take his flight, bent his head, and spoke. First of all his voice seemed like a stream of running water in the great nave, like an enormous sigh of the wind amidst the leaves. And the puff of wind gradually increased, the breeze became a tempest, the voice rolled beneath the arched roof with the majestic growl of thunder. But, nevertheless, the vicar's tone, from time to time, even in the midst of his most formidable bursts of rhetoric, suddenly became soft, casting a bright ray of sunshine into the gloomy hurricane of his eloquence.

The little baroness, at the first buzz among the leaves, had taken up the greedy and delighted attitude of a person of refined understanding, making ready to taste all the delicacy of a symphony she loved. She seemed charmed at the exquisite sweetness of the harmonious sentences at the commencement; she then followed the swelling of the voice, and the rising of the final storm, husbanded with so much science, with the attentiveness of a connoisseur; and when the voice had reached its highest pitch, when it thundered, increased in volume by the echoes of the nave, the little baroness was unable to restrain a discreet bravo and a nod of satisfaction.

Then there was celestial joy, and all devout persons were in ecstasies.

The vicar, however, was saying something; his music accompanied words. He was preaching on fasting, and was relating how agreeable the mortifications of the creature were to the Almighty. Bending over the edge of the pulpit, in the attitude of a great white bird, he sighed:

"The hour has come, my brothers and sisters, when all of us like Jesus should bear our cross, crown ourselves with thorns, ascend our Calvary, with naked feet among the flints and brambles."

The little baroness no doubt found the sentence nicely turned, for she gently blinked her eyes, as if tickled at the heart. Then, the vicar's symphony lulling her, she let herself fall into a semi-dreamy state, full of inward voluptuousness, while following the melodious sentences.

Opposite her, she saw one of the long windows of the choir, grey with fog. The rain could not have ceased. The dear child had come to hear the sermon in most abominable weather. One must of course suffer a little when one is religious. Her coachman had received a frightful downpour, and she even, on jumping to the ground, had slightly wetted the tips of her boots. Her miniature brougham, however, was an excellent one, closing well and padded like an alcove. But it is so sad to see, through the damp glasses, a line of busy umbrellas, hurrying along on either pavement! And she reflected that if it had been fine, she could have come out in her Victoria. That would have been much more gay.

At heart, her great fear was that the vicar might hurry too quickly through his sermon. She would then have to wait for her carriage, for she would certainly never consent to pick her way in such weather. And she made the calculation, that at the rate the vicar was going, his voice would never hold out for two hours; her coachman would get there too late. This uneasiness somewhat troubled her pious pleasure.

The vicar, with sudden outbursts of wrath which brought him up erect, his hair all in a flutter, his fists stretched forward, like a man troubled by the avenging spirit, thundered forth, "And above all woe to ye, sinners of the gentle sex, if you do not pour the perfume of your remorse, the fragrant oil of your repentance on the feet of Jesus. Believe me, tremble and fall on both knees on the stone. It is by coming and confining yourselves in the purgatory of penitence, opened by the church during these days of universal contrition; it is by wearing down the flags with your foreheads pallid with fasting, by becoming acquainted with the pangs of hunger and cold, silence and darkness, that you will deserve divine pardon, on the brilliant day of triumph!"

The little baroness, drawn from her reverie by this terrible explosion, slowly nodded her head, as if she were exactly of the angry priest's opinion. One must secure birches, go into some very dark, damp, icy corner, and there whip oneself; there was no doubt about that in her mind.

Then she resumed her musings, and was lost in comfort and tender ecstasy. She was seated at her ease on a low chair with a broad back, and had an embroidered cushion under her feet, which prevented her feeling the cold stone flags. She was leaning half back, enjoying the church, that great vessel pervaded with vapors of incense, and the secluded parts of which, full of mysterious shadows, were becoming rich in delightful visions. The nave, with its hangings in red velvet, its gold and marble ornaments, its appearance of an immense boudoir filled with disturbing perfumes, and lit with the subdued light of a night lamp, closed and as if ready for superhuman love, had gradually enveloped her with the charm of its pomp. It was the festival of her senses. Her pretty, plump person, flattered, petted, fondled, was indulging itself. And the voluptuousness she tasted was due above all to her feeling herself so small amidst such immense beatitude.

But without her being aware of it, what tickled her most deliciously, was the warm breath from the hot-air grating which opened almost beneath her skirts. She was very chilly, was the little baroness. The hot-air grating discreetly wafted its warm caresses along her silk stockings. Drowsiness overtook her in this delightful bath.

The vicar was still full of wrath. He plunged all the devout persons who were present into the boiling oil of hell.

"If you listen not to the voice of God, if you listen not to my voice, which is that of God Himself, I tell you truly, you will one day hear with anguish the crackling of your bones, you will feel your flesh melting on burning coal, and then you will cry out in vain: 'Pity, Lord, pity, I repent!' God will be merciless, and will kick you back into the bottomless pit!"

At this last sentence a shudder ran through the congregation. The little baroness, who was decidedly going to sleep under the influence of the warm air, which circulated among her skirts, smiled vaguely. She knew the vicar very well, did the little baroness. He had been her guest at dinner on the previous evening. He was extremely partial to truffled salmon pate and Champagne was his favorite wine. He was certainly a handsome man, between thirty-five and forty, dark, with a visage so round and so rosy, that one would have had no difficulty in taking his priestly countenance for the merry face of a servant girl on a farm. He was also a society man, played a good knife and fork, and had a smart tongue. He was adored by the women, and the little baroness was passionately fond of him. He said to her in such a delightfully sugary voice: "Ah! Madam, with such a toilette, you would damn a saint."

And he did not damn himself, the dear man. He ran about serving out the same polite attention to the countess, the marchioness, and his other penitents and that made him the spoilt child of the ladies.

When he was the guest of the little baroness, of a Thursday, she took care of him as if he were some dear creature to whom the least draught might give a cold, and to whom a bad dish would certainly give indigestion. In the drawing room his arm-chair was beside the fireplace; at table, the servants had orders to keep a careful eye on his plate, to pour out a certain Champagne, aged twelve years, to him alone, and he drank it, and he drank it closing his eyes fervently, as if he had been taking the communion.

He was so good, so good, was the vicar! While from the height of the pulpit he spoke of crackling bones and of limbs being grilled, the little baroness in her semi-state of slumber, saw him at her table, sanctimoniously wiping his lips and saying to her: "This bisque soup, madam, would cause you to find grace with God the Father, had not your beauty already sufficed to ensure your entry into paradise."

When the vicar had done with anger and threats he began to sob. Those were his usual tactics. He would be almost on his knees in the pulpit, showing only his shoulders, then, all at once, he would rise up, then bend, as if struck down by grief, wipe his eyes, with a loud crumpling sound of starched muslin, throw his arms up in the air, to the right and left, and take the postures of a wounded pelican. That was the bouquet, the final, the grand orchestral piece, the exciting scene of the catastrophe.

"Weep, weep," he said tearfully in an expiring voice; "weep on yourselves, weep on me, weep on God"

The little baroness was fast asleep, with her eyes open. The heat, the incense, the increasing obscurity had quite overcome her. She had gathered herself up into a ball, and was entirely absorbed with the voluptuous sensations she experienced, while slyly dreaming of very pleasant things.

Beside her, in the chapel of the Holy Angels, was a great fresco, representing a group of handsome, half-nude young men, with wings at their backs. They smiled with a smile of bashful lovers, and in their inclining, kneeling attitudes, seemed to be worshipping some invisible baroness. The handsome fellows had tender lips, skins as soft as satin, and muscular arms! The worst of it was that one of them bore a striking resemblance to the young Duke de P, one of the little baroness' good friends. She was wondering, in her sleep, whether the duke would look well in the nude, with wings at his back. And at times she imagined the great pink cherub was wearing the duke's swallow-tail coat. Then the dream became more distinct: it was really the duke, very scantily clad, who, from the depth of darkness, was blowing her kisses.

When the little baroness awoke she heard the vicar pronouncing the final sentence, "And that is the grace I wish you."

For a moment she was bewildered; she thought the vicar was wishing her the young duke's kisses.

There was a great noise with chairs. Every one left; the little baroness had guessed correctly, her coachman had not yet arrived at the bottom of the steps. That devil of a vicar had hurried on his sermon, robbing his penitents of at least twenty minutes' eloquence.

And as the little baroness was waiting impatiently in one of the aisles, she met the vicar, who was precipitately leaving the vestry. He was looking for the time at his watch, and had the busy air of a man who does not wish to miss an appointment.

"Ah! How late I am, dear madam," he said. "You know I am expected by the countess. There is a spiritual concert, followed by a small collation."

THE SHOULDERS OF THE MARCHIONESS

The marchioness sleeps in her great bed, beneath ample yellow satin curtains. At noon, at the smart stroke of the clock, she decides on opening her eyes.

The room is warm. The carpets, the hangings over the doors and windows, make it a soft nest, which defies the cold. It is pervaded by warmth and perfumery, and is like everlasting spring.

And so soon as the marchioness is well awake, she seems a victim to sudden anxiety. She casts off the bedclothes and rings for Julie.

"Did madam ring?"

"Tell me, does it thaw?"

Oh! Good marchioness! in what a troubled tone did she make this inquiry! Her first thought is about the terrible cold weather, the north wind which she does not feel, but which blows so keenly in the hovels of the poor. And she asks if Heaven has been merciful, whether she can allow herself to be warm without remorse, without thinking of all those who shiver.

"Does it thaw, Julie?"

Her lady's maid hands her the morning peignoir, which she has just been warming in front of a good fire.

"Oh, no, madam, it does not thaw. On the contrary it freezes harder—they have just found a man frozen to death on the top of an omnibus."

The marchioness is as merry as a child; she claps her hands, exclaiming, "Ah! So much the better! I'll go skating this afternoon."

Julie softly draws back the curtains, so that the sudden daylight may not hurt the tender sight of the delicious marchioness.

The room is filled with the bluish reflex of the snow which conveys quite a gay light to it. The sky is grey, but it is such a pretty grey that it reminds the marchioness of a pearl-grey silk gown she wore, the previous evening, at the ministerial ball. This gown was trimmed with white guipure, similar to the streaks of snow she perceives at the edge of the roofs, against the pale sky.

The previous evening she had been charming with her new diamonds. She had gone to bed at five o'clock, and her head was still a bit heavy. However, she has seated herself before a glass, and Julie has raised her mass of fair hair. The peignoir slips down, and the shoulders remain bare to the centre of her back.

A whole generation has already grown old gazing on the marchioness' shoulders. Since ladies of a merry disposition, thanks to a powerful government, have been able to wear low-neck gowns and dance at the Tuilleries, she has trotted her shoulders through the crowded drawing-rooms of the official world, with an assiduity that has made her the living signboard of the charms of the Second Empire. She has been obliged to follow the fashion and cut down her gowns, now to the small of the back, now to the centre of the bosom; so that the dear woman, dimple by dimple, has shown all the treasures of her bodice. There is hardly a bit of her back and bosom that is unknown, from the Madeleine to Saint Thomas Aquinas. The so widely displayed shoulders of the marchioness are the voluptuous coat of arms of the reign.

It would certainly be of no use to describe the marchioness' shoulders. They are as well known as the Pont Neuf. For eighteen years they have formed part of the public shows. It suffices to catch sight of the smallest part of them in a drawing-room, at the theatre, or elsewhere, to exclaim: "By Jove! The marchioness! I know her by the beauty spot on her left shoulder!"

They are very fine shoulders, for the matter of that, white, plump, provoking. The gaze of a government passing over them has increased their delicacy, somewhat in the way of those flagstones which are eventually polished by the feet of the crowd.

If I were the husband or lover, I would sooner go and kiss the glass door knob of a minister's private room, worn by the hands of favorhunters, than graze with my lips those shoulders on which the warm breath of all gallant Paris has passed. When one thinks of the thousands of desires they have awakened, one wonders what sort of clay nature employed in kneading them, in order that they might not be eaten away and crumble into dust, like those nudities of statues exposed to the open air of the gardens, and of which the outline has been devoured by the winds.

The marchioness has placed her modesty elsewhere. She has made her shoulders an institution. And how she has struggled for the government of her choice! Always on the breach, everywhere at once, at the Tuilleries, with the ministers, in the embassies, with simple millionaires, convincing the undecided with smiles, propping up the throne with her alabaster breasts, displaying in times of danger little hidden and delicious corners, more persuasive than the arguments of orators, more decisive than the swords of soldiers, and threatening, in order to gain a vote, to cut down her chemisettes until the most ferocious members of the opposition acknowledge themselves vanquished.

The shoulders of the marchioness have always remained entire and victorious. They have supported a world, without a wrinkle ever having come to spoil their marble whiteness.

When the marchioness left Julie's hands this afternoon, attired in a delicious Polish toilette, she went skating. She skates adorably.

It was bitterly cold in the wood, and there was a north wind which nipped the noses and lips of the ladies, as if fine sand were being blown into their faces. The marchioness laughed, and was amused at feeling cold. From time to time she went and warmed her feet at the braziers that had been lighted on the shores of the little lake. Then she returned to the icy air, skimming along like a swallow grazing the ground.

Ah! What delightful sport and how lucky it is there is no thaw! The marchioness will be able to skate all the week.

The marchioness, on her way home, noticed a wretched woman in one of the side avenues of the Champs Élysées, shivering, half dead with cold, at the foot of a tree.

"Poor thing I" she murmured, as if annoyed.

And as the carriage was going too quick, and the marchioness could not find her purse, she threw her bouquet to the poverty-stricken creature, a bouquet of white lilac quite worth five louis.

MY NEIGHBOR JACQUES

I was then living in the Rue Gracieuse, the garret of my twenty summers. The Rue Gracieuse is a steep lane, which descends from the knoll of Saint Victor, behind the Jardin des Plantes.

I ascended two floors—houses are low in those parts— assisting myself with a cord so as not to slip on the worn stairs, and I thus reached my hovel in most absolute obscurity. The room, which was large and cold, had the naked and dim aspect of a vault. I have experienced brilliant sunlight, however, amidst this darkness, and there were days when my heart was beaming.

On those occasions the merry laughter of a little girl reached me from the adjoining garret, which was peopled by a whole family, father, mother, and a brat seven or eight years old.

The father had an angular appearance, and a head placed aslant between two pointed shoulders. His bony face was yellow, with big black eyes deeply set beneath bushy eyebrows. This man, notwithstanding his lugubrious appearance, preserved a good, timid smile; any one would have set him down as a big child of fifty, for he became troubled and blushed like a girl. He sought the dark, and glided along the walls with the humility of a pardoned convict.

A few greetings exchanged between us, had made a friend of him. His strange features, which bore the imprint of a restless, good-natured look, pleased me. Little by little, we had' come to shaking hands.

At the end of six months, I was still ignorant as to what was the calling that gave Jacques and his family bread. He spoke little. I had certainly, in a purely disinterested way, questioned his wife on two or three occasions; but I had only received evasive answers which she stammered out with embarrassment.

One day—it had rained the previous night, and my heart was aching— as I was descending the Boulevard d'Enfer, I noticed one of those pariahs of the working classes of Paris advancing towards me, a man attired in black raiment and a black hat, wearing a white necktie and carrying under his arm the narrow coffin of a new-born babe.

He was walking with lowered head, holding his light burden with dreamy unconcern, kicking the pebbles before him on the road. It was a dull morning. This passing sadness gave me pleasure. The man raised his head at the sound of my footsteps, then quickly turned it aside, but too late: I had recognized him. My neighbor Jacques was an undertaker's man.

I watched him disappear, ashamed of his shame. I felt sorry I had not taken the other side of the street. He proceeded on his way, hanging his head still lower, and no doubt saying to himself that he had just lost the grasp of the hand we exchanged each evening.

I met him next day on the stairs. He stood timidly up against the wall, making himself small, small, humbly holding back the folds of his blouse, so that it might not touch my garments. He stood there bowed down, and I perceived that his poor hoary head was shaking with emotion.

I stopped, looked him in the face, and extended my hand to him, wide open.

He raised his head, hesitated, and in his turn looked me in the face. I saw his great eyes become troubled, and his sallow countenance showing red spots. Then, suddenly taking my arm, he accompanied me to my garret, where he at length recovered speech.

"You are an honest young fellow," he said to me; "the grasp of your hand has made me forget many a sour look."

And he took a seat and opened himself to me. He confessed that before being in the business, he felt, like others, uncomfortable when he met an undertaker's man. But since then, in his long journeys, amidst the silence of the funeral procession, he had thought the thing over, and was astounded at the disgust and fear he awakened on his way.

I was then twenty, and would have hugged an executioner. I launched out into philosophical reflections, and sought to prove to my neighbor Jacques that his work was sacred. But he shrugged his pointed shoulders, silently rubbed his hands, and, resuming his slow and embarrassed tone of voice, said:

"The gossip of the neighborhood, you see, sir, the savage looks of the passers-by trouble me little, so long as my wife and child have bread. One thing worries me. I can't sleep at night when I think of it. My wife and I are elderly people, who care no more for shame. But young girls are ambitious. My poor Marthe will blush for me later on. When she was five years of age she saw one of my companions, and she cried so, and was so frightened that I have never dared put on the black cloak before her. I dress and undress on the stairs.

I felt pity for my neighbor Jacques. I suggested to him that he should leave his clothes in my room, and come and put them on at ease, out of the cold. He took all kinds of precautions to remove his forbidding garments to my lodging. I saw him regularly from that day, morning and night. He dressed and undressed in a corner of my attic.

I had an old trunk that was worm-eaten and crumbling away to dust. My neighbor Jacques made it his wardrobe; he laid newspapers at the bottom of it, and carefully folded up his black clothes on them.

Sometimes, at night, when nightmare awoke me with a start, I cast an affrighted look at the old trunk, which stood against the wall like a coffin, and I fancied I saw the hat, the black cloak, and white necktie issue from it.

The hat rolled round my bed, snoring and jumping with little starts; the cloak expanded, and, flapping its folds like great black wings, silently flew about the room, displaying all its breadth; the white necktie became longer and longer, then began to creep slowly towards me with head erect and wriggling tail.

I opened my eyes immoderately wide, and perceived the old trunk standing motionless and dark in its corner.

I was constantly having dreams at that time, dreams of love and also dreams that were sad. My nightmare gave me pleasure; I liked my neighbor Jacques, because he lived among the dead, and brought me the acrid odors of the cemeteries. He had told me secrets, and I was penning the first pages of "The Reminiscences of an Undertaker's Man."

In the evening, before my neighbor Jacques undressed, he sat down on the old trunk to give me an account 'of his day. He was very fond of talking of his dead people. One time it was a young girl—the poor child, who had died of consumption, did not weigh heavy; another time it was an old man—this old man, whose coffin had strained his arms, was a big, fat functionary, who must have carried away his gold with him in his pockets. And I had private details about each corpse; I knew their weight, the noises that had proceeded from their coffins, the way in which they had had to be carried down, at the turns of the staircases. Some evenings my neighbor Jacques came home more talkative and with a beaming face. He leant against the walls, with his cloak hooked over his shoulder, his hat on the back of his head. He had come across generous heirs, who had treated him to "the quarts of wine and piece of Brie cheese of consolation." And he ended by displaying tender feelings. He vowed to me that when the time came, he would carry me to my grave with all the kindly consideration of a friend.

I lived thus for more than a year, with my attention taken up with the dead.

One morning my neighbor Jacques failed to make his appearance. A week later, he was dead.

When two of his companions removed the body, I was on the threshold of my door, and heard them joking as they carried down the coffin, which seemed to make a sullen remonstrance at each knock it received.

One of them, a little fat fellow, said to the other, who was tall and thin, "The biter's bit"

THE PARADISE OF CATS

An aunt bequeathed me an Angora cat, which is certainly the most stupid animal I know of. This is what my cat related to me, one winter night, before the warm embers.

I was then two years old, and I was certainly the fattest and most simple cat any one could have seen. Even at that tender age I displayed all the presumption of an animal that scorns the attractions of the fireside. And yet what gratitude I owed to Providence for having placed me with your aunt. The worthy woman idolized me. I had a regular bedroom at the bottom of a cupboard, with a feather pillow and a triple-folded rug. The food was as good as the bed; no bread or soup, nothing but meat, good underdone meat.

Well! amidst all these comforts, I had but one wish, but one dream, to slip out by the half-open window, and run away on to the tiles. Caresses appeared to me insipid, the softness of my bed disgusted me, I was so fat that I felt sick, and from morn till eve I experienced the weariness of being happy.

I must tell you that by straining my neck I had perceived the opposite roof from the window. That day four cats were fighting there. With bristling coats and tails in the air, they were rolling on the blue slates, in the full sun, amidst oaths of joy. I had never witnessed such an extraordinary sight. From that moment my convictions were settled. Real happiness was upon that roof, in front of that window which the people of the house so carefully closed. I found the proof of this in the way in which they shut the doors of the cupboards where the meat was hidden.

I made up my mind to fly. I felt sure there were other things in life than underdone meat. There was the unknown, the ideal. One day they forgot to close the kitchen window. I sprang on to a small roof beneath it. How beautiful the roofs were! They were bordered by broad gutters exhaling delicious odors. I followed those gutters in raptures of delight, my feet sinking into fine mud, which was deliciously warm and soft. I fancied I was walking on velvet. And the generous heat of the sun melted my fat.

I will not conceal from you the fact that I was trembling in every limb. My delight was mingled with terror. I remember, particularly, experiencing a terrible shock that almost made me tumble down into the street. Three cats came rolling over from the top of a house towards me, mewing most frightfully, and as I was on the point of fainting away, they called me a silly thing, and said they were mewing for fun. I began mewing with them. It was charming. The jolly fellows had none of my stupid fat. When I slipped on the sheets of zinc heated by the burning sun, they laughed at me. An old tom, who was one of the band, showed me particular friendship. He offered to teach me a thing or two, and I gratefully accepted. Ah! Your aunt's cat's meat was far from my thoughts! I drank in the gutters, and never had sugared milk seemed so sweet to me. Everything appeared nice and beautiful. A she-cat passed by, a charming she-cat, the sight of her gave me a feeling I had never experienced before. Hitherto, I had only seen these exquisite creatures, with such delightfully supple backbones, in my dreams. I and my three companions rushed forward to meet the newcomer. I was in front of the others, and was about to pay my respects to the bewitching thing, when one of my comrades cruelly bit my neck. I cried out with pain.

"Bah!" said the old tom, leading me away; "you will meet with stranger adventures than that."

After an hour's walk I felt as hungry as a wolf. "What do you eat on the roofs?" I inquired of my friend the tom.

"What you can find," he answered shrewdly.

This reply caused me some embarrassment, for though I carefully searched I found nothing. At last I perceived a young work-girl in a garret preparing her lunch. A beautiful chop of a tasty red color was lying on a table under the window.

"There's the very thing I want," I thought, in all simplicity.

And I sprang on to the table and took the chop. But the work-girl, having seen me, struck me a fearful blow with a broom on the spine, and I fled, uttering a dreadful oath.

"You are fresh from your village then?" said the tom. "Meat that is on tables is there for the purpose of being longed for at a distance. You must search in the gutters."

I could never understand that kitchen meat did not belong to cats. My stomach was beginning to get seriously angry. The torn put me completely to despair by telling me it would be necessary to wait until night. Then we would go down into the street and turn over the heaps of muck. Wait until night I He said it quietly, like a hardened philosopher. I felt myself fainting at the mere thought of this prolonged fast.

Night came slowly, a foggy night that chilled me to the bones. It soon began to rain, a fine, penetrating rain, driven by sudden gusts of wind. We went down along the glazed roof of a staircase. How ugly the street appeared to me! It was no longer that nice heat, that beautiful sun, those roofs white with light where one rolled about so deliciously. My paws slipped on the greasy stones. I sorrowfully recalled to memory my triple blanket and feather pillow.

We were hardly in the street when my friend the torn began to tremble. He made himself small, very small, and ran stealthily along beside the houses, telling me to follow as rapidly as possible. He rushed in at the first street door he came to, and purred with satisfaction as he sought refuge there. When I questioned him as to the motive of his flight, he answered:

"Did you see that man with a basket on his back and a stick with an iron hook at the end?"

"Yes."

"Well if he had seen us he would have knocked us on the heads and roasted us!"

"Roasted us!" I exclaimed. "Then the street is not ours? One can't eat, but one's eaten!"

However, the boxes of kitchen refuse had been emptied before the street doors. I rummaged in the heaps in despair. I came across two or three bare bones that had been lying among the cinders, and I then understood what a succulent dish fresh cat's meat made. My friend the tom scratched artistically among the muck. He made me run about until morning, inspecting each heap, and without showing the least hurry. I was out in the rain for more than ten hours, shivering in every limb. Cursed street, cursed liberty, and how I regretted my prison!

At dawn the tom, seeing I was staggering, said to me with a strange air:

"Have you had enough of it?"

"Oh yes," I answered.

"Do you want to go home?"

"I do, indeed; but how shall I find the house?"

"Come along. This morning, when I saw you come out, I understood that a fat cat like you was not made for the lively delights of liberty. I know your place of abode and will take you to the door."

The worthy tom said this very quietly. When we had arrived, he bid me "Good-bye," without betraying the least emotion.

"No," I exclaimed, "we will not leave each other so. You must accompany me. We will share the same bed and the same food. My mistress is a good woman"

He would not allow me to finish my sentence.

"Hold your tongue," he said sharply, "you are a simpleton. Your effeminate existence would kill me. Your life of plenty is good for bastard cats. Free cats would never purchase your cat's meat and feather pillow at the price of a prison. Goodbye."

And he returned up on to the roofs, where I saw his long outline quiver with joy in the rays of the rising sun.

When I got in, your aunt took the whip and gave me a thrashing which I received with profound delight. I tasted in full measure the pleasure of being beaten and being warm. While she was striking me, I thought with rapture of the meat she would give me afterwards.

You see—concluded my cat, stretching itself out in front of the embers—real happiness, paradise, my dear master, consists in being shut up and beaten in a room where there is meat.

I am speaking from the point of view of cats.

LILI

You come from the fields, Ninon, from real fields with their broad views and penetrating fragrance. You are not so silly as to immure yourself in a casino, at some fashionable watering-place. You go where the crowd does not go, to some leafy nook in the heart of Burgundy. Your retreat is a white house, hidden like a nest amidst the trees. It is there that you pass your springs, in the healthy open air. And thus, when you return to me for a few days, your dear friends are astonished at your cheeks which are as fresh as your hawthorn blossoms, and at your lips as red as your sweet-briar.

But your mouth is all sugary, and I would vow that no later than yesterday you were eating cherries. You see you are not a little lady afraid of wasps and brambles. You walk along bravely in the full glare of the sun, knowing very well that your sunburnt neck is as transparent as clear amber. And you run about the fields in a cotton gown and broad-brimmed hat like a peasant girl who loves the land. You cut the fruit with your little embroidery scissors, performing but a slight task, it is true, but working with all your heart and returning home, proud of the rosy scratches the thistles have left on your white hands.

What will you do next winter? Nothing. You will feel dull, will you not? You are not fond of a fashionable life. Do you remember that ball I took you to one night? You had bare shoulders and were shivering in the carriage. It was stifling hot beneath the raw light of the chandeliers. You remained sitting back in your arm-chair, suppressing little yawns behind your fan. Ah! How dull it was! And, when we returned, you murmured, showing me your faded bouquet, "Look at these poor flowers. I should die like them, if I lived in that hot air. What has become of you, my dear spring?"

We'll go to no more balls, Ninon. We'll stay at home at our fireside. We'll love one another; and, when we're weary of that, we'll still love one another.

I remember your exclamation of the other day: "Really women are very indolent." I thought all day of that avowal. Man has taken all the work and has left you dangerous reverie. Wrong is the result of much musing. What can one think of when embroidering all day? One builds castles in the air or one falls asleep like the Sleeping Beauty while awaiting the kisses of the first knight who may pass along the road.

"My father," you have often said to me, "was a worthy man, who let me grow up at home. I did not learn wrong after the manner of those delicious dolls who, at the boarding school, hide their cousins' letters in their prayer-books. I have never confused God with a bogie, and I confess I have always had more dread of causing my father pain than of being cooked in the devil's caldrons. I must tell you, also, that I bow naturally, without having studied the art of making curtsies; my dancing-master, moreover, did not teach me to cast down my eyes, to smile, or to lie with my face; I am absolutely unfamiliar with those grimaces of coquettes which form the most important part of the education of a well-born young lady. I have grown freely, like a vigorous plant. That is why the air of Paris makes me gasp for breath."

Recently, on one of those rare fine afternoons that spring reserves for us, I found myself seated in the Tuilleries gardens in the slender shade of the great chestnut trees. Children were at play, breaking the dull rumbling sound in the adjoining streets with their shrill laughter.

My eyes ended by resting on a little girl, six or seven years of age, whose young mother was in conversation with a friend a few steps away from me. She was a fair-haired child, reaching a little higher than my knee, and already had the manners of a young lady. She was wearing one of those delicious toilettes in which Parisians alone know how to deck their children: a puffed pink silk skirt, showing legs encased in pearl-grey stockings; a low-neck bodice, trimmed with lace; a toque with white feathers; for jewels a coral necklace and bracelet. She resembled her mamma, with a little extra dose of coquetry.

She had succeeded in obtaining possession of her mamma's sunshade, and was walking gravely about with it open, although there was not the smallest stream of sunshine under the trees. She was practicing walking lightly, gliding gracefully along as she had seen grown-up persons do. She was unaware that she was being watched. She was rehearsing her part quite conscientiously, trying different expressions of countenance, graceful pouts, learning movements of the head, glances, smiles. She ended by getting to the trunk of an old chestnut tree, to which she very seriously made half a dozen low bows.

She was a little woman. I was really terrified at her self-assurance and knowledge. She was not seven, and was already familiar with the arts of an enchantress. It is only at Paris that one meets with such precocious little girls, who know how to dance before they can say their alphabet. I remember the country children; they are clumsy and unwieldy; they crawl stupidly along the ground. There is no fear of Lily spoiling her beautiful dress; she prefers not to play; she carries herself very upright in her starched petticoats, finding her pleasure in being looked at, and in hearing people around her exclaim: "Ah! What a charming child."

In the meantime Lily was still bowing to the trunk of the old chestnut. All at once I saw her draw herself up and make ready; the sunshade on a slope, her lips wreathed in smiles, and with rather a giddy air about her. I was not long in understanding what it all meant. Another little girl, a brunette in a green skirt, was advancing along the broad walk. She was a friend, and it was a question of meeting her in the most elegant manner possible.

The two children slightly touched each other's hand, and made the grimaces which are usual among ladies in the same station of life. When they had gone through the customary polite inquiries, they began walking side by side, conversing in shrill voices. There was no question of playing.

"You have a very pretty gown there."

"The trimming is Valencienne lace, is it not?"

"Mamma was unwell this morning. I was very much afraid I should be unable to come, as I promised you."

"Have you seen Therese's doll? She has a magnificent trousseau."

"Is that sunshade yours? It is beautiful"

Lily turned very red. She was showing off with her mamma's sunshade because she perceived she eclipsed her friend, who had none. The tatter's question embarrassed her, as she saw that if she told the truth she would be vanquished.

"Yes," she answered graciously. "It was papa who made me a present of it."

That was the finishing stroke. She understood how to lie, as she understood how to be beautiful. She could grow up now; she was ignorant of nothing it was necessary to know to be a pretty woman. When girls have such educations how can poor husbands sleep in peace?

At that moment a little boy of eight passed by, dragging along a wagon loaded with stones. He was uttering terrible gees I acting the carter; he was playing with all his heart, and as he passed by Lily he almost knocked up against her.

"How brutal a man is!" she said disdainfully. "Observe the disorder of that child's dress!"

The young ladies laughed contemptuously. The child must certainly have appeared a very little boy to them to play at horses in this way. Twenty years hence, if one of them marries him, she will always treat him with the superiority of a woman who knew how to wield a sunshade at seven, whereas at that age he only knew how to tear his breeches.

Lily had resumed her stroll, after having carefully arranged the folds of her skirt.

"Just look," she continued, "at that great booby of a girl in a white frock over there, who looks bored to death. The other day she sent to me to ask if I would allow her to be introduced to me. Only fancy, my dear, the daughter of a small clerk. I refused, as you may suppose: one ought not to compromise oneself."

Lily pouted like an offended princess. Her friend was decidedly beaten. She had no sunshade, and no one had as yet begged the favor of being presented to her. She lost her color like a woman who is present at a rival's triumph. She had passed her arm round Lily's waist, endeavoring to crumple her frock behind, without her perceiving it. And she smiled at her, moreover, with an adorable smile, displaying little white teeth that were ready to bite.

As they walked away from their mothers, they at last noticed I was watching them. From that moment they became more sugary, and put on the coquettish airs of young ladies who wish to deserve and engage attention. A gentleman was there looking at them. Ah! Daughters of Eve, the devil tempts you at the cradle!

Then, they burst out laughing. A detail of my toilette must have surprised, have appeared very comical to them; it was no doubt my hat, the shape of which had ceased to be the fashion. They were making fun of me, literally; they were joking, with their hands before their mouths, retaining their peals of laughter as ladies do in drawing-rooms. At length I felt ashamed; I reddened, and was at a loss to know what to do with myself. And I ran away, leaving the field in possession of these two brats, who had all the gaiety and strange looks of grown-up women.

Ah! Ninon, Ninon, take those girls away to the farms, dress them in brown Holland and let them roll about in the pools where the ducks dabble. They will return as stupid as geese, as healthy and strong as young trees. When we marry them, we will teach them to love us. They will know quite enough.

THE LEGEND OF CUPID'S LITTLE BLUE MANTLE

The beautiful girl with auburn hair was born on a December morning, as the pure snow was slowly falling. There were positive signs in the air which proclaimed the mission of love she came to perform; the sun shone pink on the white snow, and over the roofs passed the perfume of lilac and the songs of birds, as in springtime.

She first saw daylight in a hovel, no doubt out of a feeling of humility, so as to show that the only riches she prized were those of the heart. She had no family; she could love all humanity, having arms that were sufficiently lithe to embrace the whole world. As soon as she reached the age of love, she left the obscurity where she had been collecting her thoughts, and began to walk along the highways and byways, seeking the hungry, whom she satisfied with her glances.

She was a tall, well-developed girl, with black eyes and ruby lips. Her flesh was of a dull, pale tint, and was covered with a slight down which gave her skin the appearance of white velvet. When she walked her body swayed gently to and fro.

She had understood, on leaving the straw where she was born, that it was part of her mission to attire herself in silk and lace. Nature had gifted her with white teeth and rosy cheeks; she was able to find necklaces of pearls as pure as the former, and skirts that were pink like the latter.

And when she was equipped, it was nice to meet her on the foot-paths, on bright May mornings. Her heart and lips were at the service of all who came forward. When she found a beggar at the edge of a ditch, she questioned him with a smile; if he complained of burnings, of sharp pangs in the heart, her lips quickly gave him alms, and the beggar's misery was relieved.

Consequently, all the poor of the parish knew her. They thronged to her door awaiting the distribution. She came down morning and night, like a charitable sister, dividing her treasures of tenderness amongst them, giving each his share.

She was as good and sweet as white bread. The poor of the parish had nicknamed her Cupid's Little Blue Mantle.

Now, it happened that a terrible epidemic ravaged the land. All the young men were attacked by it, and the majority ran the risk of dying.

The symptoms of the scourge were terrifying. The heart ceased to beat, the brain was unhinged, the victim became stupid. The young men walked about sniggering like silly clowns, purchasing hearts at the fair as children buy sticks of barley-sugar. When the epidemic attacked worthy young men, the complaint showed itself by intense sadness and excessive despair. Artists wept before their works at their helplessness, unsated lovers went and threw themselves into the rivers.

You can imagine that the beautiful child showed herself to advantage on this momentous occasion. She established ambulances, and nursed the sick day and night, using her lips to close the wounds, and thanking heaven for the great task that had been set her.

She was quite a gift from God to the young men. She saved a large number. Those whose hearts she could not heal were those who were already without a heart. Her treatment was simple: she gave the sick her helping hands and warm breath. She never asked for payment. She ruined herself with a light heart, distributing charity by the mouthful.

Consequently, the misers of the time wagged their heads, when they saw the young prodigal scattering in that manner her great wealth of charms. Among themselves they said:

"She will die on a straw pallet, she who gives away her heart's blood, without ever weighing the drops."

And, indeed, one day as she was searching her heart, she found it empty. She shuddered in terror; she had barely a few sous' worth of tenderness left, and the epidemic was at its height.

The child was beside herself; she did not give a thought to the immense fortune she had so foolishly squandered, but felt in burning need of charity herself, and that made her wretchedness the more frightful It was so sweet to go in quest of beggars in the bright sunshine, so sweet to love and to be loved! And, now, she must stand in the shade, waiting in her turn charity, which perhaps would never come.

For a moment, she had the sensible thought of saving preciously the few sous that remained to her, and spending them very prudently. But she felt so cold in her loneliness that she ended by going out in search of the May sunshine.

On her way, at the first road-stone, she met a young man whose heart was evidently withering from inanition. At that sight her sense of fervent charity awoke. She could not abandon her mission. And, beaming with kindness, superior in her abnegation, she brought the remainder of her heart to her lips, bent down slowly, and gave the youth a kiss, saying to him:

"Look, that is my last louis. Give me the change."

The young man gave her the change.

That same evening she sent her poor a circular letter, informing them that she found herself compelled to suspend her charity. The dear girl had only just sufficient left to live on in comfortable ease, with the last famished soul she had assisted.

The legend of Cupid's Little Blue Mantle has no moral.

THE BLACKSMITH

The blacksmith was a big fellow, the biggest in the neighborhood; he had knotty shoulders, his face and arms were black with the flames of the forge and the dust from the iron of the hammers. He had the great blue eyes of a child, as clear as steel, fixed in a square head, beneath thick bushy hair. His heavy jaw was replete with laughter and sounds of sonorous breath, similar to the puffing and merry creaking of his bellows; and when he raised his arms with a gesture that marked the satisfaction he felt at his strength—a gesture he had contracted while working at the anvil—he seemed to be bearing the weight of his fifty years with even greater ease than that which he displayed in wielding "the young lady," a ponderous lump weighing twenty-five pounds, a dreadful little girl which he alone was able to set dancing, between Vernon and Rouen.

I lived a year with the blacksmith, a whole year of convalescence. I had lost my heart, lost my head, I had left, going whither chance led me, endeavoring to become myself again, in search of a spot where I could be at peace and work, where I could recover my vigor. It was thus that one evening, on the highway, after having passed the village, I perceived the forge, all alone, all aflame, standing broadside at the four cross roads. The glare was such that the cart-door, which stood wide open, set the open space outside ablaze, and made the poplars which grew in a line opposite, beside a brook, smoke like torches. The cadence of the hammers resounded half a league away, in the peaceful twilight, and resembled the gallop of some iron host approaching nearer and nearer. Then, there, in the gaping doorway, in the light, in the uproar, amidst the vibration of that thunder, I stopped, happy and already consoled at the sight of that labor, at gazing on those human hands twisting and flattening out the red-hot bars.

On that autumn evening I saw the blacksmith for the first time. He was forging a ploughshare. With his shirt open, displaying his splendid chest, his ribs at each breath marking his metallic-like frame which had been put to the test, he threw himself back, gave a plunge, and brought down the hammer. And he did so, without a pause, with a smooth and continuous swaying of the body and a resolute tightening of the muscles. The hammer swung round in a perfect circle, carrying the sparks along with it and leaving a flash behind. It was "the young lady" which the blacksmith had thus set in motion with both hands; while his son, a strapping young fellow of twenty, held the flaming iron at the end of the pincers and beat it also, striking dull-sounding blows, which smothered the ringing dance of the elder's dreadful little girl. Toc, toc; toc; toc; one would have taken it for the grave voice of a mother encouraging the early lisping of her child. "The young lady" continued waltzing, agitating the spangles of her gown, and leaving the imprint of her heels in the ploughshare she was fashioning, each time she rebounded on the anvil. A crimson flame ran on to the ground, lighting up the prominent outlines of two workmen whose great shadows spread over the dark and confused corners of the forge. Little by little the blaze paled, the blacksmith stopped. He stood there black, erect, leaning on the handle of the hammer, and did not even trouble to wipe away the perspiration on his brow. I heard the panting of his flanks, which were still quivering, amidst the rumbling of the bellows which his son was slowly drawing.

I slept at the blacksmith's that night, and became a fixture there. He had a vacant room upstairs above the forge, which he offered me, and which I accepted. From five o'clock in the morning, before day broke, I associated myself with my host's work. I awoke amidst the mirth of the entire household, who continued in high spirits until nightfall. The hammers were dancing below. It seemed as if "the young lady" forced me to get out of bed by knocking at the ceiling and calling me a lazy fellow. All the modestly furnished room, with its big cupboard, its deal table, its two chairs, was creaking, shouting to me to be quick. And I had to go down. Below I found the forge already ablaze. The bellows were purring, a blue and red flame ascended from the coal—where a round star seemed to be shining—under the influence of the gusts of wind which penetrated the fuel. In the meanwhile the blacksmith was preparing the day's task. He was moving iron in the corners, turning over ploughs, examining wheels. When he perceived me he stuck his fists into his sides, the worthy man, and he laughed, making his mouth reach from ear to ear. He felt amused at having brought me out of bed at five o'clock. I believe he set hammering in the morning simply for the pleasure of hammering, to give notice with the formidable peal of his hammers that it was time to rise. He placed his great hands on my shoulders, and bent forward as if he were speaking to a child, telling me I looked better since I had been living amongst his old iron. And every morning we drank white wine together seated on the bottom of a little old cart turned upside down.

Then, I often spent a whole day at the forge. In winter particularly, when it was rainy weather, I have passed all my time there. I took an interest in the work. This continual struggle between the blacksmith and raw iron which he manipulated as he pleased, fascinated me like a powerful drama. I followed the metal with my eyes from the furnace to the anvil and met with constant surprises at the sight of it bending, extending, rolling, like a piece of soft wax in response to the workman's victorious exertion. When the plough was completed, I knelt down before it; I no longer recognized the shapeless mass of the previous day. I examined the pieces, dreaming that astonishingly strong fingers had taken them and fashioned them thus without the aid of fire. Sometimes I smiled when I remembered a young girl whom I had perceived, formerly, opposite my window, engaged whole days, twisting pieces of copper wire with her delicate hands, and then fixing artificial violets to them by the adjunct of silk thread.

The blacksmith never complained. I have often seen him of an evening, after having beaten iron for a day of fourteen hours, laughing his hearty laugh and rubbing his arms with an air of satisfaction. He was never sad, never weary. He would have shored-up the house with his shoulders had it shown signs of collapsing. He would say in the winter that it was nice and warm in his shop. In summer he set the door wide open and let the perfume of the hay enter. When the fine weather came, I used to go and sit down beside him, at the end of the day, before the door. We were half way up a hill, and from where we sat, we could see the entire breadth of the valley. He took pleasure in gazing on this immense expanse of tilled land, which faded out of sight on the horizon in the pale lilac twilight.

And the blacksmith often joked. He said that all this land belonged to him, that the forge had supplied all the neighborhood with ploughs for two hundred years. That was his pride. Not a crop grew without his help. If the plain were green in May and golden in July, it owed that change of color to him. He loved the harvests as his daughters, was in raptures at the bright sunshine, and shook his fist at a bursting hailstorm. He often pointed out to me some piece of land far away, which seemed no larger than the back of my jacket, and told me in what year he had wrought a plough for that square of oats or rye. Sometimes he set down his hammers during work-time, and went and gazed at the roadside with his hand shading his eyes. He was watching his numerous family of ploughs biting into the land, tracing their furrows opposite to him and to the right and left. The valley was full of them. To see the teams slowly moving along, one would have said they were regiments on the march. The ploughshares glittered in the sun with the brilliancy of silver. And he, extending his arms, called me, shouted to me to come and see what splendid work they were doing.

All that clangorous old iron that resounded underneath me, put iron into my blood It did me more good than the chemist's drugs. I was accustomed to the uproar; I had need of the music of the hammers on the anvil to feel myself alive. In my room, which the snorting of the bellows made quite cheerful, I recovered my poor head. Toc, toc; toc; toc; it was like the merry pendulum that regulated my hours of labor. At the hardest part of the work, when the blacksmith became angry, when I heard the red-hot iron cracking beneath the bounds of the frantic hammers, I felt the heated blood of a giant in my wrists; I would have liked to have flattened out the world with a stroke of my pen. Then, when the blacksmith's shop was quiet, all became silent in my skull; I went down, and when I saw that metal vanquished and still smoking, I felt ashamed of my own work.

Ah! How superb I have sometimes seen the blacksmith look on sultry afternoons! He was stripped to the waist, and his muscles were strained and salient, like some of those grand figures of Michael Angelo, who are straightening themselves in a final effort. In looking at him, I found that modern sculptural line, which our artists laboriously search for among the remains of ancient Greece. He seemed to me a hero made greater by labor, the untiring child of this century, who was for ever beating the implement of our analysis on the anvil, who was fashioning the society of the near future out of iron and by iron. He toyed with his hammers. When he felt in a merry mood, he took up "the young lady" and kept on thumping. He then produced thunder at home amidst the rosy flush of the furnace. I fancied I heard the sigh of the people at their task.

It was there, in the blacksmith's shop, amidst the ploughs, that I cured myself for ever of the evils of idleness and doubt.

THE SLACK SEASON

When the workmen reach the factory in the morning they find it looking frigid, as if overcast by a cloud of ruin. The machine with its slender limbs and motionless wheel, stands silent at the end of the great room; and this adds to the feeling of depression, for its puffing and vibration, in ordinary times, convey to the whole house the courage of a giant inured to the task.

The master comes down from his little private room, and with an air of sadness addresses the workmen thus:

"My good fellows, there is no work to-day—I receive no orders; countermands reach me from all quarters, I shall remain with goods on my hands. This month of December, on which I relied, this month which, in previous years, has been a very busy one, threatens to ruin the most stable firms— we must suspend everything."

And noticing the workmen looking at one another dreading to return home, in terror of approaching hunger, he added in a lower tone:

"I am not an egotist, no, I vow I am not. My position, also, is dreadful, more so perhaps than yours. I have lost fifty thousand francs in a week. I am stopping work to-day so as not to deepen the abyss; and I have not the first sou of the money I shall require to meet my acceptances on the 15th. You see I am speaking to you as to friends; I am hiding nothing from you. To-morrow, perhaps, the process-servers will be here. It is no fault of burs, is it? We have struggled on to the end. I would have liked to have helped you through this bad time; but it is all over now, I'm struck down; I've no more bread to share."

Then, he held out his hand to them. The workmen grasped it in silence. And, for some minutes, they remained there, gazing with clenched fists at their useless tools. On other mornings, the files sang, the hammers marked the rhythm from daybreak; and all this seems already to be sleeping in the dust of bankruptcy. Twenty or thirty families will be without food in the coming week. Some of the women who had been working in the factory have tears in the corners of their eyes. The men Endeavour to appear more firm. They put on a plucky look and say that no one can die of hunger in Paris.

Then when the master leaves them, and they see him walk away bowed down in a week, overwhelmed by a disaster which is perhaps even more serious than he acknowledges, they withdraw one by one, choking before they are out of the room, with lumps rising in their throats, and as disheartened as if they were leaving a deathbed. The corpse is work, the great silent machine, the sinister skeleton of which stands there in the obscurity.

The workman is outside, in the road, on the pavement. He has been running about the streets for a week without being able to find employment. He has been from door to door, offering his arms, his hands, his whole self for any kind of labor, the most revolting, the hardest, the most fatal. All doors have been closed to him.

Then, he was willing to work at half price. The doors did not open. Were he to work for nothing, he could not be employed. It is the slack season, the terrible slack season that sounds the death-knell of the garrets. The panic has stopped all trades, and money, cowardly money, has hidden itself away.

At the end of a week it is, indeed, all up with him. The workman has made a last effort, and he returns home slowly, his hands empty, worn out with wretchedness. It is raining on that particular night, and Paris looks dismal in the mud. He walks along in the downpour without feeling it, thinking of nothing but his hunger, stopping so as to reach his destination later. He has leant over a parapet of the Seine; the swollen waters flow with a prolonged noise; sprays of white foam are scattered in the air at one of the piers of the bridge. He leans more forward, the huge torrent passes beneath him, hailing him furiously to come. Then he says to himself that it would be cowardly, and he goes away.

It has stopped raining. The gas is flaming in the windows of the jewelers' shops. If he were to break a sheet of glass, he could grasp with one hand wherewith to give him bread for years. Lights are appearing in the kitchens of the restaurants; and behind the white muslin curtains he sees persons eating. He hurries along, ascends to the Faubourg, passing by the eating-houses, where poultry is roasting on spits, by the ham, and beef, and pastry-cooks' shops, by all that epicurean part of Paris, which displays its comestibles at hours when one is hungry.

As his wife and little girl had been crying in the morning, he had promised to bring food home at night. He had not dared to go and tell them he had lied, before the evening. As he walked along he was thinking how he would go in, what he would tell them to give them patience. However, they could not remain any longer without eating. He was willing to try and do so, but his wife and the little one were too delicate.

And, for a moment, he has the idea of begging. But when a lady and gentleman pass beside him, and he thinks of extending his hand, his arm becomes stiff, and he feels a lump in his throat. He stands there on the pavement, while respectable persons turn aside their heads, fancying, at the sight of his ferocious, starving look, that he must be intoxicated.

The workman's wife has gone down to the front door, leaving the little one asleep upstairs. The woman is quite thin, and is dressed in a cotton gown. She is shivering in the icy blast of the wind in the street.

She has nothing more at home. She has pawned everything. A week without work was sufficient to clear out the lodging. On the previous evening she sold the last lot of wool from her mattress to the second-hand dealer; the mattress had gone thus; now, there only remained the tick. She has hung that up before the window to keep out the draught, for the little one coughs a great deal

Without saying anything to her husband, she, on her side, had endeavored to get work. But the slack season has been more cruel for the women than the men. There are unhappy creatures in rooms on her landing that she hears sobbing at night. She met one begging at the corner of a street; another is dead; another has disappeared.

She, fortunately, is married to a good man, a husband who does not drink. They would be in comfort, if the slack seasons had not despoiled them of all. She has used up all her credit. She owes money to the baker, the grocer, and does not even dare pass by their shops any more. In the afternoon she went to her sister to borrow a franc; but there, also, she had found such poverty that she began to cry without speaking, and both of them, her sister and herself, had wept for a long time together. Then, as she was leaving, she promised to take her a piece of bread if her husband brought anything home.

The husband does not return. It rains. She seeks shelter under the doorway; great drops of water splash down at her feet, and the fine rain soaks her thin gown. At times she feels impatient; she goes out, notwithstanding the downpour,' goes to the end of the street, to see if she cannot perceive the person she is expecting coming along the road in the distance. And when she returns she is wet through; she smoothes down her hair with her hands, to wipe it; she still takes patience although troubled with short feverish shivers.

Passers-by elbow her as they go backwards and forwards; she makes herself as small as possible so as not to be in any one's way. Men stare her full in the face; at times she feels warm wafts of breath skim across her neck. It seems as if all the dubious side of Paris, the street with its mud, its raw lights, its rolling of carriages, would like to clutch her and cast her in the gutter. She is hungry, any one can take her. There is a baker opposite, and she thinks of the little one asleep upstairs.

Then, when her husband at length appears, hurrying along close to the houses like a worthless fellow, she dashes forward and gazes at him anxiously.

"Well!" she stammers.

He does not answer, but hangs his head. Then, she goes upstairs the first, as pale as death.

Upstairs, the little one is not sleeping. She has woke up, she is thinking in front of a candle end that is flickering on a corner of the table. And something monstrous and heartrending passes over the countenance of that chit of seven, who has the worn and serious features of a grown-up woman.

She is seated at the edge of a trunk which serves her for a bed. Her bare feet are dangling down, shivering with cold; her sickly, doll like hands gather the rags that form her covering, about her chest. She feels a burning there, a fire she would like to extinguish. She is thinking.

She has never had any playthings. She cannot go to school because she has no shoes. She remembers that when she was younger her mother used to take her out into the sun. But that was a long while ago. It had been necessary to move; and, since then, it seemed as if an intense chill had spread over her home. Then, she had ceased to be happy; she had been always hungry.

She is entering upon something very profound, without being able to understand it. Every one is hungry then? She has sought, however, to accustom herself to the feeling and has been unable. She thinks she must be too little, that it is necessary to be big to understand. Her mother, no doubt, knows all about this matter which is concealed from children. If she dared she would ask her who it is that puts you into the world in this way in order that you may be hungry.

Then, their home is so unsightly! She looks at the window where the tick of the mattress is flapping, at the bare walls, the rickety furniture, at all that disgraceful aspect of the garret to which the slack season conveys such a look of despair. She fancies, in her ignorance, that she must have dreamt of warm rooms with beautiful shiny things; she closes her eyes to see them again; and, through her eyelids, which have become thinner, the candlelight seems a great blaze of gold into which she would like to go. But the wind is blowing, and such a draught comes through the window that she is seized with a fit of coughing. Her eyes become full of tears.

Formerly she felt afraid when left all alone. Now she does not know whether she is afraid or not; it is all the same to her. As they have not had anything to eat since the previous evening, she fancies her mother has gone downstairs to get some bread. Then that thought interests her. She will cut her bread into very small pieces; she will take them slowly, one by one. She will play with her bread.

Her mother has returned, her father has closed the door. The little one looks at both their hands very much surprised; and, as her parents say nothing, she repeats, after a moment, in a hum-drum tone:

"I'm hungry, I'm hungry."

The father is seated in an obscure corner, with his head between his hands; he remains there, bowed down, his shoulders quivering with heavy, silent sobs. The mother, stifling her tears, has come to put the little one to bed again. She covers her with all the clothes in the place, and tells her to be good and go to sleep. But the child, whose teeth are chattering with cold, and who feels the burning in her chest more acutely, becomes very bold. She hangs round her mother's neck, and then murmurs softly:

"Tell me, mamma, why are we hungry?"

THE LITTLE VILLAGE

Where is the little village? In what dip of the ground are its white habitations hidden? Are they grouped round the church, at the bottom of some hollow? Or do they follow on one after the other along the highway? Or, again, do they climb the side of a hill, like capricious goats, ranging in terraces and half hiding their red roofs amidst the foliage?

Has the little village a name that sounds sweet to the ear? Is it a tender name, easy to French lips, or some German name, harsh, bristling with consonants, as guttural as the croaking of a raven?

And are there harvests; are there vintages at the little village? Is it a land of corn or a land of vines? What are the inhabitants doing at the present time, in the fields, in broad daylight? As they return in the evening, along the lanes, do they stay to take a glance at the bountiful crops, thanking Heaven for a good year?

I can easily picture it to myself upon a hillside. It is there, lying so unassumingly among the trees, that, from a distance, one would take it for a mass of fallen rocks, covered with moss. But coils of smoke issue from amidst the branches; on a pathway running down the slope, children are pushing along a wheelbarrow. Then, looking from the plain, you gaze at it with a feeling of jealous envy; and you go your way bearing along with you the remembrance of this nest of which you have just caught a glimpse.

No, I rather fancy it is in a corner of the plain, beside a stream. It is so small that a curtain of poplars suffices to conceal it from view. Its thatched cottages vanish in the osier-holt on the bank, like modest women at the bath. For a sward, it has a bit of green meadow; a quickset hedge encloses it on all sides, like a garden. You pass by it without seeing it. The voices of the women who are washing resound like the notes of feathered songsters. There is not a single streak of smoke. It slumbers peacefully in the recesses of its verdant alcove.

None of us know it. The neighboring town is hardly aware of its existence, and it is so humble that no geographer has ever troubled about it. It is nothing. When its name is uttered it recalls no remembrance. Among the swarm of towns with ringing appellations, it is a place unknown, without history, glory, or shame, and it stands modestly in the background.

And it is no doubt for that reason that the little village smiles so sweetly.

Its laborers live in the desert; its babes roll on the river's bank; the women spin in the shade of the trees. As for itself, quite delighted at its obscurity, it finds ample pleasure in the charm of open air. It is so far from the mud and noise of great cities! Its ray of sunshine suffices it. It takes delight in its silence, its humility, and in that curtain of poplars hiding it from the whole world.

And tomorrow, perhaps, the whole world will know of the existence of the little village.

Ah! What wretchedness! The river will be crimson, the curtain of poplars will have been swept away by bullets, the gutted cottages will testify to the silent despair of the families; the little village will be famous.

The song of women washing at the stream will be heard no more; there will be no more babes rolling on the river banks, no more harvests, no more silence, no more happy humility. A new name in history, victory or defeat, a new sanguinary page, a new corner of our country enriched with the blood of our offspring.

It smiles, it slumbers, it does not know that it will give its name to a butchery, and to-morrow it will weep, its name will re-echo through Europe with a death-rattle. Then it will remain on the earth like a stain of blood. It, so gay, so tender, will be surrounded by a dark sinister circle, it will see pallid visitors pass before its ruins, as one passes before the slabs at the Morgue. It will be accursed.

As for us, if it be Austerlitz or Magenta, we shall hear it resound in our hearts as the trumpet's blast. And, if it be Waterloo, it will roll lugubriously in our memory, like the sound of a drum muffled with crape that heads the funeral procession of a nation.

How it will then regret its solitary river-banks, its ignorant peasantry, its remote corner, so far removed from men, known only to the swallows who returned there each spring! Defiled, ashamed, with its sky overcast by a flight of carrion crows, and its slimy soil stinking of death, it will go down to posterity as a place of slaughter^ an ominous spot where two nations slew one another.

The nest of love, the nest of peace, the little village will be naught henceforth but a cemetery, the common pit where weeping mothers will not be able to go and place their wreaths.

France has strewn the world with these distant graveyards. We could kneel and pray at the four corners of Europe. Pere Lachaise, Montmartre, Montparnasse, are not our only fields of rest; there are others that bear the names of all our victories and all our defeats. There is not a corner beneath the whole canopy of heaven, from China to Mexico, from the snow of

Russia to the sand of Egypt, where some murdered Frenchman does not lie

They are silent and deserted cemeteries, wrapped in heavy slumber amidst the intense peacefulness of the country. The greater number of them, almost all, spread out beside some desolate hamlet, the crumbling walls of which are still full of horror. Waterloo was but a farm, at Magenta there were barely fifty houses. A frightful blast has blown over these infinitely small places, and the syllables that form their names, which were innocent the previous evening, have taken such an odor of blood and powder that people will for ever shudder when they find them on their lips.

Thoughtfully I cast my eyes on a map of the seat of war. I followed the banks of the Rhine; I searched among the plains and the mountains. Was the little village to the right or left of the river? Must I look for it in the neighborhood of the fortresses, or further on in some broad expanse of solitude?

And then, closing my eyes, I endeavored to picture to myself that peaceful spot, that curtain of poplar trees drawn before the white houses, that piece of meadow-land skimmed by the wings of the swallows, those songs of the women washing, that virgin soil to which war was to do violence, and the news of the contamination of which was to be brutally blown to the four corners of the horizon by the bugles.

But where then is the little village?

SOUVENIRS

I

Oh! The everlasting rain, the horrid rain, the grey rain that drapes the skies of May and June in mourning! You go to the window and draw back the curtain. The sun is swamped. Between two showers, it rises to the surface, pallid, turned green, like a heavenly body that has committed suicide in despair, and which some celestial mariner drags back with his boathook.

Do you remember, Ninon, the bitter north wind in spring, after it has rained? You leave Paris with the spring weather of the poets, the springtime one has been longing for in one's heart, a mild season, a profusion of flowers, delicious twilights. You reach your destination at nightfall. The sky is deathlike, not a spark of brightness lights up the sunset which recalls to mind a dismal grate full of cold cinders. You have to stride across pools of water in the pathways with the gnawing damp of the foliage on your shoulders. And when you are in the great melancholy room which winter has made chilly, you shiver, you close doors and windows, and light a great fire of old vine stalks, hurling imprecations against the sun's laziness!

The rain keeps you confined to the house for a week. In the distance, in the middle of the lake formed by the inundated meadows, there is always the same curtain of poplar trees melting into water, streaming with it and looking thin and indistinct in the vapor that envelops them. Then a grey ocean, a fine rain drifting along and barring the horizon. You yawn, you Endeavour to take an interest in the ducks that venture into the downpour, in the blue umbrellas of the country folk passing by. You yawn wider. The chimneys smoke, the green wood sweats without burning, it seems as if the flood were rising, that it's roaring at the door, that it penetrates through all the chinks like fine sand. And in despair you take the train again, you return to Paris vowing that sun and spring do not exist.

And yet nothing causes me more despair than those cabs which you meet hurrying towards the railway stations. They are loaded with trunks, and their occupants pass through the city with the beaming countenances of prisoners who have just been set at liberty.

I tramp along the pavements, I watch them rolling towards blue rivers, great seas, great mountains, great woods. This one is perhaps bound for a hollow amidst rocks that I know of near Marseilles; you are quite at your ease in that hollow, where you can strip as in a bathing-machine, and where the waves come to meet you. That one is certainly running off to Normandy, to that verdant nook I love, near the hillside which produces that light tart wine with the bouquet that so agreeably tickles the inside of one's throat. That other is no doubt setting out for the unknown, here or there, some place where one will assuredly be very comfortable, in the shade, perhaps in the sun, I don't know; in a word, there where I am burning to go.

The drivers flog their sorry nags with the handles of their whips. They seem to have no idea that they are whipping my dream. They are saying to themselves that the trunks are heavy and the gratuities light. They do not even know that they are saddening the hearts of the poor fellows who pass along on Shank's mare, and whose destiny it is to char the soles of their boots at Paris, on the burning pavement, in July and August.

Oh! That string of cabs, loaded with trunks, rolling towards the railway stations! That vision of the great cage thrown open, of happy birds taking their flight! That cruel raillery of liberty crossing our galleys of streets and squares! That nightmare of all my springs troubling me in my dungeon, filling me with an uncontrollable desire for foliage and cloudless skies.

I should like to become quite small, very small indeed, and slip into the big trunk of that lady with the pink bonnet, whose brougham is going in the direction of the Lyons railway station. One would assuredly feel very comfortable in that lady's trunk. I can picture to myself the silky skirts, the fine linen, all kinds of soft things perfumed and pleasant. I would lie on some pale silk; I would have cambric pocket-handkerchiefs beneath my nose, and if I were cold, faith, never mind! I would cover myself with all the petticoats.

The lady is extremely pretty. Twenty-five at the most. A lovely chin with a dimple that must deepen when she smiles. I should like to make her laugh just to see. That rascal of a coachman is very fortunate to drive her about in his box. She must be fond of violets. I am sure her linen is scented with that perfume. It is exquisite. I roll at the bottom of her trunk for hours and days together. I have hollowed out a place to lie in at the left-hand corner, between the bundle of chemises and a large cardboard box that is somewhat in my way. I had the curiosity to raise the lid of that box; it contained two hats, a small pocket-book full of letters, then things I would not look at. I placed the cardboard box under my head and made a pillow of it. I roll, roll. The stockings are on my right; beneath me are three costumes, and on my left I feel things that offer more resistance, which I fancy I recognize as pairs of little boots. Good gracious, how comfortable one feels among all these musk-pervaded chiffons!

Where may we be going to? Shall we stop in Burgundy? Shall we turn aside towards Switzerland or go down as far as Marseilles? I picture to myself that we are going to that rocky hollow, you know, where one can strip as in a bathing machine, and where the waves come to meet you. She will bathe. One is a hundred leagues away from idiots. The inlet, at its extremity, is rounded off by the deep blue of the Mediterranean. Above, at the edge of the hollow, are three pines. And, with bare feet on the large slabs of yellow stone which pave the sea, we dislodge sea snails with the points of our knives. She doesn't look stuck-up. She will enjoy the open-air, and we shall be like children. If she cannot swim, I will teach her.

The trunk is being terribly shaken; we must be ascending the Rue de Lyon. And how delightful it will be when, on reaching Marseilles, she opens her trunk! She will be very" much surprised to find me there, in the left-hand corner. I trust I shall not crumple all these flounces, on which I am lying, too much!—"What, sir! You are there, you have dared!" "Certainly, madam; there is nothing one would not dare to get out of prison "And I will explain it to her and she will forgive me.

Ah! Here we are at the railway station. I think they are booking me

Alas! Alas! It rains, and the lady with the pink bonnet is on her way all alone in the rain, with her big trunk, to go and yawn at the house of some old aunt in the country, where she will shiver, in a bad temper, at the chilly spring.

II

One must have resided in a pious and aristocratic town, one of those small places where the grass grows in the streets, and where the convent bells strike the hours in the sleepy atmosphere, to know what processions on Corpus Christi day are like.

At Paris, four priests walk round the Madeleine. In Provence the clergy have possession of the thoroughfares for a week. All the population of the Middle Ages is resuscitated on those bright afternoons, and proceeds along, singing hymns and trotting candles about, with a couple of gendarmes at the head, and the Mayor, girded with his sash, at the tail.

I have not forgotten them. They were delightful times for us college boys, who only wanted an excuse to run about the streets. To be candid, processions in those amorous towns are just the thing for lovers. The girls show off their new gowns all along the way. A new gown is indispensable. There is not a young girl, however poor she may be, who on those occasions does not drape herself in a piece of brand new printed calico. In the evening the churches are in obscurity, and many are the hands that meet.

I belonged to a musical club that took part in all the solemnities. I have heavy sins on my conscience. I tax myself with having at that period awakened more than one functionary at daybreak with a concert, on his return from Paris with the red ribbon. I tax myself with having trotted the official divinity about, as well as the saints who make it rain, and the holy virgins who cure cholera. I have even assisted the moving-out of a convent of cloistered nuns. The poor girls, wrapped up in large pieces of grey linen so that no one might see their faces or limbs, stumbled, supported each other like phantoms of the departed surprised by dawn. And tiny white hands, child-like hands, appeared at the edge of the grey cloths.

Alas! Yes, I have partaken of the vestry collations. We were not paid for what we did; they gave us a few cakes. I remember that on the day the nuns were installed in the new convent we were served by means of a turning-box. Bottles, plates of cakes followed one another in the wall as if by enchantment. And what bottles, ye gods! Of every shape, every color, containing every kind of liquor. I have often dreamt of that strange cellar which could supply such a variety of choice wines. It was a hodge-podge of good things.

I have long done penitence since those days of error, and I think I have been pardoned.

The streets which the procession is to follow are decked from early morning with flags. Each window has something. In the wealthy quarters there are old tapestries displaying great mythological figures, all the pagan Olympia, nude and pallid, coming to see Catholic Olympia pass by with its pale virgins and bleeding Christs; there are also silk quilts taken from the beds of certain noble dames, damask curtains unhooked from the poles in the drawing-rooms, velvety carpets, and all sorts of costly material that astonishes the passers-by. The middle classes show their embroidered muslins and finest linen; and, in the quarters of the poor, the good women, rather than display nothing, hang out their neckerchiefs and scarves which they have tacked together. Then the streets are worthy of the Host.

They have swept the thoroughfares. In certain corners they' have arranged halting-places, and these arouse much jealousy and hatred, which lasts for months and months. If that in the Chartreux quarter is more beautiful than that of Saint Mark, it is sufficient to turn the hair of the devout in the latter quarter grey. All the neighborhood contributes towards these halting-places. One has brought the candlesticks, another the gilded vases, another the flowers, another the lace. It is a shelter that the quarter presents to heaven.

In the meantime two rows of chairs have been placed along the narrow footways. The sightseers are waiting; they are very noisy, laughing with that south-of-France laughter which sounds like a clarion. The windows are becoming filled with spectators. The heat decreases; and, amidst the gentle rising breeze, one hears the peal of bells and beating of drums in the distance.

It is the procession that has left the church.

In front of it walk all the young bucks of the town. This promenade is a regular thing. They come there to see and be seen. The girls are at the doors. There are discreet greetings, smiles, whisperings among comrades. The young men go all round the town in this way, between two rows of flag-bedecked windows, solely to pass beneath a particular one. They look up, and that is all. The afternoon is warm, the bells peal; the children cast handfuls of broom flowers and roses picked to pieces into the street and gutters.

The road is rosy; the broom flowers form patches of gold on the pale pink. First of all two gendarmes show themselves, then comes the file of children brought up by charity, of schools, benefit societies, old ladies and old gentlemen. A Christ is borne along by a beadle at arm's length. A thick-set monk carries a complicated emblem in which all the instruments of the Passion are represented. Four buxom maidens, bursting in their white frocks, are steadying, by the aid of ribbons, an immense banner, on which a little sheep is depicted innocently sleeping. Then, above the heads, in the candle-light, which seems awed by the light of day, rise the silver incense-burners, casting flashes and leaving a thick cloud of smoke behind them, which twirls round for a moment in its whiteness, like a shred of all those muslin gowns that are passing along behind one another.

The procession moves slowly with a dull tramp, above which is heard the sound of suppressed voices. There is a clash of cymbals and a jingle of brass, followed by shrill utterances that die away, faint and feeble, in the broad expanse of open air. A muttering of lips is heard. And, suddenly, there are long silences. Now the procession glides along softly; the scene resembles a chapel all lit up, and lost in the sunshine. Distant drums are beating a march.

I remember the penitents. There were some of all colors —white, grey, blue. The latter have attributed to themselves the terrible mission of burying executed criminals. They number among them the most illustrious names of the city. Attired in a blue serge gown, with a pointed headpiece and a long veil perforated with a couple of holes for the eyes, they look really ferocious. As the holes are often too far apart, the eyes seem to squint beneath this terrifying mask. At the hem of the gown you perceive light grey trousers and patent leather boots.

The penitents excite the most curiosity of all. A procession without them is a poor affair. Here, at last, are the clergy. Sometimes small children carry palm leaves, ears of corn on cushions, wreaths, and pieces of gold plate. But the devout are turning round their chairs, kneeling, and casting their eyes to the ground. The canopy is advancing. It is monumental, hung with red velvet, surmounted by clusters of plumes, and supported by gilt poles. I have seen sub-prefects carrying this immense awning, beneath which sickly religion takes an airing in the June sun. A band of children of the choir walk backwards, swinging the incense-burners high into the air. One hears naught but the psalmody of the priests and the silvery sound of the chains of the incense-burners each time they are swung forward.

Limping Catholicism is creeping along beneath the blue sky of old convictions. The sun sets; its rosy blushes fade away on the housetops; twilight brings great peacefulness; and, in that limpid air of the south, the procession moves off with voices that are dying away, depicting the melancholy effacement of an entire age descending into the tomb.

The authorities follow in their official attire, the Law Courts, the Faculties, without counting the churchwardens, with their carved and gilded lanterns. And the vision disappears. The rose leaves, the golden flowers of the broom are crushed to atoms; and nothing now rises from the street but the unpleasant smell of all these faded flowers.

Sometimes the procession is overtaken by darkness as it returns by the narrow, crooked lanes in the old quarter of the city. The white gowns become nothing more than vague indications of something light; the penitents form a confused dark line along the pavements; the small candle flames cast will-o'-the-wisps and slowly falling stars on the blackness of the houses boxing up the narrow way. And voices are accompanied by a sort of quiver, as of fright, amidst these crosses, these banners, this canopy, the supports of which are hardly distinguishable in the gloom.

That is the time when the rogues fondle the young minxes. The organ booms at the end of the church, the Host has returned home. Then the girls go off with kisses on their necks and love letters in their pocket.

III

When I cross the bridges on these sultry evenings, the Seine calls to me with a friendly roar. It runs broad and fresh with amorous languor, offering itself to one and loitering between the quays. Water has something of the crumpling sound of a silk skirt. It is a gentle lover, and inspires one with an irresistible desire to spring towards it.

The owners of the floating bathing establishments, who had watched the persistent fall of rain in May with terror, perspire in beatitude beneath the sultry June sun. The water at last is warm. From six o'clock in the morning there is a crush. Bathing drawers are not given time to dry, and towards evening, there are no more gowns.

I remember my first visit to one of these baths, to one of these great wooden tubs, in which the bathers turn about in much the same way as straws dance at the bottom of a pot of boiling water.

I had just come from a small town, from a little river where I had dabbled with absolute freedom, and I was horrified at this trough in which water took the color of soot.

Towards six o'clock in the evening the crowd is such that one must calculate one's plunge in order not to take a seat on somebody's back, or dash into a person's stomach. There is froth on the water, the white bodies give it a neutral tint, while the pieces of cloth stretched on cords by way of a ceiling, allow a dim light to penetrate within.

The noise is frightful. At times the water spurts up, under the influence of a sudden plunge, and rolls with the sound of distant artillery. Some jokers, beating the river with their hands, imitate the tic-tac of water-mills; and there are others who practice falling backward, so as to make as much racket as possible and inundate the establishment. But that is nothing in comparison to the intolerable yells, that yelping of voices which reminds one of a school in playtime. Man becomes a child again in pure water. Grave persons walking along the quays, cast startled looks at those flapping cloths, between which they perceive great capering nude figures. Ladies pass along more rapidly.

I have nevertheless enjoyed some pleasant hours there, in the very early morning, while the city still slumbered. It is no longer the swarm of lean shoulders, bald heads and enormous stomachs of the afternoon. The bath is almost deserted. A few young fellows are swimming there in a resolute manner. The water is fresher after its night's rest. It is more pure, more virgin-like.

You must go there before five o'clock. The air is mild when the city awakens. Nothing is more delicious than to follow the quays, gazing at the water with that covetous look of lovers. It will be yours. The water slumbers in the bath. You will arouse it. You can take it silently in your arms. You feel the current flowing with a fleeting caress along your body, from the back of your neck to your heels.

The rising sun casts rosy streaks on the cloths that deck the ceiling. But the more ardent kisses of the river cause a shiver to run over one's skin, and it is then good to wrap one's self in a gown and take a walk along the galleries. You are at Athens with bare feet, the neck at liberty, and a simple robe would round you. Trousers, waistcoat, frock coat, boots and hat, are far away. You enjoy your state of nudity at your ease in this piece of linen. You are borne away in fancy's dream to springtime in Greece, at the edge of the eternal blue of the Archipelago.

But you must run off as soon as the band of bathers arrives. They bring the heat of the streets clinging to their heels with them. The river is no more the virgin of early morn; it is the noon-day girl who gives herself away to every one, who is all bruised, all warm with the embraces of the crowd.

And what frights! Ladies passing along the quays do well to hurry on. A museum of antiquities, caricatured by some witty artist, would not present anything so painfully comical.

It is a terrible trial for a modern man, a Parisian, to strip himself. Prudent fellows never go to cold baths. One day they pointed out a counselor of state to me there, who looked so pitiful with his pointed shoulders and his poor, flat stomach, that every time I came across his name in the papers, I could not repress a smile.

There are the fat, thin, tall, and short; those who float on the water like bladders, those who bury themselves in it, and seem to melt away like sticks of barley-sugar. The flesh is flabby, the bones prominent, the heads enter into the shoulders or are perched upon necks that resemble those of plucked fowls, the arms are as long as paws and the legs are drawn up like the twisted appendages of ducks. Some are all buttock, others all stomach, and there is another kind with neither one nor the other. It is a grotesque and lamentable exhibition, and pity stays the burst of hilarity one feels inclined to give at the sight of it.

The worst of it all is that these miserable bodies retain the pride of the black coats and purses they have left in the cloakroom. Some drape themselves, gather up the corners of their gowns, in the attitudes of purse - proud landlords. Others walk in their extravagant nudity, with the dignity of heads of departments passing among their multitude of clerks. The youngest put on airs as if they fancied themselves behind the scenes of some small theatre in short coats; the oldest forget that they have taken off their stays, and that they are not at the fireside, in the mansion of the beautiful Countess de B .

During an entire season, at the baths of the Pont-Royal, I saw a fat man as round as a barrel and as red as a ripe tomato, who posed as Alcibiades.

He had studied the folds of his gown before one of David's paintings. He was on the Agora; he smoked with antique gestures. When he deigned to cast himself into the Seine, it was Leander crossing the Hellespont to join Hero. The poor creature. I still remember his short torso to which the water gave violet blotches. O human hideousness!

No, I prefer my little river to that. We did not even put on drawers. What was the good of them? The kingfishers and wagtails did not trouble to blush. And we chose the holes, the "goures" as they call them in the South.

You could cross the river without wetting your feet, by jumping from stone to stone; but the holes were of a tragic character. Some devoured two or three children every year. There were most awful legends connected with them, and there were boards covered with threats which, however, troubled us but little. We used them for targets, and in many instances there only remained a bit of wood held on by a nail, which swung backward and forward in the wind.

The water was burning hot in the evening. The fierce sun heated that in the holes to such a degree, that it was necessary to allow it to cool in the first freshness of twilight. We remained naked on the sand for hours, wrestling, throwing stones at the boards, catching frogs with our hands in the mud. Night set in, and an immense sigh, a sigh of relief, passed over the trees. Then it was a bathing party without end. When we were tired, we lay down in the water, at the edge of it, where it was shallow, with our heads on tufts of grass. It was then that ushers were judged with severity, and that exercises sped away in the smoke of our first pipes.

Good old river where I learnt to float, tepid water in which the little white fish were cooking, I love thee still as a sweetheart of my childhood. You took a comrade of ours one night, in one of those holes which we laughed at, and it is perhaps that stain of blood on your green gown, which has left within me a thrill of desire for your narrow streak of water. There are sobs in your innocent prattle.

IV

I care for but one sort of sport with the gun, a sport accompanied by tranquil charms with which Parisians are unfamiliar. Here, in the fields, are hares and partridges. You do not waste powder on sparrows; you disdain larks, reserving your shot for larger birds. In Provence hares and partridges are rare; sportsmen stay abroad for feathered warblers, for all the little birds in the bushes. When they have killed their dozen beccaficos, they return home very proud.

I have often wandered over ploughed ground for whole days to take back three or four wheatears. I sank up to the ankles in the soil, which gave way like fine sand. In the evening, when I could no longer stand, I returned home delighted.

If, by a miracle, a hare passed between my legs I watched it run with righteous astonishment, so little was I accustomed to meet with such large creatures. I remember a covey of partridges getting up one morning in front of me; I remained so stupefied at that loud sound of wings, that I discharged my gun without aiming, and peppered a telegraph pole.

Besides, I acknowledge that I have always been a wretched shot. If I have killed a good many sparrows in my time, I have never been able to bring down a swallow.

That is no doubt why I prefer shooting in ambush.

Imagine a sort of small round construction sunk into the ground, and rising a little more than three feet above it. This hut, built up with loose stones, is roofed with tiles, which are hidden as much as possible by sprays of ivy. You might take it for a ruined tower razed near to its foundations, and hidden in the grass.

The narrow space within receives light from loopholes, which are closed by movable windows. The retreat has generally a fire-place and cupboards; I have even known one with a divan. Dead trees are planted round the hut, and at the foot of them are hung the cages of the decoy birds, imprisoned songsters whose business it is to call those that are free.

The tactics are simple. The sportsman, quietly shut up, smokes his pipe and waits. He watches the dead trees through the loopholes. Then, when a bird perches on a dry branch, he methodically takes his gun, rests the barrel on the edge of a loophole, and annihilates the wretched creature almost at the muzzle.

That is the only way in which people of Provence shoot birds of passage, ortolans in August, and thrushes in November.

I used to set out at three o'clock on icy cold mornings in November. I had a league to go in the dark, loaded like a mule; for it is necessary to take the decoy birds with you, and I can assure any one that some thirty cages are not carried so easily in a hilly country, along paths that are barely traced out. You place the cages on long wooden frames, where they are secured close to one another by strings.

When I reached my destination it was still dark, the tableland expanded, broad, savage, -in a mass of gloom, with its multitude of grey scrubby bushes. All around me, in the darkness, I heard that murmur of the pines, that great confused voice, which resembles the lamentations of the waves. I was then fifteen, and did not always feel very comfortable. It was already an emotion, a palpitating pleasure that I was experiencing.

But I had to be quick. Thrushes are early birds. I hung up my cages and shut myself in the hut. It was too soon as yet, I could not distinguish the branches of the dead trees. And notwithstanding I heard the harsh whistling of the thrushes above my head. Those vagabonds travel by night. I lit a fire grumbling, and hastened to get a bright blaze that shone rosy on the cinders. As soon as the sport begins not a bit of smoke must issue from the hut. It might frighten away the game. While waiting for daybreak I grilled mutton chops on the embers.

And I went from loophole to loophole, searching for the first pale glimmer of daylight. Nothing yet; the bare limbs of the dead trees were dimly distinguishable. My eyesight was bad even then, and I was afraid of firing at a black spot on one of the branches, as sometimes happens. I did not rely on my eyes alone, I listened. The silence was disturbed by a thousand sounds, those whisperings, those profound sighs of the earth at its awakening. The wail of the pines increased, and, at times, it seemed to me as if an innumerable flight of thrushes were about to swoop down upon the hut, whistling furiously.

But the clouds were becoming milky. The dead trees stood out in black against the clear sky with singular distinctness. Then all my faculties were strained, and I was bent double with anxiety.

How my heart leapt when I suddenly perceived the long silhouette of a thrush on one of the dead trees! The thrush stretches out its neck, shows itself off to the first ray of the sun, in the stream of morning light. I clutched my gun with the utmost precaution, so as not to knock the barrel or stock against anything. I fired, the bird fell. I did not go to pick it up, that might have driven away other victims.

And I began to wait again, agitated by a feeling of excitement similar to that of a gambler who has had a lucky hand, and is in doubt as to what chance may have in store for him. All the pleasure of this kind of sport is in the unforeseen, in the willingness of the game to come and be slaughtered. Will another thrush perch on one of the dead trees? The question is perplexing. But I was not particular: when thrushes failed to come, I killed small birds.

I see the little hut again now, at the edge of the great deserted plateau. A fresh perfume of thyme and lavender comes from the hills. The decoys whistle softly amidst the loud rustling of the pines. The sun shows a lock of its flaming hair on the horizon; and there, on one of the dead trees, in the white light, a thrush stands motionless.

Go you and run after the hares, and do not laugh or you will drive my thrush away.

V

I have two cats. One of them, Françoise, is as white as a May morning. The other, Catherine, is as black as a stormy night.

Françoise has the laughing, round head of a European girl. Her great eyes, which are of a pale green color, cover almost all her face. Her nose and rosy lips are coated with carmine. Any one would say they were painted like a virgin madly in love with her form. She is fat, plump, Parisian to the end of her claws. She seeks to attract attention when she walks, giving herself engaging airs, turning up her tail with the sudden shiver of a little lady gathering up the train of her gown.

Catherine has the pointed and delicately molded head of an Egyptian goddess. Her eyes, which are as yellow as golden moons, have the same fixity and impenetrable harshness as the pupils of a barbarian idol. The corners of her thin lips display the everlasting ironic smile of the Sphinx. When she squats on her hind paws, holding her head up motionless, she is a divinity in black marble, the great hieratic Pacht of the Theban temples.

Both pass their days on the yellow sand in the garden.

Françoise rolls on her back, and is very busy with her ablutions, licking her paws with the delicate care of a coquette who is whitening her hands in oil of sweet almonds. She has not three ideas in her head. It is easy to see that by her crazy-like air of a very fashionable lady.

Catherine thinks. She thinks, looking without seeing, penetrating with her gaze the unknown world of the gods. She remains sitting up erect for hours, implacable, smiling with her strange smile of a sacred animal.

When I caress Francoise with my hand, she curves her back and slightly mews with delight. She is so happy at having attention paid to her! She looks up with a wheedling movement, returning my caress by rubbing her nose against my cheek. Her hair quivers, her tail is gently waved. And she ends by closing her eyes, going off into a doze, and softly purring.

When I want to caress Catherine, she avoids my hand. She prefers a solitary existence amidst her religious dream. She has the modesty of a goddess who feels irritated and wounded at all human contact. If I succeed in taking her on my knees, she flattens herself out, stretches her neck, fixes her eyes ready to escape at a bound. Her nervous limbs and lean body are inert beneath my fingers which are fondling her. She does not deign to lower herself to the joy of love for a mortal.

And so Francoise is a daughter of Paris, doxy or marchioness, she is a light-headed, charming creature, who would give herself away for a compliment on her white coat; while Catherine is the daughter of some city in ruins, I know not where, out there in the region of the sun. They belong to two civilizations; one is a modern doll, the other an idol of a nation that has ceased to exist.

Ah I if I could but read in their eyes! I take them in my arms; I gaze at them fixedly, so that they may tell me their secret. They do not lower their eyelids, and it is they that study me. I read nothing in the glassy transparency of those orbs which open like fathomless holes, like dim wells throwing out bright sparks.

And Francoise purrs more tenderly, whereas the yellow glances of Catherine pierce me like brass wire.

Françoise recently became a mother. This madcap has a good heart. She gives the most tender attention to the one kitten that has been left her. She takes it up delicately by the nape of the neck and carries it into all the cupboards in the house.

Catherine watches her, lost in deep thought. The kitten interests her. In its presence she gives herself the attitudes of an ancient philosopher reflecting on the life and death of creatures, building up a whole system of philosophy in dreamland.

Yesterday, in the absence of the mother, she went and crouched down beside the little one. She smelt it, turned it over with her paw. Then, she suddenly carried it into a dark corner. There, thinking herself well hidden, she stood before the little creature, with flashing eyes, and quivering spine, like a priestess preparing for a sacrifice. I believe she was about to crush the victim's head between her teeth, when I promptly interfered and drove her away. As she ran off she cast diabolical, cringing looks at me in silence, without swearing.

Well! I still like Catherine; I like her because she is perfidious and cruel, like a fiend of hell. What care I for the gentle gracefulness of Francoise, her delightful airs, her ways of a madcap I All our daughters of Eve are white and purr as she does. But I have never yet been able to find a sister to Catherine, a perverse, cold creature, a black idol wrapped in an eternal dream of evil.

VI

The rose-trees in the cemeteries bear large flowers, as white as milk and of a deep red. The roots penetrate to the bottom of the coffins, to take whiteness from virgin bosoms and bright crimson from wounded hearts. This white rose is the bloom of a child who died at sixteen; this red one is the last drop of blood of a man fallen in the struggle.

O brilliant flowers, living flowers, that contain something of our dead.

In the country, the plum and apricot trees grow boldly behind the church, along the crumbling walls of the little graveyard. The warm sun gilds the fruit; the open air gives it a delicious taste. And the housekeeper of the parish priest makes preserves which are renowned for more than ten leagues round. I have tasted them. You would think—to use the happy expression of the country folk—that you were swallowing Paradise.

I know one of those little village churchyards where there are superb gooseberry bushes growing as high as trees. The red gooseberries beneath the green leaves resemble bunches of cherries. And I have seen the beadle come there of a morning, with a small loaf of bread under his arm, and quietly breakfast sitting at the edge of an old tombstone. He was surrounded by a swarm of sparrows. He picked the gooseberries and threw the sparrows crumbs of bread; and all those little creatures ate with a famous appetite above the skulls.

The graveyard looks quite gay. The grass grows thick and strong. In one of the corners clusters of wild poppies form a sheet of crimson. Fresh air comes in abundance from the plain, with puffs of all the pleasant perfumes of new-mown hay. Bees buzz in the sun at noon; little grey lizards lie in ecstasy at the entrance to their holes, inhaling the heat with open jaws. The dead are warm; and it is no longer a graveyard, it is a corner of universal life, where the souls of the dead pass into the trunks of the trees, where there remains naught but a vast kiss of what was yesterday and what will be to-morrow. The flowers are girls' smiles; the fruits are the requirements of men.

There, it is no crime to gather corn-flowers and poppies. Children come and make nosegays. The parish priest is only angry when they climb up into the plum-trees. The plum trees are his, but the flowers belong to every one. Sometimes they are obliged to mow the graveyard; the grass is so high that the black wooden crosses are lost in it; then, the priest's mare eats the hay. The villagers are not spiteful, and not one of the parishioners thinks of taxing the mare with biting into the souls of the dead.

Mathurine had planted a rose-tree on the tomb of her affianced lover, and every Sunday in May, Mathurine went and picked a rose which she placed in her neckerchief. She passed the Sunday amidst the perfume of her departed love. When she cast her eyes on her neckerchief, she fancied her lover smiled at her.

I like cemeteries, beneath a blue sky. I go there bareheaded, forgetful of my hatreds, as into a holy city where one is all affection and forgiveness.

One morning recently, I went to Pere Lachaise. The white sepulchers of the burial-ground rose in terraces against the blue horizon. Tufts of trees grew on the slope, and through the still light screen of their leaves, one could see the shining corners of great tombs. Spring is kind to the deserted fields where rest our dearly beloved dead; it sprinkles the soft paths along which the young widows slowly wend their way, with grass; it whitens the marbles with bright and childlike gaiety. The cemetery, from a distance, resembles an enormous bouquet of verdure, picked out here and there by a tuft of hawthorn blossom. The tombs are as virgin flowers of herbs and foliage.

I followed the paths slowly. What thrilling silence, what penetrating fragrance, what puffs of gentle warmth, coming from one knows not where, like the fondling breath of women whom one does not see! One feels that a whole people sleep in that agitated and mournful earth beneath the tread of passers-by. From each of the shrubs that form the clusters of verdure, from each cleft in the flagstones, escapes a soft and regular respiration, accompanied by all the peacefulness of the last sleep, as if it were that of a child crawling along the ground.

More winters have passed over Musset's slab of marble. I found it looking whiter, more sympathetic. The last showers have given it a new appearance. A ray of sunshine, falling from a neighboring tree, lit up the poet's delicate and nervous profile with lifelike brightness. That medallion, with its everlasting smile, has a charm that saddens one.

How can one account for the strange power that Musset exercised over my generation? There are few young men who, after having read him, have not preserved a feeling of everlasting gentleness in their hearts. And yet Musset taught us neither how to live, nor how to die; he fell down at every step; in his agony he could only rise upon his knees and cry like a child. No matter, we love him; we love him fondly, like a sweetheart who gives our heart feeling by wounding it.

The fact is, that he raised the wail of despair of the century, that he was the youngest and most afflicted of us all.

The willow which pious hands have planted before his tomb is still languishing. Never has that willow, in the shade of which he chose to sleep, grown vigorous and free in the strength of its sap. Its yellow foliage droops sadly, the ends of its branches hang down like heavy, weary tears. Perhaps its roots go and absorb in the dead man's heart, all the bitterness of a life thrown away.

I remained for a long time musing. Over there was the tumult of Paris. Here, the chirp of a bird, the buzzing of an insect, the sudden cracking of a branch. Then long silences, during which the breath of the tomb was heard louder. Only an inhabitant of the neighborhood, some person of small independent means, was walking softly along the path, his feet in slippers, his hands behind his back, like a worthy bourgeois sniffing the first warm air.

My souvenirs were awakening. They recalled to me my youth, that long happy time when I ran along the footpaths of my dear Provence. Musset was then my companion. I carried him in my game-bag; and, behind the first bush I forgot my gun on the sward, and read the poet, in that warm shade of the south, perfumed with sage and lavender. I owe him my first sorrow and my first joy. Even now, amidst that passion for exact analysis which has got possession of me, when sudden gusts of youth flush my cheeks, I think of that despairing one, and I thank him for having taught me how to weep.

VII

May, the month of flowers, the month of nests! The sun is discreetly smiling to-day, and I will have faith in the sun. I walk along the streets in the clear morning air, giving the whole of my attention to the merry-making of the sparrows.

If it rain to-night, heaven forgive my chant of joy which greets the spring.

This morning a young woman, a young wife who was about to become a mother, was seated in front of a lawn in the Park Monceau. She wore a grey silk gown. Her little gloved hands, the lace on her skirt and bodice, the delicate pale tint of her face, bore testimony to the elegant and opulent indolence of her existence. She was one of the happy of this world.

The young woman was watching two sparrows who were boldly hopping about the grass at her feet. First one, then the other, came and stole a sprig of hay and flew off to a neighboring tree. They were building their nest. The female carefully took each straw, plaited it with the other materials that had already been brought there, and smoothed it with the warm and thrilling weight of her throat. It was a stealthy coming and going, a labor of love in which tenderness took the place of strength.

The unknown in grey silk, watched the two lovers who were hastily preparing the cradle. She was learning the ways of poor people, who have only a few sprigs of hay and the warmth of their caresses to protect their little ones on cool nights.

She smiled with sad sweetness, and I fancied I could read her reverie in her dreamy eyes.

"Alas I am rich, and I can never feel the joy of those birds. At this moment a cabinetmaker is putting together the rosewood cradle in which a Normandy or Picardy wet-nurse will rock my child. A loom is somewhere manufacturing the woolen and linen stuffs to keep his delicate limbs warm. A work-girl is hemming the baby-linen. A midwife will attend to the newborn's first requirements. I shall be only half a mother to the dear little creature; I shall bring it into the world naked; he will not have everything from me. And these sparrows make the cradle, weave and hem the materials; they have nothing, they create all by a miracle of love; they transform the first hole they come to in a wall, into a warm nest. They are artisans of tenderness, who are envied by young mothers."

Nests grow naturally in the hedges and trees out in the country, like living flowers. They open, they bloom at the first ray of sunshine, and the sound of chirping comes from them at the time when the hawthorn exhales its perfume.

The chaffinches, goldfinches, and bullfinches select shrubs for alcoves; the rooks and magpies ascend to the loftiest branches of the poplars; the larks and fauvettes remain on the ground, in the corn and bushes. These lovers, who are jealous of their tenderness, require the great silence of the country. I know very well that there are wretches who steal nests in order to pluck the young ones, and who eat the eggs in omelettes. And so the birds hide themselves more closely each season; they go to deserted spots.

Only sparrows and swallows dare to confide their love to the walls and trees of Paris. They live and love among us. We certainly have canaries in cages that lay and sit. But what sad sweethearts they make! One would think our canaries were married before the mayor. Their enforced union, the habit of imprisoning them behind bars is as stupid as a marriage. They have pale and peevish young ones, who never expand their wings with the freedom of the offspring of love.

You should see the sparrows at liberty in the holes in the old walls, the swallows at liberty on the chimney-tops. They love and breed in the open air, and marriages among them are marriages of inclination.

The swallows make Paris their summer villa. As soon as the travelers arrive they visit the empty cradles which they abandoned at the first cold weather/ They repair the frail habitation, strengthen it, furnish it with down. And the poets, the lovers who pass by with open ears and hearts hear their little tender cries above the rumbling of the cabs.

But the real native of Paris, the urchin of the air, is the free sparrow, the fellow who wears the grey blouse of the dweller in the Faubourg. He is vulgar, perky, ashamed of nothing. His chirp is like a mockery, he flaps his wings in a bantering way; the twists and turns of his head give him a devil-may-care manner, which is both jocular and aggressive.

He certainly prefers paths that are grey with dust, the noisy boulevards, to the cool shade of Meudon and Montmorency. He takes pleasure in the racket of wheels, drinks in the gutter, eats bread, walks quietly along the pavements. He has left the fields, where the company of stupid, backward animals, wearied him, to come and live among us, lodging beneath our tiles, getting light at night from the gas, and in the daytime doing his little business in our streets, either loitering or in a hurry.

The sparrow is a Parisian who does not pay taxes. He is the spoilt child of the feathered tribe, and has a weakness for gingerbread and modern civilization.

It is in the public gardens, particularly, that you should study the lively and tender manners of the sparrows in the month of May. There are persons who go to the Jardin des Plantes to stand before bars and gaze at the animals imprisoned there. If you visit the menagerie one of these days, just look at the creatures at liberty, the sparrows that are flying about in the sunshine.

The sparrows chirp a song of triumph around the bars. They loudly extol the open air. They enter the cages with impunity, fill them with their freedom, and are the everlasting despair of the unhappy prisoners. They steal crumbs of bread from the monkeys and bears; the monkeys show them their fists, the bears protest with a swinging of the head that is full of disdainful impatience. The sparrows fly off, they are free and merry creatures in that ark in which man endeavors to confine creation.

In May the sparrows in the Jardin des Plantes, build their nests beneath the tiles on the neighboring houses. They become more caressing; they try to steal a piece of wool or hair from the coats of the animals. One day I saw a great lion stretching out his powerful head between his extended paws, and gazing at a sparrow that was boldly hopping between the bars of his cage. The eyes of the wild beast were half closed in a sweet, poignant reverie. The great lion was dreaming of boundless horizons. He allowed the sparrow to steal a red hair from his paw.

VIII

I went to the markets on one of these recent nights. Paris is gloomy at those early hours. They have not yet given it a bit of toilet. It resembles some vast dining-room still warm and greasy with the meal of the previous evening; bones are lying about, and the dirty cloth in the form of paving-stones is covered with refuse. The masters went to bed without giving orders to clear away; and, it is only in the morning that the servant sweeps up with her broom and spreads clean linen for lunch.

There is great tumult at the markets. They form a colossal larder engulfing all the food of slumbering Paris. When it opens its eyes it will already have its stomach full. Crimson quarters of meat, baskets of fish sparkling like silver, mountains of vegetables breaking up the obscurity with white and green dabs, are piled up in the quivering rays of morning light, amidst the hubbub of the crowd. It is an avalanche of eatables, carts emptied on the pavement, cases torn asunder, sacks ripped open and the contents bursting out of them, a rising flood of salads, eggs, fruit, poultry, which threatens to reach the neighboring streets and inundate all Paris. I went by curiosity into the middle of this turmoil, when I perceived women rummaging with both hands in great blackish heaps piled up on the ground. I could only see imperfectly in the dancing light of the lanterns, and I thought first of all that they consisted of scraps of meat that were being sold cheaply.

I approached. The heaps of refuse meat were heaps of roses.

All that is peculiar to the streets of Paris in springtime trails on this muddy spot, amongst the eatables of the market. On big holidays the sale commences at two o'clock in the morning.

The gardeners in the suburbs bring their great bunches of flowers. These, according to the season, have a current price like leeks and turnips. This sale takes place at night. The women hawkers, the small tradeswomen, who thrust their arms up to the elbows in heaps of roses, seem to be committing a crime, plunging their hands to the bottom of some sanguinary work.

It is now a matter of toilet. The disemboweled bullocks that are bleeding will be washed, wreathed in garlands, decked with artificial flowers; the roses that are being trodden under foot, will be mounted on bits of osier, and will have an unobtrusive perfume in their ruffles of green leaves.

I had stopped before these poor expiring flowers. They were still damp, brutally squeezed by the bonds that cut into their delicate stalks. They preserved the strong smell of the cabbages in the company of which they had come. And there were bunches in agony that had rolled into the gutter.

I picked up one of them. It was all muddy on one side. It will be washed in a bucket of water and will recover its sweet, delicate perfume. A little mud that will remain at the bottom of its petals will be the only sign of its visit to the gutter. The lips that will kiss it to-night will be less pure, perhaps, than it.

Then, amidst the abominable riot in the markets, I remembered that walk I took with you, Ninon, some ten years ago. Spring was bursting forth, the new foliage shone in the bright April sun. The little pathway following the hill was bordered with large clumps of violets. As one passed along, one felt a sweet perfume rise around that filled one's being with lassitude.

You leant upon my arm quite faint, as if the sweet smell had sent you off to sleep with love. The country looked bright, and small flies were whirling round in the sun. Great silence descended from heaven. Our kiss was so soft, that it did not frighten the chaffinches among the cherry trees in bloom.

In a field at the bend of a road, we saw some old women stooping down, gathering violets which they threw into large baskets. I called one of them to me.

"Do you want some violets?" she asked me. "How many? A pound?"

She sold her flowers by the pound! We hurried away, both of us feeling sad, fancying we saw spring opening a grocery in the amorous country. I slipped along the hedges, and stole a few sorry violets, which smelt all the sweeter to you. But then we found that violets, quite small ones that were dreadfully afraid, and knew how to hide among the leaves by means of a thousand devices, grew in the wood above, on the tableland.

You quickly threw away the stolen violets, those stupid ones that came up in cultivated ground and were sold by the pound. You wanted flowers at liberty, offspring of the dew and rising sun. For two long hours I ferreted in the grass. As soon as I found a violet I ran to sell it you, and you bought it off me with a kiss.

And I thought of those distant things amidst those fulsome smells, in the deafening riot at the markets, while standing before those poor dead flowers on the ground. I remembered my sweetheart, and that bunch of dry violets I had preserved at the bottom of a drawer at home. When I returned I counted the faded stalks; there were twenty, and I felt on my lips the delicious burn of twenty kisses.

IX

I have paid a visit to the gypsy encampment opposite the military station, at the gate of Saint Ouen. These savages must be having a good laugh at this great stupid city for taking an interest in them. I only had to follow the crowd; all the Faubourg was moving round their tents, and I was ashamed to see even persons who did not look like absolute idiots arriving in open carriages with liveried footmen.

When this poor Paris possesses a curiosity it goes into enthusiasm over it. The case of these gypsies is as follows. They came to tin stew pans and mend the cooking-pots of the Faubourg. Only from the first day, at the sight of the urchins who stared them out of countenance, they understood the sort of civilized city they had to deal with, and so they hastened to sever their connection with cooking-pots and stew pans. Comprehending that they were taken in the light of a curious menagerie, they consented with mocking good humor to show themselves for two sous. The encampment is surrounded by a paling; two men are placed at two very narrow openings, where they collect the offerings of the ladies and gentlemen who desire to visit the kennels. There is so much rushing and crushing in the place that it has been necessary to have recourse to policemen. The gypsies sometimes turn away their heads, so as not to burst out laughing in the faces of the worthy people, who forget themselves sometimes so far, as to throw them bits of silver.

I can picture them to myself counting the receipts at nighttime when the public are no longer there. What jeering! They have crossed France, amidst the rebuffs of the peasantry and the distrust of the rural police. They reach Paris in fear of being thrown into jail. And they awaken amidst the golden dream of an entire population of ladies and gentlemen in ecstasy before their rags. They, they who are driven from town to town! I fancy I can see them, draped in their tatters, standing erect on the talus of the fortifications, and giving utterance to a huge peal of contemptuous laughter at slumbering Paris.

The paling surrounds seven or eight tents, which form a kind of street. Behind the tents small, raw-boned, sinewy horses nibble the scorched grass. Low wheels of vehicles are visible beneath shreds of old awning.

Within is an unbearable stench of filth and misery. The ground is already trodden down, dusty and purulent. The bedding is being aired on the pointed palings. There are straw pallets, faded rugs, square mattresses, on which two families must sleep at ease, all the output of some leper hospital, drying in the sun. In the tents, set up in Arab fashion, very high, and opening like curtains hanging from the canopy. of a bedstead, are heaps of rags, saddles, harness, a lot of bric-a-brac without a name, objects that have ceased to have either color or form, lying there in a layer of superb filth, which is warm in tone and likely to send a painter into ecstasies.

I think, however, I found the kitchen at the extremity of the encampment, in a tent that was smaller than the others. There were some iron stew pans and three-legged cooking-pots; I even recognized a plate. But there was no appearance of cooking. The stew pans serve, perhaps, to make the Sabbath broth.

The men are tall and strong, with round faces and very long, curly black hair, which is glossy and greasy. They are attired in all the cast-off garments picked up on the road. One of them was walking about, dressed in a chintz curtain with great yellow flowers. Another had a jacket which must originally have been a dress coat from which the tails had been torn. Several have women's petticoats. They smile in their long, thin, glossy beards. Their favorite head-covering seems to be the crowns of old felt hats, out of which they have made skull-caps by cutting off the brims.

The women also are tall and strong. The shriveled-up old ones are hideous in their half-naked emaciation and disheveled hair, and resemble witches who have been burnt in hell fire. Among the young ones, there are some who are very beautiful beneath their coating of filth, with their bronzed skin and great soft black eyes. They give themselves a coquettish appearance; their hair is plaited in two thick tresses, which are looped up and fastened behind the ears, and tied tight at distances by pieces of red ribbon. In their colored petticoats, with their shoulders covered by a shawl fastened like a sash, their heads decked with a neckerchief tightened across their foreheads, they had the grand air of barbarian queens fallen to the depths of vermin.

And the children, a whole flock of them on the move. I saw one in a shirt, with a man's huge waistcoat flapping against his calves; he had a beautiful blue stag-beetle in his hand. Another, a very small child, two years old at the most, was running about naked, absolutely naked, amidst the noisy laughter of the prying girls of the neighborhood. And he was so dirty, the dear little fellow, so green and red, that you might have mistaken him for a Florentine bronze, one of those charming little figures of the Renaissance period.

The whole band is impassive in presence of the noisy curiosity of the crowd. Men and women are sleeping in the tents. A mother is suckling a little yellow-colored mite, who looks as if he were made of brass, at a bare black breast that looks like a gourd become brown by use. Other women, who are squatting down, gaze seriously at these strange Parisians who are ferreting among the filth. I inquired of one of them what she thought of us; she feebly smiled, without answering.

A handsome girl of some twenty summers strolls about among the idlers, and tempts ladies in hats and silk gowns to have their fortunes told. I saw her go through the performance. She took a young woman's hand, retained it in hers in a fondling way, until the hand in the end remained there. Then she gave the person to understand that she must put a piece of money in it; a ten-sou piece was not sufficient, she must have a couple, and she even talked about five francs. At the expiration of a few seconds, after having promised long life, children, and much happiness, she took the two ten-sou pieces and used them to make signs of the cross at the edge of the young woman's hat, and at the word Amen, slipped them into her pocket, an immense pocket, in which I caught a glimpse of handfuls of silver.

She certainly sells a talisman. She breaks a little bit of reddish stuff, which looks like dried orange peel, between her teeth; she ties it up in the corner of the pocket-handkerchief of the person whose fortune she has been telling; then, she impresses upon her that she must be sure and add bread, salt, and sugar to it . This will prevent all illness and keep away the devil.

And the hussy goes through her work with an astounding air of gravity. If one of the pieces of money that have been put in her hand is taken back, she vows that her good predictions will turn into frightful evils. The system is simple, but the gesture and tone are capital.

Gypsies are tolerated in the little town in Provence where I was brought up; but they do not excite extraordinary curiosity. They are accused of eating the lost dogs and cats, and that makes persons of the bourgeois class look askance at them. Respectable people turn aside their heads when they have to go into their vicinity.

They arrive with their habitations on wheels, and take up their quarters on a bit of waste land in the outskirts. Some spots are inhabited from year to year by tribes of children in rags, and men and women stretched in the sun. I have seen creatures of superb beauty there. We youngsters, who did not feel the same disgust as respectable persons, used to go and peer into the carts where these people sleep in winter. And, I remember that one day, when my heart was swollen with some boyish sorrow, I had an idea of getting up into one of those carts that was leaving, and going off with those tall, beautiful girls, whose black eyes frightened me, of going a long way off, to the end of the world, rolling for ever on the roads.

X

A young chemist who was a friend of mine said to me one morning:

"I know a learned old man who has shut himself up in a little house on the Boulevard d'Enfer, to study the crystallization of the diamond, in quiet. He has already made remarkable progress. Shall I take you to see him?"

I accepted with secret terror. A sorcerer would have frightened me less, for I have but little fear of the devil; but I am afraid of money, and I confess that the man who one of these days happens to find the philosopher's stone, will strike me with respectful horror.

On the way, my friend gave me some details concerning the manufacture of precious stones. Our chemists have been inquiring into the subject for a long time. But the crystals they have hitherto produced are so small, and the cost of manufacture is so high, that the experiments have, till now, been limited to the simple curiosity of men of science. That is how the matter stands. It is merely a question of discovering more powerful agents and a less expensive process, to turn the articles out at a low figure.

In the meanwhile we had reached our destination. My friend, before ringing, warned me that the old man of learning disliked inquisitive persons, and would no doubt give me a sorry welcome. I would be the first of the profane to penetrate within the sanctuary.

The chemist opened to us, and I confess that he first of all struck me as looking stupid, and of having the emaciated and down-trodden air of a cobbler. He greeted my friend affectionately, accepting my presence with a surly growl, as if I had been a dog belonging to his young disciple. We crossed a neglected garden. At the bottom of it was the house—a hovel in ruins. The tenant had pulled down all the partitions, so as to leave but one large, lofty room. Within was the complete apparatus of a laboratory and amongst it strange looking vessels, of which I did not attempt to understand the use. All the luxury and furniture consisted of a form and table stained black.

It was in this wretched hole that I was more blindly dazzled than I have ever been in my life. Set on the ground along the wall were the remains of worn-out baskets, the osier of which was bursting, filled to the brim with precious stones. Each heap consisted of one sort. The rubies, amethysts, emeralds, sapphires, opals, turquoises, thrown into the corners like shovelfuls of stones beside the road, shone with brilliant flashes, lighting up the room with their sparkling fire. They were like beacons, live coal, red, violet, green, blue, pink. And one would have said there were millions of fairies' eyes laughing in the dark, on a level with the ground. Never has such a treasure existed, even in an Arab story; never has woman dreamt of such a paradise.

I could not restrain a burst of admiration.

"What wealth!" I exclaimed. "There are milliards there."

The learned old man shrugged his shoulders. He seemed to be gazing at me with an air of profound pity.

"Each of those heaps costs a few francs," he said to me in his slow, hollow tone of voice. "I shall sprinkle them to-morrow over the walks of my garden in the place of gravel."

Then, turning towards my friend, and taking up the stones in handfuls, he continued:

"Look at these rubies; they are the finest I have yet produced. I am not satisfied with these emeralds; they are too pure; all natural ones are flaky, and I do not want to beat nature. What puts me to despair is my not having been able to produce the white diamond. I recommenced my experiments yesterday. As soon as I have succeeded, the labor of my life will be crowned, I shall die happy."

The man had become greater. He no longer appeared to me stupid; I began to tremble before this pallid old man who had it in his power to pour a miraculous shower over Paris.

"But you must be afraid of thieves?" I inquired of him. "I see solid iron bars at your doors and windows. That is a precaution."

"Yes, I am afraid at times," he murmured, "afraid that idiots may kill me before I have discovered the white diamond. Those stones which will be worthless in a short time may tempt my heirs now. It is of my heirs that I am in terror; they know that by causing me to disappear they will bury the secret of my invention with me, and that they will thus maintain the value of this pretended treasure."

He became thoughtful and sad. We had seated ourselves on the heap of diamonds, and I watched him, his left hand buried in the basket of rubies, while he made handfuls of emeralds run through his right. Children make sand pass through their fingers in the same way.

After a silence I exclaimed, "You must lead an intolerable existence! You live here in the hatred of mankind. Have you no amusement?" He gazed at me in surprise.

"I work," he answered simply; "I never feel dull When I am gay, on my days of folly, I put some of these stones in my pocket, and I go and sit down at the end of my garden, behind a loophole which looks on to the boulevard. There I from time to time throw a diamond into the middle of the road."

He still laughed at the thought of this capital joke.

"You could never imagine the grimaces the people who find my stones make. They shake, look behind them, then run away as pale as death. Ah! the poor people, what capital comedies they have performed to me. I have passed many merry hours there."

His dry voice, gave me inexpressible discomfort. He was evidently making fun of me.

"Hey! young man," he resumed, "I have enough there to purchase many women; but I am an old devil. You can understand that if I felt the least ambition, I should long ago have been king somewhere. Bah I would not kill a fly; I am good, and that is why I allow men to live."

He could not have told me more politely that if the fancy took him, he would send me to the scaffold.

Strange thoughts rose within me and rang in my ears until I was giddy. The eyes of fairies of precious stones gazed at me with their piercing glances, red, violet, green, blue, pink. I had clenched my fists without knowing it; in the left I had a handful of rubies, in the right a handful of emeralds. And, if I must say all, I was urged by an almost irresistible desire to slip them into my pockets.

I let the accursed stones go, and went off with a sound of galloping gendarmes in my ears.

XI

I had gone to Versailles, and was ascending the spacious Cour des Marechaux, a stony solitude that has often reminded me of the barren land of La Crau, where an ocean of pebbles is turning green in the bright sun.

Last winter, I saw the chateau with its bluish roof, in snowy weather, looking majestic and gloomy against the grey sky, like the royal palace of cold. It still looks sad in the summer, more melancholy, more abandoned, in the warmth of the air, amidst the luxuriant growth of the trees in the park. Each time the fine weather comes, the old trunks make themselves young again with their leaves. The old chateau is in the pangs of death; the sap of life no longer rises in its stones which are crumbling to dust; implacable ruin is at hand, gnawing off the corners, disjoining the flagstones, pursuing hourly its deadly task.

Habitations, whether they are hovels or palaces, have their complaints from which they suffer and from which they die. They are great living bodies, persons who have a childhood and old age; some are robust until the moment of their death, others are weary and shaky before the time. I remember houses standing by the roadside that I have caught a glimpse of from a railway carriage window: newly erected buildings, unpretentious pavilions, deserted country-houses, ruined keeps. And all these stone beings spoke to me, told me what sort of health they enjoyed, and what illness was killing them. When a man closes his doors and windows and leaves his abode, it is the blood of the house flowing away. The residence stands for years in the sun wearing the furrowed features of the dying; then some winter night, it is blown down by a gust of wind.

The Chateau of Versailles is dying from this desertion. Its size was too great for man to put life into it. It would require quite a nation of tenants to make vitality circulate in those endless corridors, in that long succession of immense rooms. It was the colossal error of the pride of a monarch, who destined it to ruin from its birth, by making it too large. The glory of Louis XIV no longer overspreads even the room in which he slept, a frigid chamber to which his regal ashes convey naught but a little more dust.

I ascended the Cour des Marechaux, and I saw on the right, in an out-of-the way part of that sandy tract, the old woman, the legendary Sarcleuse, who has been removing the weeds from between the paving-stones, for half a century. From morn till eve she is there amidst the field of pebbles, struggling against the invasion, against the increasing mass of wild wall-flowers and poppies. She walks, bent double, examining each cleft, singling out the green blades and straggling moss. It takes her almost a month to go from one end of her desert to the other. And behind her the grass grows again, victoriously, so thick, so implacable, that, when she recommences her everlasting task, she finds the same weeds come up once more, the same graveyard-like corners invaded by voracious flowers.

Sarcleuse knows the flora of these ruins. She knows that poppies prefer the south side, that dandelions grow at the north, that wallflowers select the clefts in the pedestals. Moss is a leper that spreads everywhere. There are plants that nothing can destroy, you may pull them up by the roots but they always grow again; a drop of blood has perhaps fallen there, an evil spirit must be buried beneath and be continually thrusting forth its reddish spikes beyond the ground. In this burial-place of royalty the dead have a strange efflorescence.

But you should hear Sarcleuse relate the story of these weeds. They have not grown at each period with equal strength. Under Charles X., they were still timid; they barely spread out like fine grass, as a carpet of tender green that softened the paving-stones beneath the tread of ladies. The court still came to the chateau, the heels of the courtiers trampled the ground, did in a morning what it takes Sarcleuse a whole month to accomplish. Under

Louis Philippe, the weeds became more bold; the chateau, peopled by the peaceful phantoms of the historical museum, commenced to be nothing more than the palace of the departed. And it was under the Second Empire that the weeds triumphed; they then grew unmolested, taking possession of their prey, threatening at a moment to gain the galleries, to overspread the large and small apartments with verdure.

I pondered, at the sight of Sarcleuse walking slowly along, with her apron full of weeds, and bending down in her old printed calico skirt. She represents the last show of pity which prevents the nettles rising and hiding the tomb of monarchy. She looks after this barren land, where the green stuff of the ditches grows, like a worthy woman.

I fancied to myself that she was the ghost of some marchioness who had come from one of the boskets of the park and who worshipped these ruins. She struggles without end, with her stiff fingers, against the relentless moss. She displays obstinacy in her futile task, and feels that if she were to stay for a moment, the mass of weeds would overgrow and envelop her. At times, when she draws herself up, she casts a prolonged gaze across the field of stones, and her eyes reach its distant corners, where the vegetation is more luxuriant. And she stays thus, for a moment, with her pale face, understanding perhaps the uselessness of her unfailing care, and delighted at the bitter joy of being the supreme comforter of these paving-stones.

But the day will come when the fingers of Sarcleuse will grow stiffer still Then the chateau will crumble down in a final sob of the wind. The field of stones will be a prey to nettles, thistles, and all sorts of weeds. It will become enormous bush, a coppice of rough, twisted shrubs. And Sarcleuse will be lost in the thickets, putting aside handfuls of twigs taller than herself, making a pathway amidst blades of couch grass as big as young birch-trees, still struggling, until the time when these blades will enthrall her on every side, will clasp her by the limbs, by the waist, by the throat, to cast her dead into this ocean, which will whirl her round and round in the ever rising wave of verdure.

XII

War, infamous war, accursed war I We young fellows did not know what it was in 1859. We were still on the forms at school. The dreadful word which made our mothers turn pale, only reminded us of holidays.

And amidst our souvenirs we merely recalled those delightful summer evenings when people made merry in the streets; the news of a victory in the morning wafted a breath of holiday-making through Paris; and as soon as it was twilight the shopkeepers illuminated their establishments and the ragamuffins let off farthing squibs in the streets. In front of the café's there were gentlemen drinking beer and discussing politics; while, there, in an out-of-the-way corner of Italy or Russia, the dead, extended on their backs, were watching the stars appear with their great, open, glassy eyes.

I remember that when I left college on that day in 1859, when news of the battle of Magenta was noised abroad, I went to the Place de la Sorbonne to have a look, to stroll about in that atmosphere of fever that pervaded the streets. There were a lot of urchins there shouting "Victory! Victory!" We sniffed a holiday. And amidst the yells and laughter I heard sobs. It was an old cobbler weeping at the further end of his shop. The poor fellow had two children in Italy.

Those sobs have frequently since then re-echoed in my memory. At each rumor of war it seems that the old cobbler, the hoary-headed people, are weeping amidst the thrilling warmth of feeling on the public squares.

But I have a still better recollection of that other war, the campaign in the Crimea. I was then fourteen, and lived buried in the country, and was so thoughtless, that all I saw in war was the constant passage of troops, whose presence had become one of our greatest enjoyments.

I believe almost all the soldiers who went to the East passed through the little town where I resided in the south of France. A newspaper in the neighborhood announced what regiments would come that way beforehand. The departures took place about five o'clock in the morning. From four o'clock we were all at the public walk; not a single day scholar was missing at the gathering.

Ah! What fine men! And the cuirassiers, and the lancers, and the dragoons, and the hussars! We had a weakness for the cuirassiers. When the sun rose and its slanting rays blazed upon the cuirasses, we fell back, blinded, fascinated, as if an army of stars on horseback had passed before us.

Then the trumpets sounded. And they started.

We left with the soldiers. We followed them along the broad, white roads. The band was playing then, thanking the town for its hospitality. And there was a savor of holidaymaking in the clear, bright morning air.

I remember having traveled leagues in that way. We marched with our books fastened to our backs by a strap, like a knapsack. It was agreed at first that we would never accompany the soldiers beyond the powder-mill; then we went as far as the bridge; then we ascended the hill; then we were all for the next village.

And when we became frightened and agreed to stop, we would climb a hill, and from there follow the regiment with the eyes, in the distance, between the dips in the land, along the winding road, and watch it lose itself and disappear with its thousands of small flashes, in the brilliant light on the horizon.

On those days we gave very little thought to the college! We played truant and amused ourselves at each heap of stones. And it was not an uncommon thing for all of us to go down to the river and pass the time there until evening,

There is not much love for soldiers in the south of France. I have seen some of them crying with fatigue and rage, seated on the pavement with their billets in their hands: the bourgeois, the sharp-nosed persons of small independent means, the stout big men of business, had refused to take them in. The authorities had to deal with the matter.

Our house was a hospitable one. My grandmother, who was a Beauceronne, smiled on all the young men from the north, for they reminded her of home. She talked with them, inquired the name of their village, and how delighted she was when it happened to be within a few leagues of her own!

They sent us two men from each regiment. We could not accommodate them, and so we put them up at the inn; but before they left my grandmother made them submit to her little interrogation.

I remember two coming one day who belonged to her own village. She would not allow these to leave. She gave them their dinner in the kitchen, and it was she who filled their glasses. I went to see the two soldiers on returning home from college; I think we even drank each other's health.

One was tall and the other short. I remember very well that at the moment of departure the eyes of the tall one swelled with tears. He had left a poor old mother in his village, and he effusively thanked my grandmother, who reminded him of his dear Beauce and all he had abandoned.

"Nonsense," said the worthy woman to him, "you will return, and will have the Cross of the Legion of Honor."

But he shook his head in grief.

"Well," she continued, "if you come back this way, you must call and see me. I will keep you a bottle of this wine which you find so good."

The two poor fellows began to laugh. That invitation had made them forget, for a moment, the terrible future, and they no doubt fancied themselves back again, and at table in that little hospitable house, drinking to dangers that were over. They formally undertook to return and empty the bottle.

How many regiments I followed at that time, and how many pale-faced soldiers came and knocked at our door! I shall always remember the endless procession of those men marching to death. Sometimes, by closing my eyes, I see them again. I recall certain faces, and I ask myself: "In what out-of-the-way ditch is that one lying?"

Then the regiments became more scarce and one day we saw the men passing by in the reverse sense, limping, bleeding, dragging themselves along the highway. Ah! No, indeed! We did not go to await them; we did not accompany those cripples. They were not our fine soldiers. They were not worth the least trouble.

The sad procession continued for a long time. The army scattered the dying along the road. Sometimes my grandmother said, "And those two fellows from Beauce, you know, are they forgetting me?"

But one evening, at twilight, a soldier came and knocked at the door. He was alone. He was the short one.

"My comrade's dead," he said as he came in.

My grandmother brought the bottle.

"Yes," he said, "I shall have to drink all alone."

And when he saw himself there at table, raising his glass, and looked for his comrade's to touch it, he heaved a huge sigh, murmuring:

"He entrusted me with the duty of going to console the old party. I would sooner have remained out there in his place."

Later on I had Chauvin for comrade at the offices of a company. We were both junior clerks and sat close together at the end of a gloomy apartment, a capital hole to do nothing in while awaiting the time to leave.

Chauvin had been a sergeant, and had returned from Solferino suffering from fever he had caught in the rice plantations in Piedmont. He swore at his affliction, but consoled himself by putting the responsibility of it on the shoulders of the Austrians. It was those tatterdemalions who had arranged him in that way.

What hours were passed in gossiping! I had found my old soldier, and I was determined not to part with him before I had extracted some truths. I was not satisfied with big words: glory, victory, laurels, warriors, which in his mouth resounded most magnificently. I allowed his flood of enthusiasm to pass. I assailed him with inquiries for details. I consented to listen to the same story twenty times over, in order to grasp the real spirit of it. Chauvin ended by confiding some lovely things to me, without imagining he was doing so.

He was as simple as a child at heart. He did not boast for his own gratification; he simply spoke in the ordinary bragging military way. He was unwittingly a humbug, a good fellow whom barrack life had transformed into a provoking blockhead.

He had stories, witticisms all ready, one felt it. Sentences prepared beforehand, embellished his anecdotes about "unconquerable troopers" and "brave officers rescued from slaughter by the heroism of their soldiers." I endured the Italian campaign four hours daily for two years. But I do not regret it. Chauvin completed my education.

Thanks to him, thanks to the avowals he made to me in our black hole, I know what warfare is without the thought of evil; real warfare, not that of which historians relate the heroic episodes, but that which sweats fear in the bright sunshine and glides into deeds of blood like a drunken strumpet

I questioned Chauvin.

"And the soldiers, did they go gaily under fire?"

"The soldiers! did they push them forward, then! I remember recruits who had never been in action, and who reared like skittish horses. They were afraid; twice they fled. But they brought them back again, and a battery killed half. You should have seen them then, covered with blood, blinded, dashing on the Austrians like wolves. They were beside themselves, howling with rage, they wished to die."

"It was an apprenticeship that had to be gone through," I said to encourage him.

"Oh yes! a hard one, I'll answer for it. You see the pluckiest of all experience icy sweats. You must be tipsy to fight well. You then cease to see anything, and strike blows before you like a madman."

And he went on with his recollections.

"One day they had placed us at a hundred yards from a village occupied by the enemy, with orders not to move and not to fire. But you see those tatterdemalions of Austrians opened a frightful fusillade on our regiment. There was no possibility of getting away. We ducked our heads at each shower of bullets. I saw some throw themselves down flat on their stomachs. It was shameful. They left us there for a quarter of an hour. And the hair of two of my comrades turned white."

Then he continued, "No, you have not the least idea of it. The thing is all arranged in books. Look here; on the night of Solferino, we did not even know if we were conquerors. There were reports that the Austrians would come and massacre us. I can assure you we didn't feel very lively. And so, when they made us rise the next morning before daybreak, we were shivering, and in mortal fear of the battle being resumed more fiercely than ever. We would have been conquered that day, for we hadn't two pennies worth of courage left. Then, they came and said to us, 'Peace has been signed,' and all the regiment began capering about, displaying an idiotic sort of joy. Soldiers grasped one another's hands and danced round like young girls. I'm not telling falsehoods, don't you think it. I was there. We were very pleased."

Chauvin, who saw me smile, imagined I could not believe that such an immense liking for peace existed in the French army. He was deliciously simple. I sometimes drew him out considerably. I asked him, "And you, were you never afraid?"

"Oh! I," he replied, laughing modestly, "I was like the others—I didn't know. Do you suppose you are aware whether you are courageous or not? You tremble and strike, that's the truth. I was once knocked down by a spent bullet. I remained on the ground, thinking to myself that if I got up, something worse might happen to me."

XIII

He died gallantly as he had lived.

Do you remember, my friends, that mild spring, when we used to go and see him at his little house at Clamart? Jacques welcomed us with his pleasant smile. And we dined in the bower covered with ivy grape, while Paris out there, on the horizon, was roaring in the falling night.

You never knew all about him. I, who grew up in the same place as he did, can read his heart to you. He had been living at Clamart for two years, with that tall, fair girl who faded away so sweetly. It is quite a story, as charming as it is painful.

Jacques had met Madeleine at the Fête of Saint Cloud. He took to loving her because she was sad and ailing. He wished to give the poor girl two seasons of affection before she entered her grave. And he went and hid himself with her, in that dip in the ground at Clamart, where roses grow as thick as poppies.

You know the house. It is a very modest one, all white, buried like a nest among the green foliage. From the threshold one breathed an atmosphere of quiet affection. Jacques, little by little, had become extremely fond of the dying girl. He watched the disease making her paler every day, with feelings of bitter tenderness. Madeleine, like one of those small oil lamps in churches, which flare up brightly before going out, was all smiles and shed luster on the little white house with her blue eyes.

The child hardly went abroad for two seasons. She filled the small garden with her charming being, her light gowns and nimble footsteps. It was she who planted the large fallow wall-flowers with which she made us nosegays. And the geraniums, the rhododendrons, the heliotropes, all those living flowers, lived by her and for her. She was the soul of this bit of nature.

Then, in the autumn, you remember, Jacques came one night and said to us in his drawling voice: "She is dead." She had died in her bower, like a child going off to sleep at the pale hour when the sun retires for the night. She had died amidst her verdure, in the out-of-the-way corner where love had soothed her agony for two years.

I had never seen Jacques after that. I knew he still lived at Clamart, in the bower, with his thoughts on Madeleine. I had been so broken down with fatigue since the commencement of the siege, that I had quite forgotten him, when hearing on the morning of the 13th, that they were fighting in the vicinity of Meudon and Sevres, I all at once recalled to mind the little white house hidden among the green leaves, with Madeleine, Jacques, all of us taking tea in the garden, amidst the intense peacefulness of evening, in front of Paris which was snoring with a rumbling, hollow noise on the horizon.

Then I went out by the Vanves gate and proceeded straight before me. The roads were encumbered with wounded. I thus reached Moulineaux, where I heard of our success; but, when I had turned the wood and found myself on the hillside, I felt a terrible pang in my heart.

Opposite me, in the trampled down, devastated fields, I saw nothing more' on the site of the little white house, than a black hole where shot and fire had passed. I descended the hill with tearful eyes.

Ah! My friends, what a frightful sight! You know, the hawthorn hedge, it was leveled to the roots by bullets. The large fallow wall-flowers, the geraniums, the rhododendrons, were lying around, cut to pieces, pounded to bits, so lamentable to see, that I felt the same pity for them, as if I had had the bleeding limbs of poor fellows of my acquaintance before me.

All one side of the house has fallen down Its gaping wound displays Madeleine's room, that chaste apartment, hung with rose-colored chintz, the curtains of which one could always see drawn, from the road. That room, brutally thrown open by the Prussian cannonade, that love-pervaded alcove that can now be seen from any spot in the valley, made my heart bleed, and I said to myself that I was in the centre of the cemetery of our youth. The ground covered with remnants of all kinds, ploughed up by shells, resembled land recently upheaved by the shovels of grave-diggers, and where in mind's eye one pictures to oneself the new coffins.

Jacques must have had to abandon this house riddled by shot. I went on further; I entered the bower, which, by miracle, has remained almost intact. There, Jacques was sleeping on the ground, in a pool of blood, his chest pierced by more than twenty wounds. He had not quitted the ivy grape where he had loved; he had died where Madeleine had died.

I picked up his empty cartridge-box, his broken chassepot at his feet, and I saw the hands of the poor departed were black with powder. Jacques, alone with his weapon, had madly defended Madeleine's white phantom for the space of five hours.

XIV

Poor Neuilly! I shall long remember the lamentable walk I took yesterday, April 25, 1871. At nine o'clock, as soon as the armistice concluded between Paris and Versailles became known, a large crowd went towards the Porte Maillot. This gate no longer exists; the batteries at Courbevoie and Mount Valerian have reduced it to a heap of rubbish. When I passed through the ruin National Guards were occupied in repairing the gate—a useless task, for a few cannon-shots will suffice to dash away the sacks and paving-stones they were piling-up there.

From the Porte Maillot you walk amidst destruction. All the neighboring houses have fallen in. Through the broken windows I catch sight of bits of costly furniture; a curtain in ribbons hangs from a balcony, a canary still lives in a cage suspended at the top of a garret window. The more one advances the greater are the disasters. The avenue is strewn with remnants, ploughed up by shells; any one would call it the vale of tears, the accursed Calvary of civil war.

I turned into the cross streets, hoping to escape this horrible high-road along which one came upon pools of blood at every step. Alas! in the narrow thoroughfares that run into the avenue the devastation is perhaps more terrible still. There they fought foot to foot with cold steel. The houses have been taken and retaken ten times over; the soldiers of the two parties have broken through the walls to effect an entrance into the interior, and they have struck down with pickaxes what the shells have spared. It is particularly the gardens that have suffered. The poor spring gardens! The surrounding walls have gaping breaches, the flower beds are up-heaved, the paths trampled down, laid waste. And over all this vision of spring, tainted with blood, a mass of lilac is blossoming all alone. Never has the month of April seen such bloom. Persons who feel curious enter the gardens by the open breaches. They carry armfuls of lilac away on their shoulders, and the bunches are so cumbrous that sprigs of them fall away at every step, so that the streets of Neuilly are soon all strewn with flowers, as if made ready for a procession.

The crowd is grieved at the damage done to the houses, at the holes in the walls. But there is something that looks still more sad. It is the removing of the inhabitants of the unfortunate village. There are three or four thousand persons hurrying away, carrying their most precious articles along with them. I see some people returning to Paris with a small basket of linen, and an enormous clock in imitation gilt bronze in their arms. All the carts for removing furniture have been retained. The people go even so far as to carry away wardrobes with looking-glass doors, on stretchers, like wounded mortals whom the slightest shock might kill.

The inhabitants have suffered frightfully. I had some conversation with one of the fugitives who had been shut up in a cellar for a fortnight with some thirty others. These unfortunate creatures were dying of hunger. One of them having volunteered to go and fetch food was struck down on the threshold of the cellar, and his corpse remained for six days at the bottom of the steps. Is not such warfare, which permits of dead bodies rotting thus amidst the living, real nightmare? Is it not ungodly warfare? Sooner or later the country will suffer for these crimes.

The crowd strolled about on the scene of the struggle until five o'clock. I saw little girls who had come quietly from the Champs Élysées playing with their hoops among the ruins. And their smiling mothers talked together, and occasionally stopped, with a delightful little look of horror. Strange people are those of Paris, who forget themselves amongst loaded ordnance, who indulge in their love of sauntering idly to and fro, and examining everything that excites their interest, to the point of wishing to see whether the shot is really in the cannon's mouth. Some National Guards, at the Porte Maillot, had to get angry with ladies who insisted on touching a blunderbuss in order to understand its mechanism.

When I left Neuilly, at about seven o'clock, not a cannon hot had been fired. The crowd was slowly re-entering Paris. One might have imagined, when in the Champs Élysées, that one was watching a late return of the public from the Longchamps races. And for a long time afterwards, up to dark, you met pedestrians, whole families, bowed down under loads of lilac There is naught at this hour on our mantelpieces, but bunches of sweet-scented flowers from the sinister village where people of the same nationality are slaughtering one another, or from the accursed avenue with houses wrecked in gore.

We have just had three days' sunshine. The boulevards were swarming with people sauntering to and fro. What causes me unremitting astonishment is the lively aspect of the squares and public gardens. In the Tuilleries ladies are embroidering in the shade of the chestnuts, children are at play, while up there, in the direction of the Arc de Triomphe, shells are bursting. This intolerable sound of artillery no longer even causes this little playful world to turn their heads. You see mothers holding young children in each hand, who go close to the formidable barricades thrown up on the Place de la Concorde, and examine them.

But the most characteristic feature is the pleasure-parties the Parisians have been making for a week to the knoll of Montmartre. All Paris has fixed a rendezvous there, in some waste ground on the western slope. This is a magnificent amphitheatre for viewing the battle which is being fought between Neuilly and Asnieres. They had brought chairs and campstools with them. Enterprising people had even placed forms there; for two sous you were seated as in the pit of a theatre. Women particularly, came in great numbers. Then there were loud bursts of laughter among the crowd. Each time they perceived a shell burst in the distance they stamped with joy, and made some good joke which ran through the groups like a squib of gaiety. I even saw people bring their luncheons there, a piece of pork-butcher's delicacy on bread. So as not to quit the spot, they ate standing upright, and sent for wine at a retailer's in the neighborhood. These crowds require sights; when the theatres close and civil war opens they go and see people die in earnest, with the same bantering curiosity as they display in waiting for the fifth act of a melodrama.

"It's so far off," said a charming young woman, who was fair and pale, "that it does not affect me at all to see them jump. When men are cut in two, one would think they were being folded up like skeins of silk or thread."

NANTAS

I

The room in which Nantas had resided since his arrival from Marseilles was on the top floor of a house in the Eue de Lille, next to the mansion of Baron Danvilliers, a member of the Council of State. This house belonged to the baron, who had built it on the site of some old outbuildings. By leaning out of his window, Nantas could see a corner of the baron's garden, across which some magnificent trees cast their shade. Beyond, by looking over their leafy crests, a glimpse of Paris was to be had: the open space left by the Seine, with the Tuilleries, the Louvre, the quays, a whole sea of roofs, and the Pere Lachaise Cemetery in the dim distance.

Nantas's room was a small attic, with a dormer window amid the tiles. He had furnished it simply with a bed, a table, and a chair. He had taken up his abode there because he was attracted by the low rent, and had made up his mind to rough it until he found a situation of some kind. The dirty paper, the black ceiling, the general misery and barrenness of this garret did not deter him. Living in sight of the Louvre and the Tuilleries, he compared himself to a general sleeping in some miserable inn at the roadside within view of the wealthy city which he means to carry by assault on the morrow.

Nantas's story was a short one. The son of a Marseilles mason, he had begun his studies at the Lycée in that city, stimulated by the ambitious affection of his mother, who had set her heart upon making a gentleman of him. His parents had stinted themselves to give him a good education; but, his mother having died, Nantas had been obliged to accept an unprofitable situation in the office of a merchant, where for twelve years he had led a life of exasperating monotony. He would have taken himself off a score of times, if his sense of filial duty had not tied him to Marseilles, for his father, who had fallen from scaffolding, was quite unable to work. One night, however, when Nantas returned home, he found the old fellow dead, with his pipe lying still warm at his side. Three days later the young man had sold the few sticks about the place, and started for Paris, with just two hundred francs in his pocket.

Nantas had inherited boundless ambition from his mother. He was a young fellow of ready decision and firm will; and even when quite a boy he had been wont to say that he was a power. He was often laughed at when he so far forgot himself as to repeat his favorite expression confidingly, 'I am a power,' an expression which sounded comical indeed when one looked at him in his thin black coat, all out at the elbows, and with the cuffs half-way up his arms. However, he had gradually made power a religion, seeing nothing else in the world, and feeling convinced that the strong are neces-sarily the successful. According to his idea, to be willing and able ought to suffice one. All the rest was of no importance.

One Sunday, while he was walking about alone, in the scorching suburbs of Marseilles, he felt genius within him; in his innermost being there was, as it were, an

instinctive impulse driving him onwards; and when he went home to eat a plateful of potatoes with his bedridden father, he determined in his own mind that some day or other he would carve his own way in that world in which, at the age of thirty, he was still a nonentity. This was no low greed, no appetite for vulgar pleasures on his part; it was the clearly-defined long-ing of a will and intellect which, not being in their proper sphere, strove to attain to that sphere by the natural force of logic.

As soon as Nantas felt the paving-stones of Paris under his feet, he thought that he had merely to put forth his hands to find a situation wor-thy of him. On the very first day he began his search. He had been given various letters of introduction, which he presented; and, moreover, he called upon several of his own countrymen, thinking that they would help him. But at the end of a month there was still no result. The times were bad, people said; besides which, they merely made promises to break them. His little store of money was swiftly diminishing—indeed, at the most, some twenty francs were left him. It was upon those twenty francs, however, that he was forced to live for another month, eating nothing but bread, scour-ing Paris from morning till evening, and going home to bed without a light, feeling tired to death, and still as poor as ever. His courage did not fail him; but mute anger arose within him. Destiny appeared to be illogical and un-just.

One evening Nantas returned home supperless. He had finished his last morsel of bread on the day before. No money and not a friend to lend him even a franc. Rain had been falling all day, one of those raw downfalls which are so cold in Paris. Rivers of mud were running in the streets, and Nantas, drenched to the skin, had gone to Bercy and afterwards to Mont-martre, where he had been told of employment. But the situation at Bercy was filled up, and at Montmartre they had decided that his handwriting was not good enough. Those were his two last hopes. He would have accepted anything, with the certainty that he would soon command success. He only asked for bread at first, something to live upon in Paris, a foundation-stone upon which he might build his fortune. He walked slowly from Montmartre to the Eue de Lille with his heart full of bitterness. The rain had ceased falling, and busy throngs crowded the streets. He stopped for a few minutes in front of a money-changer's office. Five francs would perhaps suffice him to become one day the master of them all. On five francs he could indeed live for a week, and in a week a man may achieve great things. While he was dreaming thus a cab ran against him and splashed him with mud. He then walked on more quickly, setting his teeth and experiencing a savage desire to rush with clenched fists upon the crowd which barred his way. It would have been taking a kind of vengeance for the cruelty of fate.

In the Eue Richelieu he was almost run over by an omnibus, but he made his way to the Place du Carrousel, whence he threw a jealous glance at the Tuilleries. On the Saints-Peres Bridge a little well-dressed girl obliged him to deviate from the straight path which he was following with the obstinacy of a wild boar tracked by hounds, and this deviation appeared to him a supreme humiliation. The very children impeded his progress! Finally, when he had taken refuge in his room, as a wounded animal returns to its lair to die, he threw himself heavily upon his chair, dead-beat, gazing at his trousers which the mud had stiffened, and at his worn-out boots which had left wet marks along the floor.

The end had come then. Nantas debated how he should kill himself. His pride held good, and he imagined that his suicide would injure Paris. To be a power, to feel one's own worth, and not to find a soul to appreciate you, not one to give you the first crown which you have ever wanted! It seemed monstrous to him, and his whole being revolted at the thought. Then he felt immense regret as his glance fell upon his useless arms. No work had any terror for him. With the tip of his little finger he would have raised the world; and yet there he was, cast into a corner, reduced to impotence, and fuming with impatience like a caged lion! But presently he became calmer, death seemed to him grander. When he was a little boy he had been told the story of an inventor who, having constructed a marvelous machine had one day smashed it to pieces with a hammer because of the indifference of the world. Well, he was like that man, he bore within him a new force, a rare mechanism of intelligence and will, and he was about to destroy his machine by dashing out his brains in the street.

The sun was going down behind the tall trees of the Danvilliers mansion; an autumn sun it was, with golden rays lighting up the yellow leaves. Nantas rose as if attracted by the farewell beams of the heavenly body. He was about to die, he wanted light. For a moment he leant out of the window. Between the masses of foliage he had often seen a tall, fair young girl walking with a queenly step in the garden. He was not romantic, he had passed that age when young men in garrets dream that well-born ladies approach them with their love and fortunes. Yet it chanced that, at this supreme hour of suicide, he suddenly recollected that fair and haughty girl. What could be her name? He knew not. But at the same time he clenched his fists, for his only feeling was one of hatred for the inhabitants of that mansion, glimpses of whose luxury were afforded him by the partially opened windows; and he muttered in a burst of rage, 'I would sell myself; I would sell myself, if some one would only give me the first coppers I need for my fortune to come!'

This idea of selling himself occupied his mind for a moment. If there had been such a place as a pawn-shop where people advanced money on energy and willingness, he would have gone and pledged himself. He set about imagining cases : a politician might buy him to make a tool of him, a banker to make use of every atom of his intelligence; and he accepted, scorning honor, and telling himself that it would suffice if he some day acquired strength and ended by winning the fight. Then he smiled. Did a man ever get a chance to sell himself? Rogues, who watch every opportunity, die of want, without finding a purchaser. Now that suicide seemed his only course, he was fearful lest he should be overcome by cowardice, and he tried in this way to divert his thoughts. He had sat down again, swearing that he would throw himself out of the window as soon as it was dark.

So great was his fatigue, however, that he fell asleep upon his chair. Suddenly he was awakened by the sound of a voice. It was the doorkeeper of the house, who was showing a lady into his room.

'Sir,' the doorkeeper began,' I took the liberty to come up'

Then, seeing no light in the room, she quickly went downstairs and fetched a candle. She seemed to know the person whom she had brought with her, and showed herself at once complaisant and respectful.

'There,' said she, on leaving the room, after placing the candle on the table, 'you can talk at your ease: nobody will disturb you.'

Nantas, who had awoke with a start, looked with astonishment at the lady who had called upon him. She had now raised her veil, and appeared to be about five and-forty, short, very stout, and with the face of a devotee. He had never seen her before. When he offered her the only chair, casting an inquiring glance at her, she gave her name: 'Mademoiselle Chuin—I have come, sir, to talk to you about a very important matter.'

Nantas had sat down on the edge of the bed. The name of Mademoi-

273

selle Chuin told him nothing, and his only course was to wait until she should think fit to explain herself. But she seemed in no hurry to do so; she had given a glance round the tiny room, and appeared to be hesitating as to the way in which she might start the conversation. Finally she spoke in a very gentle voice, emphasizing her remarks with a smile.

'Well, sir, I come as a friend. I have been told your touching story. Do not think that I am a spy; my only wish is to be of use to you. I know how full of trials your life has been till now, with what courage you have struggled to find a situation, and the final result of all your painful efforts. Once more, sir, forgive me for intruding upon you. I assure you that sympathy alone'

Nantas, however, did not interrupt her; his curiosity was aroused, and he surmised that the doorkeeper of the house had furnished the lady with all those particulars. Mademoiselle Chuin, being at liberty to continue, seemed solely desirous of paying compliments and putting things in the most attractive way.

'You have a great future before you, sir,' she resumed. 'I have taken the liberty to follow your endeavors, and I have been greatly struck by your praiseworthy courage in misfortune. In one word, in my opinion there is a great future before you, if some one gives you a helping hand.'

She stopped again. She was waiting for a word. The young man, who believed that the lady had come to offer him a situation, replied that he would accept anything. But she, now that the ice was broken, asked, him point-blank, 'Would you have any objection to marry?'

'Marry!' cried Nantas. 'Goodness, madame! Who would have me? Some poor girl that I could not even feed!'

'No; a very pretty girl, very rich, splendidly connected, and who will at once put you in possession of the means to attain to the highest position.'

Nantas laughed no longer.

'Then what are the terms?' he asked, instinctively lowering his voice.

'The girl has had a misfortune and you must assume responsibility,' said Mademoiselle Chuin; and, putting aside her unctuous phraseology in her desire to come straight to the point, she gave some details.

Nantas's first impulse was to turn her out of doors.

'It's an infamous thing to propose,' he muttered.

'Infamous!' exclaimed Mademoiselle Chuin, affecting her honied tones again, 'I can't admit that ugly word. The truth is, sir, that you will save a family from despair. Her father knows nothing as yet; this misfortune has not long fallen upon her, and it was I myself who conceived the idea of thus marrying her as soon as possible. I know her father; it would kill him if nothing were done. My plan would soften the blow; he would think the wrong half-redressed. The unfortunate part of it is that the real culprit is married. Ah! Sir, there are men who really have no moral sense.'

She might have gone on like this for a long while, for Nantas was not listening to her. He was thinking, why should he refuse? Had he not been proposing to sell himself a little while back? Very well, here was a buyer. Fair exchange is no robbery. He would give his name, and he would be given a situation. It was an ordinary contract. He looked at his muddy trousers, and felt that he had eaten nothing since the day before; all the disgust born of two months' struggling and humiliation rose up within him. At last he was about to set his foot on the world which had repulsed him, and driven him to the verge of suicide.

'I accept,' he said curtly.

Then he asked for clear explanations from Mademoiselle Chuin. What did she want for her services? She protested at first that she wanted nothing. However, she ended by claiming twenty thousand francs out of the dowry which the young man would receive. And as he did not haggle over the terms, she became expansive.

'Listen,' she said, 'it was I who thought of you, and the young lady did not refuse when I mentioned your name. Oh ! you will thank me later on. I might have got a title; I know a man who would have jumped at the chance. But I preferred to choose some one outside of the poor child's sphere. It will appear more romantic. And then I like you. You are good-looking, and have plenty of sense. You will make your way; and you mustn't forget me. Remember that I am devoted to you.'

So far no name had been mentioned, and upon Nantas making an inquiry in this respect the old maid stood up and said, introducing herself afresh, 'Mademoiselle Chuin; I have been living as governess in Baron Danvilliers' family since the baroness's death. I educated Mademoiselle Flavie—the baron's daughter. Mademoiselle Flavie is the young lady in question.'

Then she withdrew, after formally placing on the table an envelope containing a five hundred franc note. It was an advance which she herself made to defray preliminary expenses.

When Nantas found himself alone he went to the window again. The night was very dark; nothing was to be seen but the dark masses of shadow cast by the trees; one window only in the gloomy frontage of the mansion showed a light. So it was that tall fair girl who walked with such a queenly step, and did not deign to notice him. She or some other, what mattered it? The girl was no part of the bargain. Then Nantas raised his eyes still higher, upon Paris roaring in the gloom, upon the quays, the streets, the squares, upon the whole left bank of the river, illuminated by the flickering gaslights: and like a superior being he addressed the city, saying: 'Now you are mine!'

II

Baron Danville's was sitting in the room which served him as a study, a cold lofty apartment, furnished with old-fashioned leather-covered furniture. For the last two days he had been in a state of stupor, Mademoiselle Chuin having informed him of what had befallen Flavie. In vain had she softened and toned down the facts; the old man had been overcome by the blow, and it was only the thought that the culprit was in a position to offer the sole reparation possible that kept him from death. That morning he was awaiting the visit of this man, who was utterly unknown to him, but who had robbed him of his daughter. He rang the bell.

'Joseph, a young man will call, whom you will show in here at once. I am not at home to anybody else,' he said.

Sitting alone at his fireside he brooded bitterly. The son of a mason, a starveling without any position I Mademoiselle Chuin had certainly spoken of him as a promising youth, but what a disgrace to a family whose honor had hitherto been stainless! Flavie had accused herself with a kind of passionate eagerness, so as to acquit her governess of the slightest blame. Since the painful scene between them she had kept her room, and, indeed, the baron had refused to see her. Before forgiving her he was determined to look into the matter. All his plans "were laid. But his hair had grown whiter, and his head shook with age.

'Monsieur Nantas,' announced Joseph.

The baron did not rise. He simply turned his head and looked fixedly at Nantas, who walked forward. The latter had had the good sense not to yield to any desire to dress himself up; he had simply bought a black coat and a pair of trousers, which were decent but very worn, and gave him the appearance of a poor but careful student, with nothing of the adventurer about him. He stopped in the middle of the room and waited, standing up, but without humility.

'So it is you, sir,' stammered the old man.

But he could not continue, for his emotion choked him, and he feared lest he might commit some act of violence. After a pause, he said, simply, 'You have committed a wicked deed, sir.'

Then when Nantas was about to make some excuse, he repeated more emphatically—' A wicked deed. I wish to know nothing, I request you to explain nothing to me. In fact no explanation can lessen your crime. Only robbers break in upon families in this way.'

Nantas hung his head again.

'It is making money very easily, setting a trap in which one is certain of catching both child and father.'

'Allow me, sir,' interrupted the young man, stung by these words.

But the baron made a violent gesture.

'What? Why should I allow anything? It is not for you to speak here. I am telling you what I am in duty bound to tell you, and what you are bound to hear, since you come before me as a culprit. Look at this house. Our family has lived here for more than three centuries without reproach. Standing here, are you not conscious of our ancient honor and dignity? Well, sir, you have trifled with all that. It nearly killed me; and to-day my hands tremble as if I had suddenly grown ten years older. Be silent and listen to me.'

Nantas had turned very pale. He had taken a difficult part upon himself. He felt anxious to make the blindness of passionate love serve as his pretext.

'I lost my head,' he muttered, trying to make up some tale. 'I could not look at Mademoiselle Flavie.'

At his daughter's name the baron rose and cried in a voice like thunder, 'Silence! I have told you that I do not wish to know anything. Whatever happened matters little to me. I have asked her nothing, and I ask you nothing. Keep your confessions to yourselves; I will have nothing to do with them.'

Then he sat down again, trembling and exhausted. Nantas bent his head, feeling deeply moved, in spite of the command he had over himself. After a pause the old man continued in the dry tone of a person discussing business matters, 'I beg pardon, sir. I had determined to keep cool but failed. You are not at my disposal; I am at yours, since I am in your power. You are here to carry out a transaction which has become necessary. To business, sir.'

And thenceforward he affected to speak like a lawyer, settling as agreeably as possible some shameful case in which he was loath to dabble. He began formally: 'Mademoiselle Flavie Danvilliers inherited at the death of her mother a sum of two hundred thousand francs, which she was not to receive until her marriage. That sum has produced interest; but here are the accounts of my guardianship which I will communicate to you.'

He opened a book and began to read some figures.

Nantas in vain tried to stop him. Emotion seized him in the presence of this old man, who appeared so upright and simple, and who seemed to him so great because he was so calm.

'Finally,' the baron concluded, 'I bestow on you, by an agreement which my notary drew up this morning, another sum of two hundred thousand francs. I know that you have nothing. You can draw those two hundred thousand francs at my banker's on the day after the marriage.'

'But I don't ask for your money, sir,' said Nantas, 'I only want your daughter.' The baron cut him short.

'You have not the right to refuse,' he said, 'and my daughter could not marry a man with less money than herself. I give you the dowry which I intended for her, that is all. Possibly you reckoned on more, for I have the credit of being richer than I really am.'

And as the young man remained mute at this last thrust, the baron put an end to the interview by ringing the bell.

'Joseph, tell Mademoiselle Flavie that I want her in my room at once.'

He had risen from his chair, and now began to walk slowly about the room. Nantas remained motionless. He was deceiving this old man, and he felt small and powerless before him. At last Flavie appeared.

'My child,' said the baron, 'here is the man. The marriage will take place as soon as possible.'

Then he went out of the room, leaving them alone, as if, so far as he was concerned, the marriage were over.

When the door was shut silence reigned. Nantas and Flavie looked at one another. They had never met before. He thought her very handsome, with her pale and haughty face, and her large grey eyes which never drooped. Perhaps she had been crying during the three days that she had spent in her room; however, the coldness of her cheeks must have frozen her tears. She it was who spoke first.

'Then the matter is settled, sir,' she said.

'Yes, madame,' replied Nantas simply.

Her face contracted involuntarily as she cast a long look at him, a look which seemed to be fathoming his baseness.

'Well, so much the better,' she continued. 'I was afraid I should not find anyone to agree to such a bargain.'

Nantas could distinguish in her voice all the scorn which she felt for him, but he raised his head. If he had trembled before the father, knowing that he was deceiving him, he determined to be firm with the daughter, who was his accomplice.

'Excuse me, madame,' he said calmly, and with the greatest politeness. 'I think you misconceive the position in which what you rightly call the bargain has placed us. I apprehend that, from to-day forth, we are on a footing of perfect equality.'

'Indeed!' interrupted Flavie, with a scornful smile.

'Yes, perfect equality. You require a name, in order to conceal a fault which I do not presume to condemn, and I give you my name. On my side I require money, and a certain social position, in order to carry out some great enterprises, and you furnish me with that money and position. We thus become two partners whose capitals balance. It only remains for us to express our mutual thanks for the service which we are rendering to one another.'

She smiled no longer; indeed, a look of irritated pride appeared upon her face. After a pause she asked him, 'You know my conditions?'

'No, madame,' said Nantas, preserving perfect calmness. 'Be good enough to name them. I agree to them in advance.'

Upon this she spoke as follows, without hesitating or blushing: 'Our lives will remain completely distinct and separate. You will give up all rights over me, and I shall owe no duty towards you.'

At each sentence Nantas made an affirmative sign. This was precisely what he desired.

'If I thought it part of my duty to be gallant,' he said, 'I should assert that such conditions would drive me to despair. But we are above empty compliments. I am pleased to see that you have such a correct appreciation of our respective positions. We are not entering upon life by the path of roses. I only ask one thing of you, madame, which is, that you will not make use of the liberty I shall accord you in such a way as to necessitate any interference on my part.'

'What, sir!' exclaimed Plavie, violently, her pride revolting.

Nantas bowed respectfully, and entreated her not to be offended. Their position was a delicate one; they must both of them put up with certain allusions, without which a perfect understanding would be impossible. He refrained from insisting further. Mademoiselle Chuin, in a second interview, had given him further particulars and had named to him a certain Monsieur des Fondettes as the person to whom all the trouble was due.

Suddenly Nantas felt a friendly impulse. Like all those who are conscious of their own power, he was fond of being good-natured.

'Listen, madame,' he exclaimed. 'We don't know one another, but it would be really wrong of us to hate one another at first sight. Perhaps we are made to understand each other. I can see that you despise me, but perhaps that is because you do not know my story.'

Then he began to talk feverishly, throwing himself into a state of excitement as he spoke of his life, his ambition, and his desperate fruitless efforts in Paris. Then he displayed his scorn of what he called social conventionalism, in which ordinary men became entangled. What mattered the opinion of the world, he asked, when a man had his foot on it? He must show his superiority. Power was an excuse for all. And in glowing terms he painted the sovereign existence which he would make for himself. He feared no further obstacle; nothing prevailed against power. He would be powerful, and therefore he would be happy.

'Don't imagine that I am miserably sordid,' he continued. 'I am not selling myself for your fortune; I only take your money as a means to rise. Oh, if you only knew what is working within me! If you only knew the burning nights which I have spent, always meditating over the same idea, which was only swept away by the reality of the morrow, then you would understand me! You would then, perhaps, be proud to lean on my arm, saying to yourself that you at least had furnished me with the means to become some one!'

She listened to him in silence, without a single movement of her features. And he asked himself a question which he had been turning over in his mind for three days past, without being able to find answer to it: Had she noticed him at his window, that she had so readily accepted Mademoiselle Chuin's scheme when the latter had mentioned him? The singular idea occurred to him that perhaps she might have loved him with a romantic love if he had indignantly refused the bargain which the governess had proposed to him.

He stopped at last, and Flavie maintained an icy silence. Then, as if he had not made his confession, she repeated in a dry voice: 'Then, it is understood, our lives completely distinct, absolute liberty.'

Nantas at once resumed his ceremonious air, and in the curt voice of a man discussing an agreement, replied: 'It is settled, madame.'

Ill-pleased with himself, he then withdrew. How was it that he had yielded to the foolish desire to overcome that woman? She was very handsome; but it was better that there should be nothing in common between them, for she might hamper him in life.

Ten years had passed. One morning Nantas was sitting in the study in which Baron Danvilliers had given him such a formidable reception on the occasion of their first meeting. That study was now his own; the baron, after being reconciled to his daughter and his son-in-law, had given up the house to them, merely reserving for his own use a little building situated at the other end of the garden and overlooking the Eue de Beaune. In ten years' time Nantas had won for himself one of the highest positions attainable in the financial and mercantile worlds. Having a hand in all the great railway enterprises, engaged in all the land speculations which signalized the earlier period of the Second Empire, he had rapidly accumulated an immense fortune. But his ambition did not halt at that; he was determined to play a part in politics, and he had succeeded in getting elected as a deputy in a department where he had several farms. Since taking his seat in the Corps Législatif, he had posed as a future Finance Minister. Thanks to his practical knowledge and his ready tongue, he was day by day acquiring a more important position. He was skilful enough to affect absolute devotion to the Empire, but at the same time he professed theories on financial subjects which made a great stir, and which he knew gave the Emperor a deal to think of.

On that particular morning Nantas was overladen with business. The greatest activity prevailed in the spacious offices which he had arranged on the ground-floor of the mansion. There was a crowd of clerks, some sitting motionless at wickets, and others constantly going backwards and forwards, to the sound of banging doors. Bags of gold lay open and overflowing on the tables. There was a constant ring of the precious metal; a tinkling music of wealth such as might have flooded the streets. In the ante-rooms a crowd was surging; place-hunters, financial agents, politicians, all Paris on its knees before power. Great men frequently waited there patiently for an hour at a stretch. And he, sitting at his table, in correspondence with people far and near, able to grasp the world with his outstretched arms, was carrying his former dream of force into fulfillment, conscious that he was the intelligent motor of a colossal machine which moved kingdoms and empires.

Suddenly he rang for his usher. He seemed anxious.

'Germain,' he said, 'do you know whether your mistress has come in?'

And when the man replied that he did not know, he told him to summon his wife's maid. But Germain did not move.

'Excuse me, sir,' he whispered; 'the President of the Corps Législatif insists on seeing you.'

Nantas made an impatient gesture and replied: 'Well, show him in, and do as I told you.'

On the previous day, a speech which Nantas had made on an important budgetary question had produced such an impression that the matter had been referred to a commission to be amended according to his views. After the sitting of the Chamber a rumor had spread that the Finance Minister intended to resign, and Nantas was at once spoken of as his probable successor. For his part he shrugged his shoulders: nothing had been done, he had only had an interview with the Emperor with regard to certain special points. However, the President's visit might have vast significance. At this thought Nantas tried to throw off the feeling of worry which was weighing on him, and rose to grasp the President's hand.

'Ah, Monsieur le Due,' he said, 'I beg your pardon. I did not know you were here. Believe me; I am deeply sensible of the honor which you are paying me.'

For a minute they talked cordially; then the President, without saying anything definite, gave him to understand that he had been sent by the Emperor to sound him. Would he accept the Finance portfolio, and what would be his programme? Upon this, Nantas, with superb calmness, named his conditions. But beneath the impassibility of his face mute triumph was swelling. At last he had mounted the final rung; he was at the top of the ladder. Another step and he would have all heads save that of the sovereign beneath him. As the President concluded, saying that he was going at once to the Emperor to communicate Nantas's programme, a small door which communicated with the private part of the house opened, and the maid of the financier's wife appeared.

Nantas, suddenly turning pale, stopped short in the middle of a sentence and hurried to the girl, saying to the duke, 'Pray excuse me.'

Then he questioned the servant in whispers. Madame had gone out early? Had she said where she was going? When was she expected home? The maid replied vaguely, like a clever girl who did not wish to compromise herself.

Understanding the absurdity of the situation, Nantas concluded by remarking, 'Tell your mistress as soon as she comes in that I wish to speak to her.'

The President of the Chamber, somewhat surprised, had stepped up to a window and was looking into the courtyard. Nantas now returned to him, again apologizing. But he had lost his self-possession, he stammered, and astonished the duke by his clumsy remarks.

'There, I've spoilt the whole business,' he exclaimed aloud, when the other had gone. 'I've missed the portfolio.'

He sat down, feeling disgusted and angry. Several more visitors were then shown in. An engineer had a report to present to him, showing that enormous profits would arise from the working of a certain mine. A diplomatist interviewed him on the subject of a loan which a foreign Power wanted to negotiate in Paris. His tools flocked in, rendering account of twenty different schemes. Finally he received a large number of his colleagues of the Chamber, all of whom went into raptures about his speech of the day before.

Leaning back in his chair, he accepted all this flattery without a smile. The clink of gold was still audible in the neighboring rooms; the house seemed to tremble like a factory, as if all that money were manufactured there. He had only to take up a pen to dispatch telegrams which would have spread joy or consternation through the markets of Europe; he could prevent or precipitate war, by supporting or opposing the loan of which he had been told; he even held the fate of the French Budget in his hands, and he would soon know whether it would be best for him to support or oppose the Empire. This was his triumph; his formidable personality had become the axis upon which a world was turning. And yet he did not enjoy his triumph, as he had thought he would. He experienced a feeling of listlessness; his mind was elsewhere, on the alert at the slightest audible sound. Scarcely had a flame, a flush of satisfied ambition, risen to his cheeks than he felt himself turn pale again as if a cold hand from behind had been laid upon his neck.

Two hours had passed and Flavie had not yet appeared. Nantas at last called Germain, and gave him orders to summon Baron Danvilliers if the old gentleman were at home. Then he began to pace his study, refusing to see anyone else that day. Little by little his agitation had increased. His wife had evidently been to keep some appointment. She must have renewed her acquaintance with Monsieur des Fondettes. The latter's wife had died six months previously. True, Nantas disclaimed any idea of being jealous; during ten years he had strictly observed the agreement to which he had been a party; but he drew the line, as he said, at being made a dupe of. Never would he allow his wife to compromise his position by making him a laughing-stock. His strength forsook him as he became a prey to the feelings of a husband who requires respect. He experienced agony such as he had never endured, not even in his most hazardous speculations, at the commencement of his career.

At last Flavie entered the room, still in her outdoor costume; she had merely taken off her gloves and hat. Nantas, whose voice trembled, told her that he would have gone to her if he had known that she had come in. But, without sitting down, she motioned to him to have done quickly.

'Madame,' he began, 'an explanation has become necessary between us. Where were you this morning?'

Her husband's quivering voice and the pointedness of his question, astonished her profoundly.

'Where it pleased me to go,' she replied in a cold tone.

'That is exactly what, in future, I must object to,' he resumed, turning very pale. 'It is your duty to recollect what I said to you: I will not allow you to make use of the liberty I grant you, in a way which may bring disgrace upon my name.'

Flavie smiled in sovereign disdain.

'Disgrace your name, sir? But that is a question which regards you. It is a thing which no longer remains to be done.'

Upon this, Nantas, wild with passion, advanced, as if to strike her.

'You wretched creature!' he stammered, 'You have just left Monsieur des Fondettes. You have a lover, I know it!'

'You are wrong,' she replied, without recoiling; 'I have never seen Monsieur des Fondettes again. But even if I had a lover, it would not be for you to reproach me. What difference would it make to you? You forget our compact.'

He looked at her for a moment with wild eyes; then choking with sobs, and throwing into one cry all the passion which he had so long stifled, he flung himself at her feet.

'Oh, Flavie, I love you!'

Unbending still, she drew back, for he had touched the hem of her dress. But the wretched man followed her, dragging himself upon his knees with his hands uplifted.

'I love you, Flavie, I love you to madness! How it happened I know not. It began years ago, and it grew and grew, till now it has absorbed my whole being. Oh! I have struggled. I thought this passion unworthy of me. I called our first interview to mind. But now I suffer too much. I must speak'

For a long time he continued thus. It was the shattering of all his principles. This man, who had put his trust in force, who maintained that volition was the sole lever capable of moving the world, was crushed, feeble like a child, disarmed by a woman. And his dream of fortune realized, his present high position, he would have given all for that woman to have raised him by a kiss upon his brow! She marred his triumph. He no longer heard the gold which sounded in his office; he no longer thought of the endless procession of flatterers who came to bow their knees to him; he forgot that the Emperor, at that moment, perhaps, was summoning him to power. All those things had no existence for him. He possessed everything, save the only thing he wished for—his wife's love. And if she denied it, then he had nothing left him!

'Listen,' he continued; 'whatever I have done, I have done for you. At first, it is true, you were for nothing in it; I simply worked to gratify my own pride. But soon you became the one object of all my thoughts, of all my efforts. I told myself that I must mount as high as possible, in order to become worthy of you. I hoped to make you unbend on the day when I should lay my power at your feet. See what I now am. Have I not won your forgiveness? Do not despise me any longer, I entreat you.'

As yet she had not spoken. Now, however, she said calmly: 'Get up, sir. Somebody might come in.'

He refused, and still went on entreating. Perhaps he would have bided his time if he had not been jealous of Monsieur des Fondettes. It was that torture which maddened him. At last he became very humble.

'I see that you still despise me. Very well, wait; do not bestow your love on anybody. I can promise you so much that I shall know how to move you. You must forgive me if I was harsh just now. I am out of my senses. Oh, let me hope that you will love me some day!'

'Never!' she answered energetically.

Then, as he still remained upon the floor seemingly crushed, she would have left the room; but suddenly, beside himself with fury, he sprang up and caught her by the wrists. A woman braved him thus when the world was at his feet! He was capable of anything, could overthrow States, rule France as he pleased, and yet he could not obtain his wife's love! He, so strong, so powerful, he whose slightest desires were orders, he had but one longing now, and that longing would never be gratified, because a creature, who was as weak as a child, spurned him! He grasped her arms, and repeated in a hoarse whisper: 'You must, you must.'

'And I will not,' replied Flavie, pale and obstinate.

The struggle was still going on when Baron Danvilliers opened the door. On seeing him, Nantas released Flavie, and cried, 'Your daughter has just come from her lover, sir! Tell her that a woman should respect her husband's name, even if she does not love him, even if the thought of her own honor does not stand in the way.'

The baron, who was greatly aged, remained standing on the threshold, gazing at this violent scene. It was a melancholy surprise for him. He had believed them to be united, and he looked with approval on their ceremonious intercourse in public, considering that to be a mere matter of form. His son-in-law and he belonged to different generations; but although he disliked the financier's somewhat unscrupulous activity, although he condemned certain undertakings which he regarded as undesirable, he was forced to recognize Nantas's strength of will and his quick intellect. And now he suddenly came upon this drama, which he had never even suspected.

When Nantas accused Flavie of having a lover, the baron, who still treated his married daughter with the same severity as he had shown her when a child, advanced with a stately step.

'I swear to you that she has just come from her lover's,' repeated Nantas; 'and, look at her, she defies me.'

Flavie turned away her head disdainfully. She was arranging her cuffs, which her husband had crushed in his roughness. Not a blush was to be seen on her face. Her father spoke to her.

'My child,' said he, 'why do you not defend yourself? Can your husband be speaking the truth? Can you have reserved this last grief for my old age? The offence would fall on me as well; for the fault of one member of a family falls upon the others.'

Flavie made a gesture of impatience. Her father had well chosen his time to accuse her! For a moment longer she bore his questions, wishing to spare him the shame of an explanation. But as he in his turn lost patience, seeing her mute and obstinate, she finally replied, 'Father, let this man play his part. You do not know him. For your own sake do not force me to speak out.'

'He is your husband,' said the old man,' the father of your child.'

Flavie started, stung to the quick. 'No, no, he is not the father of my child. I will tell you everything now. This man was never my lover, for it would be at least some excuse for him if he had loved me. This man simply sold himself and agreed to hide another's sin.'

The baron turned towards Nantas, who had recoiled, deadly pale.

'Do you hear me, father?' continued Flavie, more violently. 'He sold himself, sold himself for money! I have never loved him, and he has never been anything to me. I wished to spare you a great sorrow. I bought him so that he might lie to you. Look at him now. See whether I am not telling you the truth.'

Nantas hid his face in his hands.

'And now,' resumed the young woman, 'he actually wants me to love him. He went down on his knees just now and wept. Some comedy, no doubt! Forgive me for having deceived you, father; but how can I love such a man? Now that you know all, take me away. Indeed, he treated me with violence just now, and I will not remain here a moment longer.'

The baron straightened his bent figure. In silence he stepped forward and gave his arm to his daughter. The two crossed the room, without Nantas making a movement to detain them. Then, upon reaching the door, the old man spoke these two words: 'Farewell, sir.'

The door closed. Nantas remained alone, crushed, gazing wildly into the void around him. Germain came in and placed a letter on the table; Nantas opened it mechanically, and cast his eyes over it. This letter, written by the Emperor in person, gave him the appointment of Finance Minister, and was couched in the most flattering terms. He could hardly understand it; the realization of all his ambition did not affect him in the least.

Meanwhile, in the neighboring rooms the rattle of money had grown louder; it was the busiest hour of the day, the hour when Nantas's house seemed to shake the world. And he, amid that colossal machinery which was his work, he, at the apogee of his power, with his eyes stupidly fixed on the Emperor's letter, gave vent to a childish complaint, the negation of his whole life: 'Ah! how unhappy I am! how unhappy I am!'

Then, resting his head upon the table, he wept, and the hot tears that gushed forth from his eyes blotted the letter which appointed him Minister of Finance.

IV

During the whole of the eighteen months that Nantas had been a Minister, he had been trying to drown the past by superhuman toil. On the day after the scene in his study he had had an interview with Baron Danvilliers; and Flavie, acting on her father's advice, had consented to return to her husband's roof. But they spoke no word together, except when they were forced to play a comedy in the eyes of the world. Nantas had determined not to leave his home. In the evening his secretaries came to him from the Ministry, and he got through all his work in his own study.

It was at this period of his life that he performed his greatest deeds. A secret voice suggested lofty and fruitful aspirations to him. Whenever he passed by, a murmur of sympathy and admiration was heard. But he remained insensible to eulogy. It may be said that he worked without hope of reward, with the sole idea of performing prodigies, of which the only aim was to compass the impossible. At each step on his upward career he consulted Flavie's face. Was she touched at last? Did she pardon him his former baseness? Had she still any thought save of the development of his intellect? But never did he detect any emotion on that woman's mute countenance, and he said to himself, as he redoubled his efforts: 'I am not high enough for her yet; I must climb, still climb.'

He was determined to compel happiness, as he had compelled fortune. All his old belief in his power returned, he would not admit that there was any other lever in this world; it was will which produced humanity. When discouragement seized on him at times, he shut himself up, so that nobody should witness the weakness of his flesh. His struggles could only be read in his deep-set, dark-circled eyes, in which an ardent fire blazed.

He was devoured by jealousy now. To fail to win Flavie's love was a torture; but the thought that she might care for another drove him mad. By way of asserting her liberty, it was quite possible that she might intrigue with Monsieur des Fondettes. Her husband affected not to occupy himself with her, but all the time he endured agony whenever she absented herself, even if it were only for an hour. If he had not feared to make himself look ridiculous, he would have followed her in the streets. That course displeasing him, he determined to have some one beside her whose devotion he could purchase.

Mademoiselle Chuin had remained an inmate of the house. The baron was used to her, not to mention that she knew too many things to make it advisable to get rid of her. At one time the old maid had resolved to retire on the twenty thousand francs that Nantas had paid her on the day after his marriage. But she had no doubt calculated that there would be further pickings in such a household. So she awaited her opportunity, having found, moreover, that she needed yet another twenty thousand francs to buy the long-desired notary's house at Eoinville, the little market town she came from.

There was no occasion for Nantas to mince matters with this old lady, whose pious mien no longer deceived him. However, on the morning when he called her into his study and openly proposed to her that she should keep him informed as to his wife's slightest actions, she professed to be insulted, and asked him what he took her for.

'Come,' said he impatiently,' I'm very busy, some one is waiting for me; let us be brief, please.'

But she would listen to nothing which was not couched in proper terms. One of her principles was that things are not ugly in themselves, that they only become ugly or cease to be so according to the way in which they are presented.

'Very well,' said Nantas, ' a good action is involved in this. I am fearful that my wife is hiding some sorrow from me. For the last few weeks I have observed that she has been very much depressed, and I thought that you could find out the cause of it.'

'You can rely on me,' said Mademoiselle Chuin, with a maternal outburst on hearing these words. 'I am devoted to your wife; I will do anything for her sake or yours. From to-morrow we will keep a watch on her.'

Nantas promised to reward the old maid for her services. She pretended to be angry at first, but she had the adroitness to make him fix a sum, and it was agreed that he should give her ten thousand francs upon her furnishing him with positive proof of his wife's conduct whatever it might be. Little by little they had come to call things by their proper names.

From that time forward Nantas was less uneasy. Three months passed and he was engaged upon a great task—the preparation of the Budget. With the Emperor's sanction he had introduced some important modifications into the financial system. He knew that he would be fiercely attacked in the Chamber, and he had to prepare a large quantity of documents. Frequently he sat up all night, and this hard work deadened him as it were to emotion, and made him patient. Whenever he saw Mademoiselle Chuin he questioned her briefly. Did she know anything? Had his wife paid many visits? Had she stopped long at certain houses? Mademoiselle Chuin kept a journal of the slightest incidents, but so far she had not succeeded in making any important discovery. Nantas felt reassured, while the old woman occasionally blinked her eyes, saying that she should perhaps have some news for him soon.

The truth was that Mademoiselle Chuin had indulged in further reflection. Ten thousand francs was not enough; she needed twenty thousand to purchase the notary's house. She at first thought of selling herself to the wife, after having sold herself to the husband. But she knew Flavie, and she was fearful of being dismissed at the first word. For a long time past, before she had even been charged with this matter, she had kept watch over Madame Nantas on her own account, remarking to herself that a servant's profits lie in the master's or mistress's vices. However, she had discovered that she had to deal with a virtue which was all the more rigid since it was based upon pride. One effect of Flavie's stumble had been that it had inspired her with positive hatred for the other sex. So Mademoiselle Chuin was in despair, when one day she met Monsieur des Fondettes in the street, and after they had had some conversation together, realizing that he desired to be reconciled to her mistress, she made up her mind: she would serve both him and Nantas—a combination worthy of genius.

Everything favored her. Monsieur des Fondettes had met Flavie in society and had been scorned by her. He was in despair thereat. At the end of a week's time, after a great parade of feeling on his side and of scruples on that of Mademoiselle Chuin, the matter was settled; he was to give her ten thousand francs, and she was to smuggle him into the house one evening so that he might have a private interview with Flavie.

The arrangement having been effected, Mademoiselle Chuin sought Nantas.

'What have you learnt?' he asked, turning pale.

She would not say anything definite at first. But Nantas displayed such furious impatience that before long she told him that Monsieur des Fondettes had an appointment with Flavie that evening in her private apartments.

'Very good—thank you,' stammered Nantas. And he sent her off with a wave of the hand; he was afraid of giving way before her.

This abrupt dismissal astonished and delighted the old woman, for she had prepared herself for a long cross-examination, and had even pre-arranged her answers, so that she might not contradict herself. She made a bow, and then retired, putting on a mournful face.

Nantas had risen. As soon as he was alone he said aloud, 'This evening, in her private apartments.'

Then he carried his hands to his head, as if he feared it would burst. That appointment under his own roof seemed to him monstrous audacity. He clenched his fists, and his rage made him think of murder. And yet he had his task to finish—those budgetary documents to complete. Three times did he sit down at his table, and three times a heaving of his whole body raised him to his feet again; while, behind him, something seemed to be urging him to go at once to his wife, and denounce her. At last, however, he conquered himself, and resumed his work, swearing that he would strangle them both that very evening. It was the greatest victory that he had ever won over his feelings.

That same afternoon Nantas went to submit to the Emperor the definite plan of the Budget. The sovereign having raised certain objections, he discussed them with perfect clearness. But it became necessary that he should modify an important part of his programme—a difficult matter, as the debate was to take place on the next day.

'I will pass the night over it,' he said. And on his way home he thought, ' I'll kill them at midnight, and I shall have the whole night afterwards to finish this task.'

At dinner that evening Baron Danvilliers began talking about the Budget, which was making some little stir. He did not approve of all his son-in-law's views on financial matters, but he admitted that they were very broad and very remarkable. While Nantas was replying to the Baron, he fancied, on several occasions, that he noticed his wife's eyes fixed upon him. She frequently looked at him in that way now. Her glance was not softened, however; she simply listened, and seemed to be trying to read his thoughts. Nantas fancied that she feared she was betrayed. Accordingly he made an effort to appear careless j he talked a good deal, affected great animation, and finally overcame the objections of his father-in-law, who gave way to his great intellect. Flavie was still looking at him, and suddenly a hardly perceptible glimpse of tenderness darted across her face.

Nantas worked in his study until midnight. Little by little he had become absorbed in his task, and soon he lost consciousness of everything save that creation of his brain, that great financial scheme which he had painfully built up piece by piece, in the midst of innumerable obstacles. When the clock struck twelve he instinctively raised his head. Deep silence reigned in the house. Suddenly he recollected everything. But it was a trial for him to leave his chair; he laid his pen down regretfully, and at last took a few steps as if in obedience to a will which had forsaken him. Then his face flushed, and a flame blazed forth in his eyes. He started for his wife's rooms.

That evening Flavie had dismissed her maid early, saying that she wished to be alone. She had a suite of rooms for her own use. Until midnight she remained in a little boudoir, where, stretched upon a sofa, she took up a book and began to read. But again and again the book fell from her hands, and, closing her eyes at last, she became absorbed in thought. Her face still wore a softened expression, and a faint smile played upon it at intervals. Suddenly she started up. There was a knock outside.

'Who is there?' she asked.

'Open the door,' replied Nantas.

She was so surprised that she opened it mechanically. Never before had her husband presented himself in this way. He entered the room half-distracted; his rage had mastered him while he ascended the stairs. Mademoiselle Chuin, who was watching for him on the landing, had just told him that Monsieur des Fondettes had been there for some hours. Accordingly he was determined to show his wife no mercy.

'There is a man concealed in your rooms,' said he.

Flavie did not reply at first, so greatly did these words surprise her. At last she grasped their meaning.

'You are mad, sir I,' she answered.

But, without stopping to argue, he was already looking about him. Then he made his way to the next room. With one bound, however, she threw herself before the door, crying: 'You shall not go in. These are my rooms, and you have no right here.'

Quivering with passion and looking taller in her pride, she guarded the door. For a moment they stood thus motionless, speechless, gazing into one another's eyes. Nantas with his head thrust forward, his arms opened, seemed about to throw himself upon her to force a passage.

'Come away,' he said, in a hoarse whisper. 'I'm stronger than you, and go in I will!'

'You shall not; I will not permit it.'

And as Nantas kept on repeating accusations, she, without even deigning to deny them, shrugged her shoulders, and replied, 'Even if it were true what difference can it make to you? Am I not free?'

He recoiled at these words, which struck him like a blow. It was quite true, she was free. A cold shudder ran through him, he plainly realized that she had the best of the argument, and that he was playing the part of a feeble and illogical child. He was not observing their compact; his foolish passion had made it hateful to him. Why had he not remained at work in his study? The blood fled from his cheeks, and an indefinable expression of suffering overspread his face. When Flavie saw his pitiable condition she left the door before which she had been standing, while a tender gleam came into her eyes. 'Look,' she said, simply.

And then she passed into the adjoining room herself carrying a lamp in her hand, while Nantas remained standing at the door. He had made her a sign as if to say that it was sufficient, that he did not wish to enter. But it was she who insisted now. When she had drawn aside the curtains, and perceived Monsieur des Fondettes who had been concealed behind them, so intense was her amazement and horror that she shrieked.

'It was true,' she stammered, 'it was true this man was here; but I did not know it. On my life I swear it!'

Then, with an effort, she calmed herself, and even seemed to regret the impulse which had prompted her to defend herself.

'You were right, sir, and I crave your pardon,' she said to Nantas, endeavoring to speak in her usual tone of voice.

Monsieur des Fondettes, however, felt somewhat foolish, and would have given a good deal if the husband had only flown into a passion. But Nantas remained silent. He had simply turned very pale. When he had carried his eyes from Monsieur des Fondettes to Plavie, he bowed to the latter, merely saying, 'Excuse me, madame, you are free.'

Then he turned and walked away. Something seemed to have broken within him; merely a machinery of muscle and bone still worked. When he reached his study again he walked straight to a drawer where he kept a revolver. Having examined the weapon, he said aloud, as if making a formal engagement with himself: 'That suffices; I will Mil myself presently.'

He turned up his lamp, sat down at his table, and quietly resumed his work. Amid the deep silence he completed, without an instant's hesitation, a sentence that he had previously left unfinished. One by one were fresh sheets of paper covered with writing and set in a heap. Two hours later, when Flavie, who had driven Monsieur des Fondettes from the house, came down with bare feet to listen at the door, she only heard her husband's pen scratching as it traveled over the paper. She bent down and applied her eye to the keyhole. Nantas was still calmly writing, his face was expressive of peace and satisfaction at his work; but a ray of the lamp fell upon the barrel of the revolver at his side.

V

The house adjoining the garden of the mansion was now the property of Nantas, who had bought it from his father-in-law. By a personal caprice he had refrained from letting the wretched garret where he had struggled against want for two months after his arrival in Paris. Since he had acquired an enormous fortune he had on more than one occasion felt impelled to go and shut himself up in that little room for hours at a time. It was there that he had suffered, and it was there that he liked to enjoy his triumph. Again, whenever he met with any obstacle he was wont to go there to reflect and to form great resolutions. Once there he again became what he had formerly been. And now, when the hand of death hovered over him, it was in that attic that he determined to meet it.

He did not finish his work until eight o'clock in the morning. Fearing that fatigue might overcome him, he took a cold bath. Then he summoned several of his clerks for the purpose of giving them instructions. When his secretary arrived he had an interview with him, and the secretary received orders to take the plan of the Budget to the Tuilleries, and to furnish certain explanations if the Emperor should raise any fresh objections. That settled, Nantas considered that he had done enough. He had left everything in order; he was not going off like a demented bankrupt. After all, he was his own property; he could dispose of himself without being accused of selfishness or cowardice.

Nine o'clock struck. The time had come. But, just as he was leaving his study, taking the revolver with him, he had to put up with a final humiliation. Mademoiselle Chuin presented herself, to claim the ten thousand francs which he had promised her. He paid her, and was forced to put up with her familiarity. She assumed a maternal air, and seemed to treat him as a successful pupil. Even if he had had any hesitation left, this shameful complicity would have confirmed him in his intentions. He sought the garret quickly, and in his haste he left the door unlocked.

Nothing was changed there. There were the same rents in the wallpaper; the bed, the table, and the chair were still there, with their same old look of poverty. For a moment he inhaled the atmosphere which reminded him of his former struggles. Then he approached the window and caught sight of the same stretch of Paris as formerly; the trees in the garden, the Seine, the quays, and a part of the right bank of the river, where the houses rose up in confused masses until they were lost to sight at the point where the Pere-Lachaise Cemetery appeared in the far distance.

The revolver was lying within his reach on the rickety table. There was no hurry now; he felt certain that nobody would disturb him, and that he might kill himself whenever he pleased. He became absorbed in thought, and he reflected that he was at precisely the same point as formerly——led back to the same spot, with the same intention of suicide. One evening before, in that very room, he had determined to dash his brains out. In those days he had been too poor to purchase a pistol; he had only had the stones in the streets at his disposal, but death was awaiting him now as then. Thus in this world death is the only thing which never fails, which is always sure and always ready. Nothing that he knew of was like death; he sought in vain, all else had given way beneath him: death alone remained a certainty. He regretted that he had lived ten years too long. The experience that he had acquired of life, in his ascent to fortune and power, seemed to him puerile. Why had he put himself to that expenditure of will, what purpose had been served by that waste of force, since will and force were as nothing? One passion had sufficed to destroy him: he had foolishly allowed himself to love Flavie, and now the edifice which he had built up was cracking, collapsing like a mere house of cards swept away by the breath of a child. It was lamentable—it resembled the punishment that overtakes a marauding schoolboy, under whom a branch snaps, and who perishes on the spot where he has sinned. Life was a mistake; the best men ended it as tamely as the biggest fools.

Nantas had taken the revolver from the table, and slowly raised it. At that supreme moment one last regret made him hesitate for a second. What great things would he not have accomplished if Flavie had understood him I Had she but thrown herself on his neck one day, saying, 'I love you I' he would have found a lever to move the world! And his last thought was one of disdain for force and strength; since they which were to have given him everything had not been able to give him Flavie.

He raised the revolver. The morning was a glorious one. Through the open window the sun poured in, lending even a look of brightness to that wretched garret. In the distance, Paris was awakening to its giant life. Nantas pressed the weapon to his temple.

But the door was suddenly flung open, and Flavie entered. With one movement she dashed the revolver aside, and the bullet lodged itself in the ceiling. They looked at one another. She was so out of breath, so choked with emotion, that she could not articulate. At last, embracing Nantas for the first time, she spoke the words for which he longed, the only words which could have determined him to live.

'I love you!' she cried, sobbing on his breast, and tearing the avowal from her pride, her mastered being. 'I love you, for you are truly strong.'

A Note on the Text

The task of assembling the short fiction of Émile Zola has been formidable for a number of reasons. It would be facile to say that any work rendering Zola (or any non-English writer) into English is problematic at the very least, impossible at the worst. We are simultaneously blessed and cursed with existing translations. Blessed because they introduced Zola to a much admiring public; cursed because such translations are so of their time. The Vizetelly family which has always been applauded for their efforts in this regard worked under a threat that few people in the western world face; they were not only fearful of being imprisoned, but were in fact put in jail merely for the act of translating Zola into English. As a result their translations suffer on two counts: they are expurgated almost to the point of nonsense and they are Victorian in the extreme, which is to say that they are insufferably stuffy, overblown and laden with a vocabulary that only the most forsaken scholar living in a cave somewhere and avoiding all contact with contemporary culture could understand.

Translators generally build upon each other's work and it is our misfortune that the foundation of Zola translations are the firm of Vizetelly and Co. I know this will stir the ire of mainly the British scholars of Zola because they are covetous of the prestige which surrounds the "bravery" of the Vizetellys in taking on the task in the first place. But being first does not mean doing a great job; a passable job, yes. A better than no job at all, also yes. But I can be quite certain that their translations destroyed any chance Zola had of being widely accepted in the United States and I can assure you that his influence is so potent as for any student to safely be able to assert that without Émile Zola, American literature from 1880 to 1940 would be completely and utterly different. This influence, however, is based on our American authors' ability to read the master in his original French, a talent widely accepted in the years mentioned but woefully absent today where our literati are considered learned if they have mastered MSWord. Fortunately, the same cannot be said of America's great contemporary film directors who religiously observe French films all to the general good of American cinema.

The problems with translations notwithstanding, there are even greater problems assembling Zola's short works because they were often published in newspapers and other periodicals with a heavy editorial hand. A story such as "Nantas" has at least three variations within the French language itself. So it was with some temerity that I chose the version closest in my opinion to what Zola, hopefully, intended. Most, if not all, of his short fiction was written quickly, under deadline, and with considerably less care than his novels. Many are simply sketches reminiscent of an author's working notebooks where ideas for novels are set down looking to the day when they might be fleshed out. If that day never comes, the sketches or notes will suffice to satisfy the hungry reading public whose appetite has been stimulated by the passion that intelligent readers everywhere have for the novels. Interestingly, many of his stories are so short that in their day they would have been considered ridiculous (and were by many critics.) But today, such short fiction has been "invented" in the form of what is colloquially and now in some more refined circles referred to as "flash fiction."

As a scholar of Zola, but more importantly as an adoring fan (a term I have no qualms with), I would never recommend to any reader unfamiliar with the man to start with his short stories. I think many of Thomas Hardy's short stories, most of William Faulkner's and Herman Melville's and all of Guy DuMaupassant's would make an excellent introduction to those great writers. But unequivocally, Zola is a novelist and even his best stories, while excellent by anyone's standards, pale in comparison to his full-length fiction. Nonetheless, his short works often provide an insight into his genius and, I might say, into his thought processes as a craftsman of fiction. His early stories collected in Stories for Ninon are maudlin, immature, hopelessly romantic and often vicariously embarrassing. But this could be said of any writer, great and small, who for the first time takes up his pen and presents his soul to the world. A careful reading of these stories might remind many readers of their first forays into fiction where wearing one's heart on one's sleeve was not the opprobrium it is today.

The other difficulty in a presentation of so much material is the order in which it is presented. Like any very popular author, publishers scrambled to get work of any kind into print no matter how many times it was rejected when the fellow was unknown. Profit is always the motivating force behind the publishing trade and it is little wonder that works by Jane Austen, Charles Dickens and a slew of others are foisted upon the reading public when, in fact, they were not only unedited by their authors, but not even finished! I have had the good fortune to have had access to a lengthy letter from the London firm of Chatto & Windus which had proposed to the Zola estate a publication of his complete short works. For reasons unknown, the project never proceeded. However, a proposed "table of contents" was included with a precise statement that the order was to be precisely that used in the eventual publication. While I am no fan of the Chatto & Windus English translations, I much admire their dedication to the master's works and, I might add, they even "updated" some of the expurgations and made some of them a little more accurate and a little less befuddling in the early years of the 20th century. There is a reference in said letter that Zola himself had been consulted on the matter and while there is no evidence that he dictated the order of the stories, it is my opinion that it represents a better version than one I could evolve. It would be very simple to have the order dictated by the chronology of their appearance in print. This would be very difficult indeed and would belie the fact that many were written years before they found their way into print and actually predate others which were written later but published earlier. My own opinion is that by 1900, Zola wouldn't have cared. The fact that he consented to the publication of his early novel, The Mysteries of Marseilles, proves to me at least that whatever brought in a royalty check was good enough for him. And why not? He might have seen that novel and his first, Claude's Confession, with the same affection that many writers view their early work: "Well, this isn't bad at all." His reputation was already made and he could have written a poem sang to the tune of "Yankee Doodle Dandy" and his renown would have suffered not a whit.

What little obeisance I have made to the early translations and to some of the later ones is to retain some of their now obsolete punctuation and archaic syntax. The fact remains that Zola was a writer very much of his time and his MSS indicate that, for example, he often used a colon before a piece of dialogue and not a comma as we universally do today. Sometimes he used single quotation marks, sometimes double. And perhaps his most annoying habit, at least to the eye of a 21st century reader is his absurd overuse of the exclamation point. Today, I'm afraid, we are less apt to license our writers to shout their lines at our sophisticated faces. But in Zola's time when the novel was novel, such excesses were not only permitted but encouraged. Black marks on a white page may be many things but the 19th century reader felt privileged to feel the passion the writer felt and no punctuation accomplishes that so well as the exclamation point!

These volumes of his Complete Stories were years in the making and it is my genuine hope that they entertain, amuse and enlighten the American reader to one aspect of Émile Zola they might not otherwise have encountered.

Stephen R. Pastore, 2011.

CPSIA information can be obtained at www.ICGtesting.com
Printed in the USA
BVOW05s0948110814

362415BV00001B/251/P